"Magic is Fiction."

Tara's voice trembled a bit as she spoke the words.

"Then explain to me what you saw tonight," Gregore said.

Impossible man. How the hell could anyone explain that? "You know I can't," she said.

"Magic," he said softly. "The book contains things that could turn the world to hell in a heartbeat."

Tara closed her eyes and drew in a steady breath of musky, Gregore-scented air. "Okay, let's say for one tiny minute that I believe even a quarter of what you're saying, based entirely on the fact that I'm losing my mind. Magic exists and someone bad has my book of Gypsy spells. What does this supposed villain plan to do with it?"

Gregore held her gaze for a long moment. "I don't know. That's what I need you to find out."

Tara shook her head. This was too unreal. "How did you find out about the spell book? How did *he* find out about it?"

Gregore turned away from her and paced back the few steps to his bed. He stood with his hands on his hips, staring at the wall. Tara's eyes swept over his tall frame, noting the muscles and the way his clothes clung in all the right places. What was wrong with her? She should be running the other way, not checking the guy out.

"I need your help, Detective O'Reilly," he said at last. "And if you won't help me, then I won't be held responsible for what he does with the book."

SET IN STONE

by
AURRORA ST. JAMES

The characters and events portrayed in this book are fictitious. Any similarity to real persons, living or dead, is coincidental and not intended by the author.

Text copyright: © 2013 Aurrora St. James

Cover design by Kurt Moore, copyright 2013

All rights reserved.

No part of this book may be reproduced, or stored in a retrieval system, or transmitted in any form or by any means, electronic, mechanical, photocopying, recording, or otherwise, without express written permission of the publisher.

ISBN: 1481830414

ISBN 13:   9781481830416

Library of Congress Control Number: 2013900338
CreateSpace Independent Publishing Platform
North Charleston, South Carolina

To John, because you've believed in me
every step of the way.

To Lesa Dragon. Thanks for being batty with me!
I couldn't have done it without you.

To Kristen Schubach for the writing prompt.

And to Dena Bernard, who never had the chance to
read this in print. I know in my heart you'd have
been proud. Rest easy.

Prologue

February
England 1863

"And for his crimes against our family, I demand blood for blood," Ranulf shouted, rousing the crowd to violence with his damning words. His damning evidence.

Blood for blood.
Bloodforblood. Bloodforblood. Bloodforblood.

The words swirled in Gregore Trenowyth's head, dancing around like the shadows cast by the bonfire. He knelt on the cold, hard-packed earth of the forest clearing, drenched in the blood of his beloved Zola, and stared at the flames. Around him the Gypsies called for his death; swift or slow didn't matter so much as brutal. He would suffer.

Was it no less than he deserved? He had failed to protect the one he loved. Her lifeless body lay before him, staring at the night sky and stars she had adored. His chest constricted in pain unlike anything he'd felt before. The loss was already crippling. But the night was not over.

A hush fell over the gathered crowd as if sensing his thoughts. He reluctantly dragged his eyes from the flickering flames, barely able to care for what came next. Colorful, dirty men and women with tanned skin and hate in their eyes formed a circle around the fire. Beside him, he felt the reassuring presence of Thomas and Jeffrey, his two best friends. Gregore would throw himself at the mercy of this troupe in order to spare their lives. They were innocent in this. Only he was to blame for the murder of Zola.

The crowd parted for an ancient woman of indeterminate age. Her skin was wrinkled, her hair white and flowing freely about her shoulders. Black eyes locked on him in malice. Two men grabbed Gregore from behind, holding him fast.

"Blood for blood," one whispered, though a tremor ran through him when the old woman's gaze transferred from Gregore to him.

Dear God in heaven, if her own men were afraid, what did that say for this woman? Her hateful vehemence hit him full force, leaving little doubt as to whom she was. Zola's grandmother. Even Zola had feared her. People whispered she dealt in dark magic. Not simple potions or card tricks, but true commune with evil. Gregore's heart clenched in fear. He took a deep breath and forced himself to remain calm. He would die this night, but Thomas and Jeffrey did not have to.

Gregore bowed his head to the woman. "Madame, I beg you for—"

"Silence!" She thrust her hand forward, closing it into a tight fist before his face. Suddenly his air cut off. His lungs closed and though he opened his mouth and nose, no air would come into this body. He gasped and sucked to no avail, panic taking over.

The woman looked to Zola, lying dead at his feet. His hunting knife lay on the ground beside her, coated in her blood. She transferred that dark gaze away to Ranulf.

"Blood for blood? No. That is too easy a death for three such as these. Bring me my book." Someone hurried off to grab it.

Gregore's vision receded, blackness closing over the scene before him.

"You'll not go that quick, English." Her rusty voice scraped across his nerves, seeming to finally, blessedly release the air to his starved lungs. He sucked in hard, coughing and hunching over in the grip of the two men.

His vision cleared. Clouds had thickened above, darkening the clearing and threatening a fierce storm. The bonfire illuminated the witch's face, casting her sharp features into maniacal twists of malice.

"Please," he tried again.

Ugly laughter cut him off. "Do not bother to beg for your life or that of your friends." She came to him then, and he was assaulted by the smell of sulfur that seemed to spill from her pores. He struggled to get away, but his hands were bound behind him.

She accepted a leather-bound book from a young boy and stepped over the body of her granddaughter as if it were a rotten log. Stretching gnarled fingers out, she gripped his dark hair and wrenched his head backward, forcing his gaze to meet hers.

"You believe you loved her English? You know nothing of love." She spat on his face. Gregore cringed but made no sound. "Your heart is stone, just as you shall be." She released him and turned the pages of the book, her smile cold as ice. "You will suffer for your evil deeds. Not just this night, but every night. Blood for blood? Nay. A life for a life!"

Gregore closed his eyes and prayed for forgiveness. From his friends, his father, and Zola. Prayed his father had made an easy crossing to heaven this night. His heart bled for the loss of those he had loved most. And for the loss of his life that would come.

The wind picked up, blowing so fierce it sent a shock of fear through the Gypsy tribe. Several cried out and staggered back. The wind lifted the woman's hair in a wild white cloud. Lightning streaked the sky, followed by thunder that rocked the earth beneath them. More screams followed but not from the old witch. Her wrath seemed to fuel the storm. She opened her mouth, speaking a chant. Gregore stared at her mouth and the rotting teeth within, barely hearing her words in the storm.

She slammed the book closed in time with another peal of thunder and laughed as her people ran for shelter. Rain slammed the ground like daggers, but he felt none of it. It was as if his skin were made of stone. He couldn't move.

She did.

Kneeling before him, she smiled as if satisfied with her work. "You will live long with your regrets, English. May the suffering of your soul taunt you for the remaining time you have on this earth. I condemn you to half a life, just as you have condemned me. To live without my Zola."

"Wait," Thomas cried out. "He cannot live like this. Not forever. He is innocent."

"No English is innocent," she growled. "You fear us, call us thieves and murderers when it is you who kill us. But fear not. I am not without mercy." She looked back to Gregore. "You have one hundred fifty years, English. Think you can break the spell in that time?" Her laughter grated his skin, curling like hate in his heart.

Set in Stone

He still could not move, not even his eyelids. He could only listen to the cries of his friends as they suffered under the fury of the Gypsy witch and think about his actions. It was the worst birthday of his life. And if the old woman were to be believed, one of a very many to come.

CHAPTER 1

February—Present Day
Seattle, Washington

Tara O'Reilly pulled open the door to the Mystical Moon Coffee Shop and stopped to stare.

"Interesting," her partner, Carson Holt, said as he dusted the chilly rain off his jacket and pushed past her, heading for the barista.

"Doesn't quite sum it up," Tara replied as she looked around. "Wow." Dim lights overhead illuminated the cheap plastic, glow-in-the-dark stars that decorated the ceiling, and paper mache moons of every shape and size covered blue walls. A black floor gleamed with a spiraling galaxy and enough glitter to supply a kindergarten class for a year, while classical music played in low, soothing tones. Somehow the coffeehouse managed to walk that thin line between soothing and horrifying.

Carson wanted to give this place a try, hoping to find a cheaper cup of brew than the local mega coffee shop. Not to mention it was an unusual, out-of-the-way spot to meet their contact. Tara relented, knowing that with all the syrup he had in his coffee, he couldn't taste the brew anyhow. Coffee was coffee. If it helped open her eyes, she was happy. And this coffee smelled heavenly. The scent of fresh-baked bread and pastries called her through the dark room like a magnet. She navigated her way over to Carson to order.

"Already got ya, partner," Carson said, winking at the barista. His voice rose to a frightening imitation of a woman. "Coffee. Black. Nothing fancy here."

The sorority girl behind the counter giggled and actually batted her eyes at Carson. She leaned forward, nearly falling out of the too-tight sweater she wore. He smiled, cocked his hip against the counter, and struck up a conversation.

"Casanova strikes again," Tara muttered as she grabbed a coffee cup and filled it to the rim. She took a sip and let it warm her. Not bad. Certainly not a burnt flavor like other places they had tried. She sipped more coffee and scanned the shop. A few students sat in the stuffed chairs scattered around, listening to music and reading or working on their computers. An elderly Asian man sat by the window with his coffee cup. Ordinary traffic for a late Tuesday afternoon in the middle of winter.

Carson's low chuckle reverberated through the room. Tara rolled her eyes and walked away. She stretched her jaw, feeling the muscles tense all the way to her shoulders. Carson's love life got under her skin. While he insisted the women he chased knew the stakes, it was the different face every day that drove her nuts. She'd asked him once if he'd ever wanted to settle down with just one woman.

"There's a lot of fish in this sea, partner," he'd replied. "I intend to try as many as I can."

Tara shook her head. She shouldn't let it bother her. But lately it ground on her nerves, though she couldn't say why. Carson's life was his own. She certainly had no interest in him. His blond spiked hair and casual surfer looks never really appealed. She didn't even envy him.

Liar, her inner voice whispered. After their shift she would go home alone. And Carson would likely come back here for a bit of company. How long had it been since she'd had a date?

Tara blinked as if slapped by the thought. Was it a full moon? Why was she thinking about dating? She was happy. Happy and too busy with work to play games with men. She forced her thoughts back to their objective. Dates...ha!

"Care for a reading, love?" a soft voice said from behind her.

Tara started and turned to find the female voice that had spoken. Burgundy drapes sectioned off a corner of the room she hadn't noticed before. Though in reality, she had probably been blinded by the glitter. Directly above the woman, a plaque read "Louisa, Mistress of Tarot." Louisa was a plump brunette with dark eyes, long curling hair, and a wealth of silver bracelets decorating each arm. She smiled, keeping eye contact, as she laid out her cards.

Tara forced a smile. "Thanks. I'll pass."

"Ah, come on, O'Reilly. Where's your sense of adventure? Let the lady read your cards." Carson appeared at her elbow, waggling his eyebrows.

The woman watched the two with wise eyes, gently laying each card out into a complicated cross.

Tara shook her head. She wouldn't be bullied into this. Besides, they were technically here on police business.

"Stuff it, Carson. I don't need a psychic for this case. Aside from the coffee, we're here to see Mr. Hiroshi, remember?"

"Relax, Shamus, I've got that. You just see the pretty lady about that unknown future of yours. Make sure to ask her when you'll meet tall, dark, and dreamy. Besides, we might need her later. You know that psychics and detective partnerships are on the rise. Two months time and you might not even need me anymore."

Tara scowled at him. The last thing she needed was Carson reading her mind about dating. "I only put up with you because you're assigned to me. You know that, right?"

Carson laughed. He knew her better than that.

Tara sighed and turned to decline the woman's offer.

The woman pointed to a card. "You're looking for something here. But you won't find it. Your path lies elsewhere. I can help you if you are open."

Of all the tricks to get her business…Damn it. Tara glanced back to see Carson talking with the white-haired Asian gentleman who sat by the window. If she interrupted, it could appear that the police were ganging up on the informant. She'd do best to stand aside and blend in.

"Okay," she said before she could change her mind. She took a seat at the psychic's table. "I'm game. Tell me what path I'm supposed to be on then. Enlightenment? World peace?"

The woman smiled. "You don't believe in the cards."

Tara shifted uncomfortably in her wooden chair and took a sip of her coffee to cover her expression. "I choose not to believe."

Louisa cocked her head, studying Tara as she collected the cards and shuffled.

Tara avoided the scrutiny. Carson and the Asian were talking, using their hands as well. Each looked confused. Tara grinned. It seemed only fair that Carson would also get the short straw, if she had to be tortured like this. Turning back to Louisa, she found the woman relaxed but focused as she shuffled. On the table lay a single card, a woman on a throne holding a sword.

Louisa leaned forward to capture Tara's attention with her dark, soulful eyes. She held the cards out. "Take the deck. Share your energy with it."

Tara eyed the cards and licked her lips. Just simple paper. There was nothing to fear. Squaring her shoulders, she took hold of the deck.

Almost immediately, her vision flickered. Wavered. A shadow passed over her head, like a giant bird. Tara straightened in the chair and blinked a few times, ruthlessly shoving the images away. Oh yes, she'd had her cards read before. And just like now, the visions always came. Last time...no, she wouldn't think about that. She leveled her glare on Louisa, who didn't seem to notice.

"Focus on your question while you shuffle. When you are ready, cut the deck into thirds using your left hand."

"What are the lotto numbers this week?" Tara quipped. At the teller's frown, she reluctantly focused on the silly question and did as she was told. She cut the deck, then put it back together in the way that felt right and waited.

Louisa laid the cards out in the shape of the cross. She took her time studying each picture as it appeared before her. Finally her eyes flicked up to meet Tara's. "Your past was troubled. You have lost those who—"

"Just the future, please," Tara said, shifting in her chair again.

Louisa regarded her, then nodded and studied the cards. "A stranger will come to you for help."

Tara snorted. "That's the nature of my job. I'm a detective. All kinds of strangers come to me for help."

Louisa smiled patiently. "This is not just any man. With him comes danger and here, you see uncertainty." She pointed to a card that was unmistakable. Death. "This man brings change to your life. Or transformation."

Tara shivered involuntarily. She didn't believe in this stuff, she reminded herself. She was a detective. Strangers, danger, and change came with the job. It was a part of life and she was comfortable with it.

"Tell me something I don't know." She meant it sarcastically, yet somehow it came out as a plea. Definitely a full moon.

Louisa smiled in a way that said she both pitied Tara and knew something she didn't. She tapped a long red nail on the next card.

Tara groaned. The lovers.

"You will find this man attractive," Louisa said as she studied the lovers standing nude beneath the angel. "Your association with him will expose your secrets...and his. But danger lurks with this man." The final card was an upside-down angel with two cups in hand. "It is my warning to you."

Tara grinned. Yeah, right. Before she could give voice to her reply, a hand slapped down on her shoulder.

Carson picked up the lovers card. "Ooooh, looks like someone's in for a dirty night."

Tara snatched the card from his hand and Louisa chuckled. "Get a life, Carson," Tara said. "You know this crap is fiction."

Carson clucked his tongue. "So defensive. Makes a guy think you've already got someone in mind for your sexy night out." Seeing the death glare in her eyes, he wisely switched subjects. "Hiroshi doesn't know anything. Well, at least I don't *think* he does. The man only speaks Japanese."

Tara shook her head, not quite paying attention. She couldn't ignore the shiver that went through her. Something the teller said felt right. But what? She thought over the reading briefly, then decided it wasn't worth her time.

"Let's go, gumshoe," she said to Carson. She checked her watch, amazed it was so late. If she hurried, she could hit the grocery store before her favorite television show came on. She thanked Louisa, paid for her reading, and followed Carson out.

He headed for his car and opened the door. "See you in the a.m., sunshine."

"What, no sorority girl?"

He chuckled. "Tomorrow. Tonight I have a previous engagement."

Of course. "Later, Carson."

Tara went to her blue Mini Cooper and slid behind the wheel. She drove through Capitol Hill to the grocery store for some much-needed food. Her fridge was so empty, she'd have to eat her condiments for dinner if she didn't stop tonight. Not that cooking was really her specialty. Even when Grandma Rose was alive, she'd rarely cooked. And now that it was just her, she ate takeout more often than not. She sighed and found a parking spot, though she had to navigate around a couple kissing to do so.

"Since when is the grocery parking lot the hot make-out spot?" she grumbled.

Getting out of the car, she zipped her leather jacket up to cover her badge and weapon, and headed for the entrance. A couple holding a baby hurried past to get out of the cold drizzle. Somewhere, Grandma Rose was laughing hysterically. Grandma had talked about a woman's ticking clock, but never mentioned that it might actually be a time bomb.

"I'm fine," she said aloud and just a bit too forcefully to be talking to herself. Great. Just great.

A piercing ring broke her thoughts, causing Tara to nearly jump out of her skin. She fumbled for her phone and flipped it open.

"Yeah?"

"O'Reilly, are you okay?" Captain Scott asked, his gruff voice familiar.

"Yes sir, why?" Something was wrong. The captain never called. Ever. Not even when he wanted to check in on his detectives, of which she and Carson were his top tier.

He sighed, sounding more tired than she was used to. "You better get home quick. Fire's on the scene."

"Fire? What? How?"

"Unknown. Let me know if there is anything I can do to help."

"Thanks, sir." She closed the phone and ran back to the car. Jamming it into gear, she flew out of the parking lot toward her apartment.

It was only a matter of blocks before she could see it. Thick black smoke clouded overhead like a beacon drawing her to the danger. She floored the Mini, dodging cars and ignoring their horns, as she took corners through the clogged city streets. Then she was there, and the devastation was immediate.

CHAPTER 2

Flames lapped the walls of the four-story brick apartment building, shooting through the roof and every window Tara could see. Every floor. Her heart stopped, then resumed with a sickening pound that deafened her ears. Uniformed policemen zigzagged all around, pushing back the gaping crowd as firefighters shot a forty-foot stream of useless water at the blaze. Women and children, families she had known for years, cried as their lives lit up like tinder. Tara's heart cried with them. Not for her home, but for the single object that was all she had left of the past. How could it survive this inferno? Impossible.

She parked and got out, moving slowly through the crowd, hugging her body more for comfort than against the cold winter air. She couldn't feel anything. Not the wet pavement under her feet or the icy breath in her lungs. She watched the flames lick the brick, hardly aware of her detachment. It couldn't be happening. She wasn't losing everything she owned.

Slowly Tara became aware of more flashing lights, the uniforms and firefighters taking control of the situation, moving people farther away for their safety. The crowd pushed against her but she didn't budge. Couldn't. Finally, after what felt like an eternity, the red-orange flames began to recede. Maybe it wasn't as bad as she had originally thought.

Slipping under the police line, she flashed her badge, and weaved through emergency crews in no particular direction. The smoke stung her eyes and clogged her lungs. It swirled and curled around her like a snake, trying to choke the life from her. She kept moving, trying to escape but unable to take her eyes off the leaping flame. A sudden yell, followed by a thundering crash, made her jump. Tara watched as the south section of the roof caved, just one floor above her apartment. Luckily, she wasn't on the top floor. Just one lower.

A third fire engine roared up, and more firemen jumped into motion. Tara moved out of their way, heading for the north side of the building where it was safer. Something drew her footsteps to the alley alongside the building. Certainly not a sound. She couldn't hear anything but the yelling crews, sirens, and the crackling flames. The disappearing sun cast a brilliant orange-gold glow in the clouded sky and fought with the flames for supremacy. From here she could see that the majority of the fire was on the south side. The side her apartment was on. Smoke still escaped from fissure cracks around the windows.

A beat-up Dumpster and a scattering of boxes and black garbage bags lined the alley she stood in. Tara looked around, not really seeing anything that would draw her attention. She was just beginning to think it was her subconscious playing tricks on her mind when something moved, drawing her focus up the side of the building. She thought she saw a shadow. But no, that wasn't possible. Hadn't someone called the building clear?

One tiny hand hit the window on the third floor. A second hand joined it, and a small voice pierced the noise. A shriek of terror. She knew of only one child on that floor. Timmy, the super's son. He waved wildly at her, screaming for help and beating his fists on the window. He wouldn't have long. The smoke would kill him long before the flames.

Tara couldn't hear his words over the pounding of her heart. He was trapped. Frantically she looked around. Smoke filled the alley. The fire escape was there, but the ladder was pulled up. Could she reach it? Rescuers were yards away.

"Open the window," she cried to Timmy, running for the metal ladder. "Help!" she screamed, hoping to pierce the noise and capture the attention of someone. Anyone.

Skidding to a stop, she jumped for the ladder. Her fingers just grazed it. She jumped again, still missing. Oh God, she had to get him out. She was five foot six; who the hell built this fire escape? A giant? As she backed up to take a running jump, darkness fell over the alley, followed immediately by the golden setting sunlight. The strangeness of it dragged her attention from Timmy to the sky. She gaped. Massive wings spread, beat, propelling a heavily muscled man to the building. Muscular arms and legs stretched out, ending in talons. The creature flew for Timmy's window. She opened her mouth, but the sound stuck in her throat and she choked on the smoke.

The monster (or was it a man?) landed on Timmy's windowsill, folding his wings neatly behind. One claw tucked under the window, and she saw Timmy stagger back. Tara couldn't tear her gaze away from the sight of this thing she couldn't put a name to and the mixture of hope and fear on Timmy's face. The boy had a towel at his mouth and she saw smoke as a haze around him.

"Hurry," she cried to the thing. This beast. She didn't know if it heard, but it threw open the window with such force that it shattered, glass raining down to where she stood. Instinctively she ducked, looking away only long enough to make sure that she wasn't cut. As soon as she could, Tara looked back to the scene unfolding before her. The creature reached in a mighty hand, took hold of Timmy, and lifted him out. The boy's eyes were as large as hubcaps, but he had the sense to know he was being rescued and clung to the strong arms that held him. The beast shifted, flapped his wings, and stepped off the sill. It turned a lazy circle and glanced down at her.

His face was finely sculpted with eyes above a beak-like nose. Full lips and high cheekbones, like a human male and bird combined. His eyes glowed an electric blue. Beautiful. Entrancing. He seemed to shimmer at the edges and part of her wondered if she imagined it.

Their gazes locked long enough for Tara's insides to shake with fear. Long enough to quickly realize that imagination wasn't racking her body with tremors. This was real.

He landed lightly before her. She took an involuntary step back. Those eyes captivated her, as did the texture of his skin. Stone. Marble smooth, but still stone. Exotic and intriguing. What was this thing? He was both beautiful and terrible to behold.

He studied her as she studied him, then silently handed the boy to her. Timmy's eyes were squeezed shut and his body shook.

"It's okay. You're okay," she whispered, folding his small body into her arms with care. Still, she couldn't look away from the beast.

The creature watched her with interest, then cocked his head as if hearing something far out of her earshot. Her world had gone silent the moment he reached for Timmy. Just as she realized it, sound flooded back so loud that she jumped and looked to the crowds. When she turned back, the creature had put distance between them. Sweeping his arm in front of him, he bowed low to her and launched into the air. She followed his movement as he disappeared into the lingering red and purple of dusk.

Tara tore her gaze away and rushed to deposit Timmy with the first EMT she could find. She thrust him into the woman's arms and removed the towel so Timmy could breathe better.

"He was trapped," she said. Questions from the medic flowed but she shook her head. She couldn't explain what she'd seen. Once Timmy was safely in their care, she was free, but precious minutes had been lost. Casting one last glance at the sky, Tara started running in the direction she had seen the creature go.

She dodged through the crowd and down the street, running three blocks with eyes constantly raised to the skies. Nothing moved. The sun dipped below the horizon, and the deep blue of night spread like a blanket above her.

Tara paused to catch her breath and turned in a slow circle, searching the faces of those on the street for any clues they too had seen the strange being. They exhibited no signs of terror or even surprise. People ignored her as they went about their daily lives. She walked another two blocks. There was no sign of the creature. Her shoulders sank. He'd escaped. Or maybe he wasn't even real to begin with. The alley *had* been filled with smoke. Had the light and smoke played tricks with her eyes? Was Timmy simply rescued by a fireman? Tara decided to return to the remains of her apartment building to ask Timmy herself.

She jogged back to the smoldering structure. Smoke poured white from the roof, evidence that the firemen now had the fire under control.

When she arrived, she snagged a uniform heading to his patrol car. "Have you seen Timmy?" she yelled over the noise, looking for the EMTs. The ambulance was gone. At his confused look, she added, "The boy who was with the medics."

"On the way to the hospital."

Tara barely heard the guy's response. Perhaps she could visit Timmy there tomorrow and find out once and for all what they saw.

She watched as the fire crew obliterated the last of the blaze. Uniforms blocked off the entrance to the building and asked people to stay away until an investigation could be complete. That could be days, Tara knew.

She walked back to her car, trying to focus on something practical. Like where to spend the night. Aunt Maddy came to mind, but Tara immediately discarded that idea. She honestly didn't think she could visit the old house she'd grown up in. It probably wasn't too late to drop in on her partner and ask to sleep on a couch, but reflecting back on their time at the coffee shop, she realized Casanova might have a caffeinated sorority girl for company. That really only left one option- the nearest motel. At the very least she could get some sleep. Tomorrow was going to be a hell of a day.

※

Gregore Trenowyth stepped from the shadows of a nearby building, thankful to be human for one more night. Gone were the wings and stone body that weighed him down until the hour before sunset when the change back to human began. He hated what he'd become. Hated living half a life. Each day he spent as a gargoyle took a piece of his soul. Much longer and he'd have nothing left. He forced that happy thought away and took a breath of chilly night air.

He folded his arms across his bare chest and wished for a shirt or even a jacket. But only his pants survived the change from gargoyle to human. Gregore shifted closer to the fire and lifted his eyes to the apartment building. In his other form, he could easily have entered through the flames, but there hadn't been time before he changed shape to save the boy and search for the spell book. He'd chosen the innocent boy, knowing the cost might be the loss of the one thing that could shatter his curse once and for all.

And even then he couldn't regret his choice.

The moment he'd placed the child in the beautiful woman's arms, he'd known it was too late to search the building. Maybe too late to end this shoddy half life he lived. After all Gregore had seen and done to those he loved, part of him wondered if he didn't deserve what fate had wrought.

He looked back to the woman, watching as she slipped into that impossibly small car. A slight frown tugged at his lips. She had followed him. He hadn't expected that. Or her.

Gregore had known only that she was a detective with the Seattle police department and where she lived. Up close, she was stunning in her beauty. More than that, her fearlessness impressed him. The few who had the unfortunate chance of seeing his other form had run screaming or fainted dead away. This woman had *chased* him.

As much as he hated to admit it, it piqued his interest. When most people no longer believed in magic, could he have found someone who did?

Gregore suddenly needed to know more about her.

She started the vehicle and pulled slowly through the crowds of gaping on-lookers to make a left turn onto Broadway.

Time to do some following of his own.

Gregore jogged a few steps after her, then ran full out. Preternatural speed kicked in. His feet were so light, they barely touched the pavement. Endorphins charged his blood, and he let out a cry of joy. How long had it been since he'd done this? His curse was not without its highlights, he thought with a laugh. He followed the little blue vehicle down three blocks to James and then right up the hill. She pulled into a cheap motel.

The motel was single story with a front office to the left and a dozen rooms in a row to the right. The doors faced out to the brightly lit parking lot. Why did she choose this place over friends or family? Did she just not want to bother someone? More importantly, where was the spell book?

Gregore ducked into the shadows, watching as she talked with the clerk at the front desk and accepted a key. As she walked to the motel room, his eyes were drawn to the gentle sway of her hips. Auburn curls fell to the middle of her back. His hands itched to touch the silken strands. When he'd handed over the boy, smoky green eyes had captured him, and the skin of her hands gently brushing his felt so soft. His blood heated. Another surprise. What was it about this woman?

When she was safe inside her room, she drew the blackout curtains across the window, blocking his view. The devastation of seeing her home go up in flames would undoubtedly take an emotional toll on her. She would sleep soon. There was nothing more he could do here.

He was tempted to stay. To try to see her face again—another thing that he hadn't expected. Tara O'Reilly was lovely. He could stay and learn more about her. But there were things to do. One hundred eighty-two years of his life had finally led up to this moment. He was not going to waste a second of it. Time was simply too precious.

He returned on foot to her apartment. Firefighters still tried valiantly to douse the remaining hot spots. Cops held back the onlookers and kept people from returning to their homes. He swore. Time for a change of plans. If he couldn't get into the building tonight, he'd have to try again tomorrow night.

Gregore threaded through the crowd and made his way back to the welcome sight of St. Jude's Parish. Marble walls rose to graceful turrets with a belfry at the center. The wood doors to the church were carved in an elegant pattern of Old World charm. He moved up the steps and found the doors unlocked, just as they always were.

"Let any man come who will," the priest had said the first time Gregore had attended a service there.

Gregore had. This was the place he had called home for the last four months. The priests who resided here kept his secret and for the first time in a hundred years, he felt welcome. He sighed. He didn't feel old. He didn't look old. But few people would understand what it was like to live for as long as he had. Like the marble walls of the church, he had stood the test of time. Only his time was swiftly coming to an end.

He had just eleven short days to break the curse.

Gregore entered the church and was greeted by the soft scent of candles as they burned wax for those remembered. The pews were empty tonight as they often were. He knew the priests would be enjoying their evening wine in the small house at the back of the church. Many nights he had joined them; tonight he longed to, but it would have to wait.

He walked to the back of the church, went through a side door and down the steps into the basement. His room had a bed, chair, and writing desk, with a small wardrobe of clothing. All that he needed with very little else. A musky odor filled his nose. It was a scent he had come to recognize as home. The room smelled old, but the comfort he felt when walking through the door compared to nothing.

Gregore took a shirt from the armoire and slipped it over his head, then moved to his desk to sort through the many stacks of books and papers. He hardly had space to write but that didn't matter. Only finding the spell mattered. He was close now; he could feel it. Tara O'Reilly was the last descendant he could find. She had to have the book.

Sitting in the simple wooden chair by his desk, Gregore went back through his notes. He would check and recheck every line of her lineage to be certain he hadn't missed anyone. One error now would mean his death.

⇥ CHAPTER 3 ⇤

Tara woke the next morning, still spread diagonally across the bed just as she had fallen the night before. She rubbed bleary eyes and craned her neck to find the alarm clock. Damn, 7:30 a.m. Half an hour before she had to be at work. She used the facilities, brushed her teeth with the travel toothbrush provided by the night desk clerk, and took a fast shower. Her long-sleeved shirt and jeans were completely wrinkled and smelled like smoke.

Oh God. The fire. She wouldn't have enough time to get by her apartment even if she hustled, and who knew what state her wardrobe was in. Or anything else for that matter. Did any of it survive? Her gut clenched at just the thought of having to start completely over. And what about... Tara let out a tense, tight breath. She couldn't think about that right now. She had to get to work. Fortunately she had a change of clothes at the office. She dressed quick, grabbed her jacket and keys, and headed out to her car.

The day went swiftly. She tracked down a new lead on a current robbery case and generally caught up on paperwork. No matter how hard she tried to focus on work, her thoughts returned to the fire and the creature (man?) she had seen last night. It must have been a firefighter. She'd been tired after a long day at work and stressed that everything she owned was in jeopardy. Right?

So why did the obvious answer sit so wrong with her? Why didn't she remember being that tired? The rational side of her insisted what she saw was nothing more than a trick of the light and smoke. If not, what was it really? Timmy would know.

An hour later, Tara dropped by the hospital. Timmy sat in the middle of his hospital bed surrounded by toys and stuffed animals. His parents reclined in the room's two chairs, looking far more tired than he did. Two nurses stood by the bed, taking Timmy's vitals as he entertained them with stories of the fire and his amazing rescue by a giant bird man made of stone. Tara paused in the doorway to listen.

He spread his little arms as wide as they would go. "His wings were *this* big! And then he flew us down in a circle. I wasn't even scared." The nurses smiled and gasped at the appropriate moments, clearly not believing his wild tale.

Tara stepped back into the hall. She had her answer from Timmy; the little boy had seen the same thing. She rubbed her eyes and left the hospital. Maybe she and the kid were both hallucinating last night. Men with wings only existed in comic books and cartoons.

It was nearly five when she parked in the alley where Timmy was rescued. A hulking, blackened brick structure greeted her. Part of the roof remained, looking wet from the fire hoses, and the back side of the building appeared to be intact. Good news. Maybe something survived.

Please, she thought, *let the book be safe.*

Tara ducked under the yellow caution tape blocking the front entrance and slipped through the open door without a backward glance. Bypassing the elevator, she jogged up the stairs to the third floor. Or what was left of it. The walls, once a buttery soft yellow, were now angry swirls of black soot with broken, charred doors. Grime dulled every surface, leaving her feeling dirty and gritty. Water dripped in the distance. Residual fumes and the hint of smoke hanging in the air filled her lungs and made her cough as she walked toward her apartment door. Her breath caught. The door stood slightly ajar and looked more like alligator hide than wood. Tara pushed it open a few inches, calling out, "Hello?"

"Hey, this is police business. No one should be...Oh, it's you, O'Reilly." Benjamin Toge, the fire inspector, stood firmly in the doorway, not allowing her to pass.

Tara flashed her badge. He didn't need to see it. He knew who she was. Why was he being such a bastard? "Are you gonna let me in? Or do I have to stand here?"

Benjamin turned his back on her, returning to the far wall. "Get what you need quick. This is an open investigation."

Tara turned that over in her mind. Just what the hell were they expecting to find? She stepped into the living room and stopped cold. A tremor started in her stomach, working its way through her limbs. Large bubbles of formerly cream paint covered the walls like measles. Dirt and debris covered every surface. Her television and leather furniture were melted blobs of black. To her right, the kitchen was just as bad. Insulation hung in large clumps from the ceiling, dripping water onto the floor. What cabinet doors remained hung at odd angles, the wood fuliginous. A hard lump formed in her throat. Tara tried to swallow past it, but couldn't.

She moved on stiff legs past Benjamin and went to her bedroom. One last glance showed he was focused on his work at one of the outlets in the living room by her television. She wanted to ask him what he was doing but checked her curiosity. Getting the book was more important.

She pushed open what remained of the bedroom door. Her room was damp. The smell of smoke clung to the walls and tinged the air. She coughed again. Water squished below her feet as she closed the door behind her. Parts of her living room were still visible through the splintered wood. She turned away and walked across the carpet to the bed. Once, the sparse furnishings had been nice. Good dark wood, a nice olive-green paint on the walls. Things didn't look so good in a half inch of water and scorched an ugly shade of black-brown.

She reached a trembling hand up to the old iron grate above her bed and yanked hard on it, nearly falling backward with the effort. Tara dropped the grate onto the singed green bedding and reached into the duct. Her fingers met with dust and dirt, then cool steel. The fire retardant box didn't seem to be wet, just dirty from the soot. Small mercies.

Tara dragged the box to the front of the duct and pulled her keys from her pocket. She stuck the small silver key into the box and opened the lid. Inside, the red leather journal looked no worse for wear. She sighed in relief. Hugging the book to her chest, she turned around to replace the grate and stopped short.

Familiar glowing blue eyes met hers from across the room.

><+>+<>+<+><

Gregore landed lightly in the alley next to the detective's blue car and folded his wings behind him. Fading sunlight glinted on the fire escape and reflected in the dirty windows of the apartments. He placed his hand on the hood of the car. Still warm. She hadn't been here long. This could be his only chance to talk to her about the book.

Flexing his knees, he launched into the air, and flapped his wings. He stuck to the growing shadows and rose to the third floor of the old brick building. The charred outside, blackened from soot, cloaked his brief ascent. At least the damage wasn't as bad on this side of the building. He perched on the edge of the metal fire escape landing and looked in the nearest window. A bedroom. Green walls and nice furniture were bubbled and broken. Pictures of loved ones lay shattered on a dresser. Tara O'Reilly lived simply, or had before the fire ruined her apartment.

As if summoned by her name, she entered the bedroom and glanced over her shoulder at whatever room she'd just left, then closed the door behind her. He stilled. Watched as she removed the grating on the wall and reached into the duct.

He lifted the windowpane and ducked inside. She was so preoccupied with the metal box in her hands that she didn't seem to hear him enter. Gregore stood to his full height. Tara was several inches shorter than he, with toned arms and a firm athletic build. Auburn hair hung down her slim back in waves that he ached to touch. Soft-looking hands with long, slender fingers removed the spell book.

Gregore's breath hitched when he saw it. After all this time, the leather volume looked the same, though he'd only seen it once on the night that ripped his life away. His indrawn breath must have alerted Tara to his presence because she chose that moment to turn around.

Their gazes met over the few feet separating them. Her smoky-green eyes went round and her hand stilled over the grate.

"I've come for the grimoire." He indicated the spell book still in her arms.

She clutched it to her chest and surreptitiously glanced between the door and window. He stepped toward her, fully aware he didn't look human. He kept his wings tucked behind him and tried to draw her out. "We could talk…"

"Get a grip, Tara," she muttered under her breath. She pulled her gun with her free hand and aimed it at his chest.

"I mean you no harm," he said. His voice was gravelly, but getting better. He hated that he'd had to confront her before he could make the change.

Tara shook her head. "I've heard that before." She hedged a step toward the door and yelled, "Benjamin!"

Gregore followed her. "I need the book." He didn't know who Benjamin was, but didn't want to wait to find out. He had to have that volume from her. Or even just the spell. "Please."

Her gun remained steady as she stared at him, her face unreadable. She didn't hand him the book but she also didn't pull the trigger. Seconds ticked by. Tara opened her mouth to shout again. "Ben…"

Shit. No time. He kicked into preternatural speed and closed the distance between them. Grabbing her wrist with the gun, he redirected her aim. Tara fired and missed. She rolled to the right, hitting the mattress and scrambling across. Gregore locked his arms around her waist and yanked her off the bed. Her weapon dropped harmlessly to the ground. He held her fast to his chest, ignoring her frantic struggles. Gregore could hear a man calling to her on the other side of the door.

He was completely out of time. She'd just have to go with him so they could talk. Lifting her into his arms, he went to the window and stepped carefully through. Mighty wings unfolded, and he leapt into the open air with Tara held firm in his arms.

He soared above the buildings, leaving the ground far beneath them. Tara squeezed her eyes shut and screamed. He clamped a hand over her mouth.

"We do not wish our presence to get noticed," he said.

Tara immediately stopped struggling as they soared over the rooftops of her city. She clung to him in an awkward one-armed grip that smashed the book between them. He released her mouth and tightened his arms around her, holding her close, yet gentle.

Her soft curves pressed into his chest, distracting him.

"I have to be dreaming," she said.

He agreed, but for different reasons. God, she felt good in his arms. He had to get some distance between them. First the spell.

"You are not dreaming." His voice rumbled from deep within. She shivered. "The sooner you accept this, the easier it will be for us both."

From below, the roar of a motorcycle snagged his attention. Gregore frowned as he realized the black bike took two turns, keeping up with their flight.

Tara gave a short laugh, drawing his gaze back to where she settled against his chest. "Whatever you say, buddy. Just put me down and pray that I don't arrest you for kidnapping."

He chuckled softly. "You wish me to release you now? Here?" He dipped low over a flat-roofed building, loosening his grip when they soared over the alley far below.

"Not here!" she shrieked, clutching him harder.

"I thought as much," he said, enjoying the press of her body once more.

He couldn't see the face of the person on the bike. Definitely a man, based on his build. The man continued to look up as he rode, keeping them in sight. On the west, the sun touched the horizon. Suddenly Gregore's body weight decreased as the change began. The itch between his shoulder blades drew his wings closer into his skin. He aimed for the church.

"If you drop me, I swear I'll haunt you for eternity," Tara said.

"Nonsense. I don't believe in ghosts." He flapped his wings harder, the steeple of the church a lighthouse in the dusky sky. There wasn't enough time to lose the unknown motorcyclist.

"You're laughing at me? This is absurd. A winged beast that doesn't believe in ghosts is laughing at me." She thumped his chest with her fist. "I'm lying in a hospital somewhere with a serious concussion. I don't remember how I got it, but it will come back to me eventually. All I need to do is wake up."

Gregore watched her squeeze her eyes shut again and then looked over his shoulder and down at the street beneath them. The man still followed. He cursed and beat his wings faster, heading diagonally across the rooftops to throw off the fellow. A glance behind showed the bike coming in fast. Nothing could be done now.

He landed on a narrow service walkway on the roof of St. Jude's that gave access to the tower bells and placed Tara on her feet. A rumble below pulled his attention down to the street. The motorcyclist was driving up the steps. The man swung the bike parallel to the doors and kicked down the stand, then jumped off and disappeared inside the church.

Tara pushed as hard as she could against his chest, catching him by surprise. She made a run for the door at the end of the walkway. Her arms pumped as she ran, giving her speed. She paused long enough to kick in the door and disappeared into the dark interior.

Gregore folded his wings, feeling the slight tingling at the center of his back. The sun would be beyond the horizon in minutes. He raced after Tara, dreading the scene he knew would come. He should have told her about the motorcyclist. At least then she would be prepared for the confrontation.

Tara fled down the steps, stuffing the damn book in the back of her pants. Gregore pounded down the stairs behind her, fighting to stay upright as his body shifted with each minute that passed. Below, he heard the soft click of a door closing. A thump and a grunt bounced up the narrow walls. He rounded the corner and skidded to a stop.

A blond man plowed hard into Tara, knocking her backward onto the wood plank steps. One hand went around her throat, holding her against the step while the other went behind her to grab the book. Tara tried to claw his hands away. She gasped and choked, throwing a punch blindly that barely connected with his face. The impact didn't have much force behind it, but was enough to get a grunt of pain from the man. She smiled and attempted a kick at his balls. He caught her leg.

Gregore launched himself at the man, tackling him to the floor. The guy rolled with him, landing on top. He grabbed Gregore's head and smashed it into the floor once, twice, punching his newly reformed nose. Next the man leapt up and grabbed Tara. He pulled her off the steps, and using her momentum, spun her around. He yanked the spell book out of her pants and shoved her forward into the stairway. Gregore rolled and grabbed for the man's ankles. The guy stumbled with a grunt and fled back through the door. Tara pushed herself to stand, clutching the wooden railing. She staggered out the door after him.

Gregore gained his feet and followed. Ahead, the blond dashed down the aisle with Tara not far behind. He kicked into supernatural speed and rushed through the church doors, only to find the motorcyclist riding down the steps and out onto the street. Gregore spread his wings and took a running leap into the air. He soared over Tara's head and flapped his wings to gain speed as he pursued the biker. With less than a minute left until the change was complete, he used what he could.

The guy snaked around corners at a dangerous speed, weaving around the nearest buildings. He glanced over his shoulder, then hit the gas and headed straight for a crowded section of town.

The sun sank below the horizon.

Gregore's wings fully retracted and he dropped five feet to the pavement, landing in a roll so as not to injure himself. The bike's taillights disappeared ahead.

Shit.

Whoever that guy was, he'd just stolen the one thing that could change everything.

⇥ CHAPTER 4 ⇤

Night had fallen and clouds were gathering overhead by the time Tara stopped running. She'd lost sight of them after a few blocks, but kept running down a few more streets, looking each direction for either the motorcyclist or his winged friend. A very real winged man who'd flown her over the city and deposited her on a church roof. Her skin still felt frozen from flying above the rooftops, and there was no way she could make up that fight with the blond guy.

She wanted to kick herself. She'd lost the damn book! After everything Grandma Rose had said, warning her to keep it out of the wrong hands, after hiding it and never speaking of it to anyone, not one, but two, people were after it. Okay, maybe one wasn't a person. She'd yet to determine what he was. How the hell was she ever going to get the heirloom back? Hopefully the first two numbers she'd snagged off the bike's license plate would be enough for a good lead. She'd find both men and take back her property.

Tara turned and began to walk back to her car. This trendy part of town was full of bars and intimate restaurants. People flocked the streets at all hours. Mostly young singles frequented the area, but the restaurants were known to attract the older crowd as well. Not that she felt part of either group. That's why she never came here. She moved at a faster pace than most of the people strolling along the sidewalk and frequently had to push by them.

Grandma Rose would have loved it here. They'd gone out to dinner every Friday. Sort of their own tradition since Tara hated to cook. Her heart ached. She missed Rose. Years had passed, but sometimes the loss still felt fresh. Tara filled that hole with work, but her work friends couldn't replace family. She thought of her aunt, the only family she had left, and made a mental note to call her.

Her thoughts drifted back to the gargoyle (man?) and their flight across the city. She might have enjoyed it under other circumstances. He'd held her so securely, his arms strong, except for that one brief dangle over the alley. Who or what was he? And why had he kidnapped her from her apartment? Was he simply spooked by Benjamin banging on the door? She shook her head, uncertain, but needing answers.

Her cell phone rang loud, jarring her out of her thoughts. Several people ran into her and grumbled at her to move it. She ignored them and flipped her phone open. Carson. Great. "Hey, gumshoe."

"Where are you, O'Reilly?" he asked, his tone waspish.

"Excuse me?"

"Forget it. You need to come down to the station. Captain needs to talk to you."

She frowned and started walking again. "Isn't he normally gone by now?"

Carson cleared his throat, his normally cocky tone nowhere to be found. "Must be your lucky night."

He sounded nervous and pissed off all at once. "What's going on?"

"I'm late for a date, that's what. Just get your ass in here so I can go."

"Hey, don't let me hold you back from whatever coed has your number, Casanova." Her retort met silence. She sucked in a breath. "Sorry, partner, that was uncalled for. Didn't mean to be a bitch. It's been a bad night."

"Understood." He said nothing more.

"On my way."

Carson sighed. "Thanks."

She hung up and hailed a cab to drop her off at her apartment for her Mini. The stress of no home, strange creatures, and now losing the grimoire made her testy. God, she could hear Grandma Rose now, chewing her ass for losing the book of spells, which had been in their family so long. Add to that the fact that she'd never raked her partner down like that and the guilt was just piling on her shoulders. She'd buy Carson a mocha in the morning and try to explain it all without sounding certifiable. As for the rest, well, she'd deal with it later.

Retrieving her car and weapon was the easy part. Her keys... not so much. Tara ducked under the yellow tape for the second time that day and slipped into her apartment. She located her Sig on the ground by the bed and holstered it. Five minutes ticked by as she searched her bedding, the floor, and even the fire escape for her keys, before finally locating them inside the duct, still stuck in the fire box. Suppressing a growl, Tara stomped back down the stairs and drove to the new single-story building that housed the East Precinct.

The clean brick exterior was just the next stage in the city's plan to clean up a beaten-down neighborhood on the east side. Wide glass doors and unbarred windows beckoned local thugs to break in. Not that anyone did. Most people wanted to break out.

Tara pulled open the door and stepped inside the unnaturally warm zone. The hair on her nape rose and her palms began to sweat. She'd had way too much time to wonder what had Carson worked up and why the captain would want to see her now. She marched down the empty hall toward the back offices. Was this what it felt like to walk to your execution? Just what the hell was going on? Tara quickened her step. Better to get this over with.

Carson stood outside the Captain's door, arms folded across his chest. "'Bout time."

"Didn't realize you were on a schedule."

He grunted, then inexplicably his features softened. "You need to tread lightly partner. I don't know what's going on, but take care, okay?"

She nodded and gave her thanks. Carson walked away.

Tara rapped twice on the office door and let herself in unannounced. Hell, if she was in trouble, it'd be the least of her worries.

Captain John Scott sat behind a new metal desk, twirling his pencil in his fingers. She'd seen him do it enough to know it was a nervous habit. Something to keep his fingers busy. He was also known to twirl knives, rifles, broomsticks, and pretty much anything else he could get his hands on. Captain Scott was the reason they had a new building.

One of his twirling sessions had gone slightly awry two years ago. The handle of a broom had connected with a light fixture that sparked old electrical wires near faulty insulation. The ensuing blaze had been quite a spectacle. Try explaining *that* to your superiors. Tara suspected he was pretty proud of himself for the whole incident.

The captain looked up when she entered. He didn't put down the pencil, just motioned for her to have a seat. The look on his face told her all she needed to know. He was unhappy, and in about thirty seconds, she would be too. She sat.

"Benjamin Toge, the inspector, came by with his report tonight." He watched her closely. For what, she couldn't fathom. "We're looking at arson."

Tara sat forward. "Arson?"

"I'm not finished." He thumped the pencil on the desk. "The blaze started in your unit, but I'm more concerned about where the hell you went."

"What do you mean, it started in my unit? Who'd want to set fire to my apartment?"

Scott pulled an evidence bag from his desk drawer and slid it across the desk to her. "Tell me about this," he said in response.

Tara took the bag. Through the clear plastic she could see a faxed copy of insurance paperwork made out in her name.

"What the hell is this?" Rental insurance with a national company for the full value of her goods, dated a week ago. She flicked her gaze down to the bottom. "This isn't my signature. Sir. I've never seen this before. I was with Carson when my apartment went up."

He dropped the pencil and locked his hands behind his head, leaning back in his chair. When he finally spoke, his words were slow, as if carefully chosen. "You know how I run this department, O'Reilly. I expect my officers to be above reproach."

"Sir, I—"

He held up a hand. "It's my duty to this city to investigate."

She clamped her lips shut and nodded.

"Now, you want to tell me where you went?"

Tara didn't answer.

"Okay, let's try this another way. You tell me where you went, or I will suspend you until the investigation is complete."

And she thought the day couldn't get worse? She frowned and crossed her arms. Captain looked deadly serious. Shit. She'd never known him to bluff his hand, and right now she couldn't get a read on him. Maybe she should've spent more time at the poker games Carson held each month. Whether he would follow through or not, she didn't know, so Tara sat forward and prepared to tell him the truth. Or skirt close enough to get by. She opened her mouth to respond.

"Stop right there," Scott said, holding up a finger. "Don't even think about lying. I know you went to your apartment. When Toge opened the door, he found you gone out the window and a grate cover on your bed. Whatever was inside that firebox was long gone. Now, why don't you start there and fill in the blanks?"

Cluster. Fuck. She closed her eyes and blurted out the first thing that came to mind. "A book," she said. "The only thing that mattered to me."

"A book." His doubtful tone suggested he either didn't understand or thought she was nuts.

Probably a bit of both, Tara decided with half a laugh. "My greatest treasure, sir. And the only thing I had left from my grandmother's passing."

He settled back in his chair, the leather creaking beneath him. "I know Rose meant a lot to you, and selling her possessions was tough, but why duck out the window? Why not tell Toge what you were after instead of this cloak and dagger crap? You do understand how this looks, right?"

"I didn't until tonight." She waved the evidence bag with the papers inside. "Until I knew about this."

"So you don't need me to tell you that it was stupid?"

Tara shook her head. "Not really, no."

"Then why go out the window in the first place? Why not do that thing with your lips where the vibrations come out? What's it called again? Oh, I know. Communicate." His rising voice clearly communicated all right. He was frustrated and maybe a touch worried.

The realization that he cared enough to be worried made the lie harder when it came. "I don't trust Toge. I thought he'd take the book, maybe mishandle it in an attempt to secure the evidence."

Scott snorted, but then nodded. "He does have that effect on people. You listen, though. If you ever do anything like that again, you're going to be cooling your heels far longer than you will be this time. Do I make myself clear?"

She nodded.

He waved at the evidence bag. "You have our full support. In the meantime, I think it best that you stay on desk duty until the investigation is complete." He picked the pencil back up and tapped it again. "You can go."

Tara stomped out the door and headed for her desk. There was hell to pay, and if Tara found the perp responsible for the fire in her place, she'd send him there herself. She kicked the metal trash bin beside her desk and slumped into the chair. No, she wouldn't feel sorry for herself. She may be on desk duty, but that didn't mean she couldn't do some digging of her own. Especially since some of the reports would be off limits to her in the morning.

She yawned and forced her eyes to remain open. It had been a long-ass day. Between her regular work and the emotional ups and downs she'd experienced since seeing what remained of her home and flying across the rooftops, she felt drained. Still, it was important to follow up on what she could while she had access. Captain would likely have IT block certain aspects of the investigation in the morning. Besides, it wasn't like she had anything else to do but go back to the motel.

Logging on to her computer, she brought up the report from the fire inspector. Benjamin had found a lovely little V shape coming from an outlet in her living room and upon further investigation realized that the wires in the outlet had been tampered with. Add in a few phony papers indicating she was going for a rental insurance claim and there you had it. Desk duty until investigation was complete. It was the only choice the department had, Captain had said. Tara wanted to believe otherwise. She was supposed to stay out of the investigation and work on her cases. Not likely. There was far more going on than fake insurance papers. Something—she gulped and fought off chills—supernatural.

She rubbed at the headache forming behind her eyes. No additional evidence had been found at the scene. They'd need a statement from both Carson and herself. Later. She switched over to vehicle records and entered the two first plate digits from the bike. Three hundred fifteen records returned. Or damn near every motorcycle in the area. The ache became a throb.

Taking a breath, she reviewed the events of the night. The creature had appeared in her window, which meant he knew where she lived. Could also mean that was why he was there the previous night. She stood and began to pace. The motorcyclist had appeared at the church. How had he known they would be there unless he and the birdman were in on the theft together?

She shook her head. Something didn't feel right. Maybe because she thought the two men fought at the bottom of the stairs. She turned and paced back. The church was important. The creature had known that the walkway was there and probably even that the door was open. The motorcyclist had found the stairs. And how ironic was it that the church was one she and Grandma Rose had frequented when she was a kid?

Tara grabbed a cup of coffee as she left the precinct. She had a nagging need to find out what secrets that church held and an undeniable need for sleep. Making a split-second decision, she went with her gut and headed for St. Jude's Parish. The birdman had taken her there on purpose, she reasoned, taking a large gulp of coffee. She would start with the church and hope to find some clues that would give her the identities of the two men. One had her book, which she meant to have back. Was one responsible for the fire?

She thought back to her apartment. Tara always kept the doors locked. She was trained to notice things such as scratches against the lock or doorframe indicating forced entry. There was nothing like that, she knew. That left the windows. Two in her living room overlooked the city, but had no stairs beneath. No way to reach them. Only the window in her bedroom led to the fire escape. She kept it closed and locked and hadn't checked it lately.

Could someone have figured out a way to get it open and she hadn't noticed? She drummed her fingers on the steering wheel. Anger settled deep in her bones. As a cop she hadn't made many friends and certainly had her share of enemies. Yet something told her that this was more closely related to the incident with the book. It was too coincidental.

St. Jude's rose into the night sky like a giant marble monolith. Blue moonlight dodged the thickening clouds and kissed the bell tower, casting shadows down the steps of the old building. Tara stared up at the church, searching the rooftop for a man with gray feathered wings and a piercing blue gaze. He wasn't there. She parked in the small lot and got out of the car.

Tara checked her watch. It was just after nine o'clock on a Wednesday night. Horns blared, music pumped through the velvety darkness, and people walked the sidewalks, talking and laughing. All of it faded into the distance as Tara stared up at the church. From here she could smell the sweet camellia flowers that bloomed in the garden on the east side. Tara followed her nose around the building and found the simple iron gate latched and locked. Beyond she could see the small house that the priests called home. A lamp burned in the window, illuminating a man in his sixties with silver hair and glasses bent over a text. It was the same priest from her youth. He looked up as if sensing her and gave a kind smile.

She returned to the church and swung open the large wooden door. The foyer was dim, lit only by candles. Small black and white tiles gleamed on the floor and an old wooden table held last Sunday's literature. Tara skimmed the papers with her fingers and then moved into the sanctuary.

Religion had been part of Tara's life as a kid. Grandma Rose took her to church every Sunday, where they would light a candle for her parents. She lit one now to honor their memory and another for Grandma Rose. She moved down the row of pews, taking in the stained-glass windows and the beautifully carved crucifix hanging just beyond the altar. An immense organ rose up on the second floor, its pipes lining the walls. The smell of incense permeated the air.

Two doors were set off the right and left sides of the nave just before the pulpit. The right door led to the belfry, where the biker had fought her on the stairs. She moved around the other side of the room and tried another door. It was locked.

"Good evening," a voice said from behind her.

Tara turned to see the same priest she had seen in the window.

"Hey, Father Gallagher."

"Well, bless my soul, is that you, Tara?"

"It is."

Father Gallagher smiled and adjusted his wire-rimmed glasses. "I thought I recognized that lovely dark hair. It's been too long. I'm glad you found your way back to our humble parish."

Tara glanced back around at the lovely stained-glass windows and brightly polished pews. Hardly what one would call humble. Yet humble was exactly what Father Gallagher was and always would be. If anyone could give her the information she sought, it would be he.

"Father, I need to ask you about a man. He brought me here earlier this evening but we were separated."

The older man's expression was watchful. "We have many people come to our church to seek their peace."

"This man is different." Any way she said it, she was going to sound like a lunatic. Hopefully Father Gallagher would understand that. "He...he has wings."

Gallagher smiled, humoring her. "Though many we know appear to be angels, rare few are actually seen, my dear."

"No. He's definitely not an angel. Angels don't kidnap people from their apartments." She sighed in frustration and forged ahead with the details. "He's six feet in height, has glowing blue eyes and is well built with marble-like skin. Grey and white wings sprout off of his back, and he actually flew me across the city."

Father Gallagher paled.

"He brought me here and set me down on the roof. He seemed pretty familiar with this place, and I thought, given his unusual physical appearance, that maybe you had seen him." Tara watched him intently. The old man knew something, she was sure of it. Every instinct said he was holding something back.

Gallagher seemed to reach some sort of decision as she watched him.

"I've known you since you were a wee one, Tara. Because of who you are, and only because of that, I'll show you. You best come with me." He fished a set of keys from the pocket of his trousers and unlocked the door Tara had just tried. A narrow flight of stairs on the other side led into the basement. He flipped on light switches as they went and wound a serpentine path through the large room to the back, frequently warning her not to trip over the many boxes and chairs strewn about. Tara saw a band of light underneath a door at the other end of the basement.

Gallagher knocked twice and glanced over his shoulder to give her a nervous smile.

A moment later the door opened. Amber light flooded out, bathing the man standing behind it, who propped one hand on the doorframe to block her entry. His face was in shadows, but she could feel his piercing, blue gaze sweeping over her. She shivered.

"Gregore, this is Tara, an old friend of this parish. She would like to speak with you."

Gregore said nothing, though a silent conversation seemed to pass between the two men. It ended when Gregore stood back and swung the door wide. Tara took the invitation.

"I'll just leave you two," Gallagher said and retreated.

The room was small with sparse furnishings, made smaller by the hundreds of books that crowded every available surface. They were stacked on the desk, the chair, the floor, and even the bed. Large rolls of paper were stuffed into an umbrella stand in the corner. Tara turned to Gregore. "Nice place."

He frowned and cleared off the chair for her. "What do you want?"

His voice was gruff, but familiar. Tara watched him as he cleared a space on the bed. Right height. Right build. No wings. Could she have imagined them? No, not after a terrifying flight over the rooftops. Had to be a different guy, and yet...Father Gallagher had brought her here to this man.

She looked a little closer. His thick, dark brown hair fell too long to be considered clean cut but didn't quite brush his shoulders. Midnight-blue eyes watched her and a slight five o'clock shadow hugged his jaw. He wore a navy long-sleeved tee and butt-hugging jeans. Nice. Very nice. She almost couldn't tear her gaze away from his thighs. Clearing her throat she said, "I'm Detective Tara O'Reilly and I'm looking for someone. Maybe you've seen him?"

"I don't get out much."

She ignored the chair, leveling her gaze at him. "This guy would be hard to forget. He has wings."

A dark eyebrow lifted and he smirked, crossing his arms over his muscular chest. "Detective, I think you must be—"

Lord, he was sexy with that faint English accent. He was muscular without being bulky, and though he looked relaxed, she felt his intense interest. Tingles raced through her limbs and heated her skin.

"No. I didn't dream it," she said, a bit breathlessly.

His grin widened as he stepped closer. Every enticing muscle rippled with that small movement. "I was going to say mistaken. But if you prefer a dream..." He shrugged wide shoulders that snagged her attention and held it. "Why come to me?"

Tara pushed down the most unwelcome case of rising lust she'd had in years. The man was so hot, he could have set the church on fire. Magnetic blue eyes drew her in, so she focused on his full lips instead. Another mistake. Though he lacked the beak for a nose, his mouth was just as full. He didn't have talons, though. Still, the voice, the resemblance, even his height were so close. She leaned closer to him and took a deep breath. Even his smell.

So what did all that mean? A relative? She blinked and realized that her face was inches from his neck and he hadn't moved. She licked her lips and tracked her gaze up to meet his. Gregore's midnight-blue eyes blazed with heat and his nostrils flared. He didn't look angry so much as aware. Maybe even aroused? She cleared her throat and took a step back, cheeks flaming with embarrassment. She swallowed and tried to remember what they were talking about. She squinted, then realized...Like this, she could almost see... "Holy crap, it's you!"

Gregore frowned. "As you can clearly see, Detective, I don't have wings."

Tara drummed her fingers on the desk. She had no proof, but she knew...*knew* that this man and the creature were one and the same. Everything fit and her instinct screamed it was true. Instincts that never failed her. Time to be direct. "I want my book back."

"I don't know what you're talking about."

"Like hell!" Familiar anger returned, clenching her gut. Hot or not, the man was lying through his perfect white teeth. "I know it's you. I don't know where or how you've hidden your wings. Maybe you're like Superman and have them hidden under your clothes."

His eyes sparked blue fire. "Care to see for yourself?"

Tara flushed deeper. *Yes.* She licked her lips and said, "No."

Gregore grinned. "I don't have your book," he said.

Tara blew out a hard breath and leveled him with an impatient gaze. "No? How about your partner? Does he have it?"

"I don't have a partner and I'm not married."

Cheeky. Her lips twitched. "Oh, so I'm to presume you and the mystery biker are just coincidentally after my book? A book I've never spoken about to anyone except my very deceased grandmother?"

He cocked his head to the side and studied her. "It's no coincidence," he said. Digging his hand into his pocket, he pulled out a scrap of paper and handed it to her.

"What's this?" she asked, not taking it.

"Your winning lottery numbers. Would you just look at it?"

Tara took the paper from him and smoothed out the wrinkles to look at the hastily scratched letters and numbers. "This is a license plate," she said. "Whose?"

"The biker's. I lost him a few blocks from here, but I got his plate number. I need your help."

Tara started to pace. "First you break into my apartment and then you kidnap me and fly me across the city. Oh God, at least I *think* you flew me across the city. And now you want my help? Are you out of your mind? I ought to drag you down to the station for questioning in not only theft but the fire in my apartment building. For all I know, you're trying to turn in your accomplice!"

"I don't have an accomplice. You lost a book of spells, right?"

Tara stopped the maddening pacing and turned to face him. "Yeah. At least, that's what Grandma Rose told me."

Gregore raised an eyebrow. "You don't know?"

She crossed her arms over her chest. "She warned me to keep it in a safe place and not let anyone know I had it. That's exactly what I did." Why the hell she explained it to him, she didn't know.

Gregore took a few steps toward her. She held her ground, watching him warily.

"That book in the wrong hands is very dangerous. It contains old magic. Romani magic passed down for centuries. Things that people don't believe in anymore are contained in that book."

She shifted from foot to foot. "Magic is fiction." Her voice trembled a bit.

"Then explain to me what you saw tonight."

Impossible man. How the hell could anyone explain that? "You know I can't," she said.

"Magic," he said. "The book contains things that could turn the world to hell in a heartbeat."

Tara closed her eyes and drew in a steady breath of musky, Gregore scented air. "Okay, let's say for one tiny minute that I believe even a quarter of what you're saying, based entirely on the fact that I'm losing my mind. Magic exists and someone bad has my book of Gypsy spells. What does this supposed villain plan to do with it?"

Gregore held her gaze for a long moment. "I don't know. That's what I need you to find out."

Tara shook her head and stuck the license plate number in her pocket. This was too unreal. Too *freaking* unreal. "How did you find out about the spell book? How did *he* find out about it?"

Gregore turned away from her and paced back the few steps to his twin bed. He stood with his hands on his hips, staring at the wall. Tara's eyes swept over his tall frame, noting the muscles and the way his clothes clung in all the right places. What was wrong with her? She should be running the other way, not checking the guy out.

"I need your help, Detective O'Reilly," he said at last. "And if you won't help me, then I won't be held responsible for what he does with the book."

"Just who the hell are you anyway?" Tara demanded.

"My name is Gregore Trenowyth."

"Well, Gregore Trenowyth, I don't need your help finding this guy. I'll do just fine on my own."

"Two against one are better odds. If we team up, we could find it faster."

She was doubtful. "You could lead me off of his trail."

"I could find it first."

She narrowed her eyes. "Then why work with me at all?"

"I suspect we each have strengths the other could use in this venture."

"Such as?"

He shrugged, looking like he knew something she didn't. She blew out an exasperated breath. "Say we do work together and we do find the book. What then? It belongs to me. It's precious. The only thing I have left of my grandmother's."

"I only have need of a single page. After that, I'll return it to you."

Tara paced away then back, arms folded. Why was she even entertaining the notion? She didn't need this guy. She was an awesome detective and finding her grimoire should be easy. She'd just run a background check, check his normal spots, and get the book.

"Sorry. I think I'm better off alone," she said.

Gregore ran a hand through his hair. "Why would he try to burn down your apartment?"

"What makes you so sure it was him?"

"Because he knew about the book. He knew *you* had the book. He wanted to destroy it."

"How do I know it wasn't you who set that fire?"

"I saved that little boy, remember? Why would I do that if I set the blaze?"

Tara thought that over for a minute. "Maybe you didn't want to see anyone hurt."

"Do you really believe I set the blaze and then came back for the kid?"

No. She didn't. Damn it, she didn't want to believe any of this, least of all that the very good-looking man before her was a bad guy. It was far safer to believe he was just as bad as the motorcyclist.

"You're asking me to trust you when I don't know a thing about you. Plus, you kidnapped me and you want my book of spells. Tell me how that makes you trustworthy."

Gregore paced away from her and back. "I'm cursed," he said.

"You and me both," she muttered under her breath.

"No, I'm really cursed." Gregore took a deep breath and put his hands on his hips. "Years ago, I was cursed by a Romani woman. I believe there is a spell in your book that will break it."

"Cursed how?"

"You wouldn't believe me if I told you," he said.

"Try me."

"When I come in contact with direct sunlight, I turn to stone."

"What kind of an idiot do you think I am? I *saw* you at sundown just yesterday. There was still sunlight out, and you sure as hell weren't stone then. Stone doesn't fly."

"The hour between day and night is the only time that I can stand the light. Because the sunlight is less powerful then, I can stand the effects."

"You turn to stone during the day and you have wings. So what you're trying to tell me is what? That you're a gargoyle?" It sounded so much better when Timmy said the word.

"Something like that, yeah."

"You're right. I don't believe you."

The corner of his lips twitched. "Come by tomorrow afternoon, and I'll prove it to you."

Tara patted the pocket of her jeans and headed for the door. "Thanks for the license plate number. But I can take it from here."

CHAPTER 5

Gregore slapped his palm against the door, holding it closed even as she tried to yank it open. Tara turned and glared up at him. She was so lovely with the fire flashing in her eyes. Auburn hair curled over her shoulder, accenting her creamy pale skin. She had few freckles, if any. Something that surprised him. He skimmed down the rest of her body, admiring every curve of her athletic build. She was thin, with smaller breasts. He imagined them in his hands, and it sent a jolt down to his groin. His gaze traveled back up to her chest, which rose and fell with her quick breaths. At this distance, each breath drew her delicate scent into his lungs, yet he did not step back.

He fought the urge to kiss her. She'd probably slap his face and cuff him, he thought with a grin.

"Tara," he said, looking into her smoky-green eyes, "I can help you prove that he caused the fire. Please, trust me."

"I don't trust... men I don't know."

"Do you trust anyone? Is that why you went to a motel instead of a friend's?"

"You followed me? Who the hell do you think you are?"

"A man who wanted to know more about the beautiful woman who followed him just half an hour prior."

Her eyes darted away and he knew then that he had her.

"I followed because it was my job," she said.

Gregore chuckled and leaned down to whisper in her ear, "You followed because you were intrigued. Admit it."

She stared at him and he was intimately aware of her accelerated breathing and the pulse thumping beneath her skin. She slipped out of his arms, turned, and left the room.

Damn, he wished he kept his mouth shut about the curse. He'd hoped that by laying out his cards, he could earn a bit of her trust. Enough to garner her help. She'd walked out the door before he could press further. Not to mention, she didn't seem to take well to the fact that he had wings. A logical mind like hers needed straight facts. Would the license plate numbers be enough? He didn't think so.

Despite the setback, he smiled to himself. It hadn't taken her long to find him. She would have him believe it was just her detective skills. He hoped otherwise.

Magic is fiction. He hadn't expected her to say that. The others he'd met on this journey truly believed in their gifts. Gifts every one of them had. Tara O'Reilly surprised him in so many ways. She was tough, but underneath that hard exterior he sensed vulnerability. Like how she didn't answer his question about why she'd stayed in a motel rather than seek out the comfort of friends or her remaining family member. Did it have something to do with her denial of the magic in her blood?

He added it to the list of things he wanted to know about her. Gregore decided to give her a day to utilize her contacts. After that, he'd seek her out. She needed him. She just didn't know it yet.

Gregore left his room and sought out Father Gallagher. He found the priest in the kitchen rooting through a drawer of serving utensils.

"Evening, Father."

Gallagher started in surprise. "This old heart doesn't have too many years left, son. Don't make it shorter than it already is."

Gregore smiled. "You'll outlive us all, Father. Even if I snuck up on you for the rest of your life."

Father Gallagher winked. "Then another bottle of wine won't make a difference." He pulled a corkscrew out of the drawer and waved it in the air. "Care to join me?"

Gregore nodded and followed the older man into the small dining room. The other priests were already there, passing a bowl of pasta between them. He smiled and took his customary seat beside Gallagher. He took the corkscrew and opened the bottle of wine, then poured a half glass.

"How did your visit with Tara go?" Gallagher asked.

The old man's eyes positively twinkled with mirth.

Gregore snorted. "Not as bad as it could have, but not as good as I wanted."

Gallagher chuckled and passed the salad. "That there's my girl. She hasn't changed at all. When her Grandma, Lord rest her soul, would bring her to our church, that girl could barely keep still. And the questions the child had!"

Gregore tried to picture Tara as a child. As hard as he tried, he could only see her as the beautiful woman she was now. "She is something," he admitted.

"Will you be helping her then?"

"She isn't ready for my help, Father." Gregore took a bite of his food and washed it down with wine. "You know that I don't have time to wait. How can I break through her defenses?"

Gallagher looked thoughtful. "I would appeal to her noble side. As a detective, she would want to help someone in need."

Gregore frowned. He'd tried that. "And if that doesn't work?"

Father Gallagher waggled his eyebrows. "Then, my boy, you should appeal to the softer, womanly side. I saw how she looked at you. You should kiss her."

Gregore choked on his wine.

One of the other priests pounded on his back. "You should definitely kiss her," he said.

Gregore cleared his throat and coughed again. "Perhaps I will try that." If he did, he sure as hell wouldn't kiss and tell the priests. He shook his head and steered his thoughts to a safer topic. One that wouldn't have him tracking a certain detective down tonight to see how her lips tasted.

<hr />

Nick Saints unfolded himself out of the overstuffed green chair and set the book of spells on the side table. Standing, he stretched his aching muscles. He'd been reading all night, and it felt good to focus on something across the room instead of a foot in front of him. He looked back down at the ancient red leather of the grimoire and traced the cover. At his fingertips was potentially everything he needed to destroy the gargoyle and that detective, just as the priest had said.

A faint grin teased his lips. Perfect timing, that. The old father had been on his way to his next parish. Nick had easily overpowered him and used his own brand of persuasion to find out what the man knew. As luck would have it, he'd known quite a bit about the curse the gargoyle was under and what the beast sought.

Nick blinked. Somewhere in the back of his mind he knew he should probably feel remorse for the hours spent with that old man. Maybe that morality had been Samantha's influence, lost now that she was gone. In the wake of her loss, he'd finally found purpose. And now he had the last piece needed to enact his plans.

He'd found the original curse in the middle of the book, but was so captivated by the contents that he'd read through to the end. This particular branch of the Romani delved deeper into the black arts than they were typically known for. Every spell, every curse, was meticulously inscribed on the faded pages. He could turn someone into any creature he wanted. Or better yet, end their life. The sound of his laughter was unpleasant to his ears.

He went to the kitchen and filled a glass with water, drinking down half before pausing to take a breath. Early-morning light filtered in through the window by the sink. Outside, kids played tag, their thick coats keeping them warm in the chilly February air. They laughed and teased, dancing around one another while they played.

Nick frowned. Had he ever been that carefree? Maybe after this was all over, he'd find a way to be happy again. Maybe then the constant pain in his chest would ease. He missed Samantha.

He rubbed his eyes, exhausted, but unable to sleep. Sleep brought dreams of her. The way the sunlight turned her hair to shining gold and her blue eyes sparkled with laughter and love for him.

Growling at the unwelcome thoughts, he slammed his fist into the kitchen cabinet door. The resulting sting wasn't nearly as bad as the one in his heart. He forced thoughts of Samantha aside and strode back into the living room to pick up the grimoire. He flipped it open and reread the section on ley lines. Could anyone do this shit? If so, that could change his plans considerably.

Nick closed his eyes and focused as the book instructed. He shut out the noisy kids, the leaking faucet, and even the sound of his own breathing. A single thought remained. He would destroy the gargoyle and the detective by any means necessary. With that firmly in mind, he concentrated until the world fell away.

A moment later, a dark red line appeared. Crisp and clean, it ran right through his neighborhood like a street. Nick reached out his energy to touch it. An immediate stab of shocking power had him sucking in a surprised breath, which broke his concentration. The ley line faded from sight. It worked! How the hell had it worked?

Shaking with excitement, he opened the spells and found another to try. He concentrated on the ley line, reached out his energy to draw in its power, and muttered the words of the spell. Something orange sparked bright and bold by his head. Nick snapped his eyes open and scrambled away. The lampshade nearest him had exploded in flames. He grabbed a towel from the kitchen and beat the flames out, leaving a charred black shell behind.

Holy shit!

Nick threw back his head and laughed. Things were looking brighter. Much brighter, one might say. He ran a hand over his face and through his blond hair. Damn, that was hot. He took a speculative glance at the grimoire and the dark spells it contained. An idea formed. Though he didn't understand how, he was able to cast that spell, which meant he could probably cast more. That opened up a whole new world of possibilities for punishing the detective and gargoyle.

As excited as he was to learn more about this power, he had to move. Detective O'Reilly was smart. She'd find him soon if he didn't get out. Truthfully, he was surprised she hadn't found him already. He was pretty sure the gargoyle had his license plate number after their struggle.

Nick packed the few items he cared to keep, knowing he might never return. Hopefully, he'd be back in a few days and both the gargoyle and O'Reilly would be out of the picture for good.

He carefully put the spell book in his messenger bag. His initial plan to ruin both that freak and the cop seemed horribly simple. Now that he had vast magical knowledge at his fingertips, he could, and would, do a lot more damage. He'd begin the first spell as soon as he arrived at his refuge. Closing the door behind him, Nick left his house.

The sky clouded over, threatening snow, as Nick pulled into the parking lot of the small office supply store. He headed directly toward the self-service copy center. This early, the place was nearly deserted. Exactly what he had hoped for. The bored teenager behind the counter barely spared him a glance, paying far more attention to whatever was on her cell phone.

He chose a copier facing away from her, opened his messenger bag, and removed the spell book. It didn't look like anything special. No ancient scrawling on the cover or demonic beings. Just dark red leather with yellowed pages. But within, that was where the true detail came to life. He flipped through a couple of pages, gingerly heading for a page almost direct center of the book. Colorful drawings, a delicate curving handwriting, and lists of ingredients filled each page. Incantations, spells to lure love, darker spells to bring wrath on your enemies, all contained within a book no more intimidating than a college student's journal.

Nick studied the image of a stone creature with glowing eyes carefully drawn on the page. How was it that a simple Gypsy woman could create something so inhuman? What other powers did she have and how did she come into them? Was she born with them? And how did that stupid cop come to have something so valuable in her possession? She certainly didn't seem the type to throw magic around. But what if she did have magic? Maybe that's why the gargoyle had sought her in the first place.

Darkness churned in his gut. No silly woman would stop his plans. Whether she had power or not was immaterial. What he set in motion now could not be stopped. Both would pay for their crimes against him. But just in case the worst should happen and the spell book was lost to him, he would have insurance.

Speaking of insurance…Nick grasped the top of the yellowed page with the drawing of the ugly gargoyle. He tugged, gently ripping the page from the book. No need to make it easy for them if they ever did get their hands on his prize. The girl behind the counter glanced up, then returned to her phone with a little shrug. He folded the paper and stuck it in his pocket. He'd decide what to do with it later. Opening the copier, he flipped back to the front page of the spell book and began to meticulously copy every page. He would have it bound and put it aside in a safe place.

Never underestimate the enemy. He chuckled. Maybe that brief stint in the army wasn't completely wasted. Yet he couldn't help but wonder just how much his enemy had already underestimated him. The thought brought a firm smile to his face. No, they couldn't possibly have any idea the plans he had, which made him far more powerful.

⊰ CHAPTER 6 ⊱

"Do you believe in gargoyles?" Tara asked Carson as they sipped their coffee at the Mystical Moon. She'd called her partner first thing this morning, asking him to meet her here. She sure hoped he wouldn't think she was nuts.

"You mean the ugly stone things on the tops of old churches? Yeah. What's not to believe?"

Tara adjusted a bobby pin in her hair, trying to keep the curls out of her face.

"No, I mean the old myth about them being humans and they only turn to stone during the day." She liked her hair, but trying to keep it out of her eyes was becoming more of a hassle.

"Are you feeling well? You look a little pale." Carson's forehead scrunched up in concern. His eyes lacked their usual humor. "What's going on, Tara?"

Tara decided to quit fidgeting with the pins and just let her hair be. If she ended up looking like Sasquatch, then so be it. She drained the last of her coffee and prayed it would kick in and wake her up from this nightmare.

"Someone set fire to my apartment, Carson. The inspector found evidence of arson and some phony insurance papers." She met his gaze across the small table. "I didn't do it, Carson. You know me. Hell, I thought even the captain knew me better than that." She tapped the empty paper coffee cup against the table. "He says it's just a formality until the investigation is over. I just can't believe this is happening."

Carson nodded, taking a sip of his own mocha. He always ordered the rich chocolaty brews—with whipped cream—while Tara was just a plain black coffee kind of girl.

"So then why do you ask about gargoyles?"

Tara shook her head. "Never mind, it was just a crazy thought."

"Crazy like what? You think a gargoyle set the fire?" He eyed her like she'd suddenly grown an extra head.

"Don't be ridiculous."

"You're the one who brought up gargoyles." Carson stood, grabbing his jacket from behind the chair and slipping into it. "Anyway, I better get to work. See you there?"

A bit confused, she watched him as he shifted on his feet, taking a step back and stuffing his hands into his pockets. He avoided her gaze.

"Is there a problem, partner?" she asked.

He shook his head much too quick. "No. Nothing. I just want to get a jump start on the day." He was out the door before she could blink.

Great. Just freaking great. Now her partner thought she was crazy, and he was acting like he didn't want to be within ten feet of her. She hoped to God he believed that she didn't set the fire.

From across the room, Tara felt someone watching her. She turned to see the Gypsy in the corner, Louisa, smiling at her. The woman waved.

Tara nodded, stood, and left the shop. Gypsy magic. Gargoyles. Tarot. What the hell had she gotten herself into?

She climbed into her car and drove to work. At just after eight o'clock in the morning, the place seemed remarkably busy. She pushed her way through a couple of thugs, two gang members in red scarves, and a prostitute who screamed at the top of her lungs in the squeakiest voice Tara had ever heard. It grated on her nerves. She made her escape through the door leading down the long hall to the offices. It wasn't much quieter here, she realized, and wished she had another cup of coffee to take away the dull ache in her head. Must've been a busy night.

As she made her way through the maze of desks, she realized that most of her colleagues avoided eye contact.

"News travels fast around this place," she said.

"What did you expect?" Captain Scott said, from behind her.

Tara frowned. "How about a little sympathy? Or maybe some innocent until proven guilty?"

Scott didn't comment further. "Are you okay?"

Hell, no, she wasn't okay. But she wouldn't take his head off for it. "Fabulous." She waved her hand at the piles of paperwork on her desk. "Guess I know what I'll be doing until the investigation is over."

The captain nodded and moved on. Tara sank into her chair. Not even her Casanova partner was sticking with her on this. The trouble was, she couldn't talk to Carson about her current situation. If *she* didn't believe what was going on, how could anyone else?

She pulled up her log-in page on the computer screen and selected the law enforcement network. Taking the slip of paper out of the pocket of her coat, she typed in the license plate number and watched the computer go to work. It would take just a couple of minutes to bring up all the license information on this guy.

"Bingo," she said when a match came up. "Nicholas Saints." She clicked on the link for more information, which brought up his driver's license picture and the last known address. No priors listed. No speeding tickets. Tara wrote down his address. Under normal circumstances, the guy would have looked clean. But he was definitely into something. She tapped her pen against the pad of paper, considering her options. She could send a couple of uniforms out to his place to take a look, but that might scare him off. It would be better to go out herself. She'd have to be very careful. Should she risk it?

Tara kept herself busy with paperwork over the next few hours, trying not to think about the address on her notepad. She reviewed her case file and made a few phone calls that turned up absolutely nothing. Few even answered their phones. She glanced out the window and saw the sun shining in during a (brief) sun break. Sun breaks were at a premium during the long Seattle winter and typically didn't last long.

At a time like this, who would be inside? *Me.*

Her fingers strayed to the address on the notepad. She thought about Gregore. He'd almost kissed her last night. Heaven help her, she'd wanted him to, which was crazy really, since she'd just met him. But she couldn't deny his appeal. In the glowing lamplight of his tiny room, he'd seemed to fill the space. She could still remember his musky scent and the way he'd crowded her. The way he'd touched her and the heat of his hand. She groaned. What a mess. She couldn't very well ask a stone block to go with her to scope out a perp's house, and she couldn't wait until dusk. Being stuck at her desk wasn't an option either. Twenty more minutes of paperwork and *she'd* turn to stone.

Grabbing up her jacket and Saints' address, Tara headed out of the office. She'd just take a look. No harm in that, right?

The neighborhood on the outskirts of the city looked like most others in this area. Neat yards, fences to keep the dogs in instead of the neighbors out, bright colored paint and rows of winter-blooming primroses and hellebores. Saints' house fit so well with the others that she double-checked the address to make sure she had the right place. Nothing about the light yellow paint and white trim spoke of arsonist and thief.

Takes all kinds, she thought.

She watched for several minutes, noting that in the early afternoon, few seemed to be about. Likely because the clouds moved back in, obscuring the sun and threatening snow. An older woman walked her dog at the end of the block. A man in his forties pulled his car into the garage two houses down. Nothing seemed to move in Saints' house.

Tara waited until the woman with her dog had disappeared around the corner, then opened the car door to go for a closer look. She stopped at the front door and listened for movement. All was quiet. She knocked, fairly certain that Nick Saints was long gone. Only the truly idiotic would be as brazen as Saints and then go back home to wait for the police to show up. Saints didn't strike her as idiotic. Plus, she never got that lucky.

When no one answered, she peered in the front window, noting the living room beyond. Cozy. A plush couch and chair, television, and a few photo frames. It didn't look terribly manly, as she expected.

Did Saints have a girlfriend? Wife? Before she thought better of it, Tara tried the doorknob. It was locked.

She checked to make sure she was unobserved and moved to the fence on the side. It was easy enough to jimmy the gate open and slip into the backyard. On the other side of the fence, a dog barked and snarled, making her jump. She sent up silent thanks that the dog belonged to the neighbor and not Saints, and continued on. The backyard was sparse, with just a barbecue and a single chair with a table. Maybe he didn't have a woman in his life.

Tara flattened herself against the house and took a quick peek in the first window. A bedroom—empty. She moved to the next window framed with lace curtains. The man who rode that beast of a bike would not have lace unless there was a woman in his life. Tara glanced in the window and saw a kitchen beyond. Again, empty. Finally she approached the slider door, once again cautious in case someone was within. A skinny metal frame was stuck crudely between the door and the wall. At the bottom of the frame was a pet door. From here she could see the dining room, living room, and a hallway leading back to the bedroom and probably a bathroom. She waited a full minute, listening intently for any noise or movement, but heard nothing.

Saints wasn't here.

The cop in her told her to walk away. Oh, but the woman he'd robbed struggled with herself, wanting to reach for the door handle. She wasn't supposed to be here. Hell, she'd face serious consequences if anyone found out she even looked for Saints. Tara peered into the house once more. There could be good clues in there indicating where Saints had gone. She should wait and have Carson look into this.

It was the best course of action.

Anything more would jeopardize her career.

She frowned. With the way Carson treated her earlier, would he bother? No.

Indecision warred. She might be able to track Saints down elsewhere. But how much longer would it take without the potential clues just a few feet in front of her? What would he do with the spell book during that time? Would he destroy it? Would he attempt to use one of the spells on someone? Cause them harm? Could he? If so, wouldn't she be partly responsible for any damage he did? Just the thought sent stabbing pains through her gut. She didn't know what was in that book or what he would do with it. But some small part of her conscience whispered that she shouldn't wait to find out. Tara licked her lips and went with her gut. Just a quick peek. She wouldn't touch anything.

Reaching into her coat pocket, she used the fabric to grasp the door handle. It wasn't locked, but didn't slide open. She didn't see a dowel in the track or anything other than the initial slider lock, which wasn't latched into the metal frame. She put her weight into pulling the door open, but still it didn't budge. It was worse than the slider at Grandma Rose's old house. That door always seemed to come off track when Tara least expected. Eventually, she had learned to fix it herself by pulling up on the handle and pushing the door just a touch in. Then, as now, the door popped right back into place and opened without a hitch.

Something crashed inside, out of sight. Swirling white vapor drifted toward her. Reaching for her like twisting fingers. It smelled of chlorine and something else. Tara jumped back and hit a solid wall. She yelped and spun around, free hand going for the Sig Sauer at her waist. She swore, looking up into the moss-green eyes of her partner.

"Jeez, Carson, what are you doing here? You gave me a heart attack!"

He reached behind her and closed the slider, blocking out the foul odor that tried to clog her lungs. "I might ask you the same question, partner. What in the hell do you think you're doing?" he asked in a low grumble. "And what in God's name was that white smoke?"

Tara cleared her throat and glanced at the door. "I...uh...I think it was a booby-trap. And I was just testing the strength of these sliders. You know, in case I decide to buy a house some day. Girl's gotta stay protected."

"You're the worst liar I know." He frowned. "Ever heard of breaking and entering? What if you'd gone in and breathed that shit? Tara, you can't do this."

Oh shit. This was bad. Carson *never* used her first name. He elaborated before she could ask an innocent, "Do what?"

"Listen, the captain's not a moron. Especially when you don't follow procedure and log off your computer, leaving the address of where you're going up on the screen like a newbie." The contempt in his voice hammered at her. "He knows you're up to something."

"Is that why you're here, Carson?"

"Yeah. He sent me to follow you."

She knew what was coming next. Carson could be so by-the-book sometimes. "Do I need to ask?"

He looked genuinely sad. "No, partner. I already called him. He's expecting us."

"This is going to cost me my job, Carson!" She wanted to throttle him. "How many times have I looked out for you?"

"A lot. And I haven't forgotten. For the record, he'd be more upset if you'd actually broken in. I think your job is safe. For now. Just don't do anything else this stupid, okay?" He ruffled her auburn curls and steered her back to the front of the house. Carson walked her to her car, promising to follow her back to the east precinct.

Tara slid behind the wheel, closed her eyes, and took a deep breath. *Time to face the music, O'Reilly.*

CHAPTER 7

Nick Saints traced the white pentagram painted onto the glass door of the Grand Grimoire, one of the only indications that the mystical shop was anything other than an expensive boutique. It also had the added benefit of being at the junction of three ley lines. By closing his eyes halfway and letting his vision blur, he could see the lines in burgundy, clearly intersecting at the shop. He almost laughed. His new place had more power than this.

He pushed open the door and stepped inside out of the newly falling snow. The temperature had dropped suddenly and a cold wind blew. Warmth enveloped him the moment he entered the shop. Above the door, a tinny cowbell announced his entrance. Nick took his hat off, dusted away the snow, and put it back on, taking his time to look around as he did so.

The walls were painted a rich red, with black shelves and gold and black swirled carpet. Candles in multiple colors filled the shelves to his right. Some were carved in intricate designs. Others were smooth, presumably so that a caster could carve the image needed for the spell. Cinnamon incense scented the air.

A shop girl sitting behind the counter looked up from her book. She looked about fifteen. The jail bait paused in the midst of turning a page, staring at him as if what she saw were far more interesting than an average-looking blond man who looked more at home in a coffeehouse than a mystical shop. The duplicity of that image appealed to

Nick. He smiled at her, then unfolded the shopping list written on the back of his grocery receipt and picked up a small shopping basket. Nick bypassed the typical rows of candles and tarot cards for beginners. He didn't need them. While he was a beginner, these wouldn't bring him the level of power he wanted. They probably didn't even teach the level he'd already achieved with just a few hours of practice. But other objects in the room did hold some fascination.

He headed straight for the altar section. Here he picked up an athame with a Scottish pentacle on the hilt. The ceremonial dagger gleamed in the fluorescent lights. He selected a mixing bowl, incense, both black and white salts, and a smelly magical oil that promised to enhance his mental powers. From there he wandered over to the bookshelves.

At first the sheer selection was overwhelming. Upon closer inspection, he realized that many of the books were of fairies, inspirational artwork, Wicca, Druids, astrology, and the Gothic alphabet. He wasn't interested. Nick frowned. He ran his finger along the spines of those in what appeared to be the serious spell caster's section. A green book on conjurations caught his eye. It had promise, if he wanted to try conjuring a demon. Demons of lust, general destruction, specific destruction, general chaos, specific chaos…the lists went on. He was just getting to the demon of revenge when a sexy smell tickled his nose. Briefly distracted from the book, he lifted his head and sniffed again. Closer now and smelling of vanilla warmed by skin. Shiny black hair in pigtails appeared at his shoulder.

He looked down into the crystal-blue eyes of the shop girl. Then farther down to her abundant cleavage squeezed into a black lace bra and tight, white half-shirt. This close, she was clearly not fifteen. More like a hot twenty-two. She wore a plaid skirt that barely covered her shapely ass, black knee-high socks, and boots that laced up the most amazing calves he'd ever seen. Her lips were painted a deep red, which set off fair skin and the winged black brows that framed her fantastic eyes. Her lashes went on for days. She winked at him, and he hardened with need. Nick grinned.

She reached a slim arm across his body, pressing her breasts against his chest, to pluck a different book off the shelf.

"If you're looking for real power, I recommend this one," she purred in his ear. "It doesn't spend too much time on the teachings of Aleister Crowley."

Nick tore his gaze away to look at the book she offered. In black, raised letters were the words, *Sex Magic: The Power of Passion*. Their hands brushed as he accepted the book. He flipped a couple of pages, admiring the photographs of couples locked in various stages of erotic copulation. The shop girl's delicate hand, tipped in purple nail polish, pointed to a picture of three lovers interlocked in a pose that raised his blood another few degrees. He licked his lips.

She pressed closer.

"I like what I see," she said, taking in the length of his body and lingering on his crotch. "Everything I see." She emphasized her point by rubbing against his arm. "If you do too, I can arrange for a personal demonstration. Page 69 is my personal favorite. You won't believe the power increase."

If she hadn't already had his attention, she certainly did now. But he could barely think past the mental image of those legs wrapped around his hips. "Yes-s?" His mouth no longer worked.

"Yes." She purred and flicked her tongue to his earlobe. "Come by after close."

Nick watched her saunter back to the counter, hips swaying beneath the short skirt. He gulped and added the book to his items. The cowbell over the door rattled again. Nick snapped out of his lust-fogged stupor and headed for the counter to ring up his purchase. She charged his items with detachment, barely looking at him, as if the encounter had never occurred. He started to wonder if he had hallucinated the whole thing.

Just before he left, she said, "Sir, the store closes at ten p.m. if you need to return."

He smiled, eyes lingering first on her face, then the generous swell of her breasts.

"Thank you, I will. It promises to be a spectacular night."

CHAPTER 8

"You've got ten seconds to tell me who this Nicholas Saints is and why you were going to break into his house. Start talking."

Tara sat in the quiet office of the east precinct, with the door closed and blinds drawn. She could tell by the look on Captain Scott's face that he wasn't joking. And if it hadn't been his face, then it would have been the reminder that she was now down to eight seconds. He wasn't even twirling anything in his hands. Not good. "I think Saints is responsible for setting the fire in my apartment, Captain."

He leaned back in his chair, lacing his fingers behind his head, and glanced over to Carson, who stood behind her in the corner. She didn't know if Carson was there for moral support, to bail her out, or to agree with the captain. His set features, square jaw, and hard eyes gave nothing away.

After a moment, the captain said, "Why, exactly, would you think that, O'Reilly? Did he leave a calling card that my other detectives missed?"

Tara sighed, not wanting, willing, or even daring to go into the whole truth. She'd be in the state mental ward before she could declare her name was Marie Antoinette. She settled for a portion of the truth. "No, sir. I went back to my apartment for a family heirloom, and this Saints guy tracked me down, stealing it from me."

"What?" Carson exploded. "When? Why the hell didn't you tell me about that?"

"Or me?" the captain asked conversationally.

"Maybe it was something about being assigned to my desk an hour after the incident."

Scott held up a hand to stop her before she got any further. "Which clearly affected your judgment, is that it?"

Carson snorted from his post. She glared at him over her shoulder, then turned back to her boss. "No. But you made it very clear that I was stuck here. So I made good use of my desk time and looked up the plates of the man who stole from me."

Scott rubbed his eyes with both hands, casting a pleading look at her partner. "O'Reilly, I didn't think I needed to remind you that desk duty does not mean scouting out the inside of a private residence. Especially not when the owner could potentially be a criminal and definitely Not. By. Yourself! What were you going to do if he had been home?"

Tara sat quietly, knowing all too well that anything she said would only make things worse.

The captain picked up a pen and tapped it on the desk. "I hate to do it, but you leave me with little choice. You're on leave until this investigation is over. And if you go anywhere near anyone having to do with the fire, the investigation, and especially this Saints fellow, you're out of a job. Do I make myself clear?"

Tara nodded curtly.

"Good. Now go get your affairs in order. Find a new place to live and get a change of clothes. I'll call you in a few days."

"Sir, can I at least inquire about the—"

"A few days, O'Reilly. Or Carson will be your shadow."

Tara pushed the chair out, stood, and strode out the door, vaguely aware that Carson was already shadowing her. As soon as they left the building and stepped into the wet snow, she spun on him.

"Happy, partner?"

He stood toe to toe with her. "As a matter of fact, I am. I didn't lose a partner in there today, but I'm damned lucky and so are you. So start talking. Tell me what is going on."

Tara backed up, holding up her hands. "I don't think so."

"Gumshoe," he tried again, this time in a reasonable tone. "I can't help if I don't know what's going on." He ran a hand through his spiky blond hair. "Please work with me on this."

She shook her head, remembering their conversation earlier and how he'd hardly even stayed to chat with her at the coffee shop. "You know, Shamus, life isn't always black and white. Sometimes things don't make sense. Earlier you acted like you didn't even believe I was innocent, and now you want to know what's going on. Sorry. I'm off the clock." She turned for the car.

"I'm sorry," Carson said after her.

"Not as sorry as I am," she said under her breath.

<hr />

Thomas Whetmore climbed the steps to the massive doors of St. Jude's Parish. Within, he could hear the last strains of a hymn he enjoyed long ago. He hummed along to *Holy, Holy, Holy* as he stopped before the doors, scanning the words carved above. *Come to me, all who are weary...* The words from the book of Matthew echoed in his heart. Weary was a close companion who'd walked beside him for years. No doubt Gregore felt the same. He pulled his long coat tighter against the chilled air and was glad for his warm boots.

Marble walls rose into the black sky. Above his head, a shadow in the bell tower moved, followed by the great bell ringing out nine times, clear and lovely. A half-dozen sculpted gargoyles dotted the roof and corners. Thomas felt the tug of a grin touch his mouth. This was the place all right. The old chap had family standing guard.

A few couples and the occasional businessman exited, each shaking hands with an elderly priest. They stepped into the snowy night, passed Thomas with little more than a glance, then bundled up against the February chill and headed for their warm homes.

He envied them that. Home.

Shrugging off the unwelcome thought, he entered the church and paused inside the vestibule. Candles glowed, adding an air of peace. Although the quietness surely had something to do with that. Another priest and an older couple were at the altar cleaning up from their service. Thomas made his way down the first aisle toward them.

The priest glanced his way, kind eyes assessing. "You're too late for the service, but all are welcome in the Lord's house."

Thomas nodded his thanks. "I've come to ask a couple of questions, Father."

The priest spoke a few words to the people helping him, then gingerly came down the two steps and crossed to Thomas.

"The Lord is still looking for funding to replace these old knees," the man said with a laugh. He moved over to sit on the first pew. "Now, what sort of questions do you have, young man? You'll find the Lord is full of answers. I might even have some of them." He held his hand out. "Father Gallagher."

Thomas smiled and shook the offered hand. "Thomas Whetmore. My questions are a little less celestial in nature."

Father Gallagher chuckled. "Rare few aren't, son. Ask your questions."

"I'm looking for a man. I knew him long ago as Gregore Trenowyth. He's used others, but here in this place, I think he would only use his given name. Tell me, do you know him?"

The old priest looked guarded. "Why would you think...?"

Thomas placed his hand gently on Father Gallagher's shoulder. "Perhaps I should emphasize that a bit more. I knew him *long* ago. Very long. Fear not, Father, I don't wish him harm. He and I were great friends once." When Gallagher still hedged, Thomas added, "Aren't those his brothers or children I see standing guard on your roof?"

Father Gallagher laughed long and hard, moisture rimming his eyes. He removed his glasses and wiped the tears away. "I don't think he'd care for your reference, young man."

Thomas shrugged. "At least that hasn't changed."

The priest chuckled. He adjusted his glasses back onto his face as he collected himself.

"I seem to recall Gregore mentioning a Thomas once. But tell me, if you were such a good friend, where was his family from?"

Thomas acknowledged the question with a nod. Smart man. Father Gallagher would not betray Gregore without proof that Thomas was friend, not foe.

"England. Derbyshire actually. They had a lovely estate there."

The priest nodded. He squinted in thought. "I'm trying to think of more personal questions."

"Something only the real Thomas would know?"

Father Gallagher smiled. "Yes. Forgive me, but I can't tell if you're thirty-five or one hundred thirty-five."

"Gregore and I grew up there. My family had a much smaller farmhouse, but we did well enough. He and I played in the woods surrounding his estate for years. I was there when he kissed his first girl. Her name was Elsa, I believe. We grew into dashing young men who raised hel... um, took London by storm."

The priest's eyes twinkled. "Do go on."

"We spent the season in London each year, sweeping the lovelies off their feet. The rest of the year in the countryside. It's there we met that traveling band of Gypsies." Thomas thought back to that day so long ago. That miserable day that had ruined their lives. And the day just weeks prior that began it all. He clenched his fist. "It's there that I convinced Gregore to have his fortune read by Zola. The girl who..." He flicked his gaze to meet the priest's sympathetic smile. "I am that Thomas, Father. I'm the man who brought this all upon us."

"Son, it's not your fault."

"Isn't it? Had I not been so determined to pursue a particular young woman at the fair, we wouldn't have been there. He never would have met Zola at my urging. The Gypsies would have moved on and we'd have lived our lives in peace."

"That may be true. But the Lord had a different plan." Thomas shook his head, but Father Gallagher held up his hand to stop him. "Think of this. Had you lived your life then, you would have died long ago. The things you have experienced would not be your memories. Why, you wouldn't even be here with me now. Gregore would not be here to do what must be done."

"What do you mean 'what must be done'?"

"Only that the Lord had a plan. Our Father knew the events of his time and selected those he knew could successfully thwart the evil that threatens."

"Is Gregore in some kind of trouble?" Thomas asked. *Please, not now,* he thought. *Not when Gregore needs to concentrate on breaking this curse.*

"Would it be important to you if he was?"

"Yes, Father. I got him into this. I need to get him out of it before he meets an ugly end."

"Guilt is a good motivator, eh?" Father Gallagher rose from the pew. "Gregore is our guest, but I don't see him much. We run on different hours of the day. He's not here now. He comes and goes. Shall I tell him you stopped by?"

"No, I want to surprise him."

Gallagher raised a bushy gray eyebrow. "You're not sure of your welcome." He nodded to himself. "You might try Tara O'Reilly."

"Who is she?"

The priest smiled. "Someone of interest to Gregore. Better that he tell you when you see him."

Thomas rose and gave a half grin in return. "The confidentiality of the cloth, is it then?"

Father Gallagher chuckled. "More along the lines of a friend than the cloth, in this case."

Thomas shook the man's hand and exited the church. One step closer. He had to find Gregore before it was too late.

⊰ CHAPTER 9 ⊱

Dark gray snow clouds hung low over the city the following day. Icy wind blew at Tara's clothes, sneaking past her layers to freeze everything it touched. She shivered and pulled her leather jacket closer over her new claret-colored sweater. She'd spent the morning shopping for clothes, something she hated, and scouting out apartments. By three in the afternoon, she was hard-pressed to say which was worse. Probably hunting for a new place to live. Those she could afford were dumps and those she couldn't were a dime a dozen. Finally she tucked away the apartment guide, blew out a breath, and admitted defeat.

She'd thought of Gregore more than she wanted to admit in the last few hours. Those thoughts were less volatile, and if she were honest with herself, hotter than any she had about her job. Gregore's challenge for her to trust him and visit when he was supposedly a gargoyle replayed through her mind like a movie stuck on a loop.

His eyes had glittered in the lamplight as he'd made his case. He'd saved Timmy when he had come for her spells. The fire probably wouldn't have stopped him from entering her apartment when he was stone. Instead he saved a helpless little boy. That made men heroes in her world. Heroic, but not necessarily trustworthy.

Tara needed to find out more. Curiosity often got the better of her, hence the reason she'd become a detective. That damn need to know and understand everything. Gregore was no exception. She needed to know the truth about him. He said he needed her help, and maybe, just maybe, she could use his too.

She drove to the old church and parked in the empty lot. No one was about in the vestibule or the nave. Surprisingly, the door to the basement was unlocked. She made a mental note to talk to Father Gallagher about the church's security and headed down the stairs.

No light came from under the door of Gregore's small room. She knocked lightly and waited. There was no response. Maybe he wasn't home, since he'd suggested she visit yesterday instead of today. She knocked again and this time pressed her ear to the door, trying to hear if there was movement on the other side. Tara heard a faint rustling and nothing more. Could be the wind coming in through the windows high up on his wall. Or that he was injured and needed assistance. She tried the door handle and was surprised when it opened easily beneath her fingers. She stepped into darkness.

"Hello? Gregore?"

A faint mumble came from the other side of the room. She reached for the light switch, flicking it on. Heavy, black curtains covered the windows above, keeping all light out. Gregore was stretched out on his bed, unmoving. Drawn to his side, she touched his face. As impossible as it seemed, his features were those of the creature she had seen just the day before. A sharp beak instead of a nose. The tips of his folded wings resting against the pillow beside his head. Cheekbones and lips chiseled out of stone. Now that she knew the man, she easily recognized him within the stone embodiment of this cursed creature.

Tara lifted her hand to sweep the hair off of his brow. It didn't budge. It was as if each strand was made of heavy concrete yet as cool as marble. Her brow creased when his chest rose with a deep, slow breath, as if he slept. Like a fairy tale; Prince Gregore locked in sleep. A dark combination of the frog prince and the beast.

As a girl, Tara had often daydreamed of handsome princes and ancient curses. Of being a beautiful princess breaking the wicked old witch's spell. She traced a finger over his cheek. He was cursed and definitely handsome enough to be a fairy-tale prince even in this visage. Like Beast and the frog prince, Gregore was trapped by a curse, waiting to be set free. Captivated by that thought, her eyes drifted to his lips. Before she could change her mind, Tara lowered her head and gently brushed her lips across his cool flesh. His mouth moved slowly beneath hers, bringing Tara back to her senses. She shot up off the bed and crossed the room. What the hell was she thinking?

"Tara?" Gregore's voice was gravelly and the word seemed pulled from his inner being.

"Gregore? Are...are you okay? I mean, do you need a doctor?" She returned to his side and sat on the edge of the bed. She traced his lips with a fingertip.

"Curse," he whispered, as if it took supreme effort to speak.

His glowing eyes opened and focused on her. Every movement he made was slow and forced. Unable to help herself, she touched his hair again. And then his hands. His feet. She couldn't budge them even when she put her entire weight against him. He was as immovable as a boulder.

"I don't understand," she said.

"Curse," he repeated.

"Yeah, I get that part. But how is this possible? I can't even move a strand of your hair yet your chest rises when you breathe."

He didn't respond.

"Gregore?"

His gaze moved back to her face. "You...came."

"What can I do?"

"Nothing. Sundown?"

Tara checked her watch. "Almost an hour away. Does this happen every day?"

"Yes."

How did the man survive? She had to think. A gargoyle? "Creatures like you aren't supposed to exist," she told him.

A deep chuckle rumbled slowly out of his chest and sent a delicious shiver down her spine.

"So what happens at sundown? You're suddenly a man again?"

"Mostly." Gregore closed his eyes, as if the effort to speak was too much for him.

Mostly? Just what the hell was that supposed to mean? Tara stood and paced to the door and back to the desk. It was still cluttered with books and papers. She skimmed the titles. Genealogy? History of

Gypsies and the Romani people. What looked like pages and pages of immigration records.

"What are you into?" she asked.

He didn't respond.

Tara went back to his side. She brushed her fingers against his cheek. "I'll be at the library. Come find me when you get up. We need to talk."

She heard his faint "Okay" just as she grasped the door handle and left the room.

>—⋅⟡⋅—○—⋅⟡⋅—<

A smart cop and a little bit of magic could prove to be a deadly combination. Nick wouldn't leave anything to chance. He maneuvered the bike through the slick city roads, turning onto Jackson Street. He couldn't allow that freak and the woman to discover his plans.

He drove to the warehouse and parked in a narrow alley. All around him, the neighborhood decayed. Graffiti marked every building and the stink of urine permeated the air. He opened the metal fire door, pushed the motorcycle inside and locked the door behind him. If the snow fell like the weatherman forecasted, he was going to have to find other transportation.

Removing his helmet, he flicked on overhead lights and surveyed the room. The old building was perfect for his needs. Too bad the owner hadn't accepted his offer to purchase the building when he approached the guy last week.

Nick climbed the stairs to the room he'd converted into a makeshift bedroom by laying a full size mattress on the ground, covered in clean blue sheets and an old army blanket. His duffle bag of clothes and toiletries sat beside it and another sheet was nailed across the window for privacy. Simple, but effective. He crossed to the table beside the bed and removed a candle and lighter he had purchased earlier that day. The candle flame danced until it steadied into a warm golden glow. Sliding his fingers under the mattress, he found the spell book and pulled it out. To just sit back and wait for the eight days to pass was no longer an option. He would have to be more proactive if his plans were to succeed.

He removed the gargoyle spell from his pocket, unfolding the delicate paper. At the bottom in flowing script were the words needed to break the curse. He couldn't leave this laying around just waiting to be found and put to use. Nick stuck the corner of the paper into the candle flame. The edges glowed bright green as they burned, evidence that the very essence of magic was bound in every page. He held it over the garbage pail. Small pieces of scorched paper fell as the page disintegrated before his eyes. He dropped the last piece into the can and watched it burn with a satisfied smile.

Picking the leather-bound book up, he skipped past the first few spells and went straight for the darker magic in the back. Time to try out the fun stuff.

She'd kissed him and it was about the worst thing that could have happened.

Gregore stood in a pool of light underneath a streetlamp directly facing the city library. The snow fell, swirling thicker and thicker. A thin layer clung to parked cars and the nearby buildings, promising a chilly night with more to come. The old brick library once held a trolley car turnaround and had since been restored. White columns flanked stairs leading up to welcoming glass turn-style doors. Large windows faced the street. A noisy group of teens exited the building, carrying full backpacks, and headed out to their cars in the parking lot.

He waited for a car to pass and then crossed the street. Tara was inside; he could feel her. Unsettling as that was, his thoughts returned to her visit earlier in the afternoon. At his weakest state, in a form of stasis, he was easily open to attack and took great care to make sure all the doors were locked to make it more difficult for any intruders to enter. Plus, he had the priests who regularly dwelled in the sanctuary. Tara had managed to bypass all of that with ease.

He smiled, thinking of her soft kiss. She continued to surprise him, and Gregore found that very attractive indeed. Dangerously so. He couldn't get close to her. It would be unfair to both since he only had a few days left to his life. So why did everything in his being resent that?

He pushed through the turning door, thankful he didn't have wings to get caught inside, and entered the hushed silence of the library. A stern-looking woman with gray hair and glasses glanced up as he walked in, warning him with her eyes to stay silent. He ignored her and scanned the room. Aisle after aisle of books spread out in a semicircle around him, with long polished tables in between. The air smelled of aged paper and old books. It was fairly empty tonight, with just a few students and people with their noses in the newspaper. He didn't see Tara's dark auburn hair.

Gregore sent his senses seeking outward, like his old cloak lifted around him by a strong wind. He closed his eyes and felt for her. Felt for that strong pull that brought him to attention like a new recruit. He moved through the bookcases, not seeing with his eyes but with the magic that had become an integral part of his life. He lived and breathed this crackling energy at night. Like strength and speed, his senses were much more acute. Most especially that sense that let him attune to his surroundings like a master hunter.

There. In the back corner.

Gregore opened his eyes and went to her.

Sitting at a table dimly lit by a small lamp, she was surrounded by at least a dozen books. Silken curls spilled over her shoulders and the red sweater she wore. He wanted to touch her.

As if she sensed him, she glanced up from the book. Her gaze wandered over him, taking in his leather boots, fitted jeans, black sweater, and leather coat. Her cheeks heated when she realized what she did, and she quickly returned her gaze to the book in front of her.

Tapping the page with a finger, she said, "Says here you're a water feature."

Gregore's eyebrow shot up. "Not exactly."

Green eyes that sparkled with laughter glanced up at him from under thick dark lashes. "That's what it says. How do you explain that?" She mocked his own words.

"People feared what they could not understand in those days," he said. "They used the likeness of such ugly creatures to fend off demons, sickness, and anything else they could think of."

"Is that your professional opinion?"

Gregore grinned. "Yes. Want to see my license?"

"I think I'd rather not."

He threw back his head and laughed. The librarian cleared her throat noisily.

"Shhh," Tara whispered. "You don't want to anger her."

Gregore looked at the stern woman behind him and raised his eyebrows.

Tara snickered.

He turned his most charming smile on Tara. "Perhaps we should go somewhere and talk about water features."

"All right, but I don't want to know where your hose connects." She closed the books in front of her, hiding her grin.

Her words heated his blood. He had the urge to pull her into his arms and finish the kiss she'd started. To feel her satin-soft skin under his mouth. Instead, he walked away.

Minutes later Gregore escorted her out of the library into the cool night air. She pulled her jacket tighter about her and put on her gloves. Snow crunched under their feet as they walked along the sidewalk into the parking lot.

"Should we take my car?" Tara asked.

"Yes."

She unlocked the doors to the Mini. Gregore got in, folding his legs up until his knees touched the dash. He moved the seat back to a more comfortable position and ignored Tara's laugh.

"Where to?" she asked.

His senses filled with her scent and nearness. He'd never been more aware of a person. Clearing his throat, he said, "Let's return to the church. It's safe to talk there."

"Right. Back to your lair."

"It's a church. Gargoyles don't have lairs."

She shook her head and maneuvered the car into traffic. "So what is this curse exactly?"

Gregore stared out the window, thinking about how to respond. Finally he said, "It's what you have already seen. During the day, I'm as good as dead. At night, I'm human, more or less."

"More or less? What does that mean?"

"It means that I look human, but I have certain...abilities."

"Like what? An aversion to garlic and the ability to turn into a bat?"

"That's vampires. I mean like superior night vision and speed."

"Okay, then how did you get it? The curse, I mean."

"I crossed the wrong woman."

"People just don't curse each other these days. Even Romani Gypsy women. There has to be more than that," she said.

"It was a long time ago."

She blew out a frustrated breath and pulled into the parking lot of the church. "Home sweet home."

Gregore got out of the car and headed for the front doors. He held the door for her at the entrance. "Let's go up to the roof."

They climbed the old wooden stairs and stepped onto the walkway. The flurries had subsided during the drive, but heavy snow still threatened in the thick clouds above. Tara's breath caught beside him.

"Amazing," she said, awe tingeing her voice. "It's beautiful up here. I didn't notice last time."

A million lights twinkled below them. The city lived and breathed, lights moving, winking in and out, as people went about their lives.

"Home sweet home," he said. He looked down at the beautiful woman standing so close, her arm brushed his. Her light, soft fragrance, like roses, teased his nose. Heat seeped from her body into his. Gregore wanted to pull her into his arms. See what her lips felt like when he could participate in the kiss. He admired the slenderness of her body and her long legs. He closed his hand into a fist to keep from reaching for her. She raised her chin and met his gaze. The city's glow sparkled in her eyes.

"You said before that you thought there was a spell in the book that will break the curse. Do you really think that some words in a dusty old book can truly change what happened?"

"I don't know," he whispered. "I have to try. I'm running out of time."

"What do you mean?" She reached up and brushed at the lines on his forehead.

"I've only got eight days left to break the curse."

"There's a time limit on these things? How does that work?"

Gregore laughed without humor. "Another way for that old witch to twist the knife deeper into me. She set a time limit, knowing it was unlikely I would ever be able to break the curse. It was her way of killing me slowly."

"How long?"

He leaned against the railing. What would she say to the truth? Would she walk away?

Tara put her hand on his arm, turning him to face her. "Gregore, how long?"

He locked his hand around her wrist so she couldn't leave. "A hundred fifty years."

"A hun—just how old are you?"

His lips curved up in a smile. She hadn't even tried to pull away. "One hundred eighty-two."

"Holy crap. How is that even possible? I know, I know, Gypsy magic. Okay, so you're down to just eight days. What the hell have you been doing for the last one hundred fifty years?"

He shrugged. "This and that."

"You have no idea how badly I want to smack you right now."

He laughed. The touch of asperity in her voice warred with the concern in her eyes. She continued to surprise him. Tough but compassionate at the same time.

"Tell me."

"I've been searching for the book, Tara. After I was cursed, I secluded myself from the rest of the world. I didn't know how to deal with what had happened to me. It took me nearly twenty years to come to terms with it. By the time I returned home, the Gypsies had left the area. I've been tracking them ever since. Searching through each generation to find my answer."

"How did you find out about the book?"

"An old man whispered it to me on his deathbed." That night with Ranulf changed him forever. "He was one of the original people who was there when the curse was spoken. He felt sympathy for my plight and didn't wish to carry it on his shoulders to the next world." Even now he tasted bitterness on his tongue as he said "sympathy." Ranulf hadn't been sympathetic so much as remorseful of his actions.

The old man hadn't wanted to go to his grave with murder on his hands. Ranulf was Zola's suitor before Gregore stole her away. Jealousy ran thick in his blood. It was he who riled the mob into calling for English blood. Ranulf who killed her and blamed an easy target.

Gregore swallowed and shoved the memories to the back of his mind, hands clenching the railing. "I found him in his old age. He told me the grimoire passed from generation to generation, but didn't know who had it last. It has taken me all this time to track it here. To find you."

She licked her lips as if trying to take it all in. After a time, she asked, "What did you do, Gregore? What was so awful that such a curse would be placed upon you?"

He stared into her eyes, then gave in to temptation and brushed his hand along her cheek. "Forget the past. We need to focus on the future now. We have to find the spell book before time is out for both of us."

CHAPTER 10

Tara paced to the door and back to the desk in Gregore's room, repeating the circuit as she thought. What would Nick Saints want with Gregore? And how in the world would Gregore be able to break a centuries-old curse? She couldn't deny his claims or the magic. Not after what she'd witnessed of the gargoyle earlier.

She sighed and went another circuit. A strong, logical part of her wanted to reject the very idea of magic. To shout that it couldn't be real. While the tiniest, niggling of doubt whispered that she'd known it all along. Had known it since the day her parents died. And now when so much was on the line, she finally faced the truth? Damn it.

Her stomach sank as another thought occurred to her. Grandma Rose would be disappointed in her for avoiding the Romani side of her heritage. Even more disappointed if she failed to help someone in need. Tara snuck a glance at Gregore from under her lashes. He sprawled on the bed, watching her pace. How could he be so stoic with just days left to his life? Would she be relaxing, watching someone else pace? Or would she be on a tropical beach drinking a margarita? She shook her head. No, like Gregore, she would fight for more with all she had. Despite his reclined pose, he wasn't waiting to die. She sensed him deep in thought. They had to get that book back. Tomorrow she'd pound the streets for Saints. They couldn't afford to let him slip through their fingers. Maybe Carson could help.

"Stop."

Gregore's gruff voice cut through her thoughts. She stopped pacing. "I'm trying to think this through. We have to find Saints before he's gone for good."

He stood and stretched. "You found his name from his license plate?"

She nodded, mesmerized and more than a little distracted by the flex of his muscles under the fitted black sweater.

Gregore looked smug but wisely didn't mention that she wouldn't have found Saints so quickly without his help. Instead he said, "I don't think he's going anywhere. He's too focused on his plans."

"How exactly do you know that? Are you tuned in to his thoughts? Is there some sort of cosmic force out there linking the two of you together?"

"That's it. I have a Ouija board with his name on it that allows me to contact him through my spirit guide, Zelda the Invincible."

If she wrapped her hands around his neck and squeezed, would she break her fingers? Probably. Wouldn't be worth it to find out. "Did Zelda offer anything of value?"

"She simply pointed out that his moves seem measured. He knew where to look. He has a plan."

Tara nodded and hoped he was right. She checked the time. Almost nine o'clock. "I should probably go get some rest, unless you or Zelda have anything to add?"

Gregore held his palms face up, closing his eyes. When he opened them again, he smiled. "Zelda says, 'Good night.'"

Tara turned away, muttering a few choice curses of her own. He wasn't cute. At all. Okay, he was, damn it. Before she could make it out the door, Gregore caught her hand and hauled her back to his side. All mirth was gone from his gaze.

"I don't think it's safe here anymore. Not for either of us."

"What do you mean?"

Gregore slid his fingers up and down the smooth skin of her wrist, taking his own sweet time answering her. "Only that Saints is smart. He knew where you lived and we know he's been here. I don't know specifics. What I do know is that he's done proper research. A man like that should not be underestimated."

She flicked a glance at the piles of paper and genealogy books. Raised her eyebrow. "I'll keep that in mind."

He grasped her other wrist and held both firmly against his chest. The action pulled her a step closer to him. She tried to move away but he held her fast.

"Think for a minute. What would he need the book for unless he wanted to use it? If he can make the magic work, we will have to be prepared to use magic ourselves."

She shook her head. "This is what I do, Gregore. I work with the finest men and women in the state. We'll find him before anything bad happens."

He gripped her tighter. "Be reasonable."

"I am." Tara tried to pull away once more and found herself yanked against the solid wall of his body. His mouth swooped down to cover hers in a searing kiss. Bewildered, Tara's train of thought derailed. His mouth teased against hers. She stopped fighting him, grabbing a fistful of his sweater instead. She held him to her and responded to his kiss openly, surprising them both.

Gregore's hands dipped down to her lower back, pulling her fully up against him. His heat warmed her body, making her blood rush in ways that excited her. That's when it clicked. All this bickering was because she was really attracted to the man. Gargoyle. Whatever. With a sigh, she pulled back from his kiss. "What will I do with you?"

Wicked laughter twinkled in his midnight-blue eyes. "I have an idea." Before she could respond, he gathered her in his arms for another mind-numbing kiss.

Tara enjoyed the feel of his soft lips on hers. Of his tongue sliding against hers. He tasted dark and powerful, a heady mixture that fueled her senses with passion. He smelled spicy and masculine in an intoxicating musk that was uniquely him. She buried her fingers in his dark hair and reveled in the texture.

This time it was Gregore that pulled away first, resting his forehead against hers as he gulped in air. Tara tried to kiss the corners of his mouth, but he held her away.

"No. No, we need to go. We're not safe. And if you keep doing that, we won't leave until I'm physically unable to."

That little reminder was like a blast of cold air. Stepping out of his reach, she said, "Get your things. I want to put a plan together to catch this guy."

Gregore looked at her with a tinge of regret in his eyes. Yeah, they were back to business.

>―·―·―○―·―·―<

On the roof of the old church, two figures were illuminated by the silvery city lights. From the sidewalk below, Nick couldn't make out their faces. It didn't matter. The gargoyle's height and build gave him away. The detective stood close by. Too close, actually. He squinted up at them as he considered that. He'd been shocked when the gargoyle and the detective arrived a half hour earlier in her car. Now they stood side by side as if they were old friends. Or more.

He didn't like it. Something was wrong. He hadn't pegged the detective as someone who would work with that monster. Stealing the book should have put them at odds. So why the hell hadn't it? He hadn't counted on them teaming up. It didn't bode well for his plans.

Nick pulled his jacket closer, shivering in the cold, and watched as the gap of light between Gregore and Tara closed with their bodies growing closer together. Nick swore. Initially, he'd meant to ruin them individually. If they truly had teamed up, he'd have to reevaluate. He was nothing if not flexible.

The snow began to fall again in earnest, driving the lovebirds back inside the church. If Detective O'Reilly was attempting to obtain information from the gargoyle, that would be one thing. But something in their body language said that wasn't the case. He stamped his feet, trying to put blood back into his cold toes, then paced along the sidewalk, avoiding the streetlamps as much as possible. Watching. Waiting. Freezing his ass off. He checked his watch. The Grand Grimoire closed in an hour. He didn't want to miss his date with that hot little witch from the store. Yet at the same time, his goals were far more important than a little tail.

He blew on his hands and rubbed them together, then stuck them in the pockets of his gray wool coat. Despite the fact that the creature had company, Nick had every intention of seeing this through. He'd practiced for hours to prepare for this. He pulled his hands out of the warmth of his pockets, shook them, and flexed his fingers. Magic channeled through his blood in wispy tendrils he could feel. It was indescribable and made him feel alive like he never had before. He warmed his hands again and backed into a doorway overhang across the street from the church.

Twenty minutes later, his quarry exited the church carrying a duffel bag and walked down the steps, heading for the side parking lot. Nick concentrated on the power in his blood, sent it funneling into his hands, and broke away from the building at a run. His skin tingled, though whether from the cold or the magic he didn't know.

The gargoyle's head snapped up as Nick approached. Gregore dropped the bag, took a step in front of the detective, and blocked her body from attack. Nick focused on the spell. He slid to a stop and threw his hands forward, shooting black flames from his fingertips directly at Gregore. To his delight, the air crackled and popped as heat rushed forward for his targets.

The gargoyle wrapped an arm around Tara's waist and whipped them both out of the way faster than Nick could blink. He readjusted his aim and pushed another blast of fire at them. Once again, Gregore moved them but a little bit slower. The detective cried out as ebony flames licked at her leather coat. She tore it off and tossed it aside, then pulled out her gun and aimed at him.

The creature stepped in front of her and growled at Nick. He looked human with his long leather coat and readied fighting stance, but Nick knew better. He could wear the disguise, but in hours, he'd be back to his true form. Trenowyth pulled a knife from his boot, hurtling it at Nick's chest. Nick dodged the blade and threw more fire. The gargoyle moved them again, farther into the parking lot. The detective slipped on the icy pavement and stumbled into her vehicle. A sharp blast exploded in the air as the weapon in her hand accidentally discharged.

The dance began in earnest.

The gargoyle charged, using that damn speed he possessed. Behind him, the detective scrambled to gain steady feet and aim the gun. Nick dropped short bursts of black fire at the pavement directly before Gregore, catching his clothes on fire. O'Reilly's shouts of warning filled the air. Nick ignored her.

The fire did little to deter the gargoyle's speed, and they tumbled together to the ground, rolling through the snowfall. The flames subsided instantly. Nick landed a punch to the thing's face and took one in the stomach. Using legs and fists, they struggled for supremacy. But he had one thing the gargoyle did not. Magic. Power surged into his hands and feet at his bidding. Flattening his palms on Trenowyth's chest, maneuvering his boots against the thing's thighs, he shoved with all he was worth. Superhuman force propelled the Gregore away, harder than even Nick expected. The beast slide back into the girl's car with a satisfying *thwack*. Trenowyth wasted no time gaining his feet, preparing for his next move.

Ice-cold air beat back the heat wrapped around Nick's hands. Wet, heavy snow dropped harder as they danced through the parking lot. He attacked, Gregore moved the woman and himself. Again and again. A towering yew tree caught fire, flames spreading to the nearby grass. Snow melted and made the leaves and grass hiss.

With each passing minute, Nick could feel weariness setting in. Had he ever been this tired in his life? His movements slowed. Gregore took advantage and threw a hard punch to Nick's cheek. He barely deflected the blow. Sirens screamed in the distance, growing closer. Shit. He couldn't hold out any longer. Scraping together all he had left, Nick shoved a wall of air at them. Trenowyth didn't move Tara fast enough and they were knocked backward onto their asses.

Nick ran for his motorcycle and hit the starter. The machine roared to life and he hit the throttle, back wheel sliding out to the right in the snow. He righted the bike and fled. Shit. Shit. Shit. Score one for the gargoyle.

CHAPTER 11

Gregore watched the blond speed away on the motorcycle and cursed. He would go after Saints, but Tara looked shaken and he felt the need, no, the urge, to stay at her side. Saints could have killed her in that surprise attack. Gregore might not have been able to prevent it. What if he'd failed her the way he'd failed Zola? Just thinking about it made his stomach flop over and his head spin.

So close. He'd come so close to losing another woman.

Gregore walked a short distance away to center himself. He wouldn't allow Saints to catch him off guard again. Nor would he go through the pain of another death on his conscious. Once he had his emotions under control, he knelt to pick up his blade, and sliding it back into his boot, surreptitiously studied Tara.

Pale, trembling hands returned her weapon to the holster at her side. Her eyes looked glassy and she held her spine rigid.

"What the hell was that?" she demanded as she turned to him. "I had a clean shot."

Gregore chuckled. She never said what he expected. No shrinking violet here. "Could you truly explain shooting what would appear to the rest of the world as an unarmed man?"

She licked her lips.

His eyes were drawn to her pink tongue tracing them. Hit with an unexpected flush of lust, he stood. "You and I know he's far from harmless. Does anyone else?"

"Damn it." She nodded, picked up her leather jacket, and inspected the material. Gaping holes ruined the fine grain, which had surprisingly *melted* from the unnatural magic flames.

Gregore looked back down the street in the direction Saints had traveled. Snow fell in great white flakes all around them, coating the world in a thick blanket. The sirens were closer now. "Magic changes the game," he muttered to himself.

He needed to find a way to persuade Tara to use her magic. The detective skills she boasted would do little to defeat Saints. Much more was needed to stop him. Gregore knew that. Did she?

He steeled himself to do whatever it took to bring her magic out and convince her to use it. This wasn't just about his curse any longer.

Grabbing his bag, he said, "Let's go."

<hr />

Tara rounded on him. "I'm not leaving the scene of a crime, Gregore. This is my chance to have Saints arrested for his crimes and taken off the streets."

"And you think that will protect the officers he goes into custody with?"

She ground her teeth, knowing he was right and hating it.

Gregore held up his hands, as if to pacify her, though his eyes glittered in the parking lot's single lamplight. His muscles bunched tight under his long leather coat. The sight would have been mouthwatering if she wasn't so pissed.

Tara stuffed her hands in the pockets of her jeans to keep them warm while she tried to figure out what to do. For all her bravado just now, facing someone shooting black flames was pretty damn scary. What the hell was that anyway?

Though she didn't really want to admit it, Gregore saved her life with that incredible speed. She'd never seen anyone move so fast. And, if she were honest with herself, it felt good to be protected for once. To be wrapped in the arms of a handsome man when facing danger instead of placing herself between the innocent and the miscreant.

She raised her eyes to his. "Thank you, Gregore. You saved us both tonight."

The tight line of his mouth softened.

Whatever he planned to say was cut off as her phone rang. Tara frowned at the number and answered the call.

"You really shouldn't be out at this time of night in that neighborhood, dear. You know what can happen!"

"Aunt Maddy?" she asked, stunned that her aging aunt would be calling at this hour. "What are you doing up? Aren't you normally in bed by eight?"

Maddy's tinkling laughter greeted her words. "Dear, I napped earlier so I could be awake to call you. I'm glad neither you nor that handsome fellow you're with are hurt."

Tara closed her eyes. Maddy was her only surviving relative. Dear woman that she was, Maddy had a gift of premonition and popped up at the oddest times. She cleared her throat and said, "Aunt Maddy, if you knew what was going to happen, why didn't you warn us?"

Maddy laughed. "Dear, you know I can't interfere. It has to happen and then I can help. Oh, I know. Why not bring that new beau of yours over for tea tonight?"

"Now? What beau?"

"Of course. I'm up, up, up!"

"Aunt Maddy, I really need to finish up here. I've got to call—"

"Oh, don't worry about that. That nice old priest—er, what was his name? Galahad? He called the police. In fact, I think it would be best if you came over right now." Maddy paused. "Dear, you're already in trouble with your boss. Why make things worse?"

Tara started to lose her patience. "Somebody just tried to kill us, Maddy. I've got to report this. I can't just—"

"So you'll come now? Those fellows you work with won't be happy to see you if you're still there."

"No. Tea really isn't—"

"Goodness, your grandmother was never so argumentative. Didn't she teach you to respect your elders?"

"Yes, but—"

"Right, so come over here. I have something important to tell you."

"Really..."

"Okay, but if you insist on staying, don't say I didn't warn you. You know a cop never wants to spend the night in jail."

"Jail? But I—"

"If you won't listen to your aunt, then you get what you get. Good-bye!"

And just like that, the call was over. Tara swiveled her head from the phone in her hand to Gregore. He dared to smirk.

"Family?" he asked.

Tara flipped the phone closed and groaned. She knew better than to test the limits of Aunt Maddy's knowledge. If Maddy envisioned that things would go down poorly for her, then she would do best to go to tea. Even though it went against everything in her bones. Not to mention that it was after nine at night.

"We've been invited to tea," Tara said. She ran a hand through her tangled locks and realized with some surprise that her anger had faded completely. Replaced with confusion, no doubt. "As wrong as it seems, I think we should go."

He nodded and didn't ask for further explanation. Tara found it odd, but she guided him back to her car, adding her ruined jacket and his bag to the trunk. The old ways warred with her cop instincts, but she knew better than to fight Aunt Maddy's sight. Maybe it would be useful in this case.

"My aunt wants to talk to me about something and feels it would be best if I... if we came now," Tara explained as they pulled out of the parking lot onto the snowy road. Red and blue flashing lights reflected in her rearview mirror as they left the church. A fine mess this was. Just when exactly had her life gone straight to hell, anyway? She'd never run from something in her life. Well, maybe that wasn't exactly true, but that incident didn't bear thinking on.

"How did she know?" Gregore asked.

She risked a side glance at him. Normally she'd never speak of Maddy's gift to someone. No one believed in things like *the sight* anymore. Yet with a man who was a gargoyle more than half of his life, how could he laugh at something like knowing the future? "She knows things," Tara said, still finding it hard not to be vague. "She's known things all her life."

"That could be handy," he said.

As she glanced over, she could swear she caught the corners of his lips trying to lift in a smile. How could he laugh in her distress like this? She glanced at him again and couldn't hold her own grin back. Lord, he was hot when he flashed that wicked look her way. The one that said he was teasing her and dared her to do something about it. But did she want to hit him or kiss him? Tara pressed her lips together and didn't admit that it was more of the second and a lot less of the first than she wanted to think. She could still remember the feel of his firm lips against hers. The way his mouth angled just right as he deepened the kiss between them. The heat they generated as they pressed their bodies together and mated with their mouths.

She shivered in delicious response to her thoughts and wrangled her mind back to the slick streets before she pulled over to find out just how tight the backseat of a Mini was with a six-foot gargoyle and herself in it.

"Do you think she knows something about your current situation with the cops?" Gregore asked when the silence had stretched for too long.

"With her, it's difficult to say. Half the time she sounds like a fortune cookie."

"Lucky numbers too?"

Tara laughed. "I wouldn't put it past her. We used to say she was Maddy as a hatty, when I was a kid." She smiled when a picture of her Grandma Rose's face came to mind as they giggled about their secret name for Aunt Maddy. No harm was ever meant by it, only an explanation for the eccentric ways of a woman who often didn't know if she saw the present or the future before her eyes.

"She must be quite special."

Tara turned the car onto Maddy's tree lined street and said under her breath, "Oh, you can say that again."

Gregore winked at her as they pulled into the driveway and slid his large frame out of the tiny car. She watched his muscles flex as he lifted himself out of the seat and treated herself to the delectable sight of his butt in those jeans. Snapping herself out of it, she slid from the car and locked it as the doors closed. She couldn't get involved here. Her life was already a mess. Not to mention that he was a stone tablet for twelve hours a day. Still, she'd always appreciated a rock-hard body.

Maddy stepped onto the porch in her pink, floor-length, zip-up robe and waved to them with a teapot in her hand. Her silver and white curls bobbed as she waved, and she fairly vibrated with excitement. Thankfully, it forced Tara's thoughts onto something a bit more sane, like the present and why they were there to begin with.

"Hi, Maddy. I hope you don't mind, but I brought Gre—"

"Gregore!" Maddy gushed in a way more suited to a teen than a woman of seventy. Her faded blue eyes sparkled underneath her tawny, hand-drawn eyebrows which rose like little hills over her eyes. Tara thought it made her look like she was in a constant state of surprise.

"How are you?" Maddy asked. She stepped down the two steps gingerly and held her free arm out to him for a hug.

He smiled devilishly and wrapped the woman in a gentle hug. The top of her head barely reached his shoulder. "Well enough, Maddy. Thank you for inviting us for tea."

Looking between the two, Tara had the distinct impression that these two knew each other. A tickle of unease crept up her spine at the thought.

"Come in, come in," Maddy said, shooing them toward the front door.

Tara tucked her keys into her pocket and followed Gregore and her aunt to the wide front porch of the old Victorian, with its antique rocking chairs on the left and the porch swing on the right. The oak front door was stained dark with a small glass window. She paused at the foot of the first porch step, staring up at the old house she'd once called home. A thousand memories flooded her. Playing on the old swing with her dolls, hopscotch on the walkway, and prom pictures in the front yard with a geeky boy she'd adored. Later, weekends home from college with Rose and classic movie nights in the living room. Hundreds of fragrant flowers in the kitchen with people she didn't know giving her their condolences. This was why she never visited Maddy. It was just too painful when every flower and every floorboard reminded her of Grandma Rose and how happy they'd been.

She dragged her gaze away to the door and reminded herself it was just a house. Not one that even belonged to her anymore. Gregore stood on the threshold, patiently waiting for her to join them.

Squaring her shoulders, she climbed the steps and entered Maddy's house.

Maddy toddled through her living room with the plush floral sofa and chair set and hardwood floors. She continued down the short hall past the dining room and into the kitchen to place the teapot on the trivet in the center of the round table worn from years of loving use. She waved them to sit and fill their cups while putting out the sugar, cream, and honey.

"You two got here a might quicker than I thought you would in this weather. All those years of driving those police cars must have given you a lead foot, dear."

Tara couldn't quite deny that. She'd have to watch her speed if even her old aunt noticed. She poured the steaming black tea into her china cup with the purple flowers and took great pleasure in passing an equally feminine, completely dainty cup and saucer into Gregore's large hands. Tearing her gaze away from his hands and thoughts of what they might be capable of, she turned back to her aunt, who was just settling into her own chair.

"Where's the fire?" she asked and then immediately regretted her choice of words. Just thinking of her apartment made her chest ache with loss. She'd start over once this was done. Until then, she had to focus on this Saints fellow.

Maddy gracefully sipped her tea and averted her eyes. Just when Tara thought she wouldn't answer, Maddy said, "I'm so glad you came to me. That you trusted my word means a great deal to me."

Tara couldn't miss the meaning behind Maddy's words and the look in her eyes as she spoke. A sinking feeling started in her stomach. "You're my aunt," she said in a low voice. "I may have been busy these last few months—"

Maddy shook her head. "It's been longer than that and you know it." She leaned close to Gregore and said, "She doesn't trust the sight. Or any of these things. Not anymore. "

His questioning glance set Tara on edge. Her sinking feeling bloomed into frustration. "I face down threats every single day. There are a lot of bad people out there and the world is a changed place. I—"

"You know it has nothing to do with that." Maddy looked back to Gregore to explain. "Tara hasn't been the same since our Rose died." She stopped herself and placed her finger over her lips in thought. "No, long before that even."

Tara cut her off before she could say any more. "You have a gift, Maddy. Anyone that knows you knows that. But you can't expect people to drop what they are doing to trot off at your command. You—"

Gregore laid a hand on her arm, stopping her torrent of words. The glittering midnight-blue of his eyes captured her in his spell. He slid his fingers down to touch her hand lightly, a small caress that brought out goose bumps on her skin.

Maddy laughed, clapping her hands together. "You have such charm, sweet boy."

Gregore winked at the older woman.

She waved a finger at him. "Don't think you can go charming me into telling you your fate, though. I didn't do it when you came to me a month ago and I won't do it now."

Tara's mouth fell open as the older woman's words sank in. "A month ago?" Her earlier suspicion seemed to have good root. Tara glared at Gregore, leaning closer to him. "Have you been here before?"

Suddenly the things she subconsciously picked up on came to light. He stayed behind to close and lock Maddy's front door, yet easily followed them to the kitchen. He didn't bat an eye at the china cup and saucer and even seemed to hold it in his hand without looking awkward at all. Not to mention he'd been silent during most of the exchange between herself and her aunt. He hadn't even questioned their talk of magical gifts. "You *have* been here."

Hard blue eyes glinted dangerously back at her. "I have." His tone brooked no argument.

She gave him one anyway. "How? Why? I just met you and yet you've already been to my aunt's house. Who the hell are you? Are you stalking my family?" What she wouldn't give for her handcuffs. Not that the lack of them had stopped her before.

"Oh, shush you," Maddy said. "His reasons are his own, and I'll have none of your tone in my house."

"He's a stranger to both of us. How could you have let him into your home? Were you alone?"

"Tara Ann O'Reilly, I am a woman quite capable of taking care of myself. I knew he was coming and even had the tea ready. I won't stand for you to insult my guest in my own home. He means me no harm. Surely even *you* can see that he is harmless."

Tara nearly choked on her sip of tea. Harmless? Could they be talking about the same man? She looked at Gregore, who again was more quiet than she'd ever seen him. He radiated danger and her aunt thought he was harmless? Maybe Maddy was more senile than Tara suspected.

As if picking up Tara's thoughts, Maddy blew out a frustrated breath. "Not harmless as a fly, girl. I mean he won't harm you or me."

Tara sat back in her seat and took that in. Her aunt was pretty well known for her good judge of character. On the other hand, Tara was suspicious of most. She looked at Gregore. He seemed to be waiting for her judgment of him. He held his breath, in fact. The realization shocked her. He cared what she thought of him? Before she could even ask herself why, the answer was there. Just like his hand that still sat lightly on hers. He needed her.

Suddenly she was very aware of him. The kitchen shrunk in size, until she felt the heat of his body and smelled the clean, spicy scent of his skin. Her gaze flicked to the firmness of his lips. They parted and a soft breath escaped him.

Tara's instinct was to stand and put space between them, but her legs felt too weak to hold her. Falling gracefully from her chair wasn't an impression she wanted to make on this gorgeous, yet rough, man. She sensed vulnerability in him then. He still waited for her response.

"No, you won't hurt us." She acknowledged the truth she'd been too stubborn to admit even to herself. He'd risked his life for Timmy when it meant losing the object that mattered most to him. He'd shielded her repeatedly during the fight with Saints tonight, using speed to move her out of the unnatural fire. Gave Maddy a gentle hug, careful of her small frame. He wouldn't hurt them. Tara closed her eyes and slid her fingers around his, briefly squeezing them. She heard him sigh in a soft acknowledgement that stirred her blood. The answers could wait. For now.

Maddy cut into their moment by rattling her teacup on the saucer a bit too loudly for the silence of their exchange. "Now that that's settled," she said, "let's talk about what brings you both here." She laughed in her tinkling way and the sinking feeling began anew in Tara's stomach.

⤜ CHAPTER 12 ⤛

In eight days, the gargoyle would turn to stone forever. A fact that brought Nick much pleasure. Could it be a coincidence that the creature's final day and night was the night of the full moon? He didn't think so, though how a Gypsy from the 1800s would know that, he wasn't sure. During the last months while he'd plotted revenge, he'd wondered what the man had done to bring about such wrath. And each time he'd wondered, he'd known that if it were in his power, he would have done the same. The gargoyle had it coming. If not then, now.

Tonight the moon drifted in and out of the thickening snow clouds. Every muscle in Nick's body ached from his fight with the bastard. He hoped he could get it up for the shop girl. Sex magic. He shivered in anticipation. What could it do for him that the Gypsy magic couldn't?

He parked his bike across the street of the Grand Grimoire at a few minutes after ten and dusted off the snow. Already the streets were coated in white. Tomorrow, he'd have to get a rental car. The motorcycle couldn't handle snow and ice. Nick removed his helmet, hung it on a handle, and climbed off the bike.

Inside the store, the delightful shop girl was switching off lights. She looked over her shoulder as she did, scanning the street. Was she looking for him? Did she anticipate their rendezvous as much as he did? He crossed the street as she came to the door to turn the lock.

She smiled when she saw him. Her white teeth gleamed, her eyes smoky with seduction.

"I thought you might not come," she said as she let him in and locked the door behind him.

I hope I do. "I wouldn't let a beautiful woman down," he said.

She stroked a fingernail over the bulge in his trousers "I hope not." She curled her finger through one of his belt loops and pulled him behind the counter, then into the storeroom. She waved a hand and the door closed behind them.

Nick lifted his brows in surprise. The very thought of magic was still new to him. Why should it really surprise him when he'd learned a few tricks of his own? Could he do that with the door? He was tempted to try.

Her saucy wink brought his gaze back to her lovely face. She went to her purse lying on the small break table in the corner and leaned over to dig through it, giving him a stunning view of her ass. She took her time, letting him look, no doubt, and eventually came up with a book of matches. She struck one and lit a candle on the table.

"Magic is always better with candles, don't you think?" she purred, lighting another.

He watched her circle the room, noting that there were candles in five spots.

"A pentagram," she said at his questioning look. "Drawn in our energies blended with fire. A beautiful ambiance."

Nick stared at her lips as she said "ambiance." He was enraptured with the way her full mouth moved with the word. She lifted the match and slowly blew the flame out. He could hardly think past the eroticism of her action.

"What's your name, handsome?"

She sauntered toward him. Each movement a sway of hips and long legs. "Nick," he said. His voice sounded rough to his own ears.

"Deja," she whispered into his ear, pressing her body close. "Do you want power, Nick? Do you want to feel the rush of power in an orgasm?"

He gulped. Nodded. "I do. But, can anyone do magic?" If they could, wouldn't everyone?

Deja's lips tipped up in a smile. "Most have to work very hard to accomplish even the tiniest bit of magic. To some, it comes easily."

"Why?"

"Usually it is in their heritage. Some ancestor built the power up in their bloodline." She raked her gaze over his body, lingering on his erection. "I sense you have such a heritage."

Before Nick could respond, Deja pressed her luscious lips against his. Her hands cupped his face and urged his mouth open to her passionate assault. She nipped, suckled, and licked him.

Nick had never in his life experienced a kiss like this. Her breasts pressed against his chest. She slid a thigh between his and rubbed against his leg. He was raging hard in seconds. Like a teen with his very first nudie mag.

She slowly pulled away from their kiss, sucking his lower lip as she went. "The most important thing in this magic is fire. Yours," she punctuated the word by opening the fly of his pants. "Mine." She pulled the fabric and his underwear down, releasing his throbbing erection to her gaze. "And ours." She gripped him gently and he groaned.

Deja stepped away from him. She stared at his cock and licked her lips. The muscles in his groin jumped, making his head wave. She smiled. Waved back. Sultry blue eyes finally met his. "Are you ready?"

He nodded. "What do I do?"

"Relax and enjoy the show." She moved him back a couple of inches to sit on the table and adjusted his pants further down to make him more comfortable.

Nick watched as she captured him in that smoldering look and popped a button open in the half blouse she wore. She undid the other three and dropped it to the floor. Her hands fluttered over her breasts, cupping them in the black lace bra. Then it too hit the floor. Her nipples were dark red and budded under his gaze.

"Like what you see?" she asked.

"Love it."

She lifted the tiny skirt to reveal sheer black panties. Hooking her thumbs into the strings at the side, she whisked them down her legs and stepped out, tossing them to him.

He caught the flimsy fabric and breathed deep of her scent. She moved to him and captured his mouth in another kiss. Nick dropped the panties and put his hands on her waist. He drew her close. Deja hummed in pleasure. The candlelight seemed to flicker in time to her tune, though Nick could hardly say for sure. His focus was on the soft flesh beneath his tongue and lips. Not on her ambiance. He trailed his fingers over her flat belly, down one thigh, then back to the hot juncture of her body. She was mouthwateringly bare there.

She moaned and rocked against his hand, letting him learn what she liked. Which was everything. She shuddered against him and closed her eyes in ecstasy.

Nick brought his fingers up to his lips. "You taste good, Deja."

She smiled and sank to her knees. "Let's see if I can say the same."

He threw back his head, unsure if he could last long under the heat of her tongue as she toyed with him. Just when he thought he couldn't take another moment, she would slow the pace just enough to prolong his torture. It was heaven.

Finally, after what felt like hours of delirious enjoyment, she cupped his sac and stroked him to orgasm, taking every drop in her ruby red mouth. The moment his seed went forth, his limbs felt energized. The trickle of magic he had initially felt blossomed into more. Like a river running through his veins.

Deja stood. She lifted her hands over her head and suddenly, the candle flames shoot another foot in the air. She twirled her fingers in a circle. The room warmed and swirled around them, heating their bodies even more. Her skin glistened in the dim light.

Nick marveled at the feel of pure magic both in his body and tingling on his skin as the air brushed over him. Deja's hair floated around her like a dark cloud. She brought her hands down flat, and the candle flames returned to normal.

He stared. First at the display of her power, then at her, and finally at her breasts and his penis. He could feel the power still. It hadn't drained as before. "Amazing," he whispered.

Deja skimmed her nail down his chest. "Yes. You were."

Something in Tara's past made her desperately afraid of using magic. Gregore squeezed her hand as he sat beside her in Maddy's kitchen. He let out the breath he'd been holding and acknowledged the relief he felt deep in his gut. Fear he could fight.

He flicked a glance at her, taking in the graceful curve of her cheek and the dark fan of her lashes. Perhaps it was more than relief. The knowledge that she trusted him affected him far more deeply than he could have imagined, like the surprising fear he'd felt in the battle with Saints. That unnatural black fire could have killed her and it terrified him. It made him realize that he wasn't done with her. Not yet.

Aside from the physical pull of attraction, she intrigued him. He wanted to know more about her. Wanted to spend time, getting to know her inside and out. His blood heated. Gregore ached to run his hands through her silky curls and press a kiss to her mouth. To explore her skin and heat up the sheets for days. He cursed under his breath. Days he didn't have.

He blanked the uncomfortable thoughts from his mind. Not something he wanted to dwell on.

Instead he thought about her reaction to her aunt. When faced with a threat, Tara had kept her cool. Yet the revealing of a secret rattled her like nothing else. He leaned back in the chair and considered that. Her grandmother read tarot, was a renowned healer and rumored to be the strongest of the bloodline in power. What made Tara so closed off to something that ran in her blood? What would push her enough to gain her help with the counter curse? The old witch, Griselda, would never make it so easy as to just have some words in the book like a poem to be read. There had to be more to it than that. If he didn't find out what, it would be one hell of a birthday. Nothing like wishing you wouldn't turn to stone forever when blowing out the candles on the cake.

Maddy clapped her hands like an excited little girl, breaking him out of his thoughts. Her overly arched, hand-drawn eyebrows raising to her hairline as her eyes widened. "I've got a clue!"

Tara's brow furrowed. "A clue?"

"Don't look at me like I'm senile, dear. If my gift can't help people in this world, what good is it? You should remember that with your own—"

"Is this a clue to the case?" Tara asked to cut off what Aunt Maddy had been trying to say.

Maddy's shrewd gaze cut through Tara's attempts to steer away from talk of magical gifts. She pursed her lips and said, "It is. When I knew you were coming, I spent some time scrying. There is a place associated with this gentlemen you are looking for. I could show you, if you are interested."

"We're interested," Gregore said. He cast Tara a glance and said, "I will need all the help possible to break this curse."

"Of course," she said, though she sounded far from pleased.

Aunt Maddy rose and left the kitchen, returning with a map of the city. "Are you done with your food, dears?" she asked.

Gregore stood and cleared their dishes, making room for the map to be spread on the table. Tara watched him, her expression changing from belligerent to warm. Her dark lashes fanned over green eyes and a smile touched her entrancing lips. An answering heat rose in his skin. Was it such a big thing to pick up the dishes?

Maddy placed the map on the table and leaned over it, tracing an elegant finger over its surface. She pointed to the heart of the city. "There is an old building here. Brick, I think. It holds an unusual energy."

He leaned forward to get a better view. She circled a group of city blocks in the International District. Gregore had been there once. He remembered a few warehouses in various states of disrepair. Tara would know the area better.

As if reading his thoughts, she said, "Do you know which building exactly? It's a busy area."

"Crab," Maddy said.

"Crab?"

"Yes, crab. That's what I saw."

"Crab," Tara repeated. She turned to Gregore. "A brick building with crab. Ring any bells?"

"It cannot be that difficult to find. There is little else we have to go on."

"At this time of night, the streets will be fairly quiet. We would have more opportunity to look around without people noticing. Besides that, I'd like to take you with me, big guy. As my partner tells me, two sets of eyes are better than one."

His lips twitched. "Agreed."

"You will return here when you are through, won't you?" Maddy's voice pitched higher as she spoke, the worry coming through every word.

"You don't have to put us up," Tara said.

"Nonsense," she snorted. "Are you going to go back to your apartment? You can't, can you? And I know perfectly well that a cop doesn't make much for salary. You can't live out of a motel until this is through. I won't allow it."

She was right. They could stay at the small motel Tara spent the last few nights in. But Maddy's gifts could prove useful. He suspected the older woman would be an ally in breaking through Tara's fear. "We accept," he said. Tara's mouth dropped open. Before she could voice her protest, he added, "You know she can help us. We must take advantage of that opportunity. We can't do that from a motel."

Tara took her time to respond, her conflict written in her features. At last she said, "Okay. We'll come back here. But don't go to any trouble over us, Maddy. We can take care of ourselves."

"You think it's trouble to have my niece visit? Pffft."

Tara covered her aunt's hand with her own. "Thank you." Her voice laced with warmth as she spoke.

She reviewed the intersection on the map once more, borrowed a flashlight, and checked the battery power.

Gregore kissed Maddy's cheek and whispered in her ear, "I need your help getting through to Tara. I need to know about her gifts."

Maddy nodded. "You bring her back here and you'll have your answers, dear boy. It's been too long since my Tara has been home."

<hr />

Nick Saints stretched and laced his hands behind his head, leaning back in the wooden, uncomfortable, office chair. He kicked his feet up onto the desk and admired his handiwork. A black hole smoldered in the wall directly opposite him, giving him a nice window into the hallway. He laughed, then looked down to his companion, who lay prone on the floor.

"Sorry. Did I disturb your sleep?"

The body didn't respond. Probably wouldn't since the guy was dead. The Japanese owner of the warehouse hadn't been willing to lend Nick the space. It was a shame really; he didn't have to die. It was his own fault for being so adamant that Nick couldn't buy the space. The fucking building was up for sale and all it contained was rotting crates and rats. It's not like it was the fucking Waldorf.

Nick rolled his eyes and looked through his new window. When this was over, when the freak was permanently stone and that damn detective was in jail, he was going to have to move. Murder had never been part of the plan. Now that this guy was dead, he couldn't have it linked to him, no matter that he'd killed the guy with magic. He closed his eyes and pictured a sunny white sand beach and swaying palms. Tropical would be better than this snowy shit. Maybe some place where magic wasn't feared quite so much. Some place where he could have all the power he wanted.

Just the memory of his encounter with Deja made him hard again. The power coursing through him had slightly diminished, but not so much that he couldn't play for several more hours with his newfound gift. Worse, he wanted more. More Deja, more sex, and more sweet, sweet magic. He straightened in his chair and turned to another page in the spell book. Maybe he'd try luring fortunes to him. Or casting a curse to see what happened. The options were limitless. He chuckled. Anything he wanted was in his grasp with this kind of power.

CHAPTER 13

A large crab stared down at them, beady black eyes intense and red pinchers raised. Gregore cocked an eyebrow. Maddy's vision in full color.

It was nearly midnight when he and Tara reached the International District and located the warehouse. One of two brick buildings on the block, it had a large crab painted on a wooden sign above the front door, which read "Hiroshi Crab Company." A streetlamp spread a soft glow of light in a pool by the door.

Gregore pressed into the shadows of the building across the street, watching the few cars out at this hour. Tara stood beside him, her arms folded over her chest. He tried not to notice how the action plumped and lifted her breasts, making them stand out even more. Any more notice and he might forget the warehouse altogether in favor of more strenuous activities with her. Gregore licked his lips and swallowed past his suddenly dry throat. He looked down to see if the snow around his feet was melting, because his body temperature had surged with just the thought of taking Tara to bed.

She was tough. He liked that about her. Smart too. She could have tried to leave him with Aunt Maddy (not that he would have stayed behind), but she asked for his help. And beneath her sarcastic front, he could see her love for her aunt in the warmth of her eyes, as well as a flicker of fear when Maddy tried to speak of Tara's psychic gift. Gregore knew she had at least one. Every other descendent he found from the original Romani tribe had a gift, even if it was as simple as a sixth sense about things. Tara, being of a direct lineage to old Griselda herself, would likely have several gifts. Why she refused to even speak of them, he didn't know. He would find out.

Gregore looked down at her shadowed profile. The mass of auburn curls would look unruly on most, but on her, they were lovely. He wanted to run his fingers through them and promised himself that he would soon. He intended to spend more time with her. Not because she could potentially break his curse, nor because she was beautiful and it had been too many years since he'd been in the intimate company of a woman. Something about her strength of spirit drew him like a magnet. He was captivated by a woman who could chase down a criminal without hesitation but hide from a topic of conversation that hit too close to home. A woman who used sarcasm like a sword with those she loved but left a crime scene to go have tea with them at an unusual hour. Tara's complexities fascinated him. He skimmed his gaze over her breasts once more. Not the only thing that intrigued him.

"Hiroshi. I think my partner Carson talked to the owner of this place a couple of days ago," Tara said, breaking Gregore out of his lustful thoughts. "Strange that Maddy led us back here."

Gregore didn't respond, his attention back on the old brick building across the street. It stood in the middle of the block with a narrow alley on each side. A scruffy calico cat slinked down the slush-covered sidewalk and disappeared into the shadows between buildings. All three stories were dark. For Sale signs sat in a few of the ground-floor windows. Hot pink graffiti marked the door like a child writing his name for the first time. The place looked abandoned. Even the crab sign was faded, the paint peeling away.

"I think we should take a look inside," Tara said.

"Does your spidey sense tell you that?" Gregore asked.

"Sorry. I've been avoiding the radioactive spiders. And even the nonradioactive ones." She shuddered.

Gregore smiled. Something else to add to his list of things he was finding out about Tara. She was afraid of spiders. "I suppose we should go with your gut then," he replied, gesturing toward the warehouse. "Lead the way."

They crossed the street, noting it was empty of all foot and automobile traffic. A quiet turn of the front doorknob proved it was locked. Gregore moved into the alley on the left, with Tara right behind him. A green Dumpster partially blocked the alley. Rotting food assaulted his nose, blended with the overwhelming stench of urine and who knew what else. He sucked in a breath through his mouth, maneuvered around the container and the homeless man slumbering in a newer sleeping bag against the warehouse wall. Just beyond was a door with a sign reading "Deliveries Only." It too was locked.

Before his companion could contemplate the ramifications of breaking and entering, he kicked open the door. The crunch of splitting wood woke the homeless man from his slumber. "Late-night delivery," Gregore said over his shoulder as he walked into the gloomy interior. The man peered at them briefly, then turned back to the wall and went to sleep.

"Now that we've rung the doorbell, should we announce ourselves?" Tara whispered.

"What did you have in mind? Avon calling?" Gregore's voice sounded loud. The room they stood in seemed cavernous. He sent his senses seeking out for a threat. Nothing.

"I doubt anyone would believe us."

"I doubt anyone is here," he said.

Minimal light trickled in through the broken door. Shadows drew together in the darkness of the space, wrapping around each other in growing forms that danced and blurred as he moved farther into the warehouse.

Tara flicked on the flashlight and moved the beam around. The warehouse was open to the second floor, with two roll-up doors in back and a stairway on the right leading up to the third floor, presumably to offices. No less than a hundred wood crates were stacked to various heights. Some were tipped over and broken into scrap. All bearing the name of a local seafood company. The place smelled of rotting fish magnified times a thousand. It smelled like the underside of a wharf. Beside him, Tara gagged on the odor.

He trailed his fingers over her shoulder. "Are you unwell?" he asked softly.

She shook her head. "It reeks in here."

"That it does. We should look faster."

"Definitely." They picked their way around, looking for anything of significance that would point to Nick Saints. "Let's move on to the offices," she said as she went to the stairs, "I have a feeling we'll find something there."

Gregore took her elbow, holding her back as she prepared to climb the wooden steps to the level above. He expected her to protest as he moved in front of her, shielding her with his body. She lifted an eyebrow but said nothing. He started up the wooden steps in the darkness. Reaching around his arm, Tara handed him the flashlight to light their way. It was a sweet thing. Something a partner would do as they let the other take the lead. He didn't have the heart to tell her that he didn't need the light.

The stairs ended at a landing with a door to the right. Gregore glanced back over his shoulder, making sure she was close, then went through the open doorway.

Tara followed, and walked right into his back, her hands gripping his hips. "Damn it, Gregore, your brake lights don't work. Can you signal next time?"

He didn't respond. Nick Saints was at the other end of the hall, a glowing blue orb of light shining in midair over his head.

"Well, well, this is a surprise," Saints said.

Gregore smiled lethally. He crouched low, hand snaking to his boot to lift the blade. Out of the corner of his eye, he saw Tara slip back through the doorway they had just come from. Going for cover. Good girl.

The blond man looked deceptively at ease, twirling the orb between his fingers. Each second dragged out, as Gregore waited for Saints to make a move. Around and around the orb went, with Saints apparently in no hurry to attack. His lips curled in a sneer, as if he taunted them with the threat of his magic. Gregore timed the twirl of the orb, waiting until it was farthest from the man's palm. In a lightning flash, he tossed the blade. A sure shot to hit the man's heart.

Saints waved his left hand. The knife flew wide of its intended track as if a strong wind blew through the room. Gregore didn't have time to wonder how. Saints tossed the glowing orb like a pro baseball player, straight for them. Gregore rose and stepped in front of Tara to block the magical blow.

A cobalt-blue essence slammed into his chest, causing his every muscle to convulse simultaneously.

"Gregore," Tara shouted.

His hearing faded as if she were far away. His limbs tingled. Went numb. The eyesight he used to see so clearly at night dimmed until only shadowy shapes remained. He saw one move in front of him and then run toward the other.

"No. Don't." His tongue felt thick and the words slurred.

A shuffling sound reached him. The figures melded together and dropped to the ground. He could see an arm swing out or maybe a foot, at odd angles. He heard a grunt but couldn't tell whether it was Tara or Saints. A pop. A thud.

All at once his vision brightened. His hearing came back louder than before. In a split second, he was restored and could move. He staggered under the new onslaught, oriented himself, and wasted no more time. Tara grappled on the ground with Saints, each trading blows. He ran for them.

She pinned Saints, struggled to hold him. The man wedged his knee up into her torso, pushed enough to get his foot there, and kicked her away. A blue orb sparked between his hands and pounded into Tara, knocking her to the ground with a pained grunt.

Saints scrabbled away and gained his feet. He spun to face them, throwing his hand forward, palm out as if telling them to stop.

Gregore collided with an invisible barrier. The force of the blow knocked him back a few paces and the floor shook beneath the impact. He struck the barrier with his fist and ran his hands along it. Up, down, to the side, where it seemed to become one with the hallway walls.

Saints slowly smiled. "I've enjoyed this little game," he said, strolling forward. He tapped the shield. "I wonder if I could build this completely around you? How long would it take for you to crack with no food or water?"

Gregore crowded the magical wall. "Let's see you try."

Nick chuckled. "Oh, I have other things in store for you. I'll see you both soon. Very soon." With that, he turned and ran to the opposite end of the hall, disappearing around the corner.

As soon as he was out of sight, the invisible barrier crackled, like the air itself broke. Hairline slivers cracked through the shield from all sides. Gregore kicked the barrier. The cracks spider-webbed. He kicked harder and the barrier shattered, silver dust raining down to the floor. He ran, preternatural speed kicking in, and flew around the corner. He heard Tara call his name, but paid no attention. He focused solely on Saints who was nearly at the window at the end of the hall. His point of escape.

Gregore threw himself forward, tackling Saints. They rolled, broke apart and found their footing. Gregore swung his fist, connecting with his enemy's nose. Blood spurted. Saints held his nose with one hand and materialized a second orb. Gregore kicked at his left knee, dropping Saints to the ground. He grabbed hold of him as Nick released the orb. It bounced to the side, just grazing Gregore's arm. His hand went instantly numb and raced up to his shoulder. Saints pulled himself from Gregore's grasp and punched him hard in the stomach.

Gregore flinched but wouldn't allow the pain or numbness to stop him. He launched himself at Saints, knocking them both into the wall. They went down, each punching and kicking in whatever area they could hit. Gregore's left arm was useless at his side until a lucky blow to the side of Nick's head released the spell. Seemed the man wasn't so good at holding the magic.

Saints shook his head clear, then kicked at Gregore's groin. Instinctively Gregore blocked the blow, only to be hit with a fierce left hook to the chin. He staggered, giving Saints enough time to lunge for the window. He slammed the glass pane up and ducked out.

Gregore stumbled after him, climbing through the window. He plowed into another damn shield on a fire escape. He was alone. Saints raced down the alley and out into the street. He pulled his leg back to break the shield when Tara's cry of surprise stopped him cold.

A shadow moved in the alley. Blended. Thomas Whetmore slid between darkness and light. It was his gift. The one shining aspect in his life. He had laughed at that at first. It was no longer funny.

He watched the angry, sputtering blond man race out of the alley, spewing curses at Gregore on the fire escape above. Interesting. Seemed he had that effect on everyone. Thomas wondered what the old chap had done to the other man. He watched the shadows drift across Gregore's face. He was still as a statue. Staring at the mouth of the street beyond. Another gift. Or was that a curse?

In the end, Thomas decided it didn't matter. He'd found what he was looking for.

With a dark smile, he melted back into the gloom and waited to see where his old friend would go.

CHAPTER 14

Tiny lights like fireflies twinkled and burned out all around Tara's vision in the semi-darkness. She rolled over and put her hands beneath her, pushing herself to her knees in the hallway, and stared after the two men.

Tightness pulled at her chest in a way she'd never felt before. Her lungs tried to close. She attempted to suck in air, only to cough violently, making the pain all the worse. Her heart thundered in her breast, begging to be released by the blinding panic. Her body shook like the epicenter of an earthquake. She bent until her forehead felt the smoothness of the tile floor. Breathing easier, the panic lessened. She closed her eyes to block out the last of the tiny lights.

What was that ball? How the hell had he created it?

Another few deep breaths calmed the wracking shakes of her body down to a tremble. Her mind fought valiantly to deny what she'd seen. Nick Saints used magic against them. *Real* magic. Not the fake psychic on the phone or television who said you'd meet someone tall, dark, and handsome. (Although, now that she thought about it, she had!) No, this wasn't the run-of-the-mill Gypsy fortuneteller in a run-down coffee shop frequented by the force either. This was in-your-face, freeze-you-in-your-tracks magic. The kind with the power to kill.

Even Gregore's change hadn't hit her quite like the reality of a confrontation with this magic-wielding maniac.

They were doomed.

Tara sucked in another minute of precious air and calmed her body. She straightened. She'd never been the doom and gloom type and she wouldn't start now. She was a doer. She didn't run from things, she ran after them. Though it threatened everything she'd done to build a life for herself in the last ten years, she could do that now. Somehow.

Lying pinned to the floor unable to move brought one thing home with resounding clarity. She couldn't capture Saints as a detective. The thought was almost laughable. Like bringing a plastic Spork to a gunfight.

Tara pushed herself to her feet. Out of the corner of her eye, on the edge of the shadows in the next room, lay a familiar scarlet leather corner. Her eyes widened. She jolted to the room and snatched up a book. *The* book.

"Thank you, Grandma Rose," she whispered. The grimoire felt warm in her hands. With it, she would beat Saints at his own game. She'd be a quick study, ask Maddy for help, and blow his ass off.

Tara grinned like a woman bestowed with a priceless treasure when Gregore came back into the hallway. At his look, she turned a red leather book around to show him the front. In her delicate hands was the tome he'd sought for over a century.

The tension that had built for all of those years suddenly released from his shoulders. He felt light. Free. He let out a whoop of laughter. Tara looked stunned, then joined in his laughter.

"Where?" he finally asked. "How?"

Her smile brightened and took his breath away. She was so lovely when she smiled. He wanted her to smile more often. He wanted to sing to the world.

"He must have dropped it when you jumped him. He was distracted trying to escape and didn't take the time to grab it. It was lying in the doorway there. Just waiting for me to find it." Her words flooded out in a rush of joy that equaled his own.

At last, the end of the curse was within his grasp. With only eight days to spare. He'd come so close. Had almost lost hope. But now, now he didn't need to worry. He could be a normal man again. He might even have a family of his own. Would he have to get a job? No, he'd had time to build his fortune. It would be enough. He'd already traveled quite a bit. Now that he had a normal life to look forward to, he could do those things he'd always dreamt of doing. Like settling down to a single place. Maybe a nice house somewhere. Maybe even marrying.

Tara stood close, her beautiful green eyes shining with happiness. For him, he knew. But also for herself. This grimoire was the only thing she had left of her grandmother. Family was important to her. Did she want to start a family of her own? The thought made him uncomfortable, though he couldn't say exactly why. But just the thought of another man's hands touching her, seeing that lovely smile every morning, made him sick. No one was supposed to touch her but him.

"What's wrong? Aren't you happy we found it?" she asked.

Gregore realized he was frowning, judging by the concern on her face. He cleared the troublesome thoughts from his head. He'd have much more time to pursue those things *after* they broke the curse.

"May I?" he asked, not waiting for an answer. He took the book from her and leafed through it.

"You're scowling," Tara said.

When he got to the end, he went back through it in the opposite direction.

"Now you're frowning."

One more time front to back and then back to front.

"Now you're either going to murder someone, or you already have and don't want to tell me because I might arrest you."

Her words finally broke through the building red haze behind his eyes. Gregore inhaled but it didn't take away the fear that settled into his chest like a stone. A large, permanent, gargoyle-shaped stone.

"It's not here," he said.

"What?" she cried, grabbing the spell book from him and frantically flipping through the pages. "Are you certain it was supposed to be here? How could it not be here? What did it look like?"

He closed his eyes, pinching the bridge of his nose. "Yes, I'm sure. Ranulf wouldn't have lied. His guilt was too great. It was there. But no longer."

"Then it must have been right here," she said.

Gregore opened his eyes. She traced a finger down the jagged edge of a page that had been violently torn out. "Was that there before?" he asked.

"I...I don't know. I'd never even opened...Oh God, I'm so sorry, Gregore."

He turned away, unwilling to even look at the shattered dreams in her hands any longer. His ears echoed with malicious feminine laughter from the distant past.

Griselda, that evil bitch, laughed as she cursed him. He heard it now as his final days drew near and he remembered all too clearly the joy she'd taken in stealing his life from him. The life now slipping between his fingers. His last hope was gone.

"A life for a life," she had said.

"Your kind think they are exempt from the law. That you can steal from us, ridicule us!" Griselda cried.

Gregore tried to deny it. She swore over the top of his protest, making the two men who held him clutch their hands tighter around his biceps. Holding him still. The wind whipped in the dark trees, sending the cold autumn wind down his thin shirt to chill his body.

Beside him, his best friends were equally bound, having been dragged unwillingly into his private nightmare for simply riding to his rescue. At Gregore's feet lay the body of his beloved Zola. Her eyes stared blankly, her simple gown stained dark with blood. He wanted to roar his rage at the heavens. His heart did so already. But his judgment was being pronounced. His fate lay in the hands of Zola's psychotic grandmother. All of their fates did.

Zola had feared this woman. She spoke of dark magic like she'd never seen, performed when the moon was full. Countless animals had met their ends at the old woman's hands. Sacrifices to a darker power. He felt a tremble in the hands on his right side and turned to catch a glimpse of apprehension in the man holding him. If he was afraid, then Gregore had far more reason to fear himself.

The woman neared, stepping over the body of her favorite granddaughter like trash, and held a book up. He glimpsed deep red leather binding many pages together, but nothing of the writing on them. She smiled, a rotten row of teeth leering back at him.

"You think you loved her?" she said and spat on him. "You know nothing of love. Your kind never does."

"What is my kind?" he growled.

"White, aristocratic rubbish. All of you. You fear, you hate. You persecute us for living differently. You take our daughters to your bed and send them away when they bear your offspring. Bastards, you call them. I think you all are the bastards. You think you loved her?"

Gregore looked down to the cold body of the woman he'd wanted to marry. "Yes," he whispered.

"Liar!" she yelled. "Liar. You can't love. Your heart is made of stone. As you too will be." She laughed, a little insanely to Gregore's ears.

His heart thumped hard. Zola said she'd never heard of another Gypsy tribe who practiced such dark magic. The woman before him was a lunatic. He closed his eyes and sent up a silent prayer, hoping there truly was a God up above. He prayed for Zola's spirit. He prayed for Thomas and Jeffrey, who had no part in the ending of Zola's life. Last he prayed for his father. He had hoped he'd get to see the old man once more. Now that dream shredded to nothing. Gone. Dead. Just like Zola.

Mutters and chanting brought him back to the present situation. The hands on his arms tightened once again. Griselda's face glowed like a demon and he wondered if he was looking at her true form.

She rubbed her palms together. When they opened, a silver orb glowed in her hand. It grew the more she chanted. At first it was almost translucent, with iridescent arcs of light flowing this way and that. But then the lights changed, taking more solid form. The orb turned a bleeding red, pulsing until the color changed to blue. Her eyes lit with glee.

"You'll remember this night," she said.

As if he'd forget the worst birthday of his life.

With a maniacal cackle, she threw the orb at him. It struck his chest with the weight of a boulder, knocking the wind from him. He doubled over. The sphere dissolved in liquid blue and red, spreading over his chest and down his limbs. He cried out as it climbed up his neck and over his face. Down to his toes.

He heard someone yelling to cease, but didn't know if it was his friends or himself.

"Aye, you'll remember this night," she said. And Gregore became aware that he knelt at her feet. "Every night for one hundred fifty years, you will remember. And on the last night of those years, your heart will turn to stone for good. Just like the rest of your sorry form. You'll become nothing more than *a statue for the birds to relieve on." She put a booted foot on his shoulder and kicked him over.*

Gregore couldn't move. His body felt stiff as marble. He wondered a bit wildly what would become of him and his friends. And what the old witch meant about one hundred fifty years.

"Shit," Tara said from directly behind him, snapping Gregore out of his troubled memories.

He rubbed the back of his neck and turned to find out what had Tara swearing now.

She stepped into a darkened doorway, the one Saints came out of, disappearing into the room. Gregore followed. She shone the flashlight, illuminating a silver watchband wrapped around a wrist on the floor. A dark pooling patch surrounded the arm. Blood. He could smell it.

Tara knelt by the body, shining the light on the pale white face of an elderly Asian man. His eyes stared at the ceiling as if praying for help. His shirt was ripped open, a strange symbol carved into his chest.

"It's Hiroshi," Tara said.

"You know him?"

"No. Carson, my partner, spoke with him a few days ago about a case we were working on."

"Do you think Saints had something to do with your case? Or is this just coincidence?"

"I don't know."

She closed her eyes, breathing slightly through her mouth. The stench of death only lingered near the body, and even with the record cold temperature, it couldn't have been there long. A slight quiver went through her limbs as she studied the body. The sight of death never set well with people. Especially when they knew the person whose life had so abruptly come to a halt.

Gregore nodded. The sudden use of magic by Saints, the body lying dead before them with the symbol carved in his chest, the candles in a ring around the room. Something sinister went on here. He said as much to Tara.

She didn't respond. Just pulled out her phone and made an anonymous call to the police to report a murder. She gave the address, then hung up.

"Let's go," she said, her voice barely above a whisper. "I can't be here when they show up. It will look like I'm trying to do my own investigation when I've been ordered away."

Gregore heard the pain lacing her words. Each moment they spent together, Tara turned her back on those she held dear. By pursuing Saints, she was leaving her job and those she cared about behind. Guilt pierced him like a sword. He reached for her hand, wrapping her cold, trembling fingers with his, and drew her from the room. They moved quickly down the stairs and back out the door to the alley.

He paused beside the homeless man, kneeling down to get the man's attention. Gregore removed his wallet from his jeans and handed the man a stack of fifties. "Buy yourself a hot meal and a new jacket. Forget we were here."

The man glanced between the two briefly, nodded, and took the money. His dirty hands tucked the money into the pocket of his torn and faded pants.

Gregore didn't wait to see if the man would stay when the cops arrived. He took Tara's hand once again and pulled her across the street into yet another alley. The police would be here in moments. He backed her into the shadows, keeping her safely away from the light. Fortunately, her car was far enough away that no one she knew would notice it. He pressed her back against the brick of the building, shielding her further as a couple of squad cars arrived, lights swirling red and blue in the night.

He put his finger beneath her chin, turning her eyes away from the scene to meet his gaze. Moisture rimmed her lower lashes and though she blinked them several times, the tears still spilled. The pain in her eyes was his undoing. He'd caused her to sacrifice so much. Her home had been lost, her job was on the brink, and she now hid from the one thing she should be doing. He cradled her head in his hands, holding her against his chest. She leaned in, wrapping her arms around him and silently let out her tears.

Gregore knew enough of her spirit to know she rarely cried. Too afraid to show weakness, most likely. He held her until her shaking shoulders subsided along with her tears. He moved her head back to see her eyes, then lowered his mouth to hers. He took her lips softly, trying to take the heartache from her body into his. His tongue moved over her lips, then into her mouth, taking his time. Her arms crept around his neck, pulling him closer.

He broke for air, staring into her smoky-green eyes, then dipped his head back to her kiss. Heat built between them, binding them together in the chilly winter night. He sucked her bottom lip between his, nipped, and delved back into the delightful heat of her mouth. Gregore moaned her name and heard her gasp his in return.

The screech of tires on pavement finally broke through the haze of the kiss. Gregore touched his forehead to hers, watching their breath frost between them. Something cold hit his cheek. Then again. He pulled back to see if she was crying still. Flurries fell from the sky, white in the lamplight from the street. In moments they covered Tara's lovely hair and seeped down the neck of Gregore's leather coat.

"Time to move before we freeze," she said. But instead of moving to leave, she trailed her fingertips over his cheek and across his lips.

"I'm so sorry," he said.

Her eyes questioned him.

"Not for the kiss," he said, giving her another soft press of his lips. He gestured to the building across the street. Lights were on in the upper floors. "For dragging you away from your life. Your friends. Your job. For turning your life upside down and ruining it."

She shook her head. "It will only be ruined if we fail. And we won't." Her face turned stern. "Failure isn't an option, soldier."

Gregore saluted. "Yes, ma'am."

She smiled, a little sadly, he thought, and looked back to the street. "It looks like everyone is inside. We probably have a couple of minutes until the next wave arrives."

He took her hand and led her out of the alley. Once they confirmed no one was about, they ran back to her car, nearly white with the rapidly falling snow. Gregore gave her one last kiss, then got into the car for the drive back to Aunt Maddy's.

He would make this up to her. He vowed it.

CHAPTER 15

The spell was gone and she hid from the cops. Could things get any worse? It was after two in the morning when Tara pulled the car into the sleepy neighborhood Aunt Maddy lived in. Gregore moved silently ahead of her as they entered the house, his dark eyes penetrating the shadows, looking for danger. She closed and locked the door, then followed him up the stairs, grimoire clutched against her chest.

He'd fallen silent shortly after they'd left the city, though whether from their latest dangerous encounter or something more personal, she didn't know. Most likely the latter. The one good look she had of him on that drive speared her in places she didn't dare consider. Pain and the absence of hope lingered in his eyes and made the sickness she felt hiding from her coworkers seem pathetic by comparison. God, she hated pathetic.

At the top of the stairs, she turned down the hall with Gregore. There were three bedrooms in Maddy's house. Her aunt labeled the doors of two with their names on frilly sticky notes. Tara smiled despite her solemn thoughts. Maddy was such a dear. Daffy, but still a dear.

Gregore opened the door with his name and stepped inside. He prowled around, nodding at the thick drapes covering the window. Tara stopped in the doorway and quirked an eyebrow. The room had new curtains spanning ceiling to floor, and dark wood furniture in a simplistic, almost manly design. Not a single flower in sight. Maddy clearly had prepared for their arrival at least a week in advance. Admittedly, she was surprised. But then really, she shouldn't be. Her aunt could see the future. Why wouldn't she see to Gregore's particular needs? Especially since she'd already met him.

As if reading her mind, he swung around and moved toward her. His steps, the tightness in his body, the steeliness in his eyes, were lethal. She took a step back into the hall. Fury vibrated out of his every movement. The tense man from the car turned into one radiating rage.

"Talk to me," she said and placed a hand on his arm. His firm muscles flexed beneath the long leather coat. Her awareness of him increased and she remembered his heated kisses in the alley.

Gregore opened his mouth, closed it, and gestured to the curtains. "This is my fate. Darkness. No sunlight. I should have resigned myself to it a hundred years ago," he finished with a yell.

Tara glanced down the hall toward Maddy's room, then back at Gregore, beseeching him to keep it down. "Gregore," she whispered, "we still could—"

"Good night," he snapped, stepped out of her touch, and slammed the door in her face.

She stared at the door. Well, if she'd wanted him to be quiet, she had her wish. Though not exactly what she'd intended. Never had she seen him so angry. Not that she knew him that well, she amended. It only felt like forever. She reconsidered the closed door. Part of her wanted to throw open the door and kick his ass. Tell him to quit feeling sorry for himself. Shake him until he saw reason. Maybe even kiss him until he didn't see anything but her.

She turned away instead..

He was a man facing the last few days of his life. He'd never see the sun again. Never have a family. Did he even want a family? God, she didn't know. She barely knew if *she* wanted a family. The fact was, she didn't know him. How could she ask him things like this now when he felt so hopeless about it all? Tears pricked her eyes as she realized just how much she wanted to know the answer to some of those personal questions. She licked her lips, wishing she could taste his mouth again.

Set in Stone

Tara opened the door across the hall tagged with her name and walked into a replica of Grandma Rose's room. The faint scent of lily of the valley wafted to her, swirling around like loving hands. Memories of the many times Grandma Rose had held her as a child flooded her. The soft green and pink floral print bed covers and curtains were Rose's favorites. The pink chair with the faded velour trim sat in the corner. Yet there were subtle changes.

Lace-trimmed pillows peeked out from under the comforter, inviting her to slip between the sheets. A new lamp sat on the antique bedside table. Tara gingerly set the book on the bed and slid out of her boots, socks, and jeans. Belatedly, she thought of their clothes still in the Mini and decided to get them tomorrow. It had been a long day and she was exhausted. She ditched her bra and climbed beneath the covers. The mattress was heavenly, molding to her body like it was made for it. Letting out a sigh of pure pleasure, she switched on the lamp and picked up the spell book.

The pages didn't crinkle like she thought they might. Yellowed but soft, they'd held up well over time. The scarlet leather cover felt smooth beneath her hand. A figure of a bird, maybe a raven, was the only ornamentation etched into the cover. Though no words decorated the outside, Tara knew what the book contained. She'd held this book once before, long ago. And as then, her hands tingled like all her fingers fell asleep at once.

She opened the cover.

The title page contained a single phrase: "A deed for a deed" scribed in gold letters. A chill wiggled down her back and goose bumps prickled her arms. Five words that could be the essence of maliciousness or mercy. With Grandma Rose, she had no doubt the spells were used for mercy. The old woman hadn't a bad bone in her body. But what about the ancestors before her?

The next two pages contained information on ley lines and how to draw energy from them. She studied the sketches of a map with straight lines crisscrossing over it, sometimes forming a star over a particular area. She didn't understand much about the lines, only that the book indicated they could be powerful.

Next was a list of common ingredients for potions, most of which she'd never heard of. Her mother would have recognized these. She was said to be able to cure nearly anything with her poultices. Tara swallowed over the knot that suddenly formed in her throat. Two good women, long gone from this world. They could have cured Gregore faster than Tara could draw her weapon. And the poor guy was stuck with her. Little wonder that he was angry at his circumstances. He must be pissed at the universe for sticking him with a woman who only just tonight began to believe in magic again, and couldn't begin to help him in his hour of need.

She sighed and flipped another page. No feeling sorry for yourself, O'Reilly. It would not help him and it would not help her. She'd do everything in her meager power to cure him. Tomorrow she would find out exactly how much time they had, if Gregore even knew, and they would go from there.

The pages that followed the ingredients list were full of innocent spells, like easing the pains of pregnancy, finding a lost object, and making crops grow twofold. Harmless until she reached page twenty-five. There, she found a spell to curse someone with gout. She cringed and sank a little further into the bed. She pored over more spells, amazed at the variety of things they supposedly did. This went way beyond hair of frog (or was that dog?) and eye of newt.

She yawned and flipped until she reached the middle of the book. A jagged edge protruded from the spine. She touched it gingerly, wishing she could recreate it. This was likely the place where the curse for Gregore's current condition had been. Most of the previous curses had contained the way to break them. Had this?

Gregore looked as if his heart had been ripped out along with the page when he'd seen it at the warehouse. But instead of sulking over his own—much larger—problems, he had comforted her in the alley, protected her when the homeless man could have identified them, and distracted her with kisses that even now threatened to rob her of thought. She licked her lips, remembering the feel and taste of him. Hot. A bit spicy in a way she couldn't identify but made her want more. Tingles danced in her breasts. No man's mouth had ever made her feel as Gregore's did. He poured passion into his kiss in that alley. Passion, but not his pain.

The tingles in her chest turned to an ache. She pressed a hand against her suddenly warm cheek and felt a bit ill. How could she be so selfish? His last hope for a normal life had literally been ripped away and instead of wallowing in it, he'd made sure she was okay. She should have been the one offering comfort, not taking it.

Tara flipped the book closed and slapped it on the end table, disgusted with herself. She remembered the brief melancholy on his face, how it turned to anger when he stalked around the bedroom as if it were a prison cell. The shock had worn off, she mused. Like an accident victim suddenly faced with the loss of the loved one that was in the passenger seat. Like the person who'd lost everything she owned in a fire. The ache in her chest turned to the weight of a boulder. She rolled to her side, curling up with the pillow, and switched off the lamp.

Lying in the darkness, barely able to keep her eyes open, she listened to the sounds of the old house settling. Tried to hear Gregore's movements. Her situation was hardly as bad as his, but it was still far from good. Once again she would have to put her life back together. She'd done it when her parents died and then when Grandma Rose had passed. Tara closed her eyes, feeling the pull of sleep. Her last thought was that this time she didn't want to do it all by herself. Maybe by helping Gregore, he could help her. The pressure in her heart eased as she slid into a deep slumber.

<hr>

Mottled grey light woke Tara hours later. She pried her eyes open and immediately regretted the action. It felt like the Sandman had rubbed the sand into her eyes overnight. She yawned and pushed herself up, trying to make sense of the fuzzy letters on the alarm clock. Ten minutes to noon? She blinked and glanced back at the window. The sky was dark with snow clouds. Large flakes fell in heavy waves. Seattle winters were usually more mild. Snow like this could debilitate the city. Climbing out of bed and back into her clothes from the night before, Tara resolved to grab their bags from the car even if she had to dig the Mini out of a snowdrift. Stifling a yawn, she went downstairs.

Her aunt hummed to herself as she poked a needle and thread through her cranberry tweed jacket to sew on a button. "Morning, dear!"

"Morning, Maddy. Do you have coffee?" Priorities first, then pleasantries. It was her way.

Maddy laughed, her silver and white curls jiggling. "When have I ever? But tea is ready for you, dear."

Tara nodded. Tea. Returning with a steaming cup in her hand, she sat beside Maddy on the couch. The fragrant citrus brew awakened her brain and tasted heavenly.

Maddy smiled, leaned closer as if to whisper something, then jabbed the sewing needle into Tara's finger.

Hot tea sloshed over the rim of the cup, splattering on Tara's thighs, as she yelped in surprise. "What the hell was that for?" She sucked her finger and set the delicate teacup on the side table.

"It's so you'll remember."

"Remember what? Not to sit next to you when you're armed with a needle?"

Her aunt smiled, but the sparkle didn't reach her eyes. She blinked, looking around the room, then down at her needle. "I don't remember."

"She's a fortune cookie," Tara muttered, then stood. "I'm going to get clean clothes out of the car."

"All right. I'll be here. And I want to know all about what happened last night."

Tara stalked out the front door and immediately wished she had at least blotted up the tea staining her jeans. The liquid plastered her skin with cold. She quickly retrieved the bags from the trunk and returned to the warmth of the house.

"So tell me what happened. Did you find the crab? I was quite sure there was one, you know."

Tara sipped her tea, letting it heat her back up, then nodded. "Yes, it was a warehouse with a crab on the sign."

"I knew it!" Maddy crowed. "All according to plan."

"Nothing was according to plan," Tara whispered. She shook her head, still unable to believe what she had seen. "The man who stole Grandma Rose's spell book was there. We took him by surprise. He thrust out his hand, like he was telling us to stop. And suddenly we stopped. We couldn't move an inch." The terror of being frozen in place cramped her muscles all over again. Her lungs threatened to close.

Maddy touched a soft hand to her arm. "It's over, dear. What happened next?"

"He ran and whatever held us released. I don't know how, but Gregore ran faster than I've seen anyone run. He caught the guy, taking him down at the far end of the hall.. The book flew from his hand as they struggled and the guy broke free. He got away, but not before..." She paused as her throat tightened around the words, remembering the fear of being frozen in place.

"The spell book? Did you find it?"

"I did." But at what cost? The memory of Gregore's haunted gaze still hurt. "The book is upstairs. But the page is gone. The spell is no longer there."

"Get it. Let's have a look together."

Tara retrieved the grimoire from the nightstand in her room. Her aunt's eyes misted when she saw the dark leather and yellowed pages.

"It's just as I had imagined."

"Rose never showed it to you?" Tara asked.

"No. She was afraid of the power it could wield, and kept it locked safely away, much as you did."

"Only she didn't lose it," Tara grumbled

Maddy chuckled. "True. Let's see what this can tell us." She hovered her frail hands over the leather and closed her eyes. When she opened them again, they were as lucid as Tara had ever seen them. "You're out of your league, Detective."

Tara blinked. "Pardon?" She'd never heard Maddy speak so formally. It was as if they'd never met.

Her aunt brushed imaginary lint from her pressed pants. "Your detective skills won't beat him, Tara. I've seen it."

"So I just let him go? He has to answer for his crimes."

"He shall, but only if you do what needs be done."

Tara swallowed, her throat suddenly dry. "What is that?"

"Do you truly think, after what this man did last night, that your detective skills can stop him? He is strong, Tara. Be stronger."

Tara's heart sank. She'd known she couldn't win without magic, but it stung to hear someone else say it.

"Only one of you has the time to waste on inaction." Maddy said and went into the kitchen.

Tara frowned after her aunt. She opened her stiff fingers locked on the book. Beyond whatever Maddy could see, Tara had to face the truth. What if she couldn't take this guy? What if he came after Maddy? What if he killed someone she cared about? She brushed her hand over the soft leather and cringed. She didn't want any of this. She just wanted her normal life back. Boring days with regular cases and the comfort of her Sig at her side. Even a smart-ass Casanova partner.

The house creaked from above, drawing Tara's attention to the second floor. Normal life didn't include Gregore. *Couldn't* include him. He wasn't normal in any sense of the imagination. He was too gruff and too stubborn, too strong and too fast. He was even too caring, damn it. Not to mention that men who turned to stone during the day weren't exactly date material. But he was also too honorable. Too vulnerable. And when everything in her being wanted to crawl back to the safe haven of what she knew her life to be, she just couldn't do it. Not when that too amazing man upstairs needed her. Even if it meant doing the one thing that scared her more than facing death. She traced the page edges with her finger, feeling the slight throb where Maddy had pricked her. She would help him.

Even if it meant using magic.

CHAPTER 16

Ley lines were real and crossed the earth's crust the world over, fueling magical abilities for people like Saints. Like herself, if she believed.

Tara took a sip of cold citrus tea and concentrated again. She sat in the kitchen by the window, facing Mount Rainier, though the hulking volcano was hidden behind dense grey clouds. She brought clean air into her lungs and expelled all bad thoughts. In her mind's eye, she tried to see an amber line drawn like electric current outside the house.

Nothing.

She drew another breath, exhaled, and wished she'd taken up yoga when it was the rage. Focusing again, she looked, and waited.

Nothing.

Grumbling, she readjusted herself in the straight-back wooden chair, took another breath, and focused. Either she would be the most relaxed she would ever be in her life, or she would see the damn line.

Suddenly the amber line popped into her mind, shimmering with magnetic energy. Tara jumped, ducking in surprise and nearly upending herself out of the chair. She covered her mouth, fairly certain she'd just woken the dead with her squeal. Closing her eyes, she looked for the line, and once again, it appeared with increasing clarity. Oddly, the line came straight at the house. Did that have something to do with why Grandma Rose had chosen this house and why her aunt now lived here? She made a mental note to ask Maddy later. Maybe it helped power her visions.

Tara grinned. She'd done it. One small leap for magic, one giant step for Tara.

Her heartbeat thumped in her ears. She felt triumphant, and just around the edges of that, fear. Part of her wanted to run away from her unnatural abilities. Away from darker thoughts of a day when she sat at this very table with a deck of tarot cards and her Grandma Rose smiling reassuringly. Tara's throat constricted at the memory of the phone call that followed on that sunny summer day and the lashing pain that flayed her heart.

A shrill ring snapped her eyes open and made her heart pound harder. Tara reached for her cell phone and checked the display. "Hey, Carson."

His gruff voice on the other end of the line sounded strained. "Hey, partner. Last night a body was found in a warehouse. Turned out to be Hiroshi. This case may be at a dead end."

Tara swallowed and tried to sound normal. "Shit. That's no good. Sorry I can't be there."

"Yeah, the captain was pretty firm that you're to take time off to get things straightened out." He paused and the silence stretched thin.

She hated that their friendship was strained.

"How're things going?" he asked.

"Just fine," she said in as light and friendly a tone as she could manage. She hated not being able to tell him what was going on.

"You've never done chipper, partner. What aren't you telling me?" He sounded angry.

"Nothing."

"Bullshit. Are you running a secondary investigation? You're supposed to stay out of it."

"No. Why would I investigate Hiroshi?"

"Because you can't leave anything alone. And I wasn't talking about Hiroshi. I was talking about the fire and you know it. Don't insult my intelligence."

"So what can I insult?" she shot back, suddenly pissed. "How about your dating habits?"

"Sure, you can go there. While we're at it, let's talk about that creep I hear you're hanging out with. Ring any bells?"

"He's not a creep. Wait, how do you know about—?"

"One of the uniforms saw you leave the library with some guy who looked like trouble. Said you looked pretty chummy."

"Jealous, Carson?"

"Hardly. I look out for my friends. That includes your sorry ass. So you better tell me what's going on."

Tara rubbed her eyes. He was looking out for her and she was being a bitch. "I'm sorry, Carson. I can't. It's personal."

"Yeah, right."

She cringed at the veiled fury in his words. She had the feeling she had hurt him. "Carson... I'm glad you called. I'm sorry I've been such a bitch. I need..." God, she could hardly say it. "I need help with this. I didn't set fire to my place. I think I know who did."

"Who?"

"Nick Saints. Carson, you have to find him. You have to tell me where he is before—"

"Whoa. Slow down. First, I don't have to tell you anything. You're off the case. This case and all the other cases, remember? Second, I don't know if it's the same guy. That's what investigating is about. And if it turns out that he is your guy, then I'll find him and bring him in."

"Carson, you don't understand. It's gone far beyond—"

"No, Tara, *you* don't understand. If the captain hears you're interfering in an open investigation, there's going to be hell to pay. Let me handle this."

Fear tightened her throat. "You won't tell him."

He sighed. "Not yet. But if you don't stay clear of all this, I can't help you."

She breathed relief. "Thank you, partner."

"Don't thank me yet. Thank me when you come back to work."

"Deal."

"So who is the creep you were seen with?"

Tara glanced up as if she could see through the ceiling to Gregore's bedroom above. "He's someone who needs my help."

"What's his name?"

Tara hesitated, knowing that her partner would jump to investigate everything he could about Gregore. But if she didn't say, Carson would hound her until she caved. Maybe if she told him, she'd learn more about Gregore and at the same time keep Carson busy. "Gregore Trenowyth."

"What kind of help?"

"I shouldn't betray that confidence, Carson."

He grumbled but assented.

"Carson? Can you please look for Saints?"

"Yeah, all right. I'll call you soon."

She hung up, feeling marginally better. Casanova cared, even if he had a funny way of showing it.

Tara went back to the spell book. Now that she could see ley lines, maybe she could move on to crafting a shield like Saints had used. She hated being twenty steps behind him.

Gregore woke just before twilight. He stretched and felt for the position of the sun. After so many years, he knew exactly where it was and how much time remained until full dark. He rose and walked to the window, cringing as each heavy step of his stone legs seemed to shake the very foundation of the old Victorian. He hated sleeping on a second floor. Visions of crashing through to the floor below and surprising his host rumbled through his head with each step. Made him move even slower. *No, not an earthquake. Just your guest moving about.*

He sighed and stopped in front of the window, carefully folding his wings and stilling his body, breathing slow as his form began the change in earnest. Stone melted into muscle. The tightness in his thighs, his stomach, and his arms eased. Like the proverbial weight lifting. His chest remained tight, even after his body returned to its natural human state. A heaviness remained deep within. A darkness in his soul much too familiar. It tasted bitter in his mouth. Like the flip side of his anger just hours before. This tasted of despair. Despair so deep, it settled on him like a heavy wool cloak he couldn't escape from.

It ate away at his hope like a ravenous beast, devouring all in its path. What if he couldn't escape his fate? What if he never had a chance?

On the other side of the curtain, the sun slipped behind the homes of this quiet neighborhood, bringing peaceful twilight. Tonight he didn't need to see it. He didn't want to see what twilight looked like from the window of this old house. Perhaps because it marked the passing of time in a way he couldn't control. He couldn't stop this clock and pretend he had more time. He was in trouble and only one thing could save his life.

Gregore opened his eyes and parted the curtain with a shaking hand. Dark gray clouds stretched above the houses, swallowing the last of the light and blocking the stars. As a lad, he loved the night sky. His mother would stand on the balcony of their home with him, staring up into the heavens and bidding him to make a wish on the very first star.

He made that wish now. He wished for freedom from this curse and a normal life. That was two wishes. He made them anyway.

Gradually he became aware of movement in the house below. A clatter of cup and saucer, the tap of a spoon against a pot. Tara's voice, then her rich laughter as she chatted with Maddy. A pang of regret overwhelmed what despair remained. Gregore's anger had gotten the better of him hours earlier. He hadn't treated Tara well. She was his last hope, and he'd pushed her away in a rough manner unfitting of his character. No gentleman should treat a lady as such, regardless that the world had changed since his day. Slamming a door in her face when she tried to offer comfort was wrong. His cheeks heated in shame. He would apologize.

He turned to go find her. Just inside the door to his room, he spotted the leather bag they'd brought from the church. No doubt Tara left it as he slept. Her thoughtfulness touched him. Perhaps the first order of business was a shower, fresh clothes, and clean teeth before his apology. Instead of a ruffian, he could make a better impression. Taking up the bag, he opened the door and headed for the bathroom down the hall. His steps were lighter and not just because he wasn't stone. He wanted to look good when he saw Tara. It shocked him, yet he felt the truthfulness of the thought. He cared what she saw when she looked at him. He *wanted* her to look. To see past the stone to the human man beneath. He wanted to see her eyes heat and darken with desire. Feel her soft touch on his skin.

His body responded in favor, surprising him with its sudden vigor. He closed the bathroom door, shucked his clothes, and started the shower. Tara's soft lips and warm touch filled his thoughts as he soaped himself under the hot spray, his desire for her growing. He pictured her stepping into the shower with him, her naked body glistening. Her breasts turning pink in the heated water. He dreamt of running his soapy hands over her slick flesh and moaned. His own hand found his cock and held it, not wanting to find pleasure alone. Not like this. He ached for Tara. Longed to bring her to a shattering climax, then feel himself fly apart in the searing depths of her body.

Gregore released his grip on himself and fumbled for the faucets, forcing the lust away with a shock of cold water. He finished his shower, dragging his thoughts back to reality. A woman like Tara would hardly fall into his arms. No matter what happened with his future, no matter what the next days brought, he wanted one night with Tara. Flesh against flesh. Not because he needed sex or that it had been so long, but because he felt such a deep connection with her. She felt it too, he was sure. He sensed she held herself apart from others more than she should. At times she looked alone. As alone as he. They needed each other. *In more ways than one,* he thought.

He turned off the faucet and dried with a fluffy pink towel. After using the toilet, he shaved, dressed, and brushed his teeth. Satisfied with his appearance, he dropped the bag inside his room and headed downstairs.

Tara met him at the foot of the stairs. Her eyes sparkled when she saw him, and her gaze traveled from his bare feet, up his jeans and the gray sweater he wore, to rest on his face. She too was clean, wearing snug new jeans and a sweater with a V-neck that pointed straight to her sweet cleavage. He licked his lips. *Eyes up.* The green of her eyes darkened. When she spoke, her words were huskier than he'd ever heard.

"You clean up well," she said.

"As do you," he replied, feeling his flesh heat all over again. Her lips tilted up in a small smile as if she didn't quite believe him. His

Tara needed to be wooed. He was just the man for the job. But first, he owed her an apology.

"Tara," he began, not quite sure how to convey his regrets. Women of this era were different from those he knew from his past. He couldn't very well buy her jewelry to soothe the awkwardness. Somehow he knew Tara would prefer honesty over fancy trinkets. A moment of silence stretched into two.

She raised a delicate eyebrow but didn't speak. Just waited for whatever he chose to say.

"About last night…forgive me. I shouldn't have slammed…what I mean to say is that I didn't mean…" Oh hell, just spit it out, man! The beautiful woman deserved an apology. Without thinking, he reached for her hand and fell back on the only thing he knew for such situations. He brought the soft skin of the back of her hand to his lips in a brief kiss. "It was not right to take my anger out on you as I did. Please accept my apology."

Her gaze filled with warmth. She nodded, let her hand linger at his lips a moment more, then pulled away.

"You fear the end of your life, Gregore. I understand. I worry for you too. We can't let our fears rule us. It's something I've lived by for a long time." She looked away. "Funny how somehow I still managed to ignore the one area I was truly scared of." She stepped closer and laid her hand on his arm. Determination glinted in her eyes. "But as of now, neither one of us should be afraid. We're going to break this curse. I'm going to help give your life back. Just watch me."

Gregore smiled and covered her hand with his, feeling the small star of hope in his chest go supernova. "Tara, I—"

He was interrupted by a resolute knock at the front door.

Tara turned toward the door behind her, a look of concern on her face. Maddy came in from the kitchen, wiping her hands on a towel.

"Aunt Maddy, are you expecting someone?" Tara asked quietly.

"No, dear. Were you?"

Tara shook her head and reached for her weapon. When her fingers brushed only denim, she frowned.

The knock came stronger, louder this time.

Gregore stepped in front of her as she went to the door.

"Allow me," he said. "I'm harder to hurt."

She looked like she would protest, then nodded.

He went to the window and parted the curtain, but could only see the shadowy shape of a man. He reached to flip the nearby light switch. A light came on overhead, illuminating Tara, Maddy, and himself. Tara reached past him, turning the entry light off and the porch light on. Nothing happened outside.

"Looks like your porch light is out, Maddy," Gregore said.

The man outside pounded louder, followed by a curse. The voice was somehow familiar. Gregore struggled to place the accent as he unlocked and opened the door.

On the threshold stood a blond man with an intent gaze and cocky smile.

"Hello, Gregore. Good to see you again."

CHAPTER 17

"Close your mouth, old chap. Unless you're looking for a little extra protein?" the newcomer said. He smiled and a dimple appeared in his left cheek, matching the mirth in his eyes.

Gregore clicked his teeth shut. "What the hell are you doing here, Thomas?" He caught Tara's surprised gaze and cursed inwardly. Great job, idiot. Way to woo the woman with your impeccable manners.

Thomas's smile slipped. "Just uh...in the neighborhood. You know?"

Gregore braced his arm across the doorway. "This neighborhood?"

"This neighborhood." Thomas ducked his head.

Before Gregore could respond, Tara slipped under his arm. "Can I help you?"

The smile returned with the dimple amped up one hundred percent. "Ah, now it makes sense. He always was possessive of his women."

"I'm not..." she started.

"Thomas Whetmore," the blond said, offering his hand. "*Old* friend of this gargoyle." He stuck a thumb in Gregore's direction.

Gregore didn't know who was more shocked, Tara, realizing that Thomas knew his truth, or himself.

"Tara," she replied.

"It's been a long time," he said to Thomas.

Thomas met his gaze with one almost accusing in its sudden intensity, magnifying the slight lines in his face. "Too long."

"Well, don't let that man just stand out there in the cold, you two. Can't you see he's harmless? Besides, you're letting the heat out. Can't afford to heat the whole neighborhood!" Maddy moved Gregore and Tara from the door with a shooing motion of her hand.

Gregore couldn't quite agree with "harmless," but remembering a similar conversation about himself, stepped aside. Curiosity more than anything pushed him to see what Thomas had to say. To know why his old friend had sought him out. How he'd found him here of all places.

Maddy introduced herself and led her new guest into the kitchen as if he were her closest friend. Gregore trailed along, distinctly aware of Tara behind him.

Thomas accepted a dainty china cup of hot tea with his customary charm and reached for a homemade oatmeal raisin cookie off the plate Maddy set on the table. Gregore swung a chair around to straddle and let the man take a sip of tea. He cleared his throat.

"How long has it been?" he asked Thomas. He couldn't remember the year he'd last seen Thomas and Jeffrey, only the circumstances.

Thomas gently set his cup down and flicked a glance to the women.

Gregore nodded, answering his unspoken question.

"One hundred twenty-seven years, but who's counting?" Thomas replied, an easy smile in place.

Damn. He owed Thomas a big fat apology for that night. He'd be damned if he'd kiss Thomas's hand, though.

An awkward silence settled into the kitchen. Tara studied Thomas from beneath her lashes. Maddy smiled brightly, her faded blue eyes looking from one to the next. Thomas simply stared at Gregore, waiting for a reply. Gregore pinched the bridge of his nose. Shit. He didn't need this. Not now. Not when it was so close to the end. They were supposed to leave him alone. Weren't they satisfied with just how much he'd ruined their lives? Oh no, just come back for more. Bad enough that *he* was close to the end. Now he had to drown in a hundred and fifty years of guilt to ride out those last few days. He narrowed his eyes.

"Why now?" he growled. To hell with an apology.

Thomas's gaze remained steady, though the line of his mouth flattened in determination. His friend had changed over the years. There were no new lines on his face. It was in his eyes. They reflected a weariness and age that had never once been present in the years they had been close friends. Thomas suffered.

The knowledge melted Gregore's irritation. He rubbed the back of his neck and exhaled.

"Because it's your time," Thomas answered. "Because you're not alone in this, and I won't allow you to go through this unaided."

Gregore frowned at the compassion in his friend's voice. Gone was his carefree friend with the world, and the women, at his fingertips. He had changed so much, the light gone from his eyes. And if Thomas had changed so drastically, how must he look to Thomas after all this time?

Thomas reached out and held his shoulder. "You need us, Gregore. And we need you. The three of us can beat this. We'll start with you."

"Three? There are three of you?" Tara asked in surprise.

Thomas smiled sadly. "There are. Jeffrey Kingston as well, though he keeps to himself these days. Much like someone else I know."

Gregore shoved away from the table to pace the kitchen. Guilt ate large chunks at his gut, threatening to make him ill.

"We must come back together," Thomas continued. "We were cursed together, we will end the curse together." He took another cookie and ate it in two bites.

"Oh, so exciting!" Maddy clapped her hands.

Gregore turned back to the group at the table. Questions brimmed in Tara's eyes, threatening to overflow onto her lips. He had to head them off before she could ask. He did not want to talk about any of this. Especially not with her.

"Ladies, could you excuse us? Thomas and I need some time to discuss things."

"Of course, dear," Maddy said, rising from the table.

Tara shook her head and stayed put. To further prove her stubborn point, she leaned back in her chair and crossed her arms over her ample chest.

Thomas grinned and finished off another cookie.

Gregore scowled at them both as Maddy tottered out of the kitchen. Tara didn't budge. The woman refused to be cowed and it pissed Gregore off. Even though some rebellious part of him admired that she stood up to him. He was in so much trouble.

"Do not make me remove you," he grumbled.

"Oh, I do hope you try." She fairly vibrated with challenge. Her smile told him she looked forward to his meager attempt.

Big, big trouble. Gregore cursed anew and ran both hands through his hair. "Damn it, Tara. Why won't you listen? This is between me and Thomas."

"No. I'm part of this too. You need my help. Or have you forgotten that Saints is holding all the aces and all we've got is a pair?"

Thomas's dimple appeared again as he grinned at Tara. "I like this one, mate. She's a keeper."

Tara winked back at him, a saucy smile tugging at her lips.

Gregore groaned. She was going to be the death of him. Or the death of Thomas. Because if she looked at Thomas like that one more time, he'd be across the table in a heartbeat. He'd never felt burning jealousy like this in his entire life. What was it about Tara that brought it out so fiercely in him?

Clamping a tight lid on his raging thoughts and tumultuous emotions, Gregore forced himself to nod and accept her presence there. He stalked back to the table, flipped his chair around to face forward, and took a seat like a civilized man.

"Who is this Saints?" Thomas asked.

Tara sat forward. "We don't know much. Only that he wanted the spell book. He stole it from me."

"What sort of spell book? Why would he want it?"

"Because of me," Gregore said.

Thomas jerked up straight in his chair. "The old crone's book? You found it? Here?" The excitement faded as he spoke. "And now you've lost it."

Gregore ran his hand over the smooth wood grain of the table, unable to voice his thoughts. He might just choke on the disappointment.

"Actually, we got it back last night," Tara said. "Just one problem, though—"

"The spell's gone, Thomas," Gregore cut in. "The bastard ripped it out."

Thomas paled, swallowed. "Last night. At the warehouse?"

Gregore's head snapped up. "How did you know we were at a warehouse?"

Thomas shrugged. "I followed you. Had I known...Oh God, Gregore. I'm so sorry. I could have stopped him had I known."

Gregore shook his head. "It's not your fight. It's mine. A fight I lost." He pushed the chair back and stood, unable to keep still when his insides churned. His hands tingled and his breathing sped up.

"Gregore, that's not tr—" Tara began.

He silenced her with a fierce look. "Do not pity me," he growled and stomped to the back door of Maddy's kitchen. "This fight is not over." He slammed the door behind him, rattling the entire house.

CHAPTER 18

Tara rose to follow Gregore, alarmed at his anger and surprised by the arrival of his friend. Three of them were cursed? Just what happened to these men?

Thomas stopped her with a hand on her arm. "Don't," he said in that enticing English accent. "Let his temper cool. His pride is wounded by defeat."

"But—"

Thomas shook his head. "If I know Gregore, he'll prowl around a bit and return in a couple of hours. He needs me." Thomas looked thoughtfully at her. "I suspect he needs *us* and he knows it. He'll be back."

Tara sat back down. "You must have known him a long time. Did you know him before all this?" She waved her hand. "Before the curse?"

Thomas nodded. "I did."

"What was he like back then?"

"Just as charming as he is now," Thomas said.

Tara laughed and Thomas smiled.

"My heavens. What was that racket? Who's bringing down the house?" Aunt Maddy asked as she came back into the kitchen. The hills of her penciled eyebrows rose over her eyes in surprise. "Ah, I should have guessed. That boy is troubled. Still, he needn't take it out on my poor door." She shook her head, then asked, "Who's hungry?"

Thomas turned his dazzling smile on Maddy. "Did someone say supper?"

He rose to help Maddy remove the pot roast from the oven, giving Tara a moment to study him. His dark blond hair just brushed his collar in light waves, as if he hadn't had a trim in some time. He stood about six foot and she'd hazard a guess that beneath his leather coat and shirt he was all muscle. Muscular men moved entirely different than average men. They either moved like giant blocks of cement, or in the case of Thomas and Gregore, with the grace of a lion. Strong, with a hint of prowling.

Thomas was very attractive, with his faint accent, sparkling deep-blue eyes, and the dimple in his left cheek that invited laughter. Laughter that didn't always reach his eyes. He had a few lines in his face, most deeply around his eyes and in his forehead, and somehow they made him even more handsome. Slight shadows haunted his features, but she couldn't quite put her finger on how. Whatever his curse, it shadowed Thomas as much as Gregore was haunted by his own.

She shivered at the thought of Gregore. Thomas was handsome, but his eyes didn't melt Tara to her toes the way Gregore's deep burning gaze did. Thomas could easily make her laugh. Gregore could make her go up in flames. Tara licked her lips. She wanted to burn.

Thomas caught her look and smiled. His eyes sparked with knowing, and he flicked a glance to the back door where Gregore had left.

She tried not to blush. The Irish part of her heritage, thanks to her father, got the better of her, and she felt red to the roots of her hair. It wasn't as if she and Gregore had any sort of relationship. They hadn't known each other long. The desire was there, though. Gregore felt it too. She was sure of it. Her lips quirked up. Nothing like a little hormone rush.

Maddy set the platter of roast beef before them with some vegetable sides.

"I'll save some for Gregore," she said and forked a few pieces onto a plate.

Her fork had no sooner left the roast when Thomas sat and dug in. He took a bite and closed his eyes, wonder replacing his smile. "Heaven," he said around his food. "I don't remember the last home-cooked meal I had."

Maddy patted his hand. "Thank you. You're a very sweet boy. Now eat as much as you want. We don't want the food to go to waste, and I can't possibly eat it all myself."

"Glad to help," Thomas said.

Tara grinned and started in on dinner. It was good to see Maddy so happy.

A pang of guilt stabbed her. She hadn't been good to Maddy since Grandma Rose had passed. She could count her visits to her aunt on one hand. The reasons for staying away suddenly seemed paltry and selfish. Shame heated her cheeks. What if she were in Gregore's position, with just days left to her life? Their run-in with Saints the evening before certainly brought home that possibility. Saints had the power to kill her. Last night, they'd been lucky. They might not be so lucky next time. What would become of Aunt Maddy then?

Maddy had friends, sure. But Tara was the last of her family. If things went south, Maddy would have no one. She looked at her aunt. Saw the pale skin and thin body. Her wrists were tiny. She appeared more frail than Tara could ever remember seeing her. Or was she truly seeing her for the first time? Maddy might only have a few good years left.

Tara didn't want her last relative to die alone. Gregore had given that to her. Knowing him had changed that in her. No one should die alone.

Tara struggled to swallow a bite of roast past the sudden lump in her throat. She'd been a terrible niece. She'd let years of fear of her own gifts estrange her from what truly mattered in her life.

Family.

Love.

She vowed to spend more time with the wonderful woman sitting across the table from her. No matter that the woman was nuttier than her banana nut bread. You didn't get to choose your family, but you could surely choose to appreciate them. She couldn't change the past, only the future. As Tara took another bite of food, she promised herself she'd do just that. She'd mend the bridge with her aunt and spend more time with her before she too was gone from this life.

Tara idly wondered who Gregore needed to make peace with and looked up at Thomas, who entertained Maddy with a silly tale that had her aunt laughing so hard, tears flowed from her misty blue eyes. Judging from Gregore's welcome, she suspected Thomas was that person. Life was too short to hold grudges or cling to ridiculous fears. She'd lost too many friends on the force. Too many family members. She wouldn't lose Maddy without making amends. And though Gregore might only have a short time left, she wouldn't allow him to leave without attempting to heal the wounds between he and Thomas.

She finished her dinner with renewed determination. First she would find out exactly what distanced Thomas and Gregore, then what she could do to break through Gregore's fierce defenses. She suspected she'd even have an ally with Thomas. He was here to help after all. Tara turned her attention back to her companions. Aunt Maddy yawned. Thomas smiled, his eyes half glazed.

"Food coma?" Tara asked, grinning.

"Bliss," he responded and folded his hands behind his head. "That was fabulous, my dear Maddy. You can cook for me any time."

Maddy blushed like a schoolgirl, then fought off another yawn.

Tara reached over and squeezed her aunt's hand. "I'll get the food and dishes."

"Yes, and I'll help," Thomas chimed in. "Starting with Gregore's plate. Where did you say you put that?"

Maddy swatted his hand. "You leave that dear boy be. He needs a good meal as much as you did."

Thomas grinned unrepentant.

Maddy wagged a finger at him as she rose from her chair. "You behave or my Tara may have to put the cuffs on."

Thomas shot Tara a hopeful look. "Truly?"

Tara cocked an eyebrow and gathered their plates. "Sure you want to find out?" He looked uncertain, causing Tara to laugh. "Go on to bed, Maddy. I've got this—and him—covered."

Maddy smiled and kissed Tara's cheek. "It's so good to have you here. Good night, all."

Tara watched her aunt leave the kitchen. She waited approximately five seconds after Maddy cleared the door before jumping into her inquiry.

"Thomas," she began and paused, placing the dishes on the counter. Now that she began, she wasn't sure where to start. She settled on, "Why now? Why show up in Gregore's life at what could be the very end? How did you find him? When did you start looking for him? How—"

Thomas's laughter put an end to her interrogation. He held up his hands. "I surrender. What's next? Where was I on the night when Gregore was cursed?"

She gave him a half smile. "Something like that."

Thomas joined her at the sink and started the water, adding detergent and a few plates. "That's an easy one. I was shoulder to shoulder with him waiting for a crazy woman to end our lives."

"The Gypsy woman? The one who owned the spell book?"

"The very same. The one who *wrote* the spell book," he said, handing her a clean plate to rinse.

"What happened? I mean, what circumstances brought such wrath? To not just be satisfied with killing you, but to make you suffer for so long?" She rinsed the plate and set it into the dish rack to dry, then took another clean plate from him.

He cast her the briefest glance, one she couldn't interpret, then concentrated on cleaning the dishes. She knew he tried to hide his emotions from her. It didn't work. Bleakness lined his face.

"That's his story to tell," Thomas said.

"So tell me yours."

The left corner of his lips tipped up. "Next question, please."

Tara wanted to push for the truth. She didn't know Thomas, but her gut told her she could trust him. That Gregore also trusted him, or he wouldn't have let this man past the front door into her aunt's house. She could work with that.

"Gregore is your friend. You said yourself that you had known him since before he was cursed. You must have been close."

"The very best of friends."

"So what happened? He clearly wasn't happy to see you tonight," she said as she took the last clean dish from him.

Thomas let the water drain and wiped his hands on the dish towel.

"The curse happened. After that night, we were all a little out of our minds. In one way or another, our lives were ripped away from us. Gregore was hit the worst. In one night, he lost his father, his lover, and his faith in himself. Can you understand what that is like? And then to wake hours later with the knowledge that you are some sort of freakish creature? That you can never go back to your old life?"

Tara shook her head, unable to form words past the hard knot in her throat. Her heart ached for Gregore. Ached nearly as bad as when she had lost Grandma Rose. She pushed that thought aside, unwilling to look too closely at what could prompt that sort of reaction in her.

"He went a little mad. He refused to see us." Thomas snorted. "Or simply couldn't," he muttered. Then added, "He put his affairs in order, told his family he was going to the continent, and disappeared.

"I had my own problems at the time. So did Jeffrey. I don't want to say we had an easier time of it. We can't possibly. What we did have was each other. Jeffrey and I stuck together. By the time we could manage our curses enough to travel and survive, Gregore was gone. All that was left of him was a hastily written apology."

Tara listened, watching Thomas's face as he spoke. The lines around his eyes deepened and a sadness took hold. She touched a hand to his arm. "Please continue."

His gaze met hers, and she dropped back a step under the weight of his fierceness. Determination, raw anger, and hopelessness warred within the man's eyes.

"The note was the start of the rift between Jeffrey and Gregore. Jeffrey found the apology woefully inadequate for all we suffered. Still, he and I stuck together and searched for Gregore. It took years." Thomas stepped around her to heat the teakettle and search the cabinets for a couple of cups.

"What happened when you found him?" she asked.

"Are you sure you want to hear this?"

Tara nodded. "I have to if I'm to help him."

Thomas sighed and nodded. "You care for him."

It was a statement, not a question. She didn't have an answer anyway.

"We followed his trail like breadcrumbs from country to country. Just a couple of blokes without benefit of the Internet. Much harder then. We followed strange creature sightings. Bigfoot, Godzilla, anything out of the ordinary, while hiding ourselves away as best we could during the day. It was easier in the big cities where we could keep gentlemen's hours. Much harder in the smaller countryside towns and villages, where farmers went to bed just after dusk.

"Our search eventually brought us to Italy. The rumors of a stone creature terrorizing the villagers and consuming cattle made it a bit easier to find him."

Tara paled. "Consuming cattle? Like…eating them? Raw?"

"A man wants a steak now and then," Thomas replied with a shrug of his shoulders.

Her stomach rumbled its disapproval, threatening to upheave dinner. She must have looked fairly green because Thomas burst out laughing.

"You're teasing me?" At his nod, she lightly punched his arm and growled at him. "On with the story, or so help me, you'll learn my interrogation techniques firsthand."

Thomas poured tea for them both and led her back to sit at the table. "The stories were wild but fed from superstitious imaginations. Fortunately, not everyone believed the stories. One spring night we ran into a gentleman who thought he'd seen a man matching Gregore's description up in the hills the day prior. We searched those hills for three nights and finally found a small cave with evidence that someone lived there.

"He'd been living like an animal. Just a scratchy wool blanket, a few books, and a change of clothes. Empty wine bottles littered the floor. The cave was empty other than that. Jeffrey reasoned that Gregore must have gone somewhere for food. He was right. We found Gregore at a roadside inn not half a mile from his cave." Thomas's gaze met hers. He looked older as he told his tale. The entirety of his years settling heavy on his shoulders.

"Instead of our friend, we found a man eaten alive by guilt. He was haggard. Too thin and very dirty. His once-fine clothes had holes in them, and his hair and beard looked more like they belonged on a wooly mammoth. He was miserable. And so drunk he couldn't stand."

Tara listened and tried to reconcile the handsome, strong man she knew with the picture of desperation Thomas painted. She couldn't. It was difficult to believe the tale. Thomas wasn't lying in this, though. She could read the pain in this every movement. Finding Gregore like that must have been horrible.

"We followed him out of the tavern and made ourselves known. His welcome of me today was nothing compared to that night. He yelled and screamed at us, slurring words so badly, we could barely understand him. He wanted us to leave him be. To let him drown in his drink. We tried to reason with him. We wanted to help, sure we could break the curse together if we but tried. He wanted to die, he said, and didn't care if we did the same."

Thomas frowned. "After all we'd been through to find him in the first place, Jeffrey lost it. He tackled Gregore and started swinging. I tried to break it up, but they were determined to beat the hell out of each other. I received heartfelt thanks for my efforts." He rubbed his jaw as if it ached in memory.

"The fight ended when Jeffrey…" Thomas looked away. "His curse kicked in, startling him. Gregore used that time to produce a knife, slashing Jeffrey's ribs. Gregore swore at us for fools. Said he'd ruined our lives enough and we should leave him be. Screamed at us to get out of his life for good. Jeffrey was bleeding pretty well, we clearly weren't wanted, so I helped Jeffrey up and we left. This is the first time I've seen Gregore since."

Tara blinked back the tears welling in her eyes. Her heart ached, her soul reaching out for Gregore. She touched Thomas's hand, gripping his teacup so hard, she thought it would break. The grief in his eyes told her all she needed to know. This man would give his life for Gregore and probably even Jeffrey, despite all they'd been through. A man like that made for a good ally. They needed all the help they could get.

"You're a good friend to him," she whispered. "To come here and offer your help, even though you knew he might not welcome you."

Thomas said nothing. He continued to stare into his tea as if it could reveal the future. With Aunt Maddy's tea, who knew? Maybe it could.

"You said you believed the three of you could break the curses together. What did you mean?"

Thomas traced the rim of his cup with a finger. "Only that there is strength in numbers. Together we are strong enough to conquer anything."

Tara nodded. Something fluttered in her chest. Almost a heated tickling. She had the strongest sensation of *knowing* that Thomas and Jeffrey were needed to help break the curse. As if somehow the magic inside her pulsed with that truth. There was so much she didn't know about this Gypsy magic in her blood.

"I think you're right," she said. "Somehow the two of you must be part of this." She struggled to put her finger on the elusive knowledge, to open herself up when her mind fought to close off from it.

Thomas spoke just as the back door opened. "Only together can we be strong enough to break our curses."

"Are you so certain?" Gregore almost growled from the doorway.

Thomas stood and went to him, placing a hand on Gregore's shoulder. "I'm positive, old friend. You trusted me once. Trust me now in this."

Tara could see the indecision warring on Gregore's face. She left the table to stand beside Thomas. "He's right," she said to Gregore, capturing his hand in hers. "I don't know how I know, but I can feel the truth. I've learned to listen to that instinct as a cop. We need him and Jeffrey in this fight. We need what help we can get, Gregore. I don't know if I can defeat Saints on my own."

Gregore squeezed her hand. "You never had to defeat him alone, Tara. If anything, this was my fight."

She shook her head. "No. This is our fight. He may have burned down my apartment and endangered my neighbors. He's not getting away with that."

"This late in the game, can you really afford to go it alone, mate?" Thomas asked. "What if you can't beat this by yourself? Isn't it better to have the help now than at the last moment when it could be too late?"

Tara saw the resignation in Gregore's eyes just before he said, "No. But if even one of you gets in harm's way, all bets are off and I take him down alone."

She opened her mouth to argue, then snapped it shut. She'd pick her battles. Or, more to the point, she'd pick when to fight them. Because if Gregore thought he'd lay down the ultimate sacrifice due to a little scuffle, he had another thing coming. Something about the look Thomas gave his friend seemed to say the same. Gregore may come to regret his decision tonight, even though it was the right one. She'd just found this strong, brave, incredible man and she wasn't about to lose him. No matter what he had to say about it.

Gregore pulled her to him, wrapping her in a brief hug.

She took the comfort he offered. He smelled of the crisp night air and deep forest. Her body fit right into his like she was made to be there. She touched her lips to his neck and wrapped her arms around his back, holding him still against her. It felt right. Too right. And the banked embers of her passion roared to life. She wanted him and that scared her.

She reluctantly broke the embrace and stepped back. "How about dinner?" Not waiting for a reply, she turned to reheat his food. She watched with interest as two men who hadn't spoken for a century sat down at a kitchen table and tried to make peace. This was where she would start to help Gregore heal. Now that she had at least a glimmer of understanding of him and what he'd been through, she could help him make his peace with Thomas. Hopefully, he'd even have time to bring that friendship back to life.

The men were silent until she brought Gregore's plate to him. She deepened her voice as she dropped into a chair beside them and tried for a faint (although terrible) British accent. "So Gregore, how have the last one hundred years treated you? What's new?"

Thomas chuckled under his breath.

Gregore didn't smile, but mirth appeared in his eyes all the same. He swallowed a bite and replied, "Oh, not much. Last week I went to the cinema. Amazing how films can change in a couple of decades..."

Thomas smirked. "So much better than the silent films."

They both laughed and the floodgates of camaraderie opened.

Tara sipped her tea and listened as they laughingly remembered past times before the curses had stolen so much. Boyish pranks pulled on each other and unsuspecting parents, wild rides on horseback through the countryside. Trips to London and the guilty pleasures found in the more illustrious brothels. Thomas, oddly enough, spent more time talking about those particular days.

"You always were the man the ladies flocked to," Gregore said with a smile. To Tara he added, "Jeffrey and I were invisible when Thomas was in the room."

The smile faded from Thomas's lips. "Now it's quite the opposite, isn't it, old chap?" he said quietly.

Gregore frowned. "Sorry, Thomas. That was thoughtless of me."

Thomas turned to Tara. "I don't suppose I could see the spell book? Maybe I could find something useful to my ah…affliction."

"Sure," she said. She burned to know what Thomas's curse was, but allowed him his privacy. She rose and snagged the spell book from the coffee table in the living room. The men were silent when she returned. "I hope it's here," she said as she handed it to Thomas.

He took the scarlet leather volume in hand with a mixture of hope and dread on his handsome face. "Thank you." He opened the book and began to thumb through the pages.

Tara took Gregore's empty plate to the sink. She felt the heat of his body before she heard his approach. His hands settled on the counter on either side of her, blocking her in. She turned into him.

"Thank you," he said. "For making me see reason."

Tara reached up to trace her fingers over the smooth skin of his cheek. "Don't do this alone, Gregore."

He turned his mouth to place a kiss on her palm. "You make me want to never be alone again," he whispered.

Likewise, she thought, but didn't get the chance to say it.

"It was a fool's hope," Thomas said, closing the book with force.

"I apologize," Gregore said, resting his forehead against hers.

"As am I, mate."

"We'll break your curse, whatever it is. Don't lose hope," Tara said. She looked between Gregore and Thomas. "Don't either of you lose hope. Not yet."

Gregore nodded and stepped away from her.

Thomas rose and ran fingers through his hair. "Right. Gregore first. He has the least amount time." He laughed bitterly.

"Thomas…" Gregore started.

Thomas held up a hand. "Save it. I'm going to get Jeffrey and bring him. We need all three of us together."

"Where is he living?" Gregore asked.

"He's holed himself up in a remote cabin east of here. Strange that you both settled so close to each other. Anyway, it may take me a couple of days."

"Why so long?" Tara asked.

Gregore answered. "Because Jeffrey has no desire to ever lay eyes on me, let alone help me in any way."

Thomas nodded. "He can be convinced. Just give me a little time."

"A little is all you have," Gregore said.

"Then I won't waste any more of it." Thomas clasped Gregore's hand. "I'll see you in two nights' time, old friend."

Gregore kept the hold of the handshake just a moment longer. "I'll be waiting." He looked an odd mix of uncomfortable and grateful. "Thank you, my friend."

"Don't thank me yet. We may not succeed." With those parting words, Thomas left the house.

CHAPTER 19

Church bells rang through the crisp, clear Sunday morning air. The cold wind coming through the open window blew away the scent of blood in the third-floor office of the warehouse. Outside, the inches of snow that fell overnight had turned to ice, keeping most people at home. Even the cops didn't seem to be out. That worked for Nick. He'd slipped past the police tape last night and reclaimed the warehouse as his own.

He sat in his desk chair, playing with an orb. Shooting his hand out, he drew on his power to channel a blast of energy at the metal wastebasket across the room. The contents within should have erupted into flames. A tiny waft of smoke twisted up instead. Fuck it.

Magic trickled in his blood once more. The roar of power he'd experience with Deja just two nights ago was gone. Lost after the unexpected battle with that damn freak Gregore and the detective. What the hell were they doing there anyway? How did they find him? Who was helping? Or was this one of the woman's magical gifts?

Nick needed to replenish and get back to work. Self-pleasuring only increased the power a fraction. He needed to feel that zing of magic shooting through his limbs and over his skin. He'd thought of little else since that night. Magic and power. Power and magic. He'd practiced and pleasured himself and practiced some more until he could control the flow of energies. Until he could wreak destruction on small items. It wasn't enough. To decimate his enemies, he needed more. He needed that feeling again. He needed Deja.

If oral sex brought as much power as it had, intercourse was going to rock his world right off its hinges. He walked over to the desk and pulled out an old copy of a phone book. He thumbed through, looking for the number to the Grand Grimoire. Grabbing the phone up off the old desk, he dialed and listened to it ring.

He couldn't remember the last time he'd called a woman for an amorous encounter. Years. Before Samantha. Her sunny smile and laughing eyes came to mind. Making love to her in the sunlight. On the beach. Lying in a hammock in…He pushed thoughts of her aside. He'd think about her when this was all over.

The call connected and Deja's sexy voice came on the line.

"It's Nick," he said. "I'm ready for another lesson."

Her throaty laugh filled his ear, making his skin tingle and his heart thump. "Think you're ready for the real thing?" she asked.

"I know I am."

"The power…it's intense. Think you're up for that?"

"Definitely. Can you come by after work tonight?"

She sighed sweetly in his ear. "I'll be there."

He read off the address, said an appropriate good-bye, and hung up.

He spent the next couple of hours cleaning up the office he'd turned into a makeshift bedroom. He lit candles in a pentagram on the floor, put fresh sheets on the bed, and lit some incense.

She knocked on the door just as he put on the finishing touches. It almost looked like a home, if you ignored the warehouse condition. He opened the door and took a step back to let in a leather-clad sex kitten in four-inch stilettos. The blood rushed from his head south, leaving him slightly lightheaded.

"Wow," he said, easing her up the stairs to his bedchamber.

She smiled like a siren and strolled past him, looking around the room. "Nice place." Turning to him, she unzipped her jacket and let it fall to the floor. Beneath it she wore a sheer black blouse with no bra. The black leather miniskirt followed the jacket. "Let's get this party started."

Mouth watering, he closed and locked the door. He shed his shirt and jeans, watching her remove the blouse until she stood only in her lace panties and heels.

She crossed to stand in front of him, pulled his shorts down, and wrapped her strong fingers around him.

Nick threw his head back, already feeling the power surge. He moaned in delight. Deja chuckled in his ear. He wrapped his arms around her, cupped her ass, and lifted her up until she wrapped her long legs around his waist. Kicking his boxers aside, he carried her deeper into the bedroom. The candles flared as they passed. Light bulbs shattered. Electricity blazed over their skin, making anywhere flesh touched burn.

He laid her on the bed and ripped the panties from her. She rolled over onto her hands and knees, cast a naughty glance at him, and whispered, "Come and get it. This power is yours for the taking."

Nick wasted no time meeting her every demand. The full, compelling power of their passion fueled the magic within, filling him to bursting with a force of energy that tempted him to take everything he wanted, with no thought to consequences.

He was a god.

Tara stifled a yawn and tried not to look at the kitchen clock. She sipped more hot tea and rubbed her eyes. Normally she would be at work right now, having a morning cup of coffee with Carson. Instead, she'd crawled into bed at nearly four o'clock after spending hours poring over the spells. She'd practiced with the ley lines and even managed a simple spell of lighting a candle.

She smiled and remembered Gregore's face when not a moment after the words had left her mouth for the very first time, the wick caught fire and a lovely yellow light filled the room. He hadn't been surprised. He'd been proud and confessed to not having any doubts in her abilities. How amazing was that?

Even now, a candle flickered on the table in front of her. Magic was simply coming easier. Like once she'd put her mind to it, the floodgates had opened, and everything she'd dammed up inside was released in a torrent.

She shivered. She didn't have time to be afraid. Even if she weren't helping Gregore, her gut said Saints wasn't going to stay away. She didn't know what he planned, or anything about him, really, but her instinct said he had something larger at work.

Tara opened the spell book and gathered it into her lap. She turned pages yellowed with age, reading every spell. What was Saints planning? Was it a personal vendetta against Gregore? Or was it on a bigger scale? The grimoire seemed more in line with the personal vendetta. Within these pages were more than a dozen ways to kill or maim someone, not to mention all the ways to make a person ill, ruin his life, or just take everything he owned.

A recipe for disaster. Or evil.

Every spell was written in the same hand. She flipped back to the beginning, studying the difference between the everyday spells and the others with a darker undertone. The first of such spells started around the twenty-fifth page, which cursed someone with gout. The prior page held a spell for enhancing crop growth. The following cursed a person with memory loss. And so it went, each worse than the last. Almost as if something had happened to the woman who wrote this book. Or was it that the magic corrupted? She needed to talk to someone who knew more about these things. Someone other than Maddy.

Tara rose from the kitchen table and walked over to the antique oak telephone stand by the back door. Maddy kept a copy of the phone directory there. She pulled it out and thumbed through a number of different options, looking for magic. Or anything that didn't include gags and rabbits in hats. There were three shops in Seattle that seemed a likely fit, the closest being a place called the Grand Grimoire. She pulled her cell phone out of the pocket of her jeans and dialed. The phone rang twice and the sultry voice of a young woman answered.

"Do you carry books on magic? Not the kind with card tricks, but the real thing," Tara asked.

"Sure, we have a good selection. What particular subject are you looking for? Wicca? Black arts?"

Tara glanced to the book on the table. "I have a Romany spell book already. I'm looking to learn more about magic in general. Maybe learn something...defensive."

"Ah, I have just the thing," the woman replied. Her tone was assured. Confident.

Tara found a pen and pad, then jotted down the store hours and hung up. She glanced at the phone in her hand. It shook and it took her a moment to realize that her hand trembled. There was one other call she needed to make.

The kitchen clock said it was nearly eleven. Bright sunlight pouring through the window, framed in bright yellow curtains, confirmed it. She yawned again and thought about crawling back into bed. Or maybe she should open the book and practice some more spells. She'd seen one in there for a magical shield. Possibly even the same Saints used. She had to learn that quickly.

Or maybe you should stop delaying that call, her mind whispered.

They were friends. Had been for years. And she had no reason to avoid him. Fortified, she hit the speed dial for Carson and prayed her partner would speak to her. God knew he hadn't exactly been kind last time she spoke to him.

"Carson" he answered in a clipped tone.

With caller ID, there was no way he didn't know who called. Yep, that bite to his voice was just for her. Excellent.

"It's me. How are you?"

"Fine."

Tara swallowed, feeling a spark of anger in her breast. What had she done to deserve this? "What could I gain by setting fire to—"

"I know," he interrupted.

"You know?"

"Yeah, I know."

"Then what the hell is this cold shoulder crap about?"

"You fucked up, O'Reilly. You went to a crime scene and disappeared—"

"It was my place—"

"You took potential evidence—"

"Wait, how do you know—"

"Now you're investigating the case even when you've been ordered to stay away."

Tara pressed her lips together. Carson would tell her to go fly a kite, but not so nicely, if she continued her argument. She needed his help. "Okay, you're right. I've screwed up."

He blew out a frustrated breath. "Listen, partner, I've got your back. But if you jump off a bridge, I'm not going with you, you get me?"

"Loud and clear."

"So tell me what's going on." When she didn't reply immediately, he said, "Please trust me. I'm your partner and your friend."

"You walked away from me a couple days ago, Carson. At the station, remember?"

"Yeah, I remember," he said quietly. "About that, I was pissed and didn't know what to think. We've had new evidence come in that cleared you."

"What evidence?"

"O'Reilly…you're not getting out of the conversation that easily. Now tell me what's going on."

"Grrr." She frowned at the phone, wishing he could see it. "I went to my place to see the damage for myself."

"What did you take?"

"How do you know—"

"When we entered your bedroom, we found the metal vent plate on the bed."

"Ah. Busted." Damn it. She wanted to be pissed that Gregore had kidnapped her that day, allowing Carson to find the plate where she'd dropped it on the bed. Somehow she couldn't. If he hadn't taken her, she never would have forced herself to face her heritage. She wouldn't be here with him. He stirred things inside her she hadn't felt in a very long time.

"I'm waiting," Carson prompted.

"I took a family heirloom. It was the one thing I couldn't leave behind. I had to know that it survived the fire."

"What was it?" His voice had the familiar edge that told her he wouldn't drop the line of questioning.

"A book."

"You risked your career for a book?"

"I know you don't do more than Dr. Seuss, Carson, but some of us like to read."

"Ouch," he said.

"Sorry," she mumbled. Then added, "I haven't been myself since this whole thing started. Seeing everything I owned destroyed… was tough." She cleared her throat of the sudden lump that formed. "The book belonged to Grandma Rose."

"Oh," he said with sudden understanding. "I know how important she was to you."

"That book is one of the only things I have left of hers," Tara said. Pain stabbed at her heart, as if she'd lost Rose yesterday.

"Why is that? Didn't she leave her estate to you?" Carson asked.

"Yes. I had to sell nearly everything. I had just finished at the academy and was still job hunting when she died. I couldn't afford the mortgage payments. But I didn't have the heart to sell the house she loved."

"What happened to the place? You must have eventually sold it, right? Or you wouldn't be living in an apartment."

Tara looked around the kitchen with its sunny yellow curtains and worn table. It had been home for most of her life. Until Rose passed. "Maddy lives here now."

Silence on the other end of the line. At last he said, "I understand. Now tell me what else is going on."

Tara was grateful for his change of subject. Talking about Rose, about the house, was uncomfortable. "Saints stole the book that same night. I got it back, but he ripped out a very important page."

"You're telling me someone stole the book your grandmother left you on the same night you retrieved it?" he asked, skepticism in every word. "What the hell is so important about this book?"

She cringed. He'd never believe her now. "I don't suppose you could check out Saints more for me?"

"O'Reilly, spill."

No way in hell was she giving him anything other than the condensed soup version. Even mentioning Gypsy curses and gargoyles would get her committed. A rubber room could seriously hinder Gregore's timeline for success. "It's an old book of Gypsy spells that Rose had from her ancestors. This guy Saints thinks he can use it for something."

"Sounds like a real crackpot. Is he planning to turn someone into a toad?"

Tara laughed, hating the hollow, fake sound. "Maybe."

"So how does the other guy fit into this?"

"Other? Oh, Gregore."

"You seem pretty familiar. Have you slept with him?"

"What? None of your damn business." But oh, she wanted to. Not that she'd tell Carson that.

"Testy. In a sexually frustrated way," he mused. "Good. Don't sleep with him. I've got a bad feeling about this guy."

"You don't know a thing about him," she snapped.

"Yet. Listen, O'Reilly, I'm just looking out for you. Like it or not. It's what partners do. Or have you forgotten the time that psycho chick stalked me and practically lived in the lobby of my building? You took her to task. I swear you scared her so bad, she moved out of the state."

"I hate it when you make sense."

"I'd thought you'd have been used to it by now, since it happens so often each day..." He laughed aloud at her growl. "Meet me at your new favorite coffee shop tomorrow at noon. And come by yourself, just in case I find out things you need to hear about your new boy toy."

"I'll be there."

"Bring cash. You may need to have that psychic reconsider her cards on your love life."

"Better bring your own. Or did Sorority pull through?"

"She pulled and—"

"Sorry I asked." Tara chuckled and hung up after promising to come alone. Her heart felt light in her chest. The strain of her partner not believing in her had pressed like an unseen weight. One she hadn't even realized she was carrying until it lifted.

Maddy came into the kitchen, humming a little song and bopping her head, causing her silver curls to dance. "It's a clear day. I bet those lines are shining nice and bright." She waved her fingers and twirled in a circle. "What better day to practice some magic?"

Tara couldn't hide her grin and didn't try. "I know just where to start."

CHAPTER 20

A light blue oval as tall as himself shimmered in the air, fading in and out of focus as if it were no more substantial than a thin cloud. As Gregore watched, silvery cracks splintered through the shield, fracturing it into a thousand pieces of colorful dust that disappeared as they hit the ground.

"What's wrong?" he asked from the shadowed corner of Maddy's living room. Agitation slanted Tara's eyes and tightened her mouth into a thin line.

She slapped the book cover closed and shoved the spell book away, movements jerky. It slid across the coffee table and teetered on the edge. Pushing her hands through her hair, she squeezed her eyes shut. "I don't know what I'm doing." She waved to where the shield had been. "Why won't that work? And how did *he* learn it so quickly?"

He bent and retrieved the book. They'd been practicing for hours. Both agreed that their gut instinct said they hadn't seen the last of Nick Saints. Tara pushed herself hard, trying to learn magic at a fast pace. He admired how she threw herself into her work. Clearly it took a toll on her. Gregore set the grimoire on the side table and went to her. He took her hand in his, earning a surprised look from Tara.

Her skin was soft beneath his. He stroked his thumb over the back of her hand, marveling in the texture of her skin. Touching her soothed something inside him, and at that moment he realized how very much he'd wanted to hold her. This strong woman who braved so much for him, a virtual stranger to her. He brought her palm to his lips and pressed a soft kiss there. Her eyes darkened to a deep emerald and her lips opened invitingly. Gregore accepted the invitation.

The kiss was hungry and explosive. Their mouths moved together, building the passion to burning heights. He wrapped his arms around her and pulled her flush against his chest. Tara drove her fingers into his hair, trying to pull him closer, until nothing separated their bodies. He wanted nothing between them, he realized as his erection strained against his jeans. Nothing but hot skin and slick sweat as he made love to her in ten different ways. Getting lost in her body for days.

Days he didn't have.

Gregore broke the kiss and reluctantly set her back. He stroked the smooth skin of her cheek and felt the silky strands of her hair. "You move me," he said, not ashamed to admit it. When facing the last days of your life, you didn't have time to not say what you meant. "I want more time with you." He adjusted his erection to a more comfortable position in his pants, drawing her heated gaze.

Tara stared at the bulge in his jeans until he thought he would explode, then dragged her eyes up to meet his. She cupped him, stroking lightly, and said in a husky breath, "I want you too." She leaned forward and nipped his bottom lip, then soothed it with a kiss.

Her breasts pushed into his chest, and it was all he could do not to take them in his hands, his mouth. Gregore cleared his throat and struggled for a modicum of control. He stroked a hand up and down her firm back, unable to let go just yet. "Then we should break this curse. I don't think I'll be satisfied with anything less than a month in bed with you."

That earned him a chuckle. Tara kissed him once more, a soft press of lips, then pulled away before he could deepen the kiss. "A month it is. Which means I have work to do to make sure we have that month."

Gregore nodded, enjoying the sparkle in her eyes that was just for him. That small break seemed to renew her energy and focus. "Try again," he said.

He stepped out of her space, back into the corner of the room. Tara concentrated her energy and held her hand up in front of her, palm out. Electric blue shimmered into an oval that tripled in size in the blink of an eye. In seconds the oval changed from the size of her hand to a shield three feet high. Sheer color solidified and held. Gregore moved closer, touched the firm substance.

"It feels like glass," he said.

"I'm holding it," she said in wonder. "It's staying."

Gregore met her gaze, feeling pride. He had no doubt she'd be able to do this. The woman was nothing if not determined.

"Good job, dear!" Maddy said from the doorway.

Tara jumped and the shield dissolved. "Thanks, Maddy."

Her aunt smiled brightly. "You're welcome. Just came in to see the progress before I start dishes."

"She learns quickly, Maddy," Gregore said.

Maddy waved his words away. "As if it would be any different." She tottered back off to the kitchen.

"She's right," he said. "I expected no less." He bent to lift the spell book and thumbed through a few pages.

She gave a noncommittal grunt.

The yellowed pages of the book flowed through his fingers. Earlier she'd examined every spell, every word. Looking for some clue into the mind of a crazy Rom woman. Something to help or guide them to the answer.

"Did you find anything at all?" he asked.

"Not yet. But I'll never lose my keys again. There's a handy find-something-lost spell here." She chuckled without humor.

"What can I do?" he asked quietly. Going to her side, he knelt and laced his fingers through hers.

Tara looked at their linked hands then gave a brief squeeze.

He drew in a quick breath, surprised. They had kissed, but that one small movement felt far more intimate. It was a sign of trust. Of kinship. Hope. Something he dare not have. The sands of his hourglass were falling too quickly now to give in to the luxury of hope. No matter his words indicating otherwise.

Tara turned her hand, stroking her fingers along his. She glanced at him from beneath her lashes. Frustration no longer lined her features, replaced by sparks of heat and desire.

Caught in her spell, Gregore parted his lips. Leaned forward. Waited desperately for her to come to him this time. Praying that she would.

She pressed her lips to his.

Tara's kiss wasn't hesitant. She went into the kiss as she dove into action. Hands in his hair, she pulled him to her and met him with rekindled hunger. Her mouth moved against his. She nipped his lower lip, then licked the sting away. She demanded entrance and he gave it. Her warm tongue caressed his, exploring, taking all he had and giving it back without reservation. She held him close. Breaking the kiss only to draw in air and then engage his mouth for more.

Heat seared his blood to all parts of his body. He ached for her. Needed her naked skin against his own. He slid his hand from the silken strands of her hair down to the satin skin of her neck, feeling the fast pulse of her heart beating beneath his palm.

Her eyes glittered with heat. Her skin warmed beneath his hand. Gregore moved his fingertips lower, tracing them over her chest to dip inside the open neck of her shirt. Smoothing over the swell of her breast. Lower to skim the satin of her bra.

She leaned into his touch. A breathy sigh escaping her lips.

He settled his mouth over her dancing pulse and moved his fingers lower, brushing the nipple that hardened just for him. He closed his palm around her full breast, aching with the need for more. To touch more. Taste all of her.

A loud crash from the kitchen jolted him out of the haze of lust. His fogged brain recognized it as a metal pan hitting the floor.

"It's okay dears," Maddy called.

Gregore slowly removed his hand from Tara's breast, cursing himself for forgetting that they were not alone.

Tara brushed her fingers over his cheek. Her eyes sparkled with promise. "Let's pick this up later," she whispered.

He nodded, not sure he could even find words. Nothing compared to the feel of her. The flush of desire she brought out in him. Not even Zola, he realized, with no small amount of shock.

"Do you need help with something, Aunt Maddy?" Tara called.

Gregore rose and paced back to the corner. Even more than Zola? The lover who made him what he was today. Had his feelings for Zola faded after all this time? Or were his desires for Tara more powerful? He ran a hand through his hair. God, he just didn't know.

"I'm fine," Maddy replied, ambling into the doorway. She dried her hands on a dish towel. "Just finishing up in here. Find anything yet?"

Tara shook her head. Glossy auburn hair reflected the lamplight, mesmerizing him. She was so lovely, she made him ache in areas he thought long dead. Gregore rubbed a hand over his chest and turned away from the enticing image she made, with a smile on her lips and a graceful profile.

"Not yet," Tara said. "I just don't know what I'm looking for."

Maddy smiled. "You'll find it. I know you will. Things that are lost always have a way of reappearing. Even when you least expect it."

Tara frowned and glanced at the spell book.

Maddy looked very pleased with herself. Too pleased.

"Do you—" *Know something,* he started to ask.

"Well, I'm off to bed in just a few minutes. The next few days may be quite long."

Tara rose. "Do you have plans? Why not let me help clean up?"

Maddy paled and patted her silver hair. "Not plans exactly. Not my plans anyway. I do hope things go all right." The pensive expression melted under her forced smile. "No need, dear. I've only one pot left to do and I'm all done. You finish what you're working on and don't worry about me. Breaking the curse is far more important than a few dishes. Wouldn't you agree, Gregore?"

"Yes, ma'am," he replied.

Tara looked between them and then sat back down. Maddy returned to the kitchen.

Silence settled in the small living room. Tara blew out a breath and ran her fingers over the cover of the spell book.

Gregore listened as Maddy hummed a tune and scrubbed her pan, then rinsed it and set it into the dish drain. Moments later, the water drained in gurgles down the sink.

She reappeared in the living room, coming to kiss his cheek. "Good night, Gregore. Don't despair. My Tara will help." She moved to Tara, kissing her temple and said, "Believe in yourself. Good night, all."

"Good night," Tara said softly.

They remained silent until after Maddy retreated upstairs and the door to her bedroom clicked closed. Finally, they were alone.

"Tell me about the night you were cursed," Tara said.

"What?"

"Tell me about that night. I need to know what happened. Exactly."

Gregore folded his arms across his chest. This wasn't what he wanted. Now wasn't the time to talk. He wanted her back in his arms, feeling softness beneath his palms. He sure as hell didn't want to talk about his greatest failing. "Why?" The word came out rougher than intended.

"Why?" She bristled, eyes narrowing. "Because I'm trying to help. Because I can't figure this out unless I know everything. And not from Thomas's mouth, but yours. I need you to tell me what happened in every detail you can recall."

"In every..." He rubbed the back of his neck. She brought him to the brink and teetered him on the edge. And now this? "What do you want to hear? That I left my father's bedside while he breathed with a death rattle to go tryst with my lover? Or would you rather hear that when I gathered her in my arms that same night, my knife stuck out of her back? Or is it better to tell you that both my father and my lover died that night, but I couldn't save either? Is that what you want to hear?" he growled. No other woman tied him up in knots, spun him around, and dangled him over an emotional cliff.

Tara stood and crowded his space. "Yes. I want to hear that. That and everything else that happened. Don't think you can scare me off. You can't. You won't. So you weren't there when your father died? Your lover? You think you failed them? You think that will make me run screaming into the night? I see people every day who fail their loved ones. I see people who've killed their loved ones for nothing more than interrupting while they watched television. I've seen death and greed and the ugliest emotions human nature has to offer every single day."

Damn it. "I don't want you seeing those things in me," he ground out.

She laid a hand on his chest. "The day my parents died, do you know what I was doing?"

He shook his head.

"I was practicing reading tarot cards in Grandma Rose's kitchen. She was watching me while my parents were at the ballet. It was a cold winter day and ice had crusted the road from the night before. I remember trying to read my own cards and turning over Death. It scared me, even when Grandma tried to assure me the card only meant transformation. But my fear grew. I knew something was wrong. When I closed my eyes, I saw a terrible car crash. I could hear the sirens and feel the blood slip through my fingers. I couldn't breathe.

"She shook me out of the vision. I was screaming. A short while later, we got the call. They'd been on their way home, hit a patch of black ice, and careened into a semi. The force of impact made the truck swing until both crashed into the guardrail at top speed. They died before they even made it to the hospital.

"What if I hadn't been practicing tarot? Would they have lived? Did I cause it? Or did I just channel it?" She lifted her hands, studying her palms. "Did I kill them with the Gypsy magic running through my veins? I've thought so for a long time. I understand about guilt. It claws at me from the inside out."

He blew out a breath and pulled her into his arms. What a fine pair they were. Two souls blaming themselves for the deaths of those they loved most. Would anyone else ever understand him as she did in that moment? Unlikely. And yet when she'd asked an innocent, clarifying question, he'd been a jerk. "You're so strong," he whispered against her hair, then, "I'm sorry."

She shook her head in denial. "I'm practical. I know I can't save the world. I couldn't save my family. But I can help."

He cupped her cheek, lifting her eyes to his. "I've never met another like you, Tara O'Reilly. Your courage and passion are amazing to me. There will never be another like you, will there?" He brushed his thumb over her lower lip.

Tara's lips parted, hot breath caressing his thumb. "Perhaps not. We're each given a certain number of days, Gregore. Most of us don't know how many are left." Her lips tilted in a smile with no humor. "What will you do with yours? Will you die, drowned in your guilt? Will you reap revenge? And if so, what will you have to show for it?

More blood on your hands?" Her eyes implored him to think beyond himself.

He shook his head. "What could I possibly do or accomplish, other than what has driven me these years? Do not ask me to hope for more. My heart couldn't take the crush of that dream."

Tara curled her fingers in his hair, pressing her body closer. "And spare no thought for a future? What if? What if we break this curse? What if you have more than a handful of days to live?"

"What if Saints has taken the only shot I had away from me? What if these are my last days?"

"What if they are?" she whispered. "What do you want from your last days on earth?"

Gregore stared into the deep green of her eyes, aching for her. Not just his body but his soul wanted hers tied up in him. Holding her in his arms was a dream. "Are you an angel?" he asked.

She laughed and the husky sound rippled over his skin. The sparkle in her gaze turned wicked. "Do you want me to be?"

"I just want you." He lowered his head and took her mouth in a fierce kiss.

She brushed her hand over his chest, moving it up to curl in his hair. Her hips moved to fit herself better into his body. Gregore's breath caught. His blood surged through his veins, roaring in his ears. He moved his hand down the curve of her spine, pressing her closer against him. Her breasts pushed against his chest. Delicious. In moments he was hard as steel with wanting. Cupping her bottom, he rubbed himself lightly against her. Whatever they had been talking about melted away into unimportance. Holding her against him with one hand on her backside, cupping her head with his other, Gregore opened her mouth wider and tasted her spicy essence.

Tara's response was fierce. Her mouth moved against his with intense hunger. Her tongue touched his, tangled and fought for dominance. He drank from her like a man starving for water. Taking all she gave and wanting so much more. He tasted the delicate skin under her chin, licking his way to her ear. He sucked and nipped her earlobe, then moved lower to the warmth of her neck. She purred and arched her back and head, giving him more room.

He gripped her hips and lifted her, wrapping those amazing legs around his waist and brushing the heat of her body against his hard-on. He moved blindly to the chair and sank into it. Arranged her legs over the arms of the chair, her core flush with his erection. Gregore took her mouth again and blindly fumbled for the lamp on the table. He found the switch and turned it off, casting them into dark shadows.

Tara pulled back from his mouth, adjusting herself into a more comfortable spot. Her movements rushed more blood to his groin. He groaned as she ground against him. "You're killing me," he whispered.

Her throaty laugh brushed his ear. "Not yet, but soon." Leaning forward, Tara reached behind him and shifted herself up to part the curtains for the window. Her breasts filled his vision. He cupped them and squeezed gently, just as moonlight spilled into the living room and bathed her in silver.

He heard her gasp as he found her nipples beneath the fabric of her dress shirt. It seemed a lifetime ago since he had touched her flesh and the hard bud of her nipple. He wouldn't wait a lifetime more. Settling her back into his lap, he kissed her neck and slipped a button open in her blouse. Another opened, revealing her tender flesh to his gaze. He followed every button with his mouth, sampling her sweetness.

Tara sighed and held his head closer as he moved down, leaning her backward to flick his tongue over her flat stomach and circle her belly button. His hands roamed her warm skin, heating it more with each stroke of his palm. Her shirt hit the floor and revealed her delectable breasts encased in a simple black satin bra. He traced the edge with his lips before he even had the thought to do so. She moved against his groin, the warmth of her burning through his jeans to superheat his erection.

"I want you so badly," he murmured. "I shouldn't..."

"Yes," she said. "Do."

"No, I—"

"Don't think," she commanded. Tara unhooked her bra in the back. She moved his hands to cup her breasts over the satin and kissed him hard. "I need you, Gregore. Don't hold back. Show me who you really are."

SET IN STONE

A cry burst from his throat. The vocal reaction to the dam bursting a leak within. His hands were everywhere, caressing, tweaking, tossing her bra over his shoulder as he kissed and licked and nibbled her skin. She wrapped her arms around his neck and held him close. "Yes," she purred.

Gregore cupped one of her breasts in his hand and rubbed his thumb over her nipple. He brought it to a firm peak, amazed at her reaction to him. "God, you're beautiful," he breathed. She glowed in the moonlight. As if her skin lit from the inside out. Lowering his head, he kissed his way down and sucked the tight pink peak into his mouth.

She moved her hips in a circle, rubbing against him until they both panted with need. He kissed his way to the other breast for the same treatment. Tara held him tighter, keeping her breathy sighs as quiet as she could.

"I need to feel you against me. I need…"

"Yes," she said.

"Not here."

"No. Up."

"Yes. Let's go." He lifted her off his lap and nearly moaned with the loss. She gathered her bra and blouse off the floor.

"Your room," she said.

Scooping her up into his arms, he kicked in preternatural speed and had her pinned against the wall in his room in less than a few heartbeats. Tara laughed. Delight bubbled out of her, and her eyes sparkled in the moonlight. He grinned back, feeling ridiculously happy. The weight of his curse evaporated from his body, replaced by something he couldn't name. The woman turned him inside out just with a smile. A laugh. What was happening to him?

He kissed her, then broke away to close the door with a quiet click and locked it for good measure. When he turned back, she held up a small foil package. A condom. "Prepared," he said.

She grinned and pointed to his nightstand, where a slim box was open. "I think Maddy is hopeful." He crossed to the bed. The box had a bright pink sticky note on it that read: *Something told me you might need these. Be safe, dear!*

Gregore shook his head. Imagining Maddy picking these out at the pharmacy made him chuckle.

Tara slid her hand down his back and cupped his backside, drawing his attention back to where he needed it. On her. He drew her back into his embrace for a kiss. He couldn't get enough of her soft skin, the flavor of her mouth, or her breasts pressing into his chest.

Her nails tracked under his shirt, scoring his back in light lines. She sighed against his mouth and brought her hands forward to stroke his chest, then down to his stomach. Gregore broke away and pulled his shirt over his head. Her hands found the waistband of his pants and dipped inside to run a finger inside the elastic of his boxers. She nipped his chin, then soothed it with her mouth.

"What have we here?" she purred, sliding the zipper of his fly lower.

"Have where?" he asked, all innocence, as he kissed the shell of her ear and flicked his tongue within.

"Here."

He gasped as her warm hand made contact with his erection. Exactly where he needed her most. He cupped her hand and held it against him in pleasure. He couldn't remember the last time he'd been touched by anyone other than himself. Had it ever felt so good in his entire life?

She grasped him in her strong fingers, her stroke firm, but gentle. He nearly shouted when she ran a fingertip around the tip of his head.

"Stop, stop," he begged and caught her hand back in his. "Or I'll be done before we've started."

Her siren's smile nearly did him in anyway. "Should I come back tomorrow?"

"Just try to make it to the door." Gregore pulled her flush against him and gloried in her firm curves. He ran his hands over her backside and breasts, between her legs and over her hips. Scooping her into his arms, he laid her on the bed and divested her of her socks. She wiggled her toes at him and gave an impish smile. He chuckled. Pressed kisses to her stomach and lower, opening her jeans as he went. She lifted her hips to let him slide them down her long legs and onto the floor. Never had he seen such creamy skin.

Gregore kissed her insole and moved his way up. He sampled the tender skin behind her knee. The inside of her thigh. Her heated fragrance shot a pure jolt of need to his cock. Yet tonight was not just about him. He moved higher and nuzzled the valley of her breasts. Tara arched into his mouth.

"Don't stop now, handsome," she said, her breath brushing his ear in an erotic caress.

He laved one nipple, sucking it into his mouth until she moaned and writhed against him. She pushed briefly at his jeans.

"Off," she whimpered, still arching into him.

"As my lady wishes," he said. Gregore nearly ripped the clothing from his body, tossing the boxers aside while he was at it. "Shall we finish the job?" he asked.

Tara nodded. He lowered his head to her other breast and tugged her panties off. Matched the black satin bra, he thought as he tossed them over his shoulder.

"Now," she said. Driving her hands into his hair, she gripped his head and pulled him into the curve of her body.

He gasped into her mouth as their flesh came together. She moaned and rubbed against him.

"Are you ready for me?" he murmured against her lips.

Tara took his hand and guided it between her thighs.

"So wet." Blood pulsed and throbbed in his erection. He was so hard, he physically hurt.

"Come to me," she whispered.

"Yes."

"Gregore," she said and unrolled the condom onto his thick shaft. "Love me."

His last thought as he sank into her wet heat, was that maybe, just maybe, he could.

CHAPTER 21

Tara gripped Gregore's shoulders and stared into the deepest blue eyes she'd ever seen. Like staring into the twilight skies. A dark lock of hair fell over his brow and his lips curved in a sensuous smile. There was something tender in the depths of his eyes. A look she'd never seen before. Here in the darkness of his room, they existed in another world, apart from the worries of real life. Like being held within a snow globe, encased in a magic all their own. She smiled back and guided him to her entrance.

He needed no further invitation. Gregore rubbed himself between her slick folds, then pressed slowly forward. Tara gasped and arched, taking him inside. "Yes," she breathed.

He pushed in, then wrapped her leg around his waist and pushed to the hilt. Retreated and pushed in again.

Tara bit her lip to keep from crying out. "Feels so good."

He nodded, a drop of sweat dotting his temple with his restraint. Tara touched her finger to the moisture and kissed him. Tonight wasn't a night to hold back. Who knew what tomorrow would bring? Locking her legs on his hips, she pushed off the bed and flipped him onto his back.

Gregore let out a surprised laugh.

She tugged her lip between her teeth and straddled his hips. Rising up on her knees, she sank slowly back onto his shaft. He groaned in ecstasy.

Set in Stone

Tara laced her fingers through his and planted their combined hands on either side of his head. A roll of her hips increased their pleasure. "Mmmm," she purred. "Rock hard."

Gregore's lips parted on an expelled breath. His hips bucked as she continued her slow torture.

But slow wouldn't do at all. Not on her watch. She wanted this too bad, and by the glazed look in his eyes, so did he. Bending forward, she nipped his chin. Surged forward until he nearly pulled out, then crashed back down onto him.

Tara clenched her teeth to keep from crying out and waking Maddy, who slept just down the hall. She rocked her body on his. A fast pace that had each moaning softly, gasping for air.

He released her hands to knead her breasts. Ran the pads of his thumbs back and forth across her nipples until she panted and writhed on him. Sliding his hands down her sides, he grabbed her hips and pulled her up and off.

Tara whimpered at the loss until he slid out from under her and wrapped his body around her. He pushed his length into her from behind. Drew her hips up to meet him and plunged as deep as he could. She dropped her forehead to the sheets, trying desperately to remain quiet when all she wanted to do was scream out her pleasure. Her muscles tensed, heat spiraling through her every limb and curling into a tight point right where he thrust.

"Come for me," he demanded, pushing her hard.

She was so close. Damn close. Teetering on the brink.

Gregore sensed her there and tweaked her nipple. He slid his other hand down her stomach into the curls between her legs and parted her folds. The moment he found what he sought, rubbing her moisture over it, she trembled and crashed over the ledge into an intense orgasm. Her muscles clenched his shaft, tugging him with her into oblivion. He buried his head in her hair, pumping madly as he moaned, his release shaking his whole body.

Wrapped around her as he was, Tara gloried in the contact. How he trembled and moaned. She had done that. Brought him to an orgasm that seemed never ending. He continued to pump, and a flick of his fingers over her sweet spot sent another orgasm sweeping through her.

They collapsed together, a tangle of limbs and slick skin. Gregore rolled aside long enough to pull the blankets open and slide her in. He gathered her to him, pressing her back to his chest and curling his legs around her. His breath warmed her neck. She sighed and wrapped his arm around her waist.

"You're the most beautiful woman I've ever beheld," he said.

Tara snuggled closer. "That was amazing." Truly the best sex she'd ever had. It wasn't the positions; those were normal enough. Or just the unexpected frenzy. She trailed her fingers over the back of his hand, thinking. Not even the afterglow could account for the beating of her heart or that feeling that swelled deep within. Normally she would have avoided looking too closely at such feelings, but something felt different about it.

Gregore. It wasn't the sex that was different. It was him. He made the whole experience different. He brought about that special weight in her chest. She felt a kinship like she'd never felt with another. Even when making herself vulnerable, talking about her parents' death. About the vision. Instead of revulsion, he'd shown her compassion and understanding. She licked her lips and settled against him. It was more than just connecting about the guilt they both felt over the loss of their family, though she hesitated to specifically name that feeling. Not yet. After all, it was probably just a deeper infatuation than normal.

She'd had a few lovers in the past, but nothing really serious. Maybe this time with Gregore was just stronger because of the life and death situation they were in. Yes, that had to be it. Studies showed that men and women in such situations tended to have a brief bond that they thought was love but was merely a reaction to the situation at hand.

Satisfied, she closed her eyes and let her mind drift. Still, her inner voice whispered, he was incredibly special. Not just what he could become or what he could do. He was heroic. Not in an everyday way that she saw with the other guys on the force. But through and through. Here was a man who didn't run from what he was. Didn't use it to do wrong. He'd saved Timmy, the super's kid, without a thought for himself. He'd saved her from Saints in the warehouse and outside the church.

He made her want to fight her own fears. Like magic. "Strong," she whispered. Strong enough to pull himself out of a drunken stupor born of self-pity and make himself into a man determined to find answers.

"You're thinking too hard," he said from behind her, rubbing his warm palm along her arm.

Tara chuckled. "Perhaps." She turned in his arms and kissed his lips. "Any other man would have broken under this curse. But you're strong, Gregore. That strength is what will beat it."

He traced a finger against her soft cheek. "I can't do it without you."

She smiled. "Lucky for you, you don't have to."

He leaned forward and kissed her. "That's not the only reason I'm lucky."

She rested her head against his chest and yawned.

"Rest," he said. "I know that the magic takes your strength."

"You do?"

He traced her lips with his finger. "I can see the exhaustion in you. Sleep. You're safe with me."

Tara closed her eyes. What he said was true. She'd never felt safer in her life. How remarkable. She breathed deep, smelling the warm musk of his skin. What would it be like to wake up or go to sleep in his warm embrace for the rest of her life? Oddly, it was a welcome thought. One that carried her all the way into her dreams.

She ran barefoot over grass damp with dew. Dark grey mist swirled about her in eddies so thick, she was lost. Turning in circles, looking for a way out. There was danger nearby. The back of her neck prickled with the knowledge. Somewhere in fog as thick as a London night, the hunter tracked her.

She picked up the pace, jogging toward nothing at all. Her breath blew out in white puffs of air as she ran, her body feeling heavier with each step. A rustle of leaves and the scratch of an animal in the shrubs jerked her around to a stop. She grabbed for the Sig on her hip and came up empty. Her fingers touched satin. Tara looked down to find herself in a white nightgown, barefoot. Suddenly the damp grass and the cold night air sent shivers down her spine. She moved away from the bush, peering through the fog for any landmark. Something to tell her where she was.

A footstep fell behind her. Close. Too close. Tara lifted the skirt of her nightgown and ran. The wind picked up, blowing from behind like a bad omen. Her auburn hair flew into her face, momentarily blinding her. She paused when she realized it was very long hair. Much longer than her current locks. This went nearly to her hips.

"I'm Rapunzel," she murmured.

A noise nearby snagged her attention. It sounded like something spinning in the air. She kicked back into motion. Fear tickled the back of her neck. Leafy tree limbs broke through the mist. Just as she passed the first thin sapling, the spinning blade shot by and slammed into the bark with a thwack. The hilt vibrated madly under the impact.

She yelped and stumbled, staggered to her feet and ran. Ahead, a yellow orb appeared in the fog. It was higher than her head. She ran for it, hoping for some sign of where she was and who was following. An old, iron lamp with intricate scrollwork appeared in the gloom. A flame danced within, casting a ring of gold in the fog.

Tara slowed as a shape took form beneath the lamp. She looked about for anything she could use as a weapon. Nothing surrounded her. Only trailing mists of fog.

The shape didn't move. Not an inch. She crept closer, casting a glance behind her for the unknown threat. She heard nothing. A crisp breeze still tugged at her, bringing the distinct scent of decaying leaves. With the short grass beneath and the lamplight, it had to be a park. But which one?

The unmoving form before her became clearer. The fog seemed to part, revealing stone. Sharp points rose above her head and a hand extended to her. Suddenly the curling fog ringed around her, opening in a wide circle nearly twelve feet in diameter under the lantern. The figure was clear.

Tara stood toe to toe with a towering gargoyle. With Gregore.

His face was carved in pain, mouth wide as if he cried out and his folded wings rose above his head. His hand extended toward her, palm up. Tara realized two things simultaneously. In Gregore's hand were her car keys and she wasn't in her own body. She traced a long, tan finger over his stone form. Tan? She looked closer. Lightly tanned olive skin instead of white, Northwest skin. Her hips flared more seductively and her breasts were fuller. She raised *her head to Gregore's pained expression and extended hand, offering her keys, yet somehow pleading for her help at once.*

She looked around. It was night. He should be...

Oh God. Ohgod ohgod ohgod...He should be human. They'd failed. She'd failed. He was stone.

Husky feminine laughter sounded in her ear and echoed around the park.

"You're too late," cried a singsong voice. "Too late. He got what he deserved and there's nothing you can do about it."

Tara whirled to face the wild eyes of Grandma Rose. Silver bangles clinked on her arms and dangling earrings danced as she shook her head. "Too late!"

Her voice was deeper. Wrong. Could this... could this be the old Romany woman? The Gypsy who'd started it all?

Tara lunged for her, only to have her disappear into a cloud of mist. She staggered forward and came face to face with the muzzle of a gun. It cocked and on the other end was a hulking blond man. Saints.

"Good-bye, Detective. Our little game was fun." The muzzle exploded.

Tara jerked upright, a scream lodged in her throat. Gregore's arms came instantly around her.

"Shhh," he said, rubbing his hands up and down her arms. "It was just a dream."

She shook her head. Too real. It was too real. And something told her to listen. She was going to lose him if she didn't break the curse.

CHAPTER 22

Tara curled onto her side. Gregore pulled her against him, wrapping himself around her body. He stroked her arms up and down, up and down. He kissed her temple and breathed deep of her silky hair while she trembled in his arms. He remained silent. She would not want him calling attention to what she'd likely think a weakness.

"It felt so real," she said.

"It wasn't. You're here with me. Feel my arms around you, Tara. Know that you are safe."

She leaned back into him, taking the solace he offered. "I ran through fog so thick, I couldn't see. Someone chased me. God, they got so close, I could feel the hot breath on my skin. I was in a park, running at night but I wasn't myself. It wasn't my body. And then suddenly there you were."

"Rescuing the fair maiden?" he asked, pressing a kiss against her cheek.

Tara shook her head. He watched her throat work as she swallowed. "No. You were stone."

"But that's not possible. Not at night. Not unless..."

Tara turned in his arms and pressed her fingertips to his lips. "No, don't say it. Please. Like you said, it was just a dream, right?"

He nodded and gathered her closer still, holding her and pressing his cheek to hers until it was unclear who trembled more. He didn't want to let her go, he realized. Not now. Perhaps not ever.

"Grandma Rose was there. Actually, it looked like her, but it couldn't have been. This woman was insane. And I...I think it was..." She shook her head. "You never told me what happened that night you were cursed."

Gregore released her and rolled to his back. He ran a hand through his hair. "I'm not ready."

"I need to know."

He felt pressure in his chest, as if someone was squeezing his heart. He rubbed the spot. "I..."

"You won't make me run, no matter what you say," she said, stroking his cheek gently with a delicate fingertip.

He pulled her back into his arms, needing the contact, the comfort her touch offered. "My father was ill. Had been for months, but that last month he'd taken a turn for the worse. We knew he wouldn't last, and my mother and I took turns nursing at his side. My brother was far too young and so my sister spent her time with him."

As he spoke, the day that Thomas and Jeffrey visited returned to mind. He could see their easy camaraderie as they lunched and teased one another. Swapping tales of exploits, no matter how outlandish. Bittersweet memories.

"Jeffrey and Thomas were my closest friends. They visited, intent on turning me back into the man I was before my father's illness. They dragged me out to a country fair."

"That doesn't sound so bad," she said.

"Turns out the real reason we went was because Thomas planned to meet a woman there. Jeffrey and I stood no chance with the ladies when Thomas was with us. That day was different. There was a group of Gypsies who had come in and set up a few tents. Practicing their cards and entertaining. It's the day I met Zola.

"She was the loveliest girl I'd ever seen. Her skin was tanner than the women of London, whose fair skin was fashionable at the time, and she wore her hair long and loose about her shoulders. The way she moved, her eyes, everything added to the mystery that surrounded her. It drew me like a moth."

He fell silent, thinking about that day. How the sun made her hair shine. Her smile and laugh as she twirled about. "She was alive when all I'd seen for a month was near-death."

"What happened?" Tara asked quietly.

"She read fortunes. Thomas saw my interest and nearly shoved me into the tent to have my cards read. He paid her a small fortune to read damn near anything about me she could." He chuckled. "She wasted no time. We kissed that very day. Yet another thing that was far different from all the other women I knew. From that day on, I met with her every spare moment I had. I would sneak out in the middle of the night to meet her in the woods, only to stumble home at dawn, sleep an hour, and go back to my father's bedside. We spent weeks in rendezvous. I suppose we always knew we courted danger. Just never quite how much. Or the jealousies roused from our love."

"Jealousies?"

"The Rom society was so far removed from our English society. Especially her particular family and the things they valued or did not. The entire group looked out for one another to the point of having her followed. They spurned outsiders like myself. I was to inherit an earldom and for the first time in my life, that wasn't good enough for a prospective mate. Good enough for her but not her family. If she were to marry at all, it would be from within the Romany community. Anything else was unacceptable." He shifted, drawing Tara closer. "One of her suitors discovered us. It was he who followed us into the woods one night."

Tara stroked a hand down his chest, silently asking him to continue.

"He devised a plan. In truth, I knew Zola was scared of her grandmother and her family. She said often that the old woman was mad and into dark things that ought not to have been disturbed. I foolishly shrugged it off as no more than any other Gypsy troupe. Cures for what ailed a person and fortunes and the like." Gregore rolled to his back, tucked his hands behind his head, and stared at the ceiling. "Zola was right all along. The woman was mad. She'd been collecting and creating dark spells for years. Who knew what sacrifices she made under the full moon?" He frowned and whispered the one thing that had darkened his heart for these many years. "God, I wish I'd never met Zola. I wish I'd never left my father's side that night."

Tara placed a hand on his arm, her touch soothing. "Tell me the rest."

"I snuck out to see her. She was all I could think of day and night, and I could barely wait for the time to pass until I could be at her side. I remember thinking that my father's breathing sounded worse." He chuckled, the sound full of guilt and self-recrimination. "Not even that could keep me from Zola. I was obsessed. Her touch. Her scent. I couldn't get enough. I thought I loved her. I went to her at our usual meeting spot in the wooded acreage between the border of my home and where her family made camp. She waited for me in the clearing, wearing a white dress. I remember thinking she looked like a lost moonbeam. She was afraid she'd been followed, but I hushed her with kisses and gathered her into my arms." Gregore glanced at Tara. "Does it bother you to hear the details?"

She shook her head and traced her fingertips over his chest. "I need to hear them, Gregore." She touched her teeth to her bottom lip in thought. "Was the dress white satin? Did her hair hang to her hips?"

He nodded. "How…?"

"She was shorter than me. More voluptuous?"

"Yes." Gregore pressed a kiss to the soft skin under her chin. She smelled like lavender. Breathing her in, he knew he didn't miss Zola. Had probably never loved her.

"In my dream, I was Zola," she said. She watched for his reaction.

He wasn't surprised. Nothing about the Gypsies surprised him anymore. "Like reincarnation?"

"No. More like past and present colliding. I saw Saints in it. The dream means something. I wish I knew what." She turned away from him. "Magic is so new. I…I'll figure it out. Tell me the rest."

Gregore pulled her into the curve of his body, spooning her from behind. He didn't want to say the rest. She needed to know, but the words were like acid in his throat. He trudged on with the truth, hating every second of it.

"I don't remember telling her I loved her. I was too busy kissing her. Wanting her. When she stiffened in my arms, I thought she wanted to hear pretty words first. I pulled back to see her mouth open with shock. Fear made her eyes wide, and at first I didn't understand why. She weakened in my arms, her weight no longer supported, and as she slipped in my grasp, my hands hit the hard handle of something in her back. She tried to speak but no words came past her lips. She sagged and I sank to the ground with her, watching helplessly as the life faded from her eyes.

"I don't know how long I sat there with her. I cried and begged her not to go. I was a madman howling in the night. It's how Thomas and Jeffrey found me. When Mother couldn't locate me in the house, she went to them as my guests and closest friends. They agreed to find me. To give me the news that my father had passed.

"I can't recall anything they said to me when they found me. I do remember Jeffrey demanding to know what I'd done. Why was my hunting knife in the back of my lover? That's what jolted me out of the fog. I hadn't used my knife in months." He closed his eyes.

"Are you certain it was your knife?"

"Absolutely. It was a birthday gift from my father a couple of years before. The handle was ivory with my initials carved in the base. Someone from her family was able to sneak it out of my home. Ranulf, Zola's Rom suitor, followed her that night. I was his target. He threw the knife, but just as he released the blade, Zola came into my arms for a kiss, shielding me from the killing blow. She never knew she saved my life or that her kinsman took hers.

"When Ranulf realized what he'd done, he ran back to their camp and swore he'd seen Zola murdered. A dozen men returned with him to where I still held her body, with my knife damning me for the crime. Thomas and Jeffrey were merely collateral damage. The Romany men dragged us back to their camp. Ranulf carried Zola and laid her at the feet of her grandmother."

Gregore shuddered, recalling the black, lifeless eyes the woman possessed as she stared at him with utter malice. She hated him to the core for what she believed he'd done. Even if he'd not given the killing blow, it didn't matter. Zola had died because of him.

"The woman regarded us with such hate as she heard Ranulf's absurd tale and the demand for our deaths. The old witch wouldn't let us go. We were meant to suffer, she said. I pleaded with her to listen. I begged her to let Thomas and Jeffrey go. The more I spoke, the more anger darkened her face. She called for her book and swore we'd never know another moment of happiness."

"Judge and jury," Tara whispered.

"No trial. We were guilty if for no other reason than that we were English."

"What could make a person deliver such a brutal sentence without any real proof?" Tara demanded.

"She had all the proof she needed. She had my knife dripping with Zola's blood and the word of Ranulf. As for why, she'd lost her favorite grandchild to a race of people she despised."

"It's so harsh. I don't understand what breeds such hate in people. How they do what they do to one another."

"Zola once told me that the reason her family hated us so was not strictly because of persecution. It was far more personal for her grandmother. The woman had been repeatedly raped by an Englishman. Zola thought she'd gone mad shortly after the attack." Gregore shrugged. "Who can say for sure?"

"Tell me what happened when she cursed you."

"I was out of my mind at that point. Several men held us in place, making us kneel as if we were not worthy of the woman. I remember the look of pure disgust on her face as she spit the words of the spell at me. She cast her hand out, and I remember feeling that something hit me square in the chest. I struggled as a tingling came over my body, spreading to all of my limbs and making them go numb. I panicked because my legs and arms felt like dead weights. I thought she was killing me. She stepped over Zola's body like she was trash, leaned into my face, and cast her curse."

"Tell me what you remember of it," Tara said.

"I don't remember any of it. It was so long ago, only the images remain."

"What about Thomas or Jeffrey? Do they—"

"No. They don't recall. I've asked. Don't you think I've asked?" He scrubbed a hand over his face. "Without the spell it's over."

"That spell or another. I'm not giving up. You can't come into my life, stir things up, and then give up hope when the situation doesn't turn around immediately. I never pegged you for a quitter."

He turned his head to her with a sharp glare.

"Are you?" Tara asked.

"No," he said, eying her bare breasts with renewed interest.

"Then get your ass up. We've got work to do."

He rolled on top of her, pinning her with his hips, erection pressing into her heat. He rubbed against her until she gasped and her green eyes deepened to emeralds. "Later," he said against her lips. "I have something else in mind."

CHAPTER 23

Wet snow caked his windshield, falling so fast that Thomas could barely keep it clear with the windshield wipers on high. He shifted the truck from third to second gear and coaxed it toward the mountain summit. "Thank God for four-wheel drive and chains," he muttered.

The heater ran full blast but hardly kept the chill at bay. The winding highway was dark. No other cars on the road at such a late hour or in such horrid weather conditions. Smart of them, he thought with a smirk. Only the desperate were on a black mountain road in the middle of a blizzard.

He laughed, knowing exactly what that said about himself. "Playing with the ladies instead of standing in line for brains, Whetmore?" he asked aloud. He adjusted the heater to blow onto the windshield as the windows began to fog and rubbed his sleeve on the glass to clear a hole to see through. What miserable weather. If it weren't for Gregore, he'd be nice and warm, perhaps with some company, sharing a fine glass of scotch for a nightcap. Not driving over a godforsaken mountain. "And he better be grateful once we break that damn curse."

The road curved and began a sloping ascent. He couldn't see the lines dividing the lanes. Instead he aimed for the middle and tried to keep out of the snow banks. "Man dies in snowdrift. Disappears in daylight. Story at eleven," Thomas muttered, then winced. Could he sound like more of a baby? This was his friend. "Buck up, chap. And maybe stop talking to yourself while you're at it."

All in all, the confrontation with Gregore went well. Better than expected, entirely thanks to Tara, no doubt. Good to see he wasn't hitting the bottle and had cleaned himself up. That would go a long way with Jeffrey. He ran a hand through his blond hair and over his chin. With Gregore, he'd known he wouldn't be well received. With Jeffrey, he'd be received but would have to argue his case. What a bloody mess.

He wiped the windshield again and thought about Tara. The woman had spunk and determination, just what they all needed. She just might be the key to fixing all this shit. If he was wrong, they were screwed.

He passed the ski lodge at the top of the mountain pass and began the torturously slow descent down the other side. Somewhere around here was a nearly invisible turnoff. After what felt like an hour, he spotted the markers, hit the brakes, and skidded a couple hundred feet past the turn. "Bloody hell." Thomas put the truck in reverse, carefully backed up, and turned onto a small logging road.

He followed the road for miles up the side of another slope. The truck trudged on through six inches of snow, the snow chains on the tires working well past their grade. He'd be lucky to make it. Why the hell Jeffrey settled in a place so remote was anyone's guess. He half expected to find Grizzly Adams in place of his friend.

Still, it would be good to see Kingston again. Like Gregore, it had been too long. Just not quite as long, as at least Jeffrey and he were still on good terms. He hoped. Thomas thought back to the last time they'd seen each other. What year was that? Was it 1992 or 1998? The problem with living so bloody long was everything really began to run together. Especially in forgettable decades.

Lord, whatever had happened to them? That Gypsy broad had ruined three decent men, turning them into—and here he laughed without humor—shadows of themselves. In his case, literally. Regardless, it was long past time to glue their lives back together and live. Really live. Not just exist as half-human fairy tales.

Near the top of the next crest, he slowed and turned the truck onto a small gravel driveway. The thickest snow was cleared away and only the fresh flakes stuck to the rocks. Thomas stopped the truck halfway down the drive. Just beyond the tree line lay a cabin with smoke curling from the chimney. Lights glowed between mostly closed curtains, allowing only small streaks of gold to escape. The framework of the house looked sound, with hand-hewn wood and a sharp, sloping metal roof to let the snow slide off. A porch ran the length and width of the first floor. The second floor held a small balcony overlooking the valley.

A shadow moved fast in the window upstairs. Blocking the lamplight quick and then was gone. So fast, he would have believed it imagination had he not known better. Guess the old chap was home. And watching. Thomas flashed his headlights twice. He hoped it signaled friendship. Or at least not an enemy.

He pulled forward and parked in front of the cabin, killing the engine. He sat a few minutes, gathered his hopes, and opened the truck door. He went up the porch steps and noted the rocking chair. Kingston didn't strike him as the rocking-chair type and picturing his friend in it brought a smile to his face.

He rapped on the door. Waited. There was no sound from within. "Don't play coy with me, Jeffrey," he said, knocking again.

Minutes ticked by. He rubbed his hands together and blew onto them for warmth.

"It's bloody cold out here. I don't want to freeze to death."

Another minute.

"Actually, I don't even know that I *can* freeze to death, and I didn't drive all the way out here to sign up for a science experiment."

Thomas heard a snort on the other side of the door. A moment later it opened. Jeffrey stood on the other side, blocking part of the lamplight. What wasn't blocked revealed dark hair sticking in all directions and an unshaved jaw. He wore flannel pajama bottoms. But no smile.

"What are you doing here?"

"Out for a stroll?"

Jeffrey snorted. "Try again."

"Snowshoeing and lost my way?"

Jeffrey shook his head.

"Heard rumors of this terrifying, scaled beast that occasionally sprouted feathers and had to come see for myself."

Kingston sighed. "I suppose it would be polite to let you in?"

"You suppose correctly. And offering a warm drink would get you everywhere with me."

Jeffrey tried to close the door.

Thomas let out a sharp laugh and blocked it with his foot. "It's been years, man. I've come a long way. Surely you can let me in for a brief time."

Jeffrey opened the door and almost smiled. "Brief. But get your own damn drink."

"Show me the way, mate." Thomas walked in to a warm cabin.

Rich golden wood trimmed the walls and bookshelves. Plush leather chairs and a couch nestled up to the fireplace that heated the room to a comfortable temperature, compared to the chilly weather outside. The cabin was cozy. Stairs led up from the living room to a hallway on the second floor which had a few bedrooms and a bathroom. It smelled musky, with a hint of the burning wood.

Thomas went to the fire and warmed his hands, then turned to warm his backside. A couple of table lamps cast off the gloom of the living room and reflected in Jeffrey's eyes as he studied him. A thick book lay on the coffee table beside a glass with a tawny liquid in it.

"I'll have one of those," Thomas said, pointing to it.

Jeffrey grunted and went to a sideboard, lifting the stopper off a crystal decanter that looked a lot like…

"Isn't that your mother's decanter?" Thomas asked. "I've never seen another with the swirling smoke etched in glass like that."

Jeffrey nodded. "I brought it from her estate after she passed. That and a few other small items."

Thomas accepted the glass of scotch and took a sip, letting the heat of the liquor scald him while he thought about that. Out of them all, he'd never pegged Jeffrey for the nostalgic type. "The curse changed us all, didn't it?" he asked.

Jeffrey took a sip of his drink and set the glass back on the table. Lowered himself into a chair. "So what brings you out, *mate?*"

Thomas settled onto the couch. "No need to be an ass."

Jeffrey didn't respond.

"Okay, fine. Be an ass. But you're still my bloody friend, so get over it."

Jeffrey's lips tipped up as if he couldn't help it. "I wouldn't have it any other way." He finished the scotch and twirled the glass between his palms. "But I know what year it is. You've come here about him."

"You used to be best friends."

Jeffrey snorted. "Ancient history."

Thomas took another sip of his drink. "You should hear me out."

Jeffrey closed his eyes.

Thomas waited, patient. When Gregore had turned on Jeffrey that night so long ago in Italy, it had seemed the worst sort of betrayal. After all they had done to find him, Jeffrey's anger was warranted.

Jeffrey nodded. "For you, mate."

Thomas finished his drink and lifted the glass. "Refill?" At Kingston's nod, he took both glasses to the sideboard and gave them each a healthy splash. He had a feeling they'd need it.

Once he was settled back on the couch, he took a sip and decided where to start. "You know he's only got a few days left. What you don't know is that the chap actually located the old witch's spell book."

Jeffrey sat forward. "Griselda's? How the hell did he find it?"

"Enough genealogy to put a professor to sleep. He tracked it down to a woman who appears to be a direct blood relation."

Kingston shook his head. "He could track down that old bat himself and it still wouldn't make a difference."

Thomas smiled. "This woman wants to help."

"Why would she want to help us? What's in it for her?"

"I think she likes our boy."

Jeffrey looked uncertain. "How old is she? He doesn't have to, uh...sleep with an old lady, right?"

Thomas roared with laughter. "If it broke the curse..."

"If it broke this damn curse, *I'd* do her and give her the best damn lay of her life. Fortunately, that's not an option."

Thomas sobered. "No. But for the first time, we have an option. Isn't that worth something?"

Jeffrey thought for awhile. Long enough that Thomas thought he might actually say no.

Jeffrey eventually nodded. He stood and paced to the front window, staring over the snowy landscape. "What aren't you telling me?"

Thomas rose from the couch and went to find Jeffrey's kitchen. "Have anything to eat in this place?" he called over his shoulder.

Behind him, he heard Jeffrey sigh and follow him. "Now you want a meal as well? Whatever did I do to the fates to deserve such company?"

Thomas let out a throaty laugh. "That's between you and them." He poked around in the refrigerator until he found eggs and bacon. Pulling them out, he snagged a pan off the pot rack and started the gas stove. "Breakfast okay?"

Jeffrey nodded, leaning his hip against the counter. "Still waiting."

Thomas laid the bacon into the pan and snagged another pan for the eggs. He grabbed a couple slices of bread and put them in the toaster. "There are complications. Things like curses are never easily broken, right? Otherwise they wouldn't be the stuff of legend. The first and biggest complication is that the actual spell was stolen."

"What? You came all the way out here to tell me that there's a way to break the curse, but it was stolen? What kind of fool do you think I am?" Jeffrey ground out.

"Would you like that answer alphabetically or chronologically?" Thomas winked at his growling friend. "I'm confident Tara can find the answer. She's determined and she has the bloodline."

Kingston didn't look mollified. He'd be even less once Thomas finished telling the rest. May as well get it all out there and hope some food quelled the gathering storm. He didn't really want to fend off Jeffrey's beast. Kingston's eyes were wider, his breathing a bit faster. Sure signs that his emotions were rising.

"Take a breath and calm down," Thomas added. Jeffrey drew a few deep breaths and visibly settled down. "Another challenge is that our girl hasn't used her magic since she was a kid. And then there's the matter of the man who stole the spell. He seems to have some sort of twisted vendetta against Gregore."

Jeffrey snorted and ran his hand in his hair, tugging on the strands as he squeezed his eyes closed. The skin of his arm rippled, silver-green scales flashing and disappearing. "Is there any good news or did you just come to torture me?"

"I told you the good news. Tara can break this curse. And if she can break his, she can break ours," Thomas said, taking the crisp bacon out of the pan and flipping the eggs. The toaster popped up and he snagged the bread slices.

"No," Jeffrey said.

"No what?"

"No, I'm not going to help or whatever it is you want from me." He sounded tired. Resigned.

Thomas handed him a plate of food and fished through the kitchen drawers for silverware. "Don't be too hasty."

"You can't seriously think to drag me back into this. I spent years tracking that bloody idiot through seven countries. I still bear the scar from my last run-in" More scales rippled, this time flashing over his neck and hands.

Thomas sat and took a bite of bacon, savoring the flavor. "Eat. You'll feel better." He motioned with his fork for Jeffrey to sit.

His friend reluctantly sat and shoveled a forkful of food into his mouth. The scales receded.

"Good." After a few more bites, Thomas said, "Gregore is nearing the end of his time. The man I saw was part resigned to his fate and part determined to beat it. I think Tara is giving him hope. I get the sense he hasn't had much of that. She's feisty, which is just what he needs. I think he might be falling for her." He could tell that Kingston listened even though he didn't respond. "The thing is, mate, if this were you, I'd move heaven and earth to be there. I'd fight with you to the end, if that's what it took. He would too."

Jeffrey scoffed. "Like he did before?"

"Can you truly say that any one of us has acted completely logical since becoming what we are? He lost so much that night. I think it really messed his head up. He's a changed man. I can see it." Thomas looked squarely at his friend. "Only together can we break our curses. Are you really going to risk all of our lives out of stubbornness?"

"Would it be any less than you deserve?"

"No. Hardly the point, though, is it?" Thomas said, lips twitching.

Jeffrey took his empty plate to the sink and rinsed it off. He put his hands on the counter and stared out the small window. Finally he turned. "I need time to think this through."

Thomas nodded and added his plate and the pans to the sink. "I thought you might. But make it quick. He's only got a couple days left." He turned on the faucet and plugged the sink.

"I'll do those since you cooked. And I'll have an answer for you tomorrow."

"Great, I'll just go grab my gear from the truck. Shall I set up here, or do you have a spare room?"

"What is this, the Plaza? Get the hell out. I'll contact you tomorrow."

"How? You don't even know where I'll be. And would you really kick your best friend out in the middle of a bloody blizzard?"

"Fuck it," Jeffrey rumbled. "Spare bedroom upstairs on the right.

Thomas laughed all the way to the door. "I'll grab my bag. Don't lock the door behind me."

Jeffrey grunted and nodded. A reluctant smile curled his lips. "It is good to see you, old friend."

Thomas clasped arms with him, ducked into the steadily falling snow, and ran to his truck. He knew Jeffrey would come around. No question. He had to, or they would all perish.

~ CHAPTER 24 ~

"Maddy!" Tara screamed, jolting upright in bed. Her heart pounded, sweat dampened her skin, and her breath sawed in and out of her lungs. She took a couple of slow breaths, trying to calm herself. Stretching out her arms and legs that felt cramped from straining. The sheets tangled around her legs, around a sleeping Gregore, and trailed off the end of the bed. She brushed her hair back from her face and fell back against the pillows. A nightmare. One she could barely recall. Just fleeting glimpses in her mind of Maddy.

Tara tried to think, to pull the dream back to the forefront of her mind. Thinking it through, changing the outcome had always banished the night terrors before. This dream remained elusive. Something about Maddy and magic. Relaxing stiff limbs that still ached from their lovemaking, she let her mind drift back to the dream. Maddy sat in a chair surrounded by darkness. Orange. She remembered an orange glow. It surrounded Maddy, making her aunt afraid. No, not afraid, resigned. Like she knew it was going to happen. The rest of the dream was lost. She couldn't remember any other details, just the unsettling feeling that Maddy was harmed.

Focusing, Tara tried to change her aunt's expression to joy, the orange to red. Green. Brown. No matter how hard she concentrated, the tainted memory of the dream remained. Like the dream in the garden, this too seemed relevant to the situation. She hadn't had dreams like this in years. Why now? Was it Gregore's presence or the opening of herself to the magic running through her blood? Her head throbbed, making her rub her temples. Maybe coffee would bring clarity.

Beside her, Gregore slept soundly, his chest rising and falling in slow, even breaths. She reached out to touch him and felt her breath hitch. She'd seen him in repose once before, just days ago. He'd been hard as marble and in full guise of the beast. She clearly remembered the wings curving over his head, the talons. It was far different to wake up beside him. Gregore's stone felt cold under her fingertips. Her heart shuddered. How could he live half a life like this?

Tara slipped from the bed and padded to the window. She pushed the dark curtains aside to stare out at the white blanket of snow. The sun shown bright, and though it was clearly still freezing out, a bit of water dripped nearby from the roof. The snow would be gone soon as warmer temperatures moved in. She'd miss it. The city didn't get nearly as much snow as she'd like. Probably for the best, she decided. Seattle had no idea what to do when the snow hit. The city would literally shut down if there was too much and it froze. Buses and cars stranded on the side of the roads, ice everywhere. It was a traffic cop's worst nightmare. Guess she'd have to stick to the mountains if she wanted a real winter.

Thomas said Jeffrey didn't live too far, somewhere off the main highway up in the mountains. He probably had a spectacular view of pristine white snowcaps and tree branches heavy with their winter burden. Maybe when this was all over, if Gregore and Jeffrey could restore their friendship, she and Gregore could go visit.

That thought brought her up short. Whoa, O'Reilly. Making plans for a future? She barely knew the guy. As soon as the words hit her brain, her heart protested. No, that wasn't entirely true. She knew him to be strong and caring. He looked after her aunt. He was considerate and very smart. He would have sacrificed his life to save his friends the night they were cursed. The guilt he carried for his actions showed a depth of self-awareness and remorse few people these days had. He wasn't selfish. Not to mention, he had rock-hard abs. One might even say marble hard. Those abs weren't the only thing hard about his impressive body. Tara pictured him in bed with a tent pole under the sheets. She snickered. Chuckled. Gave in to full laughter at the thought.

She must have cracked her skull while thrashing around in that nightmare. Either that or she needed a sleeping pill stat. Tara pulled away from the window and looked longingly at the bed. At Gregore. The alarm clock said it was after nine a.m. Much as she would like to crawl back in with him and pull the covers over her head, she had a meeting with Carson, who should have some details on Saints. Hopefully he wouldn't interrogate her about Gregore. She couldn't readily admit what she felt about him to herself and damn sure wasn't ready to share it with anyone else.

She needed coffee. Aunt Maddy's tea wouldn't quite cut it today. Maybe she'd get one of those triple-shot mochas that Carson always drank, with enough caffeine and sugar to shoot her into outer space. It sounded heavenly and put a spring in her step.

Tara showered and dressed, then went downstairs to where Aunt Maddy was watering her plants.

"Morning, dear. Did you sleep well?"

Tara poured herself a cup of tea and added an extra tea bag. Couldn't hurt to get a jump-start on that caffeine hit. "No. I had a bad dream."

Maddy paled. "What was it about?"

Tara pursed her lips, realizing her mistake. She wasn't going to tell Maddy she'd dreamed the woman had been hurt. She shook her head instead. "I hardly remember. Probably just whatever I ate last night." She waved a hand around her stomach. "Nothing to worry about."

Maddy patted her silver hair, looking uncertain. "If you say so. Sometimes dreams come true. Or are portents. You should check out that book on dreams I have on the bookshelf in the living room. It's very good." The old woman stared back out the kitchen window.

Tara glanced over Maddy's shoulder, but saw nothing in the backyard that would draw her aunt's attention. "Sure. I have to go meet Carson for lunch in a bit, so maybe later."

"Carson?"

"My partner, remember? Maddy, are you okay? You seem distracted."

Maddy smiled brightly. Too brightly? "Of course. I, ah, just didn't sleep well myself. Just part of getting old." Her aunt looked around the kitchen a moment, then smiled again. "Well, I'm off. It's bridge day at the club, and ol' Doris hates it when I'm late. Says it throws off her luck or some such nonsense." She took her coat off a peg by the kitchen door and put it on, then added her hat. "Of course, she doesn't know it's not my being late that gives her the bad luck, but that little charm I gave her for her bracelet last year."

"Maddy, that's cheating!" Tara said, smothering a laugh.

"Oh hush. I'm just making things more even. That Doris and her partner have the most amazing luck. Goldie and I wouldn't have a chance otherwise. And who wants to play when you always lose?" Maddy nodded her head as if it made perfect sense.

Tara shook her head as her heart warmed. She'd missed her aunt. "Will you be okay driving out there? The streets are pretty icy."

"What kind of psychic would I be if I didn't know it was going to snow? I'm a better forecaster of the weather than those silly weathermen on the television. Why, I had snow tires put on my car last week." She gathered her purse and keys. "Well, I'm off! Do look for me later, dear," she called as she left the house.

Tara chuckled and finished her tea. She settled into the chair at the old wood table and closed her eyes. A bright beam of light was waiting for her there. The honey ochre ley line. Loud and clear and without any effort. She focused that energy within her body and whispered, "*Ascensor.*" A china plate rattled, then was quiet. Tara opened her eyes to see her teacup floating right in front of her. She snagged it out of the air and grinned. "This could really come in handy."

She set the cup down and wiggled her fingers. Her skin tingled from using the magic. It seemed to be a side effect of some sort. Like a magical endorphin rush. She felt alive. Powerful. Using the magic was…fun!

Focusing on the amber ley lines, she mentally drew the magnetic power to her hands and cast the magic out like a wall in front of her. "*Solida.*" Solid. The shield came just as easily today and remained until she dropped it.

Tara rose and put her cup in the sink. Sure, she could float it over, but she didn't want to get lazy and use magic for everything. Power corrupted. True in the political world and no doubt true in the magical world. Look at Gregore. Wrong place, wrong time, wrong Gypsy girl, and suddenly he's a block of stone half the time. If that wasn't misused power, she didn't know what was.

Tara practiced crafting the magical shield a few more times, pleased that each time, the shield appeared faster than the last. Power shot through her limbs, racing along her nerve endings, fuller and stronger than yesterday. She felt invincible. Like she could do anything. Pulling the magic into her hands, she crafted a snapping, crackling ball of amber energy. Flames danced over it, licking at her, until her hands warmed. She jerked in surprise and lost the connection. Could she keep the energy from burning her? More determined than ever, she decided she would.

An hour later, she did. Exhausted, she staggered upstairs to get ready to meet Carson. Gregore still rested. Tara bent to kiss his forehead, whispered she'd be back soon. She crossed to her room, put on her boots, then spent a few minutes hunting for her keys. She finally found them on a table by the front door, under a stack of Maddy's mail and scarf.

"Damn it, O'Reilly. Can't you at least put them in the same place every day?" she muttered. Yeah, probably not. Was it possible that losing things repeatedly was in her DNA? Better to add the ingredients of the remembrance spell to her shopping list, she decided, and left the house.

A cool wind blew, digging under her sweater to any exposed areas of flesh. She shivered and ran for the car. Or where the car was supposed to be. It was covered in snow. She brushed the snow off as fast as possible and tried to think warm thoughts. An eternity later she opened the door and slid behind the wheel. Her boots were caked with slush. Too cold to care, she started up the ignition and cranked on the heat. Hopefully the roads would be better today.

Tara made her way through the neighborhood out onto the main arterial roads, thankful the sanding trucks had been through the night before. She glanced at her watch while waiting for a light to change. Not quite eleven o'clock. She had an hour before meeting Carson, and the Grand Grimoire bookstore wasn't far. She'd just make a quick stop. No harm in that, right?

Nick wiped the moisture off the inside of the windshield of his rented Ford Escape and watched Tara leave the house. She moved as much snow as she could, climbed into her small car, and carefully backed out of the drive.

He waited until she was half way down the block before he started the SUV and followed. She drove through the city at a crawling pace. He kept a few cars between them as they traveled the frozen streets.

This little journey was about knowing his opponent. From his prior research, he'd known where Tara lived, where she worked, who her only relative was, and the people she descended from. Finding the aunt's residence had been easy enough. He correctly assumed that she would turn to family when he'd set her apartment on fire. But that was before she'd hooked up with that freak.

Before Tara had changed the game.

She turned corners, leading him past Seattle University and then down Pike Street until they came to a familiar neighborhood. Suddenly, he knew exactly where she was going. The Grand Grimoire.

No doubt she'd felt inadequate at the warehouse. Out maneuvered. She must have come here in search of more about magic. Interesting that she'd chosen this particular store to look for something to defend herself and that hunk of rock she was partnered with.

Nick waited for her to park on the street and circled the block. By separating herself from the gargoyle, Tara had unknowingly presented him with a unique opportunity to remove her from the game. He planned to take full advantage.

He parked several cars away. And waited for her to leave the shop.

CHAPTER 25

Tara parked her Mini across the street from the Grand Grimoire, situated on the east side of the city in the Capitol Hill neighborhood. Known for its retro and funky shops, the area drew a unique clientele made of a mix of college students, artists, and those who never really fit in with the nine-to-five crowd. Tara liked it immediately. She waited for a car to pass, then stepped into the street to cross.

The hair of her arms stood on end. Tingles spread through her skin, leaving goose bumps in her wake. She stopped mid-step, unsure what was happening. Her body felt tense here, though there didn't seem to be a reason. This was different than her gut instinct that alerted her to danger. This was something far different.

A horn blared close by, jolting her from her introspection. A car was heading for her, honking to remind her to get out of the road. *Snap out of it, O'Reilly.* She jogged the short distance across the street to the sidewalk and looked around, unable to shake the strange feeling. She didn't smell or hear anything other than exhaust and the crunch of tires on snow. She didn't see anything, yet the odd sensation remained. Could it be her newfound magical abilities were even more heightened here?

She stood at the edge of the sidewalk and looked around. Only a few shoppers were out. Closing her eyes, she tilted her head back to the sky and gasped. Emblazoned in the sky was the most spectacular sight she'd ever seen. Glowing arcs of burgundy light intersected above. Never had she seen so many ley lines at once. Three lines crisscrossed here, right where the store was located. Definitely not a coincidence. Was the difference in the color of the lines due to the amount? Like everything else magic related, she didn't know.

Tara opened her eyes and turned back to the front door of the store. Bright red curtains framed the front window, showcasing a group of books, candles, and mystical wares. A pentagram was painted below the store name. Bells chimed overhead as she entered. A young woman with black pigtails and heavily black-lined eyes looked up from the cash register.

"Let me know if I can help you find anything," she murmured as she went back to her book.

The store was surprisingly large. Crimson walls with gold and black swirled carpet made the place feel more like a sensuous boutique. There was a large candle section off to the right and directly ahead, a display of tarot cards and books. Bookshelves lined the walls, filled with books, jars of different ingredients, and a variety of different figurines. There was also a section of clothing and jewelry. Gathering her self-control, she avoided the tempting jewelry and headed in the opposite direction to the rows and rows of glass jars.

She took out her small shopping list. This morning, while getting ready, she'd decided that the spell for remembrance would be ideal for Gregore. Perhaps if he could remember everything that happened and was said the night of the curse, it would give them everything they needed to break the curse. Not to mention the spell to find lost items. If her keys were any indication, she'd need it daily. She picked up several candles in black, yellow, and white. She needed a couple mirrors, periwinkle, lilac, zinnias, everlastings and rosemary. She also needed a mortar and pestle. Strange, none of the jars on this shelf had ginkgo leaves. Maybe that was a vitamin store purchase.

Vanilla scented the air. Tara sniffed and looked around. The storekeeper walked up behind her. She wore a skin-tight black dress with a deep V neckline and knee-high lace-up boots. Tara admired her gumption. She'd never have the courage to wear that.

"Find what you are looking for?" the girl asked.

"I'm not sure," Tara said. She looked at her list again. "I'm new to all of this. I have a spell book and I want to try a couple of spells. I...well, I have a list of ingredients, but I don't see some of the items here." She felt awkward, though she couldn't say why.

With sensual grace, the girl leaned forward to take the list from Tara. "These are old names. No wonder." She opened a couple of jars, removing different flowers. "So what kind of spell are you trying?" the girl asked.

"I want to help a friend remember something that happened a long time ago. And a spell to find something lost."

"Oh, that's a handy one. I never remember where I leave things." The girl dropped the packages of ingredients into a handheld basket. "You want to be very careful when casting spells over people's memory. If you don't get the spell exact, you could do more harm than good." She cocked an eyebrow. "Unless that's the intention."

"No. I don't want to hurt him." Just the thought of wiping out more of Gregore's memories, of hurting him in any way, made her gut clench with fear. Maybe this wasn't such a good idea. What if she messed things up so completely that she wiped his mind clean? What if he couldn't remember who he was in the final days of his life? What if...no. No. She tamped down that overwhelming fear. She wouldn't hurt Gregore. She was helping him. She was his only shot to break this curse, and she wouldn't let fear of using magic hold her back. Not this time. She glanced at the girl's name badge. "Thank you for the warning, Deja. I really need this spell to go perfect. Can you give me some pointers?"

Deja nodded and picked out the candles Tara needed, adding them to the basket. "Sure. Judging by your list here, you'll mix the ingredients, then burn them like incense."

Tara nodded, surprised. "Yes. How did you know?"

"Casting is my specialty. Let's go look at the books."

Tara followed Deja to an impressive selection of books, categorized by hundreds of subjects. She pointed to a section on casting. "Here are the basics. Things you need to know before you begin." She added two books to the basket. "Do you have a place to cast?" At Tara's blank look, she said, "You need a quiet spot. Some place you can concentrate without interruptions when you're new. Once you've been at it awhile, you don't need it. Oh, and I recommend a fire extinguisher. Can't tell you how many newbies have set their drapes on fire."

Tara felt a blush heat her face and cleared her throat. "Yeah, wouldn't want that." She made a mental note to buy new curtains for Maddy while she was out today. And to not practice drawing fire by flammable material.

"Do you have an athame to carve the candles with?" Deja asked.

"No? What is it?" She felt terribly out of her comfort zone. Like some clueless kid overwhelmed with all the choices in a candy store.

Deja laughed. "A ceremonial dagger. We've got a good selection. Blessed, non-blessed, whatever you need."

"I don't know what I need."

Deja selected a curved blade from a glass display cabinet. She showed Tara the ivory handle. Carved into the grip was a woman with flowing hair, arms raised to the moon and magic flowing from her fingertips. "She almost looks like you," Deja said.

Tara traced a fingertip over the carving. "It's beautiful. So I guess a regular butter knife doesn't work quite as well?"

The shop girl chuckled. "It works, but it's like using a hacksaw when you really need a chainsaw. So what kind of spell book do you have?" she asked, handing over the shopping basket.

Tara took the basket with a nod of thanks. "It's an old family book of Gypsy magic."

Deja's gaze swerved to hers. "Really? I thought they were more into tarot and that sort of mysticism."

"This group was different," Tara murmured. "I'm going to look around a little more."

Deja left her to go back behind the counter. Her eyes tracked Tara throughout the store, far more interested than she had been just a few minutes before.

Tara felt watched, but ignored it. Some part of her instinct told her not to say more about the book. Perhaps it was simply Grandma Rose's original warnings not to share it with anyone. She shook off the strange interaction with Deja and put a few more things in her basket. She purchased another book of magic and a few more innocuous ingredients like salt. A quick check of her watch said that it was almost time to meet Carson. She walked to the counter to check out.

Deja said no more, but cast a few glances to Tara from beneath her lashes as she rang up the items. Tara avoided her look and glanced down into the glass display case under the cash register. Her breath caught. An old tarot deck was there. One just like her Grandma Rose's. Just like the one she tried to read as a child. The day her parents died. Her throat closed tight. She tried to swallow over the strong knot of emotion. Her eyes stung, but she refused to cry.

"Where did you get those?" Tara asked, tapping the glass with her finger.

Deja looked down at the cards. "I bought them from an estate sale years ago. Never seen another deck like it."

"Where? Where was the sale?" Tara knew before she even asked. On the left side of the deck was a red line from a marker. One she'd accidentally made when putting them away for Grandma.

She didn't hear Deja's answer. Didn't need to. "I want them."

Deja's eyebrows rose. "You sure? You haven't even asked the price. The stuff in this case is more expensive than the rest of my merchandise."

"I'm sure. I...These were my grandmother's."

Tara cringed when Deja said her total, then paid and left the store. What would Grandma Rose think of the changes in her granddaughter? She hoped she'd be proud.

Ice-cold air enveloped her as soon as she stepped onto the sidewalk. The warmth of the store disappeared as the door closed. She hurried across the street and made a note to buy herself a new jacket today. Fingers shaking with the cold, she dug her keys out of her pocket and promptly dropped them in the snow.

"Damn it," she muttered and bent to retrieve them.

Something hard slammed into the side panel of the sedan next to her head. It sounded like a frozen snowball. Tara jumped at the noise, dropped her bag, and looked up to see dagger shaped icicles protruding from the metal. Too close. A high-pitched whistle of something slicing through the air had Tara diving around behind a car. She braced her back against the wheel just as more icicles hit. The front tire of the car deflated and dropped a couple inches. She snuck a glance around the bumper and swore. Saints. He didn't appear to have a weapon in hand. So how the hell was he throwing icicles that would cut through metal?

As she watched, he scooped more snow into one hand while chanting. With his other, he picked up what looked like clear throwing stars from his palm and in three quick throws, impaled them in the car she took cover behind.

Incredible. And terrifying.

Around her, the nearest shoppers retreated into doorways, a couple with phones to their ears. Shit. If she drew her Sig Sauer and tried to hit him, she could accidentally shoot a bystander. Was it worth the risk? Her only other options were the shaky magic she barely had use of or to wait for backup to arrive.

She took another look around the bumper to find Saints readying more ice daggers. He smiled at her just before he threw them.

Tara ducked back behind the wheel and weighed all three shitty options. If she drew her gun, she might hit a bystander. If she used magic, she might blow a bystander up. If she waited for the police, Saints might take a bystander hostage in order to force her hand. She swore words she'd never used in her life and made a decision.

This might be her only chance to take out Saints. A quick sweep of the area showed her three ley lines. She took a deep breath. She could do this.

Tara drew the crackling energy from the ley lines into her body and crafted an amber ball of flame. Swinging around to her haunches, she peered over the hood of the car, and tried to time her throw to deflect Saints' ice weapons.

He tossed the daggers with deadly accuracy.

She tossed the ball of flame at the same time. It hit two of the daggers, melting them on impact. Unfortunately, it missed the third. She dove to the ground as it soared over her head and clanked onto the sidewalk behind her, breaking into three pieces of ice.

Gathering more energy, she created another amber ball. She aimed and threw it at Saints.

He shielded himself with magic and deflected the fire back into a snow bank.

Tara was already gathering magic as she ticked off a couple more options. With Saints on the other side of the street, it was only a matter of time until a bystander was caught in their battle of magic. She didn't know what her fire would do to a body and didn't want to find out. She would have to draw him closer.

Shops lined his side of the street, while cars lined hers. Behind her, about fifty feet away was the entrance to a small park. It should be empty in this weather.

Tara tossed another flame at him. As soon as he deflected it, she stood and ran for the park. A glance over her shoulder showed Saints in pursuit.

Icicle stars and blades sunk deep into a wooden railing beside her.

She tried to gather more energy into an amber flame ball but found it difficult to focus as she ran. Another dagger hit the tree trunk beside her. Tara dodged right and hit a patch of black ice on the path. Her feet went out from under her. She landed hard on her ass.

Saints bore down on her at a fast clip, readying another ice weapon. He stopped a foot from her. His smile was pure evil. "You've made this too easy. Your paltry magic can't defeat me. But don't worry, I'll pass your regards onto that freak and your aunt."

He aimed and threw the dagger right for her chest. She threw her hands up and nearly cried in relief when the shield came at her bidding.

The dagger bounced harmlessly to the ground.

Saints growled and bent to scoop more snow just as she gathered more flame to herself.

She readied herself for his attack as he chanted over the mound of snow in his hand. If she struck first, in this close quarters, she might strike him before he could cast a shield to protect himself.

She raised her hand to throw it just as he loosed another dagger. She awkwardly turned to try to avoid it. Sharp, stinging pain hit her before she could release the ball and it fell from her fingers to dissipate on the ground. She looked down to find ice shards sticking out of her thigh from where the dagger had sliced as it flew past like a missile. Blood welled around the wound and began to melt the ice.

He chuckled as he gathered more snow.

Tara reached for more magic. It wavered and danced around her, but she couldn't concentrate enough to draw it into her body. She held her hands up, praying for a shield as he fashioned the snow into a dagger before her eyes.

He held his arm back, the tip of the ice reflecting the sun.

Suddenly a thick snowball, slammed into Nick's face.

"Ha ha! I got your back lady! Let's get him." a kid called out.

Tara looked behind her to see a couple kids no more than eight years old readying another round of snowball ammunition.

"Run," she yelled at the kids. Gaining her feet, she rushed Nick Saints and tackled him to the ground. Ice coated his fair hair and eyelashes. Pulling back her fist, she punched him in the face twice, then gained her feet again. She kicked him as hard as she could in the ribs. Gathering the flame, she threw it at him.

Saints huffed out a pained breath, his shield not quite blocking the blow.

Damn it. She couldn't battle him here with the kids and she didn't have the magic to best him.

Tara ran back to her car, hoping he would follow and leave the kids alone.

She glanced back to find Nick slowly pushing himself up, shaking his head as if dazed and holding his ribs. He didn't even glance at the children as he started to follow her.

He'd live.

She couldn't stay and fight, not out in the daylight with all these people around. She gathered her bag of supplies and dug for her keys in the pile of snow where she'd dropped them when diving for cover. Why oh why did they have to be in four inches of snow part way under the sedan? Cursing her luck, she got behind the wheel of her car as fast as she could, stuck the key in the ignition with shaky fingers, turned it over, and hit the gas. The Mini slid, found traction, and jolted forward onto the street with a shudder that matched her nerves.

CHAPTER 26

Nick swayed as he watched Detective O'Reilly peel out like the hounds of hell were on her tail. No matter, he'd learn what she purchased from Deja.

He was calm, if not pained, as he entered the store, confident in his new plan. Let the detective think she could win this war. He had planned for too long not to succeed. He'd ruin their lives.

Nick grinned. Thanks to the prostitute he'd had last night, power flowed freely in his body. Hummed in his veins like a fine, vibrant tune. It wasn't enough. Never enough. Sex ramped the power up high, but he couldn't sustain it. The current amount would be used up in the first spell or two. Why settle for that when he could have so much more? What he needed was an orchestra in his veins. A bonfire of power in his body that would last days, no matter the number of spells he cast.

Nick checked his watch. Maybe Deja would have some ideas. Multiple partners, perhaps? His blood heated at the thought. Multiple partners at once? He thrummed with desire, the thought of all that flesh generating all that power making him giddy.

It was time to start the final phase of his plan.

Carson arrived ten minutes early to his meeting with O'Reilly. Fortunately, most people were staying home since the snow still stuck to the roads. He got out of his car and went into the Mystical Moon Coffee Shop. There were a few patrons, but the girl behind this counter drew his interest. She looked up from the espresso machine and gave him a shy smile.

"Morning, Elena. You look pretty today." He winked at her and relived a brief memory of their time together. She was particularly limber. A pleasant surprise that worked for both.

She blushed. "What can I get you, Carson?"

"Give me a big mocha. Extra chocolate," he said.

She giggled. "I remember how much you like the chocolate sauce."

"Maybe you can come back over tonight and we'll explore more uses for it."

"You are so on," she breathed and started his drink. "Coffee's on the house."

"Thanks, babe." When she was done, he took his coffee, intentionally brushing his fingers over hers. He walked to a table by the window to wait.

Carson finished his mocha and was just contemplating a second when Tara came into the coffeehouse.

She headed straight for the coffee counter, not stopping to look his direction. Or any direction, for that matter. She gave an order to Elena and handed over her money. Carson waited. Strange, it looked like Elena was making something at the espresso machine. O'Reilly always took her coffee black. Stranger still, his partner looked rumpled. Her clothes were normally a bit wrinkled, but today her bottom left pant leg was soaked and her sweater had a rip in the hem. Dirt smudged her cheek. Either she was living on the streets or she'd been in a fight.

He raised an eyebrow when Tara limped over to him. "Are you okay?"

"What?" she said as she sat. "Oh, the coffee. I haven't had coffee in days. I've been staying with my aunt and all she has is tea. I didn't think I'd make it another day. How are you, Carson?"

"I'm good. But I meant your clothes and the blood on your jeans. Are you hurt?"

Tara took another sip of coffee and avoided his stare. "Fine. Just slipped on the ice earlier."

He'd allow the lie, for now. "Any luck finding a new place? You look like you fought someone for his cardboard house and lost."

She ran a hand over her hair. He leaned forward and wiped the dirt off her face.

"Ah, no. Not yet," she said. "You know how the housing is here. Either you can afford it, but you don't dare live there, or you can't afford it, but you wish you could."

"It's been years since your grandmother died, O'Reilly. Can't you live at her old house with your aunt?"

"I told you the other day. It won't work. The memories are still too strong."

He shrugged. "Maybe you just need to start making some new ones there."

Tara's gaze drifted to the window as she thought about that. A small smile formed on her lips. "Maybe you're right."

Damn it. Based on the blush on her face, she was thinking about that guy she'd been seeing. That definitely wasn't where he wanted her to go with that comment. "Listen, partner, I checked out that guy you've been seeing. There's no Gregore Trenowyth in the system. I think this guy's been lying to you. You need to back away."

"Carson, he hasn't been lying to me. He's been truthful from the start. Don't you think I'm able to tell a lie after years on the force? That I wouldn't check him out a bit myself?"

"So if you checked him out, what did you find?"

"I found that he's from England. That's why he's not in the system. And I've checked out other things he's told me. Trust me, partner. Please."

Carson frowned. "I don't want you getting hurt."

"Thanks."

She didn't sound the least bit thankful. "Just be careful. Make sure you know what you want before doing anything stupid."

"Like you, Carson?" she scoffed.

"Hey, I know exactly what I want when I get involved with a woman. Be smart and do the same." She didn't respond. Just sipped her coffee.

"Damn it, O'Reilly. Don't tell me you've slept with him already." A couple of people in the coffee shop looked his way.

"Say it a little louder," she hissed. "I don't think the captain heard you. But God knows everyone else did. How about this? Why don't you drop it? Maybe you could tell me what you found on Saints instead?"

Her shoulders tensed, and she leaned forward as she spoke, green eyes flashing. All the hallmarks of an O'Reilly who was stubborn as hell and would clam up if he kept talking. Better to retreat and go at this from a different angle.

"Fine. There's nothing on Saints but a couple of speeding tickets. Nothing that says he's out to burn down your place for some old book so he can turn people into toads with eye of newt." He sounded like a jerk to his own ears, but fuck it. She pissed him off being so reckless.

"Any idea where he's been or why he'd be out for me or Gregore?"

"Nothing. No connection I can see. You'd probably have better luck with Louisa, mistress of the tarot, over there." He pointed to the curtained-off corner. Louisa was just setting her bag down and pulling out her cards."

Tara looked over at the fortune-teller. He expected her to deliver a snappy retort. She didn't. When she looked back at him, she said, "You're right."

That set him back. "I am?"

"Yeah. Maybe I will get more out of her since you clearly didn't put any effort into my request." She rose and Carson snagged her wrist before she could leave.

"Sit."

"Pardon? I'm not a damn dog, Carson."

"Please."

She slumped into the chair, radiating the irritation he already felt. He stuffed it far down so he could ask the question that had been on his mind.

"Since you haven't found a place, why not stay with me for awhile?"

She rolled her eyes. "Get serious. I'd have to invest my retirement savings in earplugs every time you had a date."

Her shot hit its mark. "At least my dates are honest about who they are," he bit out.

Tara leaned forward, lips parting to blast him. He cut her off.

"Look, I didn't come here to fight. I care, damn it. Even when you make me wonder why I do. This guy is trouble. He's making you do what you normally wouldn't."

"That's where you're wrong, Carson. I help people. It's my job. He's a good man. He's helping me face my fears. Maybe you just don't know me as well as you think." She stood and stalked across the cafe to sit by the fortune-teller.

Carson watched her take money from her purse and give it to Louisa. What was the world coming to? He would have laid a substantial bet that she'd never willingly do that. The first time had been a fluke and he knew it. His partner was changing. He didn't know why, but something was off with her. It had to be that guy she was seeing.

He shoved away from the table and left the shop. O'Reilly was right. He hadn't done enough research. But not on this Saints character. He needed to do more on Trenowyth. That passport had to be fake. He'd find it and confront her with the truth.

CHAPTER 27

Tara toweled off from the shower and reached for the hydrogen peroxide. She flinched at the sting as she poured it over the wound in her thigh. It bubbled, clearing out any infection. Now that she'd washed the blood away, she could see that the ice dagger had sliced across her skin a couple of inches. Damn thing hurt, but she didn't think it was too bad.

She prodded the cut, checking to see how deep it was. One portion looked a bit deeper than the other, but probably not enough to need stitches. After cleaning off the peroxide, she smeared some topical antibiotic on it and applied a gauze bandage. It would do for now.

She put away the medicine, washed her hands, and released a shaky breath. The damage could have been exponentially worse. One thing was clear though. She needed to keep working at her magic or she'd die at the hands of Nick Saints. Tara fortified her resolve to learn more magic and pushed aside all thoughts of Saints. She reached for the bag of items she'd purchased earlier and lifted out the sheer black nightie.

A smile curved her lips as she slipped it over her head. She'd been thinking of Gregore from the moment she left the coffee shop, eager to climb into bed with him just as he woke for the night. The gown clung to her like a second skin and ended just below her bottom. It accentuated every curve she had. Turning to the side in the mirror, she wondered at the image of the siren staring back at her. Gregore

Set in Stone

had done this. He made her feel sexy and beautiful. Wanted. Like the way she wanted him.

Tara left the bathroom. It was time to claim her lover.

>―◁>―○―<▷―◁

Gregore woke in darkness and immediately knew two things. One, the sun had set and his body had completed the change. Two, and more importantly, he was not alone. Someone touched his sides, sliding hands around his waist to hold him from behind. He looked down to feminine hands, soft skin, and trim nails. He traced a finger across her skin.

"Tara," he breathed.

"Mmmm," she murmured, trailing those fingertips lower to trace the top of his boxers.

His body reacted immediately, coming to life and aching for her caress. Leaning back into her embrace, Gregore relaxed and encouraged her to explore him further. Every moment spent in her company only made him hunger for more. Not simply her form, but her sharp mind.

And her mouth.

Tara's tongue flicked out to trace his earlobe. He moaned, then turned in her embrace to capture her mouth with his.

She chuckled against his lips and deepened the kiss.

Gregore molded her body into his. He kissed across her jaw and down her neck to nip the delicate skin between her neck and shoulder.

"Gregore," she purred. Tara pressed tight against him, her arms wrapped around his waist and a long leg entwined with his. Something scratched at his thigh as their legs brushed. He looked down to see a white bandage covering her fair skin.

"What is this from?" he asked.

"Later," she breather in his ear. She kissed his neck and dipped a hand below his waist to tease his thigh.

Later worked. He cupped the back of her neck and brought his lips to hers. Sliding a hand under her, he maneuvered her onto his body, once again pressing her to himself as in his dream. He cupped her bottom and startled to realize that his hand embraced bare skin.

Gregore broke the kiss to look down her body. Sheer black fabric clung to every amazing curve and ended just below her bottom. Shifting her onto his body had scrunched the fabric up to reveal glorious white skin for his touch.

"My God, you're beautiful," he whispered.

Tara scooted aside and slid the covers off of his body. "Show me what you've got in exchange."

He rolled onto his side and propped a head on his hand, waving the other down his length. "Will this meet with your satisfaction, ma'am?"

"Oh no," she chuckled. "You don't get to call me ma'am unless I've got the handcuffs out."

His eyebrows shot up. "Is that an option with this particular outfit?"

She moved a long lock of hair off her shoulder. "Sorry, those are with the naughty policewoman outfit."

Gregore traced a fingertip over one of her nipples, barely covered in the sheer fabric. "I'm intrigued. Just how naughty is she?"

Tara took his lips in a hungry kiss, showing him with her mouth how much she wanted him. She ran her hands over his shoulders and down his chest, then back up to tangle in his dark hair and pull him closer to her lips.

Gregore drank in her passion, responding with his own hunger. He pressed his erection to the heat of her body and reveled in the feel as she rocked her hips against him. He broke the kiss and whipped the flimsy nightie off of her, tossing it away. He cupped her breasts. Rubbed his thumbs over her nipples until she dropped her head back and moaned. Leaning forward, he laved her tight bud. Tara's rosy nipples tasted like heaven.

She sank into his embrace. Gregore rolled her over onto her back and let his hands glide over her silky skin. He followed with his mouth, tasting every inch. He dipped his head to nip below her belly button, making her squirm and pant. He kissed the inside of her thighs and inhaled her intoxicating scent, tasting her until she begged mindlessly for him.

Gregore pushed her over the edge at his own pace, then rose over her and settled between her thighs. Tara wrapped her legs around him and scored his chest lightly with her nails. He leaned into her for a kiss and gasped when she flipped him onto his back once more.

"Two can play that game," she purred and slid down his body, taking his boxers with her. She claimed him with her mouth, driving him higher and higher, then pulling back unexpectedly.

"That's not naughty," he groaned. "That's evil."

Tara laughed and reached into his nightstand for a condom. "Think you're ready for me?" she asked as she rolled it down his length.

"I need you. Now." Gregore lifted her up and slid deep inside her body. They both moaned at the contact. He moved as slow as he could at first, building her pleasure back up while desperately trying not to shatter in a climax.

He waited until she was writhing on him once more. Gregore moved his thumb down between their bodies and teased her over the edge, then pushed his release along with her. He cried out with pleasure and belatedly remembered that Maddy might be home.

Tara dropped her head onto his chest and breathed in deep. "And here I thought I was going to rock your world." She glanced up at him. "No pun intended."

His lips quirked. He wrapped his arms tight around her and held her close. It felt so right. Which was why he should push her away. He couldn't in good conscious entangle her heart only to leave her at his death. He'd lived through that once. Nothing hurt more than losing those you loved and facing the rest of your life without them. He wouldn't do that to her. He couldn't seem to release her either.

Gregore rubbed his hands up and down her back, feeling her heartbeat against his. "You're amazing." He hadn't meant to say it, but it wasn't any less true. Could any other woman have taken the last few days in stride like Tara had? He didn't think so. Certainly none he'd known before. Each day she tried to overcome the fear of her magic for one reason. To help him. She could have gone her whole life without using it.

She'd also put her life on hold. Even now, she should be out pounding the pavement to find a new place to live. To find Saints, whom she suspected of burning her apartment. Instead she lay in his arms, glowing from his lovemaking.

He gripped her upper arms and slid her up his body, pressing her lips to his. He kissed her, taking his time. Gregore explored her mouth, felt the flames of his desire start to build. Tara nipped his lower lip and kissed the sting away.

A door closed somewhere downstairs, bringing Gregore back to his senses. "Maddy?"

Tara nodded. "She must be home now. She was playing cards earlier with friends." She sat up, the hot center of her body so close to where he wanted her.

Gregore grasped her hips and maneuvered her onto his shaft. "She'll just have to wait for us."

CHAPTER 28

Mottled gray light filtered through the curtains onto the kitchen table where Tara sat and yawned. Her sleep schedule was way off after being up all night with Gregore a couple of nights in a row. Grandma Rose's tarot deck fanned out in front of her in a sea of blurry pictures. She blinked to clear the images in her eyes, thinking of all she'd learned.

Carson's sarcastic invitation the day before to sit with Louisa had been exactly what Tara needed to do, even if she didn't know it at first. Actually, she'd done it more to piss Carson off than to actually get information from the tarot reader. Once she'd thought about it, she realized there was a lot she wanted to know.

She'd gone to the Grand Grimoire in hopes of learning more about magic in general. But something about the shop girl had warned her off. Tara had the opposite reaction around Louisa, who exuded warmth and trust. Tara felt safe talking to her. They had talked for over an hour before the actual reading commenced.

The woman allayed her fears about the cards. Tara couldn't possibly have been responsible for the death of her parents, just as Gregore and Grandma Rose had said. Neither were the cards. If she had seen them or had a premonition about the accident, it simply meant she was gifted and learned the truth about their deaths instead of being lied to, as adults sometimes did to young children.

Sitting with Louisa was akin to sitting with Grandma Rose. It brought back the memories from before her parents' death. When the world of tarot and the possibilities that magic brought with it were exciting. It could be again. She knew the dangers. She was older and knew when to draw the line. To not let the power suck her under until she no longer controlled the magic and was herself controlled.

And what a powerful reading. They used Rose's old tarot deck. With each shuffle, Tara felt more connected. Louisa directed her to lay out the cards in an astrology pattern, asking her question. As when she was young, a vision shimmered to the surface of her mind. Instead of pushing it away, Tara opened herself to the image.

What she saw would forever haunt her.

She stood in the middle of an inferno with heat beating against her skin. Gregore lay still at her feet and Maddy was tied to a chair close by. Darkness descended over the scene and Saints stepped through the flames. Madness flared in his eyes. He drew a carved knife and launched it at Maddy. At that moment, she had felt herself thrust out of the vision, back into the tiny coffee shop. Back to Louisa's table.

Louisa had finished the reading as if nothing had happened, saying something about uncertainty and a break from what Tara knew before. Her knowing eyes had instantly picked up the worry in Tara's. She'd listened as Tara poured out the details of what she'd seen and offered a single bit of advice. To remember that the future was always uncertain and could change at any moment.

Louisa also reminded her of another important detail. Today they lived in a digital age where anonymity was very hard to come by. Just because Saints didn't have a criminal record didn't mean he was anonymous. More than likely, he could be found online.

If it hadn't been for her plans for Gregore yesterday, Tara would have driven to the library right then to use the free computer. She missed her laptop. Hopefully her renter's insurance would cover the cost of a new one.

She refocused on the kitchen clock. She should play it safe and wait for Gregore, but the need for information about Saints burned in her gut. Before she could talk herself out of it, she grabbed her new jacket, spent eight minutes hunting for her keys before finding them on the bathroom floor, and left for the library.

She parked, went inside, and found an empty computer. The library was nearly deserted. With the winter storm waning, most people still hadn't left their homes. Even the students were absent.

Opening an Internet web page, she pulled up a popular search engine and typed in Nicholas Saints. About four million references to Santa Claus came up. Narrowing her search to Seattle didn't help. She scrolled through a couple of pages before giving up that avenue and going to the online version of the city's newspaper.

Twenty minutes later she found an article written six months ago. A dark picture of an ambulance and a distraught blond man accompanied the piece. The caption read, "Nick Saints, fiancé of the victim." Barely more than a couple paragraphs, the article said the robbery critically injured the victim but didn't name the person. Tara noted the date of the article and tried unsuccessfully to find more. She logged off the computer, and went to the reference desk. The old newspaper copies were bound to have more. Her gut said this was what drove Saints in his actions now. But what did she and Gregore have to do with it?

The old library was surprisingly updated in technology. All of the papers were scanned, the librarian said as she guided Tara to a table and computer in the back. Using the reference password, she logged into the scanned files and searched for August second, the day after the article she found online. The paper would cover any news from the night before, with updates to the story. She found the article and scanned for updates.

Three men approached the victim, Samantha Peters, while she waited outside a local restaurant. Police described the incident as a robbery turned violent, where the victim was brutally beaten and stabbed several times. She died in transit to the hospital.

Tara studied the picture of Saints standing on the sidewalk behind an officer she knew, staring at the ambulance as a paramedic loaded the victim inside. Pain, worry, and fury lined his features, clearly visible even though it was a night shot. The scene looked familiar. She zoomed in on the photo, moving the screen around, trying to figure out what tugged at her memory. Nothing stood out, although admittedly there wasn't much to the picture besides a few bystanders, paramedics, and an ambulance. Perhaps it was just a familiar scene. Someone gets hurt by crime and all the family can do is stand aside and watch with hope that their loved one will live.

She printed the article and scanned the following day's paper. The only additional mention of the incident was a note that all three suspects had turned themselves in the same night. The policeman providing the quote noted only that they seemed incoherent at the time, babbling about a monster with glowing eyes and wings.

"Gotcha," she said. The connection to Gregore. Right there in black and white. She printed the screen, paid for the pages, and left the library.

She pulled her cell phone from her jacket pocket and flipped it open to call Maddy. Did Gregore remember the incident? Had he been there when the woman was mugged? She doubted it, or he would have stopped the attack. Come out of the dusk like a superhero and saved that poor woman from an early death. Much as he had saved Timmy from the fire. She remembered that first glimpse of his gargoyle form. The lazy spiral he made bringing Timmy down to her. The glint in his eyes even while they blazed an electric blue.

Shivers tracked down her spine, making her tingle. Not from fear. No, she didn't fear Gregore. Even in that form, he was incredible. All those solid marble muscles. The incredible sculpted features and firm lips. Her breath caught. His big hands as they trailed over her sensitive skin, warming her. Heating her with hot kisses in a snowy alley. After all she'd been through with Saints, Carson, and Louisa, her nerves were fried and her emotions were on overload.

No, she amended, she wanted Gregore. It wasn't quite four o'clock. Perhaps he'd still be in bed. Maybe she'd wake him first. Share the news later, after she'd shown him that she missed him. With a wicked grin, she flipped the phone closed. Her blood pumped, sang with anticipation. Her stomach fluttered and she could practically feel his hot skin beneath her already. When had she last felt this good? This confident in herself as a woman. A smile settled onto her mouth. Gregore had done this for her. He'd come into her life and dragged her out of her comfort zone, forcing her to know herself. To know him.

Now it was her turn.

>·⊢◆·O·◆⊣·<

A steady, insistent pounding broke Thomas from his dreams like a battering ram. He rolled over in the darkened room and stuffed a pillow over his head. Not that he wanted to go back to his dreams. The past held nothing for him but nightmares now. Encroaching on his peace the moment he closed his eyes and haunting him through the day until the sun began to set. Just once he'd wanted to banish the nightmares and slip into black oblivion for a few hours. Just once.

The pounding stopped.

It started again before he could breathe a sigh of relief.

Thomas pulled the blankets over his pillow and head, burrowing half into the bed. At least the pounding muffled. No, now it sounded more like someone yelling.

"Oh, for the love of...," Thomas growled and yanked the pillow off his head to sit up.

"...Make me wait out here all damn day. You're the one who came to me, remember?" someone shouted from the other side of his door.

"What?" Thomas yelled back.

"Get your ass out of bed, Whetmore, and answer the fucking door," Jeffrey barked.

"All right. All right! I'll be right there." Thomas crawled from the bed and stretched. "Someone's grumpy today," he muttered as he located his discarded boxers and pulled them on. He stomped to the door and pulled it open. "You could at least have tea if you're going to give a guy such a rude awakening."

"Pansy," Jeffrey grumbled. "You hungry?"

Thomas ignored the gibe. "Is that your way of apologizing for waking your guest at an ungodly hour?"

Jeffrey snorted. "Get some clothes on. There's a half-decent diner down the road. I'll buy you a cup of coffee. But no tea."

The Horse Hitch Cafe was a quaint greasy spoon on the edge of town. Decorated in antique barn gear and wagon wheels, the place held a certain Old West charm mixed with furniture from the 1950s.

Thomas slid into a sparkling, red vinyl booth and had to smile. "I always feel more at home in a place built around the same time I was born. Don't you?"

Jeffrey looked around. "No. But this place does have its charm. Good evening, Fern," he said as a cute waitress came to their table.

"Evening, Jeffrey," she said, twining a short lock of red hair around her finger.

Thomas sat back and watched his friend turn the charm on for the cute girl. Great legs, that was for sure.

"Coffee," Thomas said when it became apparent that the waitress hadn't even noticed he shared a booth with Jeffrey.

Fern flashed him a grin then. "I'll make that two. I know Jeffrey likes his coffee black," she said and sauntered off with a definite swing to her hips.

Thomas watched her go, appreciating the view. "Cute. I guess you come here often?"

"Often enough."

Thomas studied his friend. "She likes you."

Jeffrey shrugged.

"Enough to not even notice you had a guest at the table," Thomas pushed.

Jeffrey grinned. "Jealous? Strange turn of events. You always were the ladies' man."

Thomas's smile faltered. "Times change. We know that."

The waitress came back and set the coffee in front of them, promising to give them time to look the menu over.

Jeffrey opened his menu. "I recommend the steak and eggs. It doesn't get better."

"Sounds good." He took a sip of coffee. The silence between them stretched and Thomas hated every moment of it. "It's not like we are the ones estranged, my friend," he said quietly.

"No, we're not. For that I'm glad."

Thomas nodded. "I missed your friendship. I know that Gregore has also." He watched Jeffrey for signs of his intent. He'd become a master poker player, face never giving a hint of what went on behind his mask.

"You want my answer."

"I do."

Jeffrey drank his coffee, saying nothing for long moments. "I don't want to help."

Thomas's heart sank.

"But I will," Jeffrey continued. "What you said was true. None of us stands a chance without the other."

CHAPTER 29

A dozen candles flickered in the back room of the Grand Grimoire, illuminating the writhing skin of two lovers on the floor, pillaging power from one another. Deja arched her back. Her legs, framed in over-the-knee patent leather boots, spread on each side of Nick, heels digging into the ground on either side of his head.

He held back his release, keeping it as long as he could. Power sizzled in his veins, stinging as it whipped along his limbs, adding pain to the pleasure. A strange haze obscured the edges of his vision as the magic grew. Blood-red sparks shot out of his fingers. His toes. The haze bled into his vision, turning his view of Deja crimson.

His senses went into overload. He could smell the burning candle wicks as if he'd buried his nose in them. Every drop of sweat was numbered as it trickled down his chest and forehead. Deja's sweet essence tasted like ambrosia in his mouth. Nick let loose when he couldn't breathe any longer. The crescendo of his senses snapped off the moment he came, turning his world completely black.

A shallow hissing sound broke through the void. Nick recognized it as his breathing. In its wake was awareness of the heat of Deja as she sprawled over his chest. Golden light edged back into his vision, illuminating her beautiful body.

He rubbed a hand down her back. Watched his skin illuminate where he touched her. The glow spread up his arm to his shoulder and across his chest, down the other side. Deja lifted her head and gave him a lazy smile.

"I've heard of post-coital glow, but this is new." She waved her hand under his body.

He no longer touched the floor. Nick glanced down. They hovered nearly four feet off the ground. "What the—"

"Cool. Never seen that before. Can you get us back down?"

Nick chuckled. With the amount of power flowing through him, he could do anything. Get them down? Sure. But why, when he could take them higher? He wrapped her arms around his neck and mentally pushed higher. She let out a surprised laugh and held him tighter. He lit the remaining candles in the room and swayed with Deja back to the ground, setting her on her feet.

His body sizzled with electricity, with power waiting to escape. He pointed at a nearby table and mentally let loose. A lightning bolt ripped from his finger, flashed across the room and slammed into wood. The small table exploded into kindling. His eyes lit with excitement. Shit!

He opened his palms and allowed three crackling balls of blue energy to spring up in each. A nudge from his mind and all six twirled on the surface of his skin in a dizzying merry-go-round of light. On a whim, he slapped his palms together and crushed the balls. A deafening roar crashed through the building like thunder, shaking the walls on their foundations. Deja's eyes went round and she took a tentative step back.

Nothing was out of reach. Money was his for the taking. He could crush anyone who stood in his way of anything he wanted. No more scraping by. No more working for some loser with his head up his ass. He felt like a king. Hell, maybe he'd make himself a king. Anything he wanted, anytime.

Deja stepped away and slid into her miniskirt and tank top. She twirled her panties around her finger and studied him. "Feeling invincible, are we?"

He smirked.

"Too bad that euphoria doesn't last, eh?" She tossed the panties, hitting him in the chest.

Nick caught the red lace and pocketed the pair. He frowned when he realized she was right. A third of the power had drained from him. Much faster than it did with his hand jobs, which didn't build as much intense power as intercourse. "Perhaps not, but nothing a little sex can't cure."

"Going to have sex twenty-four/seven? That's a lot of tired women." Her eyes blazed, narrowed on him.

He tossed his head back and laughed. Deja almost looked jealous. Intriguing. "Perhaps I had something else in mind."

"A lot of tired men?"

Nick captured her wrist and tugged her against his chest. He swatted her butt. "I was thinking more of a party line."

The wicked light of interest sparked in her eyes. He had her then. Anything he wanted. What a heady concept.

"Have you ever made love as a gargoyle?" Tara whispered in his ear.

Gregore opened his eyes, aware of the setting sun, and smiled at the siren curled up beside him. He wanted to wake like this every day for the rest of his life.

She trailed her fingertips up the marble smooth skin of his chest, over his shoulder, and along the edge of his wing.

Rare few had seen him like this and none had touched him. "No," he said. "The few who know me like this are either men or afraid."

"Don't you think we should rectify that before breaking your curse?" She leaned down to trail her lips from his ear to his collar. "I think you should have the full gargoyle experience, just so you can say you did once this is over."

A rusty chuckle worked its way out of his chest. She never said or did what he expected. She was remarkable.

The sun dipped beyond the horizon and the change began.

Grasping her waist, he pulled her onto his chest. "You would make love with the beast?"

Tara shook her head. "I would make love with you. In a different form."

Something melted inside his chest. Her words touched him as nothing else could. He opened his mouth to say that when her lips twitched.

"You're already hard for me."

He snorted. Despite the desire darkening her eyes, he would wait a few more minutes until the change was through. He wouldn't risk hurting her with the heaviness of his limbs. Slipping a hand around her neck, he drew her down for a kiss. Their lips melded. Passion built until he felt it was safe. Flipping her over onto her back, he kissed his way down her neck. This time he would go slowly and savor every moment spent in Tara's embrace.

Later, Gregore watched Tara as she pulled one of his tee-shirts over her head. She looked good in his shirt. Especially when she bent over to pick up her discarded clothes. He reached out and caressed her bottom, earning him a gasp.

She laughed and swatted his hand away. He grabbed her hand and pulled her back to bed.

"Tell me about the bandage," he said, tracing his fingertips over the white gauze on her thigh.

Tara cleared her throat. "I, uh, went out yesterday. I found a store that sells things for different spell ingredients so I checked it out. When I was leaving, I ran into Saints."

Gregore stilled. His heart stuttered and his fist clenched. He would not lash out at her. Yet. "Tell me."

"He surprised me, slinging weapons he'd created out of the snow." She picked at non-existent lint on the sheets. "I drew him away to a nearby park, hoping to keep the civilians out of the crossfire. I held my own, but he got a lucky shot in. It's just a scratch. It's fine. Really."

He traced his fingers over the gauze, then pulled the edge up to look for himself. Her skin was sliced a couple of inches, the wound red and scabbed. The edges looked okay but one end was starting to swell. He replaced the bandage and sat back against the headboard.

"How did you get away?"

"Couple of kids came through and thought Saints and I were having a snowball fight. They distracted him long enough for me to get away. He didn't keep fighting, so I might have injured him."

"And the children?" Gregore asked. He kept his anger in check, but just barely.

"Fine. Saints staggered after me but I made it to the car. I'm fine, Gregore. Don't worry."

Don't worry. Those two words detonated the anger he'd held back. "He could have killed you and no one was there to back you up. You've seen the power Saints has and his vendetta against me. He knows you are helping me and you think for one moment that I won't worry for your safety? I don't want you going out alone again."

Tara drew herself up and faced him. "I'm a grown woman, Gregore. I can take care of myself and I don't need you dictating my actions. I managed fine without you."

Gregore's head snapped back, feeling the strike as if it had been physical. What could he say to that? He dare not acknowledge the pain her words caused.

"Gregore, I'm so sorry. I didn't—" Tara started.

He waved her words away. "Your leg proves otherwise." Gregore stood from the bed and went to the window, parting the curtains to look out at the sprinkle of stars just lighting the sky.

She came up behind him and wrapped her arms around his waist, pressing her body against his back. "You're right. It was terrifying. I'm just not used to someone worrying about me, looking out for me. Gregore, I can't do this alone. But even if I could, I don't want to. You're important to me."

He turned in the circle of her arms and lowered his head, capturing her mouth in a possessive kiss that said what he couldn't put into words. He let his fear for her pour through their mouths until she melted against him. Until the kiss changed and heated, passion ramping up to something more.

"I'm going to go get dressed," she whispered as she pulled away from him.

"Is there an option B?" he asked with a wolfish look.

"No. We've got work to do. Get dressed. There's a spell I want to try out." She tiptoed from the room then, giving Gregore a great view of her legs.

When she was gone, he reached for his pants and tugged them on. The spicy scent of Tara filled his nose, made him ache to have her again. He pulled on a clean shirt and padded toward the door. As his hand closed around the knob, he looked back at the rumpled bed where they'd made love, and became aware that something was different.

It was more than that she kept him off balance. He acknowledged that he very much wanted to wake up with Tara in his arms again. Though that didn't seem quite what stirred this new feeling. A lightness filled his chest.

He felt alive.

Stunned, Gregore stopped cold. Alive? Awake. He felt like he never had before and the feeling was indescribable. The sensations had been building for these last few days. Tara had changed him. Made him want more.

He wanted her. He wanted to go to bed beside her and wake up with her. He wanted to hear her laugh and listen as she talked about her day. Gregore ran his hands through his hair and closed his eyes. He imagined holding their child in his arms and was hit with an intense longing that nearly brought him to his knees. Once he'd dreamt of having children. Zola had inspired such desires until her death and this wretched curse had stolen such whimsy. He'd ruthlessly buried his dreams then. He thought them dead.

Until now.

Gregore swore. The implications of the track his thoughts took were almost too much to bear. He had two days left. A future was impossible if he didn't live to see it. First they had to break the curse, then he could consider more with Tara.

Wrestling his determination back into submission, he forced himself to open the door and go into the hall. Tara was just exiting her bedroom. She smiled brightly and kissed him. She still wore his shirt but slid into jeans that hugged her legs. Her hair flowed in dark auburn waves around her shoulders and her green eyes sparkled with tenderness. For him.

Gregore cupped her cheek and feathered his thumb over her lower lip. Then he turned and walked down the stairs. He heard her jog to catch up.

"Everything okay?" she asked.

He nodded as they stepped into the living room.

"Gregore, what's—"

He stepped off the landing, then grabbed her hand and pulled her out of the way of the door as it swung open. Maddy came in with a few shopping bags. Her odd eyebrows lifted in surprise.

Gregore took them from her and headed into the kitchen. Behind him, Maddy chatted about her day and what she bought, with Tara giving distracted replies. He unpacked the milk and put it into the refrigerator. The rest of the groceries looked like ingredients for a meal. Perhaps dinner. He filled the teakettle and put it on the stove to start heating. Making Maddy a cup of tea gave him a chance to put his mind on things other than Tara and his curse. He was just taking a cup out of the cupboard when the ladies came into the kitchen.

"Well, I think that is a wonderful idea, dear. A spell like that should be easy enough and who knows, you might learn something that will help. Don't you think, Gregore?" Maddy asked.

He half turned to look at them. "What idea is that, Aunt Maddy?"

"The spell to remember the night of the curse. She didn't tell you?" Maddy looked between Tara and him.

His heart tripped and his stomach plummeted. Gregore turned to Tara. "You want me to remember the night of the curse?" He could hardly believe... "Do you have any idea what it took for me to forget it? Why in the hell would I want to relive those terrible memories? Isn't losing my family once in my life enough?" His voice rose with each question. What kind of sadistic game was she playing? He pushed aside the niggling notion that it was easier to be pissed than reflect on his heart.

Tara flushed. "I know it will be painful..."

He opened his mouth to give a terse reply, but Maddy cut him off. "Don't you think it will help to know the exact words of the curse? Maybe it will help with the reverse."

Gregore clamped his mouth closed. He hadn't thought of that. He'd only thought of the emotional pain he'd have to endure with reliving the memories.

"Trust me, Gregore," Tara said quietly. "I don't want you to be hurt, but this may be what we need for the counter-curse. If you can remember every word the Gypsies said, maybe we won't need the spell from the book."

He was silent as he thought over her proposal. She was right, but not just about the spell. He hadn't trusted her when she mentioned it. He'd lived with the guilt of his actions for so long. Trusting Tara in this, when she had put aside so much to help him already, was right. If he didn't trust her now, he'd live with the guilt for the rest of his very short life. That was unacceptable. She didn't deserve that.

He nodded. "You're right. I do trust you."

Her lips trembled a bit as she smiled. Their eyes locked and he remembered the shared moments in his bed just a little while ago. He trusted her more than he'd trusted anyone in years. He was just slow to see it. Facing down their enemy, he couldn't afford to be slow in trusting his friends. Gregore pulled her to him and kissed her.

"Just don't trust my cooking," Tara said with a wink when she pulled back.

The teakettle whistled, startling them.

"Oh, you shouldn't have, you sweet boy." Maddy took her teacup from him and added her favorite tea. "Now off with you. I'll get dinner started, then be right there to help out."

Tara took Gregore's hand and led him to the living room. Laid on the table were several candles, two mirrors, a mortar and pestle, and several bags of herbs of some sort.

"What, no crocodile tears?" Gregore remarked.

"Well, the spell does call for it, but the shop didn't have any, so we'll just have to make do with salt water. Don't worry, it's the same, right? What could possibly go wrong?"

CHAPTER 30

"You're evil," Gregore groaned. "You can't help it, can you? It's in your blood."

Tara laughed. She gestured for him to sit on the chair. "Try to relax, this won't hurt a bit."

He snorted and the corners of his mouth tipped up.

She gathered the candles and put them into brass holders on the table. "You were right to say what you did," she said. "I didn't think about what it would be like to relive the events, even in your memory."

He closed his eyes and drew in a breath. A crease formed between his brows.

"Listen, if you don't want to do this..." she began.

"No," he said. "We must." Gregore opened his eyes and reached for her hand. Slid his thumb over the back of her palm. "Last night and this evening made me want..." *You.* "Things." He flicked a heated gaze up to her. "I want a real life. Not just half of one. I can't do that if I'm going to die in two days."

Tara squeezed his hand.

"I didn't come this far to fall short because of fear. I won't stop now. This is the best chance we have." He pressed a kiss to her palm. "Let's do it."

She sat beside him on the couch and leaned forward to open the bags of herbs. "You know I was kidding about the crocodile tears, right?"

"I hoped. That smells good. What is it?"

"Mostly flowers. The purple petals are periwinkle, lilacs, and everlastings. Those tiny dark-pink petals and the orange ones are from zinnias." She held up a bright green fan-like leaf. "These are ginkgo leaves, which are good for memory." Tara opened the last bag and poured out fragrant dark green leaves that were thin and nearly an inch long.

"Rosemary," he guessed. At her surprised look, he added, "I've cooked spaghetti for the priests every Friday for the last few months."

Tara chuckled. "I'm glad one of us can cook. At least we won't starve anytime soon."

Their eyes met.

Her words sounded like a promise of a future. He rubbed a hand over his heart to stem the ache that began. Would a woman like Tara settle for a man like him? She was everything he wanted and everything he didn't deserve.

She swallowed and he watched her lovely throat flex. "What happens when we break this curse?" she asked.

He lifted his hand and traced a long finger down the curve of her cheek. "If we—"

"When," she corrected.

"When we break this curse, I'll have to figure out once again where I belong in this world. I've spent so long looking for a cure, with barely a glimmer of hope that I would break the curse. It didn't seem wise to plan. It still doesn't."

"Even when you're this close?"

"Especially this close," he said.

She nodded. "I can understand not wanting to get your hopes up. The loss would be greater should we fail." She grinned impishly. "Since we won't fail, I suggest you start thinking about the rest of your life. You could do anything you want. Short of murder. I'd hate to bring you this far only to throw you in lockup for doing something stupid."

"I appreciate your candor, Detective."

Tara nudged him with her elbow. "I'm serious. In two days you'll be deciding your fate instead of gracing Maddy's garden."

"If I'm going to grace any garden, I'd rather grace yours, if it's all the same."

She sobered a little. "I don't have a garden. Not yet."

The weight of guilt settled on his shoulders. He frowned. "I've taken time from you. You should have been looking for a home instead of helping me."

She shook her head. "No. By helping you, I am helping myself. I know that Saints is the one who torched my place and planted those insurance papers. What I don't know is why or how to prove it."

"There must be some reason he is out for blood. Yours and mine. Or in my case, stone."

"Oh! I stopped at the library today." Tara stood and rummaged through her bag by the front door. "Here it is," she said and pulled a folded piece of paper out. She waved it and handed it to him. "A wise woman reminded me that anonymity is scarce these days."

He accepted the paper and studied the article and picture she'd printed. It showed a crowd gathered on a sidewalk in the setting sun. An ambulance was parked on the street, and two men loaded someone into the back of the vehicle. He could just make out the sign of the donut shop that was three blocks from the church. "I think I remember this scene. It looks familiar. I definitely know the neighborhood."

"I found a related article indicating that the three suspects turned themselves in, raving like lunatics about a stone creature. The officers gladly booked them."

"That would have made for an interesting story." He definitely knew that night. The thugs had tried to mug a woman, or possibly do more. She had fought back, been stabbed, and fell into the street. Straight into the path of an oncoming car.

"I think we know why Saints is targeting you. He was the fiancé of the woman who died."

"I made sure those thugs had their own ride to the police station. Why would he target me for that?"

"First, you're assuming he is sane. Second, and more importantly, who knows? But this is the connection. I know it. Like I know the scene is familiar to me also. I just can't figure out why." She folded the paper back up and set it aside, then surveyed the ingredients laid out on the table. "Ready to try this?"

No. "Yes."

Tara picked up the spell book and flipped a few pages. When she found the right page, she set the open book on the table. Flowers in different colors bordered the delicate script of the spell.

"It doesn't look too bad, if the flowers are anything to judge by. They aren't poisonous, are they?" he asked.

"Don't worry. You don't have to eat them."

"That doesn't answer the question," he pointed out.

Tara ignored him. "Read the flowers off to me."

He did so, watching her add them to the mortar. "Wait, those are purple."

She raised her eyebrow.

"Those are purple."

"True, but they're still periwinkle flowers. The color shouldn't make any difference. That's all of them, right?"

"Yes. Are you sure...?"

"Of course. Now the candles." Tara struck a match and lit the white and yellow candles. Reading from the book, she said, "Add the flowers and rosemary. Burn until only ash remains."

She struck a new match and set it to the mixture. A blue smoke curled up from the concoction, filling the room with an odd smell. Not smoky but certainly not the floral and rosemary scent he expected. They burned quickly down.

"Now take this mirror," she said and handed one to him.

"What do I do with it?"

"Hold it up and look at your reflection." She walked around behind the chair and leaned over his shoulder, holding the second mirror up. "Look into your mirror and try to see mine."

Gregore adjusted his mirror a little and nodded.

"Great," Tara said. From her angle, she could see the fine lines around his eyes. And the deep blue mesmerized her. She could see herself in the reflection of his mirror, her face side by side with his. It stirred something within her, seeing him there. She needed to succeed.

"Hold the mirror and look. Focus on the night you were cursed."

Drawing the power into herself, Tara repeated the words of the spell. "I call the past into the present. Force grey shadows to the past.

Bring what's lost to meet the light. And remember wrongs to make them right."

A punch of air slammed into Gregore, snapping his head back and making his vision swim with stars. One by one they winked out until all that remained was darkness.

Air expelled from Tara's lungs like she'd landed hard on her back with the wind knocked from her. She choked, unable to draw breath back in. Gregore's head fell back against her shoulder and his eyes closed. Breath shuddered from between his parted lips. He stilled. Tara struggled within her body, panicked. She couldn't breathe. Couldn't move. The edges of her vision dimmed.

Focus! Breathe.

She struggled until only pinpoints of light filled her sight. No. No, she needed to see the mirrors, needed to control the magic. This wasn't right. Her mind stilled, near passing out.

Stillness released her panic. Suddenly her lungs opened and beautiful air filled her body. Light replaced the darkness and the mirror came back into focus. Her eyes locked on the silver reflection, unable to see anything else.

Dark grey mist swirled in the oval mirror, turning and swirling like a maelstrom. The misting clouds turned black like a growing thunderstorm. Silver tinted the edges, making them glow as if with a life of their own. They twirled faster in the center, then stretched out, past the pane of glass. Curling fingers of mist floated toward her, filling the room until there was nothing but dark clouds.

Cold. She was so cold. Watery vapor touched her skin. It smelled clean, but dark in a way she couldn't describe. As if she was on the edge of the worst storm of her life. The edge of a tornado come to blow everything she knew away. Gregore was there with her. She could feel the press of his body against her chest. He took slow, shallow breaths, but otherwise didn't move.

Tara considered trying to wake him, then quickly discarded that. Hopefully he was learning what he needed to of the original spell.

Thunder crashed so loud in her hears, she jumped. She couldn't see anything but the dark clouds. Another thunderbolt. This one closer than before. The small hairs on her body rose with electricity. They were near, so near the storm. Too near.

Tara wrapped her free arm around Gregore and held him close.

A flash of silver blinded her. Thunder rattled the ground, shaking her in place. As the last tremor passed, a faint breeze blew in, and the black-grey clouds parted.

She smelled fresh, clean earth. The damp leaves of a forest. (Forest? That didn't make sense...) A drop of water slid down her throat and into the collar of her sweater. An owl hooted from somewhere nearby. She moved her arm from around Gregore to place her hand on his shoulder, keeping the connection but giving her freedom to look around more. Flickering firelight from a campfire lit the dark of night. They were in a clearing. Dozens of watchful black eyes stared at them. They were surrounded by people. Angry people with murder in their eyes.

With a flash of dread, Tara realized her mistake. She'd been caught in the mirror. Now she too would see the past.

Gregore moved then. He sank to his knees and bowed his head. Two men were forced to their knees beside him. A quick glance showed one was Thomas. The other, she assumed, was Jeffrey. Dark hair spilled over his face, obscuring his features. The fabric under her fingers changed, turning to linen. Gregore's hair was longer. His shoulders shuddered under her touch.

"I'm sorry," he whispered, reaching a hand out toward something on the ground in front of him.

Tara looked over his shoulder and found the still body of a young, beautiful woman. Her features were perfect. Plump pink lips, a perfect nose, and long black lashes. Her black hair fanned out all around and would easily reach her hips were she alive. Her figure was perfect too. Her breasts were full, and she had a flat stomach, hips perfectly proportioned. A Gypsy Barbie doll. No wonder Gregore had loved her.

Tara felt a pang of jealousy. Seeing the lovely Gypsy in the white dress laid out before him twisted a knife in her gut. She'd never be that perfect. She didn't look like a model, like this woman, and she certainly wasn't docile. Not overly feminine. She was tough. Most days, she was proud of that.

Looking at this woman, Tara admitted that today was not one of those days.

A low chant started. Blood for blood. Blood for blood. *Bloodforblood. Bloodforblood. Bloodforblood.*

Gregore tensed. She had only a moment to look at him before she realized what caused his reaction. The sea of faces parted to reveal a woman with wild white hair and eyes filled with rage and malice.

Tara's heart stuttered. Grandma Rose stepped forward. Or at least, her very likeness. The rage and malice in this woman's eyes had never been part of Rose's expression. But the wild, flowing white hair, thin lips, and strong but thin body were nearly identical.

The woman raised a bony, pale finger and pointed at Gregore. "You dare bring destruction to my family?"

Two men came forward and forced Gregore to stay on his knees. The woman seemed delighted by the roughness of their hands on Gregore. Tara tried to break their hold on him, but her hand went straight through. She was a ghost, caught in a dream. Unable to help Gregore, to shield him from this, she stood by his side. Every part of her ached at her helplessness. At his.

He opened his mouth to respond. "Madame, I beg you—"

"Silence!" She thrust her hand forward, closing it into a fist.

Tara felt power shoot from that wrinkled hand and envelop Gregore in its grip. He gasped and choked.

The woman looked to the dead girl. Her gaze flashed from pain to cold and emotionless so quick, Tara wondered if she'd imagined it. The woman now looked as if she'd never cared for the girl. Tara suddenly felt sorry for Zola. What must this girl's life have been like?

The witch finally released Gregore and he dragged in air. Clouds thickened above, blocking any sliver of the moon. The old woman smiled. There was no humor, only dark intent in her gaze.

Tara felt her heart lurch. She knew what would come next. What she and Gregore both needed to hear.

Gregore glanced at his friends, fear for them in his eyes. "Please," he whispered.

His plea fell on deaf ears. A boy shuffled forward and placed a familiar, red, leather journal in her hands. Newer, but no less frightening. Especially in the hands of this woman. She laughed an ugly sound, and stepped over the dead body of her granddaughter. She yanked Gregore's head back. Forced his gaze to meet hers.

"You believe you love her, English? You know nothing of love." She spat on him. "Your heart is stone, just as you shall be." She released him to open the book and turned to the page she sought. "Blood for blood? Nay. A life for a life."

A roar of approval went up from the surrounding crowd of onlookers. Thunder echoed overhead. Fierce wind blew through the clearing, lifting the woman's white hair in a wild cloud. Her eyes glinted in menace and her wrath seemed to fuel the storm. She began a low chant, allowing it to grow with the storm. Icy rain slammed all around them, soaking through clothes to skin.

Tara shivered and stepped closer to Gregore. His eyes were tortured, tearing at her heart.

The old Gypsy, the one who looked so much like her dear Grandma Rose, finished her chant and slammed the book closed.

She taunted Gregore, letting him know he would suffer for what happened that night. Then she uttered the words they wanted to hear. "I condemn you to a half life, just as you have condemned me."

Thomas cried out, begging her to stop. Gregore was innocent. They all were.

The woman scoffed, her hate of the English shining through. "I am not without mercy," she said.

Tara would have laughed, if her heart wasn't already breaking. This woman had no mercy in her. Not an ounce of love. Nothing but hate and revenge and darkness.

"Think you can break my curse, English? I give you one hundred fifty years to try."

Gregore struggled in his captor's arms. He briefly broke their hold, only to have more men capture and hold him still.

The witch lifted her hands, channeling the power of the storm. The wind roared, the thunder boomed, drowning out her words.

"No!" Tara yelled, struggling against the storm. The gale winds blew her back, keeping her from advancing much farther. She strained to hear the words. Tried to read her lips. Only snatches of the curse came through.

...the power of Gypsies...By the power of...I see...dead and hollow... craft a curse...back...revenge then...three...

The rest of her words were lost as the storm clouds descended, closing around her like a shield. The last thing she saw was Gregore struggle, then fall to the ground, Thomas right behind him. There was a blur of motion, then swirling darkness.

"Tara."

A hand shook her shoulder. "Tara, wake up, dear."

She cracked her eyelids open, her vision filling with Aunt Maddy's worried gaze. "Maddy?"

Maddy took her hand and pulled her up. Only then did Tara realize she had been flat on her back on the floor. "What? What happened?" She felt moisture on her cheek and wiped the tear away.

"The spell. Did you learn anything?"

Tara looked for Gregore. He lay in the chair, his head tipped back against the cushion. A mirror dangled in his fingertips. He breathed easy, as if he was just sleeping.

She shook her head. "No. Not enough." She couldn't bring herself to voice the thing that pained her nearly as much as being there. The woman had looked identical to Grandma Rose. She wouldn't bring that pain to Maddy. Couldn't.

"I don't know what happened, Maddy. I wasn't supposed to be there. Gregore was supposed to remember. And when it came time to hear what I needed, the wind was too loud." She fisted her hand. "Damn it, this should have worked," she ground out. *I screwed up*, she thought. Her stomach hurt and her chest ached.

The mirror dropped uselessly from Gregore's fingers, clattering to the floor. "Is he okay?" she asked.

Maddy nodded. "Sleeping."

"Damn it," Tara muttered, angry with herself. "I should have listened to him. He knew that the flower color mattered." She righted her clothes, went to Gregore, and placed a hand on his cheek. "Wake up, handsome."

He didn't stir. His breath was shallow and slow. Shallower than if he'd been in a deep sleep. She shook his shoulder. "Gregore, wake up."

Still no response. Goose bumps slid down her arms. What had she done?

"Gregore!" She shook him hard.

He didn't even flinch.

"Oh God," she whispered, sinking to her knees in front of him. "Maddy, what have I done? Why won't he wake up?" She shook him harder, calling his name over and over.

Nothing.

Maddy pulled her back from him. "Stop. Stop!" She captured Tara's wrists and pulled her around to look at her. "He sleeps. He is caught in your spell, dear. He won't wake until the spell wears off."

"But then why am I awake? Isn't it over?"

Maddy shrugged. "Getting even one thing wrong changes a spell. It works. It doesn't work. It gives unintended consequences. All you can do is wait."

"How long?" Tara whispered. "How long until you think he'll wake?"

"I don't know, dear. All you can do is wait."

CHAPTER 31

Bong...Bong...Bong...

Tara peeled an eyelid open, looking for the obnoxious sound. The hall clock. It was just past three in the morning. She sat up too fast, and her head spun. She blinked a few times to clear away the cobwebs from sleep and looked to Gregore.

He still lay slumped in the chair, exactly as he had been since the spell had gone so horribly wrong. Her brow furrowed. *What if he doesn't wake up? No. He will. He must, or I'll haunt his dreams for eternity.*

She stretched, then rose and tucked the blanket back around his shoulders. He looked terribly uncomfortable, with his head back on the rest and his body tilting to the side. She and Maddy hadn't been able to move him. She was strong, but two hundred muscular pounds of dead weight were more than she could carry. They'd propped his feet up on the coffee table and tried to make him look more comfortable. She frowned, fairly sure he wasn't. He was going to wake with an awful pain in his neck.

Grabbing a small throw pillow off the couch, she tucked it under his neck and gave him more support.

Damn fool, she muttered to herself. *You should have listened to him about the flower color.* Then, *Please let him live through this. I'd never forgive myself...*

He couldn't end up like her parents. It would kill her. Because as much as she didn't want to admit it, the big lug meant something to her. She wanted to spend whatever time she had left with him. Whether that be one day or one thousand. She took a breath. No, she wasn't a child anymore. Just like being more in control of her body, she could control the magic.

Tara sank back onto the couch where she'd fallen asleep watching him. She pulled the pink crocheted blanket back over her legs and lay down on her side. He was peaceful. If he didn't wake before his time was up, at least she gave him that.

Please let him wake. I don't want to take on Saints alone.

Nick Saints was powerful. Maybe more powerful than herself. What she needed was strength in numbers. Maybe even the element of surprise. She needed Gregore to wake and Thomas and Jeffrey to show. Saints might be strong in magic, but he was only a man. If they could overpower him, she could arrest him. Tomorrow they'd find Saints and end this.

She watched Gregore until her eyes grew heavy. Thinking about all the things they had been through. Sliding a little further into the cushion, she decided she wouldn't let a colossal screw up like this change things now when so much mattered.

>―◆>―O―◆―◁

Nick watched the Wednesday afternoon commuter traffic filter out of the city from the window of the warehouse. He swept a blond lock of hair off his forehead and wiped the perspiration away. The offices in the warehouse were warmer than usual tonight, thanks to a little magical help. He wanted the witches very comfortable for the night he had planned. He'd purchased some mattresses and fitted them with black satin sheets, then added some of those fancy throw pillows women liked and a lot of candles. He even hung sheer fabric in different colors from floor to ceiling, making the room more appealing than an abandoned office in a decrepit old building. After lighting some incense to banish the smell of seafood, he laid out a few specialty items he'd picked up at the local adult store, and stepped back to admire his work.

It looked like a Gypsy tent or maybe a harem. Maybe he'd have his own harem, he thought wolfishly. A place where women would feed his need for power day or night. He needed the feel of the magic in his blood. Not the weak Gypsy magic he'd started with in that ridiculous book, but the real thing. The true power he'd discovered, thanks to Deja.

Nick licked his lips. If she wanted to stay with him, she could. He'd allow that. So long as she didn't get in his way. If she did, well, he'd deal with her then. First he had to take care of the gargoyle and that detective once and for all. Then he'd ruin them. He owed Samantha that.

He swallowed the bile that rose just thinking her name. She wouldn't want this for him. She wouldn't want...He ruthlessly thrust the thoughts away. She was dead and it didn't matter what she wanted anymore. All that mattered were his wants now. And he wanted to burn.

The door downstairs closed, pulling him from his thoughts. He checked to make sure the wine was ready, since he'd added a special ingredient, then left the room and went to the top of the stairs, overlooking the warehouse floor.

"Ladies. Please join me." He beckoned to them, willing them to want what he wanted.

Six women of all different colors, all in their early twenties, smiled at him. Deja led them up the stairs.

Nick escorted them back to his chamber and held the door. When Deja passed, he took her arm and pulled her close. "You've outdone yourself, sweet."

She winked at him. "We're ready to play when you are."

"I'm more ready than you know." Nick closed the door and turned some music on low. The ladies looked around his newly designed room, slipped out of their ridiculously high heels, and sank into the pillows. He poured wine into goblets and passed one to each woman. "A toast," he said, "to a very pleasurable evening."

⊰ CHAPTER 32 ⊱

The lily pads never moved on the lake, Gregore noticed with a frown, even though a slight breeze drifted. He sat outside his estate in England on the soft green grass, facing the lake, unable to leave. Caught in a dream that hazed around the edges of his vision.

What he needed was a gale. Hurricane force, preferably. Something to make the frog go away.

"I don't care if you are Sleeping Beauty. I am not kissing you," the frog said.

Gregore blanched. "I don't want to be kissed. I want you to go away."

"You invited me," the frog grumbled, sounding vaguely familiar.

Gregore stared at the frog, trying to place the creature's voice. He'd heard those deep tones before. "Can we go back to when you just stared at me and croaked?"

"Croaked," the frog said, drawing the word out as if he had no idea what Gregore meant. As if Gregore were crazy.

He glared at the frog.

The frog was unmoved by his fierceness.

"You do know that they serve frog legs as a delicacy in some places."

"Frog le…I think it's past time for you to snap out of it," the frog said.

It almost sounded like…no. That wasn't possible. Was it? "Jeffrey?"

"Yeah. And before you ask, that old witch Griselda didn't turn me into a frog. So I'm not kissing you. You're not my type."

Gregore blinked, the lily pads and frog fading from sight and replaced by a man he hadn't seen in ages. Thomas stood behind Jeffrey, wearing a wide grin that promised Gregore would never live any of this down. Someone squeezed his left hand. Gregore looked down to find soft fingers wrapped around his, and followed them back to the beautiful sight of Tara's face.

"He's back," Jeffrey said and clapped him on the shoulder. "For a minute there, I was worried. You start making googly eyes at me, and I'd have had to hit you."

Thomas threw back his head and roared with laughter.

Gregore's cheeks heated, though he admitted it felt good to be teased. Like old times. He rubbed his eyes and refocused on Maddy's living room. He felt pretty rested. "When did you guys get here?"

"About half an hour ago," Jeffrey said.

"While you were getting your beauty sleep," Thomas added.

"You might want to sleep more," Jeffrey said. "It didn't work."

"Why did we invite them?" Gregore asked Tara. She smiled, but faint lines tightened around her eyes. He cocked his head. He'd never known her to be quiet. He sat up fully and turned to her, holding her hand. "What is it?"

She shook her head. "I...I just worried about you," she said. "You were out a long time. The spell backfired." She slipped her hand from his. Tucked a dark strand behind her ear. "I thought you wouldn't wake up in time."

"Hey, it's all right," he said, taking her hand back.

"No, it's not," she said and glanced at Thomas and Jeffrey.

Thomas caught her gaze and cleared his throat. "Uh, Jeffrey. How about some tea?"

Jeffrey didn't take his eyes off Tara. "No, thanks. I'm good."

"I think you want some tea, Jeffrey. You really want tea. In fact, how long has it been since you've had some? A hundred years?" Thomas grabbed his friend and pushed him from the room. He winked at Gregore over his shoulder.

Gregore shook his head. "Jeffrey hates tea," he said when his friends were gone. "Hated the stuff in England, probably hates it even more now." He slid his palm over the top of her hand, still held in his other. "Tell me."

She closed her eyes and swallowed. When she opened them again, she seemed stronger, the worry gone from her eyes and replaced with a strength of determination. "I hate being weak."

Gregore wrapped a hand around the back of her neck and pulled her toward him, kissing her mouth with exquisite tenderness. "You are the strongest person I know," he said against her lips. "Strong. Smart. A pain in the ass. Perfect."

She snorted. "Perfect enough to screw up a spell and nearly make you sleep through the last hours of your life."

"Not everyone gets to go in his sleep. I'd have been lucky."

She moved into his lap. "Lucky? Hardly. Killed by the family that cursed you."

He traced a finger down her cheek. He couldn't brush her words off. She'd see the lie for what it was. "Neither one of us know what the next hours bring. You've made the last days the best of my life. Do you understand? Nothing can take that away. And if the worst happens, I'll go knowing I spent my time with the woman I…" He what? Loved? He couldn't say the word. "Care for."

She buried her head in his neck. Placed a kiss against his skin. "I care for you too."

Her lips lingered, heating his flesh. He reacted as he always did, with instant desire. He pulled her closer and lifted her lips to his. She opened her mouth and accepted his kiss, taking him deeper. Gregore pressed her body flush with his, cupping her bottom.

A throat cleared.

Gregore pried himself away and glared at the throat.

"Do not tell me I'm holding a ridiculous cup full of vile acid just so you can make out with your girl here," Jeffrey rumbled from the door to the kitchen. He held a delicate pink, flowered cup in one hand and a matching saucer in the other.

"Oh, I think that is exactly what you're doing, mate," Thomas piped up from behind him. He sipped his own tea and grinned. "But since Gregore is clearly finished licking her tonsils for the moment, I think it's a fine time to talk about what's what."

Tara tried to rise from Gregore's lap. With her cheeks flushed pink, her color matched Jeffrey's teacup. Gregore anchored his hands on her hips and held her in place. "Stay," he said. She cocked an eyebrow at him, but then settled back against his chest. To Thomas and Jeffrey he said, "Sit. We'll talk."

Jeffrey scowled.

Thomas laughed.

Jeffrey set the pink abomination of god-awful tea on the coffee table and sprawled on the couch. Thomas plopped down beside him.

He looked around the small living room. It was cozy, with a floral couch and chair, coffee table, and lace curtains. A musty scent tickled his nose. Mothballs and the elderly, steeped in fragrant roses. Gregore's woman, Tara, watched him with interest. She was pretty, with those green eyes and dark curls. Her body wasn't as voluptuous as Zola's, but Gregore didn't seem to mind. Intellect flashed behind her eyes as she studied him and Thomas. She shifted slightly, placing herself in front of Gregore. Protecting him. Interesting.

He sat forward, shifting his thoughts to Gregore. He was clean and well groomed, wearing clean dark jeans and a sweater. He didn't smell of even a smidgen of alcohol. Jeffrey would have been able to detect it at a distance. Gregore looked well.

"I'm here," Jeffrey said. "Talk. How do you think the three of us can break the curse when we couldn't before?"

"It's not that simple," Gregore said.

Jeffrey closed his eyes. Ran a hand over his face. "It never is. Tell me, don't you have a birthday coming up?"

Tara's eyebrows rose and she looked between Gregore and himself. "What? When's your birthday?"

Gregore muttered something that sounded suspiciously like "same damn day every year."

She pinched him. "Be nice. When's your birthday?"

"Two days," Gregore said. He pressed his lips into a thin line. "I was cursed on my birthday by that evil bitch. If she has her way, I'll die on it." To Jeffrey he said, "I found the spell book. Actually, Tara had it."

Jeffrey nodded. "So Thomas said. He also mentioned that someone stole the spell."

Tara flushed, but straightened her spine. She faced Jeffrey fully. "We found the spell book, but the spell's been ripped out."

Ice crawled down Jeffrey's spine. He glared first at Thomas and then Gregore. "The spell book was found. Then stolen and found again, but you don't have the spell. How do you propose to break this curse?"

Thomas shifted on the couch. "Tara is a direct descendant of Griselda. She can break the curse."

Jeffrey stood and paced away, running his hands through his dark hair and tugging at the strands. He drew in a deep breath and let it out. "Listen, you've got to give me something more." He waved to Tara. "Something more than we can do this together and this woman is a direct descendent, blah, blah, blah. You've got two days, Gregore. Two days and then this conversation is pointless."

"Kingston," Thomas started.

Jeffrey cut him off with a glare.

Gregore's eyes creased and his jaw set. "All right, you want it straight. Is that it? Here you go." He moved Tara off his lap and stomped over to Jeffrey, getting in his face. "I fucked up. First, I got us cursed. Then I pushed away the only friends I had, the only people I could rely on. Once I got my hands on the book, it was literally ripped away within minutes and the last hope for all of us went with it. I met this amazing woman, turned her life upside down, and nearly got her killed."

"It's about time you realized that you've dragged more than your sorry ass through the mud," Jeffrey growled back. "We're tired of eating dirt in your wake."

Gregore looked away. He took a step back and dropped his head.

Jeffrey swore. He felt like an ass. Gregore was ashamed. What kind of a friend was he, rubbing in something none of them could have seen coming. Jesus, he should walk now. But damn it, he couldn't. Not yet.

"You're right. I'm sorry," Gregore mumbled. "I've got nothing and I know it."

SET IN STONE

Tara stepped in between them and thrust a finger in Jeffrey's chest. "Hey, buddy. Do you know what this man has been through just in the last few days? He's trying. It's my fault we lost the damn spell, so if you're going to make anyone feel like shit, it should be me."

Jeffrey held up his hands, palms out. He didn't want to admit it, but he admired anyone that cute who would get in his face. "Noted."

Then she turned her wrath on Gregore. "How long do we have?"

Lines of pain bracketed Gregore's eyes as he said, "Hours at best. Once the sun is up, we just have the remainder of the day. After midnight tomorrow..." He shrugged. "It's anyone's guess."

"Then we have to get to work."

Jeffrey stared at Gregore over the top of Tara's head. Pain and sadness mixed in his friend's eyes. Gregore glanced down at Tara, and his countenance changed, softened. When he looked back up, there was the barest trace of hope. He cared deeply for her, Jeffrey realized. He'd never seen Gregore look at Zola like that.

Tara put her hands on her hips, unaware of the silent exchange. "Well?" When no one spoke, she said, "Fine. I'll figure it out. You guys just sit around and glare at each other for awhile." She stalked out of the room and disappeared into the kitchen.

Jeffrey watched her go. "She's something else."

Thomas's eyes glittered. "Maybe if Gregore strikes out, you can have a go. Say three days from now?"

"You won't touch her," Gregore barked.

Thomas threw his head back and laughed.

"Your woman is safe from me," Jeffrey said. "But I'd keep an eye on Thomas, were I you."

Gregore scowled at them both with a look that said, *she's mine.*

Thomas waggled his eyebrows.

"You're killing me," Gregore said with a groan.

Jeffrey crossed his arms over his chest. "You don't need our help with that. You're well on your way."

Gregore's face darkened and he worked his jaw, visibly keeping his lips clamped together.

Jeffrey pushed him, needing to finally get this off his chest. "I'm not here for a repeat. Thomas and I chased after you for years and what did we get for it? A bunch of bruises, a nasty scar, and a broken rib." He pointed at Thomas. "If it weren't for him, I wouldn't be here. I owe you nothing. The friendship we had was over the night you turned on us for trying to help."

"Then why are you still here?" Gregore asked. "I've already said I fucked up. I've already said I was sorry. What the hell more do you want?"

Jeffrey leaned in close and said in a low voice, "I want that man sitting behind you to not suffer anymore." He jerked his head at Thomas.

"I want that too," Gregore replied.

Jeffrey nodded. "I'll help if there is any hope of breaking that curse. But tell me now if there isn't. Can your girl do this?"

"If there is a way, then she will." Gregore's mouth lifted in a half smile. "Never seen someone more determined."

"You care for her."

"I do. Perhaps too much for so late..." His eyes glazed as if in memory. When they refocused on Jeffrey, he added, "I know you owe me nothing, but I would ask a final favor. In honor of the friendship we once had."

"You can ask." *But I don't promise...* remained unspoken.

"If things go wrong, if...if it's too late, will you watch over her? She's strong, but vulnerable. Maddy is the only family she has left. I don't think she has close friends. She needs someone to look out for her, even if she doesn't know it."

He didn't want to commit. Damn, he didn't want to commit. Jeffrey swore to himself. He knew a dying wish when he heard one and this was one hell of a request. He kept to himself in his cabin. He only saw people when he was sure he could keep his own demon under control. He was perfectly damn happy on that big damn mountain with no damn people. Traipsing around after a woman who wasn't his in a big city was a nightmare to even contemplate. What if his demon got loose? What could happen to the innocent bystanders? Why was he even considering this?

Jeffrey looked to Thomas, who sat in the corner watching the exchange. Thomas gave a slight nod. Damn. Damn, damn, damn. Thomas was right. This wasn't about him. This was about honoring his longtime friend and making sure a woman didn't get hurt. And if he started to change... "Thomas and I will do it," he said.

Gregore expelled a breath, his shoulders sagging slightly. "You have no idea what this means to me."

"I know what it means to *me* now," Thomas griped under his breath. Jeffrey chuckled.

"She'll be in good hands," Gregore said. "I trust you both."

"Of course she will. I have great hands," Thomas said as he stood. "If you don't plan to be around much longer, then perhaps I'll go acquaint her with them now." He laughed at Gregore's glare. "I meant give her a hand. With the research. So touchy!" He shook his head and went to find Tara.

"There is nothing he wouldn't do for you. You know that, right?" Jeffrey asked.

Gregore nodded. "He could have easily stayed away. Let this happen. He didn't have to come find me." He laid a hand on Jeffrey's shoulder. "Neither did you."

"What can I say? I'm a softie." *Or a sucker*, he thought.

Gregore snorted. "All the same, it means a lot to me." He paced away to the front window. "I never meant to hurt you. Either of you. If I could turn back time, I would change everything."

"Everything? Even Zola?"

"Even Zola," Gregore replied. No hesitation.

"You loved her. Do you really think you could walk away from her if you were to do it all again?"

Gregore shook his head and turned to lean against the glass. "No."

Jeffrey pursed his lips and nodded. "I didn't think—"

"No, I didn't love her," Gregore corrected. "I thought I did at the time. I thought she was perfect."

"But no longer?"

Gregore shook his head. His gaze skated to the kitchen.

Jeffrey rubbed the back of his neck. Had it been time that dulled his friend's feelings or the new woman? He'd ask, but he wasn't here to talk about their feelings. He shuddered. If they started down that trail, he may as well order a couple of lattes and go buy a purse.

"I don't deserve your forgiveness," Gregore said, returning to the original conversation. "I'd like it anyway."

Jeffrey stuffed his hands in his jeans. He couldn't. Not yet.

CHAPTER 33

Gregore was going to die and it was Tara's fault. She paced the length of the kitchen, wracked with pain because she couldn't help him. Her family started this and her limited magic was going to end it in the worst way possible. She stopped in front of the refrigerator and thumped her head against it a couple of times. Her eyes stung, watered, but not from the fridge. Her heart ached for Gregore.

"Don't hurt yourself," Thomas said absently as he considered the cookie jar.

Tara cursed herself and returned to the grimoire on the kitchen table. She slumped into the chair and idly turned the pages until she came to the ragged edge of the removed spell. She'd exhausted all of her and Maddy's knowledge for breaking curses and had nothing to show for it.

As if on cue, Maddy wandered into the kitchen in her pink robe and bunny slippers, yawning. "My, those boys are a hot lot. Makes a woman want to be twenty years younger." She fanned herself with her hand.

Thomas grinned and winked at her elderly aunt.

Tara mashed her lips together to keep from laughing.

"What are you doing up, Maddy? It's late," she said.

"I was thirsty. Besides, I'm not so old that I have to sleep through all the excitement."

Tara grinned. Trust Maddy to chase away her insecurities with silliness, even if only temporarily.

"I'd ask why you weren't out there with Gregore and the other man, but I think I know. You'll figure it out. I have every faith you can break the curse."

She accepted a hug from her aunt. It was comforting in a Grandma Rose kind of way. "I'm glad you believe, Maddy. I have my doubts."

Thomas cocked a hip against the counter. "Don't. You can do this. We're counting on you."

"But no pressure," Tara mumbled to herself.

Maddy patted her shoulder and then went to the cupboard for a glass. She reached into the refrigerator for milk.

"Rose would be so proud." Tara said to her aunt. "You've made this house a home again,"

Maddy's eyes glistened with moisture. "Oh, I do hope so. Do you like your room? I never did ask you."

Tara swallowed around the lump in her throat. "It's just exactly as she had it when she was alive. At first, it was tough. But now it is comforting instead of painful. I think... I think maybe it's time I let go."

"She would want that for you, dear. I know she's looking down on you even now, happy for the man you've found." Maddy wagged a finger at her. "She believes in you too, so don't you forget it."

"Of course she does," Gregore said from the doorway. "We all do."

He entered and rested his large hand on Tara's shoulder, gently squeezing. Jeffrey came in behind him.

Thomas stealthily opened the cookie jar and sniffed the contents like a shark hunting out blood.

She chuckled and rose from the chair. Knowing Thomas, he'd sweet talk Maddy into cooking something for him and Jeffrey.

"I should grab my phone to see if I have any messages from Carson. He was checking into Saints."

Walking to the front door, she paused at the entry table and grabbed her purse. She rifled through it and frowned. Her phone was there, but where the hell were her keys now? She didn't need them at the moment, but it drove her crazy that she'd misplaced them again. She checked under the pillow on the chair, the floor, and the coffee table. No keys.

Grumbling, she went up to her room to search the side table, vanity and dresser drawers. Nothing. Gnomes. Gnomes were real, very much alive, and constantly stealing her keys. That was the only explanation for the fact that they were never where she left them.

Tara snapped her fingers. The spell for finding something lost. At least she knew where that was. She returned to the kitchen and slipped into her chair. As she suspected, Maddy had finished her milk and now had a skillet on the stove. She regaled the guys with a story about her and Grandma Rose in their days as young women as she chopped up a green pepper.

Tara grinned and flipped to the front of the spell book. This particular spell was in the section she liked to think of as BP. Before Psycho. Before the writer sought ways to harm people.

It was fairly simple really. All she needed was a candle, more incense for ambiance, and something resembling the object she wanted to find. If it worked, she could use this for all kinds of lost things. Keys, money, anything that was missing.

She stilled, her hand on the page. Anything? Even paper?

Excitement pulsed through her blood. Keys forgotten, she grabbed a napkin and bookmarked the spell to find lost items, then flipped to the curse. She ran her finger over the jagged edge of the page and dared to hope.

"Gregore," she said, barely containing her excitement. "I know how to get the spell back!"

Everyone fell silent. Gregore turned. "If this involves confronting Saints..."

Tara's heart melted at the worry on his face. She stood and went to him, wrapping her arms around his neck and dragging his head down for a kiss. She'd expected his interest, his excitement that she could get the spell. This was what he wanted. What he'd been trying to find for over a century. Instead, his first response was clear concern for her. How could she not lo...care for this man? She broke the kiss and cupped his cheeks.

"It doesn't," she said.

His shoulders relaxed beneath her hands.

"I can recreate the page. I can't believe I never thought about it before. It's so simple. We can finally do this."

Midnight-blue eyes stared back at her with heat. Then he was crushing her to him and plundering her mouth with kisses. His hands roamed over her body, up her back and down her sides, settling at her waist. He lifted his head and cupped a large hand against her cheek. "No matter what happens with the curse, I've never cared for another as much as you."

She smiled and kissed his palm. "You've never done or said what I expected. Now let me do this. Let's break the curse."

"Sounds good to me," Thomas said. "It's getting a little too hot in here. Much more of the mushy stuff, and I'll have to throw open a window." He stepped around Gregore and clapped a hand on his shoulder. "Jeffrey can help you. I'm working with Maddy on food."

Jeffrey rolled his eyes, but nodded.

Tara looked between the four people and saw trust and belief on their faces. She could do this.

Gregore kept his hands on Tara as she danced with excitement about the spell.

She smiled and took his hand, giving it a squeeze. "I've got a few things to gather first. I want all the help we can get."

"What can we do?" he asked.

"Can you find me a candle and some incense?" Tara asked. "I will find some suitable paper."

Gregore retrieved the items from the living room and brought them back to her. She set the candle and incense beside a blank sheet of paper.

Maddy tapped the spoon against the skillet. "You probably need some quiet, don't you dear?" To Thomas she added, "Be a love and get us some plates. We'll take the food to the living room and give Tara a chance to concentrate."

"Thanks Maddy," Tara said. "I definitely don't want to screw this one up."

One by one, they filed out. Gregore was the last to leave. He leaned down to nuzzle Tara's neck. "You can do this," he whispered. "I have faith."

"What if I—"

"You won't. Once this is all over, maybe you and I can go somewhere. Just the two of us."

"That sounds nice," she said. Tara turned in her seat and pressed a tender kiss to his lips. "I'll hold you to that."

Gregore cupped her cheek, pressed a quick kiss to her lips, and left the kitchen.

Jeffrey and Thomas sat in the living room with Maddy, who listened avidly to a tale of their youth. Maddy laughed so hard, her eyes watered. Even Jeffrey cracked a smile.

Gregore accepted a plate of pasta from Maddy and took a seat on the floor. To Thomas he said, "Don't forget the part where you agreed to wear her dress if she would—"

"We're not telling that part of the story," Thomas quickly interjected.

Maddy doubled over with laughter. "Oh but you must tell us now."

Thomas reddened. "All right, but you must swear to never repeat this."

Gregore grinned. He had just stuffed another bite into his mouth when he heard Tara swear. He set the plate aside and went to her.

Stepping into the cozy kitchen space, he found Tara in tears.

He was beside her in an instant, wrapping his arms around her. They'd been gone five minutes. What the hell could have happened in that time? Crying women were a mystery, no matter how old a man was. He took in the scene around him before he asked. A lit candle was on a plate on the table and the spell book was open to an ugly picture of a winged creature that looked familiar. Nothing that would induce tears. Gregore stroked her back. "What is it?"

She wiped a tear away. "I thought I'd done it. I thought this was it and I'd break the curse." She waved to the grimoire. "The spell worked, but it didn't help. I... I'm sorry, Gregore." She trailed off and pushed past Jeffrey and Thomas who stood in the doorway.

Gregore watched her disappear up the stairs, then turned back to the book.

"That's new," Thomas said, bending over the pages.

"What is?" Jeffrey and Gregore asked in unison.

"That ugly image of your mug," Thomas said. "There wasn't a picture of you in the book before, Gregore. She did it. She restored the page."

They crowded around the new sheet.

Gregore drew in a tight breath. "She did it." He traced a finger over the brittle paper, perfectly recreated as if it had never been torn out. In that moment, he knew why she cried. Disappointment. Crushing disappointment. The new page held the original spell and what amounted to a riddle.

By the power of Gypsies and mages
By the power of mavens and sages
By the moon and through its stages
By the Sphinx and through the ages
By the night of darkness and sorrow
I see your heart be dead and hollow
I see your blood turn murky black
I craft a curse upon your back

I reap revenge then cast times three
I twist your greatest vanity
Your heart is soft, your love a waste
You fly aloft, and run with haste
You must atone, no longer free
Your body stone, so shall it be!

Only by my blood and tears
Freely given with no fears
Wrapped in a love you can see
Only then shall ye be free.

Each stared at the page.
"I hate riddles," Thomas said.
"I hate psychotic old witches," Jeffrey added.
Gregore couldn't have agreed more.

When Tara didn't come back after a few minutes, Gregore went to find her. She sat on her bed, hands clasped in front of her and staring out at the melting snow dropping off the roof.

"You did everything right," he said. He sat on the bed and scooted behind her, nestling her between his legs and wrapping his arms around her waist. She laid her head on his shoulder but didn't look at him.

"I should have thought of this earlier. Why didn't I think of this before now? I mean...find something lost. How hard is it to connect the dots? I'm a detective! I connect dots all day long!"

"Stop now. A week ago you wanted nothing to do with any of this. Today you recreated a page we thought lost forever. At every step you've amazed me. You've made me laugh and had more courage than most men I've known. This is a small setback, nothing more."

She snorted. "Yeah, small. We've only to figure out a riddle older than you before you turn to stone."

"You make it sound so simple," Gregore agreed, trying for lightness he didn't feel.

That earned him a watery laugh. She wiped the remaining tears from her face.

Gregore placed a kiss on her neck, lingering. "Tara, you are more than I ever thought you would be. The magic of the Gypsies truly does flow in your blood. I know you can still break this curse. For me. For us."

She shivered. "For us. I like that. You truly believe that I can do this before time runs out."

"Mmmm," he agreed, trailing his lips down the warm skin of her neck. He brushed his palms up her flat stomach, cupping her breasts. She arched into his hands and speared her fingers into his hair. His body responded, needing to give her the comfort she sought. He pulled back and whisked her pink sweater over her head. Laid her down in the soft blankets of the bed and covered her body with his own. "Let me give you this," he whispered against her mouth. "Won't take long."

She nodded and opened herself to him. Gregore settled himself against her and kissed away her pain.

Later, Tara stretched and rubbed her naked body against Gregore's. "I feel so energized," she said. "Stronger. Like each time we make love, you increase the flow of my magic."

He winked at her. "Guess I'm just that good."

She laughed and thumped him with a pillow.

His lips tipped up in a smile. "Come downstairs and whip us old men into gear." He slid out from behind her, taking her hand and pulling her to her feet.

"We might not have *that* much time."

He swatted her butt. They dressed and he followed her downstairs. He hadn't lied. He knew she could break the curse. But a small voice whispered that it wouldn't be that easy. Griselda meant him to suffer. So did Nick Saints.

No. It wouldn't be easy at all.

CHAPTER 34

His coffee was cold, damn it. He'd already ordered a refill and a warm-up on the current cup. Short of heating it himself with a flash of his own power, this cup couldn't be saved. Nick raised a hand and signaled the cafe waitress.

She took her time circling back to his table. Nick frowned and turned his attention back out the window. Cars packed the small lot of the senior center across the street. A few old blue hairs had tottered out of the building fifteen minutes ago, but since then, nothing. He drummed his fingers on the table. He hated waiting.

"More coffee?"

He flicked an irritated glance up at the waitress and considered lighting her hair on fire or something equally shocking. Maybe a jolt of electrocution next time she set the coffee pot down on the burner. Something to propel her brain cells into action. He swallowed the urge to do either and nodded. She topped off his cup and stepped away.

"How about a fresh cup?" he called after her.

She turned on her heel, glaring at him. "You couldn't ask that when I was there? All right, I'll get it for you."

"Thanks."

A man in a walker exited the senior center. A couple of ladies followed behind.

The waitress set a new cup in front of him and filled it with coffee. "Anything else?"

Your blood through my fingers? he thought. Probably not on the menu. Nick asked for the check and waved her away. He glanced at his watch. He'd been here an hour longer than anticipated. What the hell was taking the old bat so long?

He finished his coffee and slammed the cup down on the table. A few diner patrons turned his way. He glared at them. One by one they returned to their meals.

Fifteen minutes later she walked out of the senior center.

"About goddamn time." Nick threw five bucks on the table and left the diner. He owed more than that for the coffee, but didn't care. She was lucky she'd brought the coffee. Otherwise there would be serious consequences.

He stalked across the street, dodging a couple of cars. They honked but he kept walking. The old woman looked up at the sound, finding him as he crossed the street. Awareness flashed in her eyes, followed by fear.

Good. That was very good.

She said good-bye to her friends and came toward him. Her steps were hesitant but she raised her chin as she neared. He met her in the parking lot.

"Oh, how brave," he said, taking her by the elbow.

"You should let go. Stop now, before it's too late." The drawn line of her eyebrows rose in emphasis.

Nick tried not to stare at them. Either she never had eyebrows to begin with or she shaved them to make her own. It was unlikely the makeup she used to draw her eyebrows had ever matched her natural hair color. He shook his head.

"It's too late now." He hustled her to his rented Ford Escape, parked in the small lot.

"She'll come for me. You know she will. She'll make you pay."

"Dear Madeline, I'm planning on it."

"Hey, Maddy, who's this?" A younger woman approached and looked pointedly at his hand on Maddy's elbow. "I haven't seen him before."

"I'm her nephew," Nick snapped. "Not that it's your business. Or does she need to be checked in and out of her card game?"

The woman's spine straightened. "We watch out for our guests. Sir, I don't like your tone. Maddy, why don't you let me take you home?"

Maddy opened her mouth to respond. Nick tightened his fingers on her elbow. She gasped in pain. He pushed a minimum amount of magic into his free hand and reached for the young woman. She jumped at the amber glow on his fingertips, but didn't react fast enough to avoid his touch.

He gripped the side of her head and let the power flow into her skull. "You'll forget this encounter," he said roughly. "Madeline is no concern to you."

Madeline protested beside him, but he maintained his grip on her elbow. Releasing the young woman, he turned his attention back to his captive. "Let's go." Nick smiled and guided her into the front seat of the SUV. He closed the door and held it with a little spell that barely wicked off any of his power. "When your niece comes, she'll bring a friend and I'll be waiting."

The bleary ring of a telephone tugged Tara from sleep. She cracked her eyes open against the blinding sunlight and instantly wished she hadn't. She threw one arm across her eyes and waited for the sunspots to go away. The phone rang again. She grumbled and reached for her cell.

"Whatchya got, Carson?" she mumbled, turning away from the sun so she could open her eyes without pain.

"Expecting someone else?" asked a smooth, cocky male on the other end of the line.

Tara glanced at her phone display. Unknown number. "Who is this?"

"Don't recognize my voice? I'm hurt, Officer O'Reilly. Or should I just call you Tara, since we know each other better now."

She sat up and pushed the hair from her face. She didn't recognize the voice. It was bright out, at least noon, so it couldn't be Thomas or Jeffrey. "I'm sorry, but who...?"

"Oh yes, you are. You don't even know how much. Let's change that. Say hello to someone for me."

Tara's heart kick-started with a mighty jump in her chest and set out a frantic pace. She no longer needed the phone display.

Dread settled with a sickening weight in her stomach. "Saints," she whispered.

A scratchy, panicked voice came on the line. One she'd know anywhere. "Tara, dear. Don't you listen to him. Stay away and be—"

The line rustled as if there was a scuffle on the other end. Suddenly there was a crack and Maddy cried out.

"Saints!" Tara shouted into the phone. "Don't you dare hurt her, or I'll hunt you down."

He chuckled in her ear. "I look forward to the hunt then. But let's up the stakes. I'll give you twelve hours to find her. If you don't, harming her will be the least of your concerns."

The line went dead.

Tara choked out a sob. He must have grabbed Maddy while she was out. He could kill her. Oh God. He had to be stopped, even if it meant killing him. First she had to find them.

Carson. He could help.

Her fingers shook hard as she dialed Carson and held the phone to her ear. She sat forward and put her head between her legs, drawing in air. She never panicked in a tense situation. Not like this. But this was the last of her family. The only person she could call her own. She couldn't lose Maddy.

The phone rang once, twice. "Please pick up, Carson. Please. Oh God, please." The phone rang a third time. A fourth, then clicked into voice mail. "Carson! You have to call me. No, you have to run a trace on the last number received on my phone, then call me. It's an emergency. Carson...He has Aunt Maddy." Her voice cracked. Tara struggled to pull it together. "Call me," she said and hung up.

She lunged from the bed and raced down the hall, throwing open Maddy's bedroom door. "Maddy!" she cried. The room was empty. She ran back to the stairs and down the steps, taking them as fast as she could. She rounded the corner, past the dark living room, and into the kitchen. It too was empty.

A single sheet of paper lay on the wooden table with Maddy's flowing script. She'd gone out to the senior center for bingo.

Back soon. Love, Maddy.

Tara clutched the note and ran back through the living room to the staircase. She was halfway up when she remembered that Thomas was supposedly asleep on the couch, and she was running around in a tank top and lace panties. She couldn't quite bring herself to care. She looked over the railing but didn't see Thomas. Perhaps he had left with Jeffrey.

She raced up the steps and across the hall to Gregore's room. She burst into the darkness and stumbled forward to the bed. She ran into it and fell forward, crashing onto Gregore's stone form. "Ow!"

A breathy grunt released from him.

"Gregore," she said, pushing to her hands and knees and crawling up the bed to reach for his face. She traced a hand down his marble-smooth cheek. "Can you hear me?"

"Yes," he rasped.

"Saints has Maddy. Oh God, Gregore. Maddy! You saw what he can do. I can't…I can't beat that. I almost put you in a coma. How can I defeat a dark wizard who is so far beyond my magic level?" Tara curled up beside him, resting her head on the pillow next to his. She reached down and wrapped her fingers around the cold marble of his hand.

"Special."

She snorted.

"Special," he repeated.

She sighed. "Twelve hours. That's how long I have to find her. He called from an unknown number and didn't give me any idea where he was calling from. How can I find her in twelve hours?"

"Friends."

She squeezed his hand and prayed that Carson called back soon. "I need you, Gregore. I can't face this guy alone."

"Never alone," he mumbled.

An hour and five more frantic calls to Carson later, Tara still hadn't heard from her partner. She had crawled from Gregore's side, dressed, and returned to the spell book. She now sat in the kitchen, trying to concentrate on pendulum dousing while surreptitiously looking at her phone and praying it would ring.

While waiting, she made an interesting discovery. She'd found Thomas's curse. He was invisible, or nearly so. When she grabbed the tome from the living room, she'd seen the faintest of outlines of a man on the couch. She would have thought her eyes played tricks on her, were it not for the gentle snore emanating from him. Fascinating.

She returned her attention to Maddy and focused on the pendulum. The grimoire made brief mention of this type of searching, saying that a person could locate anything with a crystal pendulum.

Picking up her aunt's quartz on the silk cord, she dangled it over a city map from her glove box. Third try was a charm, right? The crystal spun, swinging to and fro, and circled the map. It slowed, stopped, pointing to downtown. She dropped the cord and shoved the map away. This was useless. She didn't know what she was doing. Tara rubbed her eyes and pushed trembling hands into her hair. She had to find Maddy. She'd gone through the spells in the book with no luck. Scrying didn't work either. Every time she closed her eyes, her nightmares and the visions returned in Technicolor. Flames and burning fear in Maddy's eyes. Gregore at her feet.

If Carson didn't come through...The hell with that. She couldn't give up.

She looked around absently. This old house had seen such love. When Rose passed, the house had come to Tara. She hadn't been able to step inside then. It was easier to let Maddy move in. Not much had changed. Still looked like it did when Rose was here.

Tara looked at the tarot cards next to her on the kitchen table. She straightened her spine and reached for them with no hesitation. Anything for her aunt. Shuffling the cards, she focused on finding Maddy. In a blink, a vision filled her mind, flashing in and pushing all other thoughts away.

Smoke. So much smoke that she coughed. Maddy struggled against the ropes binding her, eyes watering and tears streaming down her cheeks. Flames sputtered and crackled, closing in on her elderly aunt. An instant later she was thrust from the scene. Shit! Nothing but the same scene she had seen at the coffeehouse. Where was Maddy? And where the hell was Carson?

Tara glanced at the phone again. Then her watch. Then the kitchen window. Half an hour until sundown. *Hurry, hurry, hurry,* she thought. She had to rescue Maddy, arrest Saints and remove any suspicion about what happened at her apartment.

She stood and paced to the stove, then back to the table. Checked to see if the phone had turned itself off. Or broken. No such luck. Was Carson ignoring her or what?

In fact, the hell with Carson. She didn't need his help. She snapped up the phone and called Captain Scott.

"We were just discussing you," he said.

"Well, hello to you too, sir. Who is 'we'?"

"Carson and I."

"That's why he hasn't responded to my five emergency calls?"

"I'm why he didn't call back."

"I...wha...excuse me?" she sputtered. "My aunt has been kidnapped, the only link I have to her is the last number called to my phone, and you—"

"We've got what you need, O'Reilly. The number and more," Scott said smoothly.

"Then why the hell have you left me waiting? Sir."

"Your tone, O'Reilly."

"Is warranted," she growled. "The life of my only living relative is in question."

He sighed and she heard something tapping against his desk. No doubt a pencil or pen, whatever he normally would be twirling in his hand. "We recovered the video from the hallway and front door of your apartment. Were you expecting flowers?"

"Flowers?" Her apartment? She wanted to shout that none of that mattered. Nothing mattered but finding Maddy. Instead, she sucked it up and answered the question. She knew from experience that answering his questions got him to the point faster and would get her the important answers. "No, sir. I don't know anything about flowers. It's not my birthday, I wasn't dating anyone, and no one would be sending them anyway."

"I thought not. The card was blank."

Tara blinked. "What's this about?"

"The evidence shows a man bringing flowers to your door. From the video vantage point, we see him from behind. He knocks on your door. We can't see what he does, but a minute later, he enters your apartment. He never leaves. Not from the front door anyway. We think he went out a window onto the fire escape."

Tara stopped in the middle of the kitchen, realizing she'd been pacing the small kitchen. "Blond? Shoulder-length? About six feet and an average build?"

The captain cleared his throat. "That's right."

"Saints. I knew it."

"We never see his face, O'Reilly."

"This man stole from me, sir. First my apartment, then my book, and now my aunt. The apartment is gone and the book was damaged. I am *not* losing my aunt to this man."

"You found your stolen property? When?"

Shit. She wasn't supposed to let that slip. She'd been ordered away from the case. Scott had been on the force for twenty years. He could sniff out a lie like it was dirty laundry. But how much truth should she tell him? Certainly not that she'd been at the warehouse. That she'd been at the scene of a crime and made an anonymous tip? Bad news.

"You were at the warehouse, weren't you?" he asked.

Tara nearly choked.

"Uh…"

"We talked to a resident of the city who gave a description of you and another gentleman in exchange for a hot meal."

Damn, damn, damn. This was bad. The "resident of the city" must have been that homeless fellow they'd seen in the warehouse alley. Guess you couldn't count on people to be quiet when food was at stake. Not that she blamed him. She ran a hand through her hair and tried to think of what to say. Fortunately, Captain Scott saved her the trouble.

"Listen, O'Reilly, don't sweat it. We know you were there. We've got your fingerprints and a rough timeline. Aside from breaking into private property, the victim was dead hours before you arrived. Give us a statement and you're in the clear. Do it again and you're off the force. Understood?"

"Yes, sir."

"I think you better tell me what is going on. What makes you think this Saints guy is behind all of this?"

"I got the plate number off his bike the night the book was stolen. He chased me to St. Jude's Parish and grabbed it. I got an up-close encounter with the guy, so I know what he looks like. My friend and I followed a lead to the warehouse, where we ran into him again. We didn't know about the murder."

"What kind of lead?"

She cleared her throat. "A psychic saw a vision of the warehouse."

"A psychic? Detective, you of all people have never used a psychic in your career. I've heard you blow them off as fakes more times than I can count. What's really going on?"

"She's, uh, she's family, sir. Hard to ignore that."

Scott laughed. "That actually explains a lot. But not why you think this guy has your—what is she? Aunt?"

"Psychic aunt?" she heard Carson say in the background, with a snort.

Could this call get any worse? "Yes, my psychic Aunt Maddy. He called me, threatened to hurt her."

"I see," he said in a way that made Tara cringe. "I want you off this case, Detective. You're emotionally invested and could make a mistake. Let Carson and I handle this one."

Apparently it could get worse. "Hell, no. Sir." She struggled to maintain a respectful tone, knowing she walked a fine line with him. "She's my family and this guy is dangerous."

"We deal with dangerous every day. You could get her killed, O'Reilly. Is that what you want?"

"Of course not."

"Then let us handle it. Carson's got the call data and will follow up. He'll take backup and scope out the building and exits. If he can't extract your aunt, we'll go from there."

"Sir, I have to be there. She's my aunt. There are circumstances you aren't aware of."

"Then make me aware."

She couldn't. He'd never believe her. She'd scoffed at anything mystical for so long, they'd either laugh her off or lock her up. Plus, who'd believe in a rogue magician terrorizing the city? Only in the movies, right?

"Please," she said quietly. "I don't want you or Carson hurt."

"Don't worry, O'Reilly. Carson can protect himself. He's a fully trained officer. Now, I don't want to see you anywhere even close to this. Do I make myself clear?"

"Yes, sir. Understood," she ground out.

"Good. When this is over, you and I will be having a long discussion about your future as a detective. I won't have rogues on my force. You're a good cop, O'Reilly. Don't make a bad choice." He hung up.

SET IN STONE

Tara pursed her lips and felt her heart sink into her stomach. She'd just lost her job. Because despite the captain's warnings, she'd already made the choice. If she didn't do something, Carson and Maddy could both die. They had no idea who they were up against. She had to find and stop Saints before he hurt anyone else.

The vision was the key. She reached for the tarot deck again and pictured her aunt. The scene popped up in sharp relief. She focused on every detail she could see. Maddy was tied to a chair in a dark room, and flames were way too close to her thin body. Gregore was solid stone on the ground, his features pained. Smoke filled the space and fire spread from crate to crate. She honed in on each section one at a time until finally coming to the wood crates that circled Maddy. She could just make out a word.

Hiroshi.

Tara's eyes snapped open. Crates like those at Hiroshi's crab warehouse. She was such an idiot. She'd assumed that the place was still closed by the police investigation. It never occurred to her that Saints would return to that place. Suddenly she knew that's exactly what he'd done. He was hiding right under their noses. Carson and Captain Scott knew it. They were in danger, but didn't want her help.

Too bad. They were getting it anyway.

Strangely, the thought of losing her job didn't bother her as much as she thought. A week ago she would have railed and done everything in her power to keep her status as detective. It's who she was, after all. When had things changed so much? When had it become less important to her? She looked up at the ceiling, trying to picture Gregore in his room. He'd come into her life, brought a few new friends, and turned everything upside down and inside out. Surprisingly, Tara wasn't sorry. After all she'd been through, she'd come to realize just what was important to her.

She checked her watch. The sun would set in about ten minutes. As soon as Gregore and Thomas rose, they would plan. She'd use every available resource and blast Nick Saints straight to hell.

"I'm waiting. What did Saints say?" Gregore growled. He flexed his hands, trying not to fist them at his sides as he paced the kitchen. If Saints had laid even one hand on Maddy, he would die. She may not be Gregore's aunt, but she was family nonetheless.

Tara rubbed her temples and squeezed her eyes closed.. "You said Jeffrey would be here shortly. Once he is—"

"Once he is, we'll already have a plan in place and can be ready to act," Gregore finished.

She nodded. "Okay. He said I have until midnight to find Maddy. He gave me no clues as to where she's located. I've found her but... the sick bastard is acting like this is some sort of game. What's worse is that my partner knows where she is and is bringing the police in."

"They'll be massacred. You know that, right?" Thomas said. "We have to stop Saints."

"No. *No.* I am not facing that man with three half-human men whose curse kicks in when the sun comes up. What if the worst happens?" Tara said.

"Then it will happen overnight. We'll save her," Gregore said, confident. "We'll bring her back before the sun comes up."

"Gregore, if she's right and something does happen, you might not make sun up."

He glared at Thomas, wishing the man would shut the hell up. The doorbell rang and stopped his response.

"That must be Jeffrey," Thomas said and headed for the front door. Gregore followed.

Thomas held the door open and let a gruff Jeffrey inside.

Jeffrey looked between the two. "What?"

"You want the good news or the bad?" Thomas asked.

"Why would I want the bad?"

"Noted. Good news only. Tara was cleared of setting her building on fire."

Jeffrey nodded and nearly smiled.

"Tara's aunt was taken earlier today and we have to get her back," Gregore added.

Creases lined Thomas's eyes as he frowned a bit. "Bad news anyway. Sorry, old man. But while we're at it, if we don't do something soon, then the police will be in the picture, if they aren't already, and more people could die." He clapped his hands together. "Well, I think that about sums it up. Tea?"

Jeffrey narrowed his eyes. "You're not funny."

"Oh, I might be. Depending on who you ask." Thomas's grin was back, bigger than ever.

"Don't ask me," Jeffrey groused.

Gregore nearly groaned. Wonderful. Two cavemen and the court jester. This had the makings of a bad movie. He almost felt sorry for Tara, having to put up with them at a time like this. "We need a plan and we need it now. Otherwise a certain detective will go in without us, and I will not allow that to happen."

"Poor Gregore," Thomas said to Jeffrey. "Always was a business-before-pleasure sort of fellow. Hopefully Tara can break him of that."

Gregore shook his head and returned to the kitchen. Judging by the footsteps pounding on the floorboards behind him, Thomas and Jeffrey were ditching the jokes and joining him. His heart warmed in his chest. In these last hours, knowing his best friends were with him meant more than he could say. After all they had been through, the curse and the falling-out in Italy, and now this, it was a miracle.

Tara paced the kitchen, wiping away tears. Once she saw them with Jeffrey, she squared her shoulders, lifted her chin, and said, "Let's go save Maddy."

Thomas clapped his hands together. "Right on. Bring on the death magic!"

"Death magic?" she asked, sounding very uncertain.

"Don't tell me you were planning to arrest him?"

She shook her head. "I don't think I thought that far ahead."

"Now is your opportunity," Jeffrey said.

She nodded, but Gregore didn't see conviction there. She wouldn't take a life unless her life, or that of someone else, was in jeopardy. That's who she was. Better to start with what they knew and build a plan. "Did your police friends say where he was holding Maddy?"

She pursed her lips. "No, but I know where she's at. Saints has her back at the warehouse."

"Chinatown," Gregore filled in for the others. To Tara, he asked, "How did you know?"

She waved to the tarot cards on the table. "Another one of my gifts, it seems. I had a vision of her. She was..." Tara cleared her throat. "She was surrounded by flames. We need to hurry. He's going to hurt her."

Gregore took her hand and squeezed it. "Let's go get the son of a bitch."

⇥ CHAPTER 35 ⇤

"We're so fucked," Jeffrey muttered as he rubbed the back of his neck.

Tara couldn't have agreed more. This rescue mission had just become *Mission Impossible*.

Black and white patrol cars dotted a full block of Chinatown, centered around a crumbling warehouse with a crab on the sign. Tara, Jeffrey, and Thomas watched as patrolmen rushed around, setting a perimeter and holding back the gathering crowd. A broken streetlamp brought shadows to the alleyway they stood in.

She closed her eyes, blocking out the scene before them to the one that only she could see. Her body tensed and tingles raced over her arms, centering in her chest. This was ten times stronger than when she'd felt it at the Grand Grimoire. And no wonder. Six ley lines intersected in a glowing, ochre star so powerful she could barely draw breath.

"Any more people look over here, and someone in charge is bound to notice," Jeffrey added darkly, breaking her out of her thoughts.

In the midst of the crowd, Tara saw just the man who'd notice. Captain Scott. He was slightly shorter than Carson, but managed to command attention as he barked out orders to the guys.

"It won't take long to notice us," she said. "That man has a radar like no one I know."

"Can you see an entry point?" Jeffrey asked.

She shook her head. Gregore was scouting the back of the building, using his supernatural speed to get there as no more than a breeze. "We'll need cover until Gregore returns. Maybe we should move—"

"I got it," Thomas said, stepping up to the mouth of the alley.

Tara thought she heard him mutter, "Damn curse may as well be good for something."

His blond hair glinted in the moonlight, then dimmed and faded. She blinked. Looked closer. At first she thought Thomas was disappearing like she'd seen earlier on the couch. But no, he wasn't disappearing, the alley was.

"What the...?" she said, stepping forward. Darkness cloaked them like a blanket, hiding them from view. She could see through it when she concentrated. Like being in the dark and narrowing on a single pinpoint of light. She could see the activity on the other side of the veil, just as sure as she knew they were invisible now to prying eyes.

"Wow," she said.

"Parlor trick," Jeffrey grunted.

"Like to see you try it, Scales," Thomas said.

"Scales?" Tara asked. Jeffrey glowered and she decided not to press it. The man made Grumpy look like Happy. "Right, never mind. Can Gregore see through this?"

"No, but he's familiar with the *Shade*. He'll know where we are."

They watched another five minutes, cataloging the flow of people. Which uniforms went where, listened to what they could hear of Captain Scott over the occasional siren, and hoped for a sign of life within the building.

"Here he comes," Jeffrey said from behind her.

Tara had no idea how he knew. Gregore stepped through the inky shadows moments later.

His face was stricken. "I found a way in."

Jeffrey rubbed his hands together. "Excellent. I could use a good fight."

Gregore held up his hand. "There's more." He turned to Tara and put a hand on her shoulder, drawing her into his arms. "You need to prepare yourself to see Maddy. He roughed her up."

"You saw her? Is she okay? I'm going to kick his ass!" The words tumbled out of her mouth with a vehemence unfamiliar in its intensity.

Jeffrey chuckled behind her. "My kind of woman. No wonder you have a thing for her, Trenowyth."

Gregore's fingers gripped her, keeping her focused. "There is a fire escape in back with too many policemen in the alley, no doubt to make sure Saints doesn't escape out the back when they decide to go in."

She nodded. "Right now they are trying to negotiate with Saints. Get him to release Maddy and come out."

"I wouldn't," Thomas said.

"Neither will Saints," Gregore said. "We can't enter from the back. I have a plan, but we need to wait for an opening."

The wait was the longest of Tara's life. She wanted to run to Maddy. Doing so would draw attention to them, so she waited and pretended that everything she cared about was not in jeopardy.

Focus, she repeated over and over again in her mind. If she didn't, her fear of losing both Maddy and Gregore on the same night would overwhelm her. Bring her to her knees. Her enemy had the upper hand magically, but she had the motivation he didn't. She wouldn't lose anyone she cared about this night.

"Oh shit," Jeffrey said.

Jerked out of her thoughts, she followed the line of his gaze. An emergency vehicle roared up and the amount of officers surrounding the building doubled. How the hell would they get in now?

⊱┈┈┈◦❀◦┈┈┈⊰

As plans went, it was a bad one.

Gregore took in the scene, formulating his idea. They had to get into the warehouse. The alley dead-ended behind the building, with no other way to it from here. With the front and back so heavily patrolled, they couldn't use either. Even if they could get to the fire escape with Thomas *Shading* them, they might still be seen. Gregore wished for his wings . At least then he could get them to the roof without causing his friend pain.

Jeffrey stepped up beside him. "What do you think?"

"I think we've only got one option," Gregore said. Last time, he'd lost his two best friends. Would they understand now? He'd make them. Maddy was most important here.

He motioned them deeper into the shadows. "Thomas?"

"Got it," Thomas said, spreading his hands and letting the shadows darken around them.

"What are we doing?" Tara asked.

Gregore glanced at Thomas, nodded, and turned his attention to Jeffrey. "I want you to stay behind," he said. "Guard us from the back in case something goes wrong."

Jeffrey whipped around. "What?"

Gregore understood his friend's confusion. They'd previously planned to use Jeffrey as a distraction to Nick. Make him taunt Saints while Thomas and Gregore attacked and Tara rescued Maddy. They still would, but first they needed wings and only one man had them. Trouble was, Jeffrey could only bring them out under extreme emotion. Something he worked very hard to control. Gregore would break that control and pray his friend forgave him.

"Four of us will be too much," Gregore said. "Stay here and guard Tara. Thomas and I can handle this. I've got a plan."

Jeffrey squinted, his lips thinning. He took a deep breath and his face relaxed. "You want me to babysit your girlfriend while you and the invisible man go save the day? Please. You need me."

Gregore shook his head. "We'll be fine." He looked at Thomas again, hoping to convey what he was doing. Thomas watched him closely, all the while holding the *Shade* at the mouth of the sidewalk.

"Gregore," Tara said. "Remember what happened last time we saw Saints here? We need all the help we can get."

"No, you're wrong. And you're staying here with Jeffrey. That's final. He'll be better off here and so will you." Jeffrey's lips inched back down into a frown. Gregore pushed harder, needing his friend at the point of losing control. "Saints is no match for Thomas and me. I'll distract him while Thomas gets Maddy. Jeffrey, you're better suited to staying behind. You've always been a loose cannon and we don't need that in a tense situation."

Jeffrey clenched his fists. Released them and shook out his hands. "I'm not here to babysit. I'm here to break my fucking curse, and we can't do that until this woman is rescued. Do I look like I get paid hourly?"

"You look like you're about to pop. Maybe you should stay here, old man. There's nothing wrong with taking care of the ladies," Thomas piped in. He winked at Gregore.

"Excuse me?" Tara all but snarled.

Jeffrey took a step toward Thomas, growling, "You too?"

Gregore hid his smile. Time to play it hard. "You heard me. Thomas and I will take it from here. We. Don't. Need. You."

Jeffrey closed the distance between them, getting in Gregore's face. Pearlescent scales flashed in patches over his nose and cheeks, his arms. Jeffrey grabbed Gregore's shirt in the middle of his chest, black-tipped claws ripping into the cotton, and hauled him close. "You need me and you know it. You two sissies couldn't tackle a mouse."

Gregore breathed in the salty scent of the sea, which poured from Jeffrey when the change was upon him. He was close, but not close enough. They needed those wings. He'd hoped words would push his friend over the edge. Instead, it became clear he needed action. If he backed off, Jeffrey would calm and that's not what they wanted.

"What did you say?" Gregore demanded, getting in Jeffrey's personal zone.

"You can't do it without me."

"You called me a sissy."

Jeffrey nodded once. "I did."

Gregore smashed his fist into Jeffrey's face. He followed his friend back against the wall and threw a few more punches, pounding his stomach, whatever he could land a blow against.

Jeffrey erupted in rage, shoving Gregore back and growling. Wings exploded from his back and his nails elongated. Glossy white scales flowed down his limbs, followed by a light line of fluffy feathers.

Thomas laughed. "Damn, I hoped it wouldn't come to that. Ah well. Good work, Gregore."

"What?" Tara asked, rounded eyes glued to Jeffrey.

"We needed a lift to the building," Thomas said. He waved a hand at Jeffrey's wings. "Now we have one."

"You're a bastard, Gregore," Jeffrey said. His voice distorted when in this form, as if it were mixed with a bear growl and cut with glass. As far as Gregore knew, Jeffrey had never figured out just what he was. What *this* was. One thing they did know, this was only half the change. He still had human form, which was a testament to his extreme control.

Jeffrey pointed to Thomas with a black claw. "And I'm going to kick your ass later. Count on it."

Thomas threw back his head and laughed. "Come find me at noon."

"Funny," Jeffrey barked. Thomas would be nothing more than a shadow at noon. He wouldn't have an ass to kick. "Let's get this over with. Who's first?"

"I am," Tara said. She stepped to Jeffrey's side and faced Gregore. "Don't even think about telling me no."

"Not just no, hell, no," he replied. "I go first to scout the roof."

She sputtered, surprise and fury blinking over her face. "Who is the officer here?"

"Who is indestructible?" he countered. He didn't let her reply. To Thomas, he said, "Keep an eye out for anything unusual until Jeffrey returns. Bring up the rear."

Tara crossed her arms over her chest and muttered something about insufferable men.

Gregore ignored the comment. "I'll see you soon," he said, brushing a fingertip over her cheek. She glared, but her anger wouldn't last. She would realize he was right in this. He wouldn't risk her safety going into an unknown situation.

Jeffrey wrapped his arms around Gregore, flapped his white wings, and lifted into the air far over the heads of the police.

"Can you forgive me this time?" Gregore asked as they glided unnoticed over the heads of the cops.

"Sure, what's to forgive?" Jeffrey said "Friends always punch friends instead of talking to them."

"Do you need a hug?"

"Do you need a lesson in gravity?"

Gregore chuckled. This must be what Tara felt like the first time they'd flown together. "No, I remember gravity well. I'm sorry, Jeffrey. I should have talked to you. I thought if I did, it would be harder to rile your emotions."

"Just being in this situation riles my emotions." He sighed, scalding breath brushing past Gregore's ear. "I understand why you did it. Do it again and I'll rip your head off your shoulders. We clear?"

"Clear."

Jeffrey landed lightly on the roof, setting Gregore on his feet. "Good. Let's do this so I can go back home and pretend none of this ever happened." He flapped his wings and returned for Tara and Thomas.

Gregore scrubbed a hand down on his face. He'd deal with Jeffrey later. Right now they had to save Maddy. He spent the next few minutes checking for entry points.

Soon after, all four stood on the roof of the warehouse. A domed skylight of mud-caked glass ran a dozen feet across the top of the building. There wasn't a hatch of any kind in the glass to enable a quiet entry.

"We'll have to go in fast because we're definitely going in loud," Jeffrey observed.

Tara peered through a lighter section of glass. "I can't see anything. The falling glass could hit Maddy," she whispered.

"It's a risk we have to take. Let's try to keep it minimal," Gregore said quietly. "Thomas, can you shade us as we enter so that our numbers at least will be disguised?"

He nodded. "What's the plan to get in? If we go in one at a time, that will be too slow. The breaking glass will alert whoever is in there."

Gregore cursed. Thomas was right. "Time check, Tara?"

"Just after ten," she said.

"Isn't this the place in the movie where someone pulls a rope out of nowhere?" Thomas asked. He looked pointedly at Tara. "I don't suppose you could do that?"

She patted the pockets of her jeans. "Sorry. I seem to have left the rope behind. I don't think we have time to get any."

Jeffrey muttered under his breath. "No fucking breaks, huh?"

Tara planted her fists on her hips and looked around. "Shoelaces."

Gregore cocked an eyebrow. "What?"

"Give me your shoelaces," she said. "We don't have rope, but I can make it work."

"You're going to need a lot more than shoelaces if you want to get in there," Thomas said. "Oh, and my boots don't lace up."

She waved his words away. "Details. Just trust me."

Gregore bent and removed a lace from his black boot. Jeffrey followed suit. Tara took the laces and laid them down. "I saw this spell in the grimoire to extend objects. I hope it works."

She knelt, drawing her fingers over the strings. Amber light followed her movements, disappearing into the fabric. She lifted one end of each and handed them to Gregore. "Hold this tight."

He did, fascinated with the change in her. She seemed in perfect control and not the least bit intimidated by the magic in her blood.

"Pull," she said.

Gregore complied and the laces stretched. Wrapping the laces around his elbow, he continued to pull and pull. In no time at all, he held thin, but sturdy, ropes.

Thomas and Jeffrey stood at his sides, their jaws open. Gregore felt a flush of pride for his woman. "Hands off, guys, this lady is mine." He pulled her into his arms and took her lips, reveling in her strength.

All too soon, he lifted his head. "We've got one shot," he said. "Let's get Maddy."

CHAPTER 36

Nick stood at a boarded-up third-story window, looking through a narrow hole in the slats. Half a dozen cop cars remained out front. They still hadn't figured out if there was a hostage situation at hand. He'd cast a spell to scramble their minds, making everything they thought they knew uncertain. They couldn't hold on to any particular thought for more than a few minutes. Damn, what fun. They ran around like little mice out there, each trying to find the cheese but not able to remember what they were doing. The magic would wear off in another hour or so, but by then he should have things under control.

The soft warmth of a feminine body pressed against his back. A thigh wrapped around his, the arch of her foot sliding down his calf.

"Deja," he rasped.

She came around his side, never letting the touch of her body leave his. She smiled, her red lips darkly seductive, and ran her fingers through his shaggy blond hair. She wore a red lace bra and short black skirt, with nothing underneath. Spiked stiletto boots ended the outfit. Nick pulled her close and kissed her hard. He slid his hands under the skirt and felt his power grow, among other things.

She moaned into his mouth, pressing closer. "Can we?" Her sultry voice came out needy and breathless.

Nick leaned back against the wall, taking her with him. Her heat rubbed at just the right place on his pants. His power was nearly full, having just sated himself on three witches. Everything was on hold until the detective and the creature arrived. He glanced at his watch. Two hours to midnight. Surely a little more couldn't hurt. He flipped their positions and pressed her against the wall. Lifted her leg to wrap around his hip.

Just as her fingers brushed his zipper, glass shattered out in the main warehouse.

Nick released Deja's breast, planted a quick kiss on her mouth, and set her away. He held a finger to his lips and then moved quietly to the doorway. He slipped into the hall and out to the top of the stairs. He felt Deja come up behind him. She pointed at what he'd already seen. An unnatural blob of shadow the height of a man and width of three drew the darkness closer, even in the center of his candles.

Finally. They'd come.

He motioned Deja to stay hidden, to wait. They'd go for the old woman. He didn't doubt it for a moment. Didn't even have to wait long.

The shadows separated, dimmed, and shapes formed within.

"Two more men with them," Deja whispered as she pulled a shirt over her head.

Nick smiled without humor. "So predictable. She's a detective. Of course she'd bring backup."

Deja chuckled softly. "Good thing you've got your own backup."

He shot her a dark look.

Her smile vanished. "If...if you need it, that is."

"Not right now," he said and moved farther down the stairs. He kept to the shadows. He'd left the warehouse purposely dark. A couple of ritual candles flickered on different crates, dispelling just enough of the darkness to be able to see. Nothing more.

The cement floor was marked with ritual symbols. The old woman was tied to a chair in the center of a ring of sugar. The sugar was only for show, meant to make them think it was a ritual circle. She was gagged but struggled and muttered all the same.

All was ready.

Nick crouched down, waiting. Watching. Listening.

"Tara, be careful," the gargoyle said. He put a hand on her back.

Such familiarity. Nick wanted to puke. How could she even touch that creature without vomiting?

Tara moved to the outer circle of the sugar in front of Madeline.

Closer. Just a little closer. Nick's patience stretched thin. The three men cast wary gazes around, as if waiting for something to jump out at them. They edged near to the two women, fanning out in a semi-circle around them.

Nick grinned. Exactly where he wanted them.

Gregore scanned the vast warehouse, expanding his senses to find the threat. It was there, he knew it, even as the hair on his nape stood up. The crash of broken glass when they entered should have alerted Saints, yet no one came running. Maddy sat tied to a chair, silver tape over her mouth and terror in her eyes. Her silver curls framed her face in wild disarray and highlighted the purplish-black bruise forming under her left eye. Abrasions covered her right cheek as if she'd skidded across concrete on it. Crates were stacked a dozen feet around her, all at varying heights and forming a circle. Lit candles topped some, bringing just enough illumination to dispel complete darkness.

His vision sharpened, adjusting to the dark. He peered into the blackest of shadows for the enemy, seeing nothing. Yet he sensed them. Any other time he could pick up a definite direction of where the hunted hid. Tonight it was as if they hid in all directions. Maybe because Nick's essence had settled into the building with the days he'd spent here. Clearly the crates had moved from the haphazard stacking he'd seen the last time he and Tara had been here.

Frustrated by the lack of a trail, he crept forward, hoping to pick up something. Tara started forward with him. Gregore held his hand out and motioned to stay back. She paused just long enough to pull her weapon and start forward again, completely ignoring him. He grabbed her arm, hauling her back to his side.

Tara glared, leaned in, and said, "I'm going to get her. I won't leave her there a second longer."

"You know this is a trap. She's bait. Don't be foolish."

She pulled her arm from his grip. "Yes, and I'm trusting the three of you to back me up while I go in." She stomped off, heading for Maddy.

Gregore swore under his breath and signaled to Thomas and Jeffrey. She was thinking like a cop, not someone who used or defended herself with magic. She was going to spring the trap. He only hoped they could minimize the damage.

Jeffrey and Thomas signaled back and fanned out in opposite directions to explore the shadows.

He followed Tara, long steps eating up the distance between them. Suddenly, not bringing a weapon other than his knife seemed like a really bad idea. He cast around for anything larger. The ground was clear of debris. Even the surrounding crates were intact. Saints prepared for them well, he'd give him that. Gregore wouldn't risk further alerting Saints by breaking a crate. Not yet. They may be undetected and he planned to keep them that way as long as possible.

Tara stopped a few feet shy of Maddy. She knelt and inspected the warehouse floor. Gregore moved up beside her. "What is it?" he whispered.

"A circle. Looks like a fine white powder. Probably salt. Maddy is directly in the center of it. The circle can either keep magic in or out." She stood. "I'm thinking in."

"What's the plan?"

Tara's gaze swept the room. "The candles provide pretty dim lighting. I think that Saints is hoping I won't see the circle. I should be able to break it and we can get Maddy out of here." She paused.

"But?"

"But I'm concerned that we haven't seen Saints. There is no way that the police are providing such a distraction that he didn't hear all the noise we made breaking in. He knows we're here unless something else has happened?"

Gregore pinched the bridge of his nose. Did they dare go for it and hope Saints was distracted elsewhere? Should they find Saints first? Or move in fast and hard to rescue Maddy and be ready for the inevitable battle?

Tara made the decision for him. She pointed the toe of her boot and pushed it through the salt, breaking the continuous circle.

Gregore lifted an eyebrow. "I'd expected more. Maybe a shockwave of power or some shimmering lights or something."

Tara frowned. "I did too. But I'm not wasting the time to find out."

She stepped forward, placing a foot inside the circle.

All hell broke loose.

CHAPTER 37

A sharp cry of pain rang out from the right. Thomas.
A grunt, groan, and roar from the left. Crates crashed and a heavy thump hit the ground on the left. Jeffrey.

Candle flames shot high, nearly a foot, sparking down onto the crates circling Gregore, Tara, and Maddy. Fire erupted, shrieking along the wood planks and enclosing them in flames. Heat enveloped them.

In seconds, they were trapped.

So much for damage control, Gregore thought.

"He used accelerant on those old crates," Tara said, moving back toward Maddy. She stomped through the powder on the floor. "Shit. He put that circle there to distract me. Damn rookie mistake."

One that could cost them.

For the second time in less than an hour, Gregore wished he had his wings. He'd fly the women over the top of the flames. Odd, really. He'd spent so long wanting to be human again. Nothing more than a normal man, never realizing how much he'd come to rely on those special abilities he'd been cursed with.

Sadly, they didn't have to worry about being discovered now, and his potential weapons were on fire. Jeffrey might be their only hope. He prayed the earlier groans didn't mean his friend was down permanently. Gregore kicked at the nearest set of stacked crates. Jeffrey could be injured, and Gregore would be damned if he would sit around and fry on his last night on earth. He kicked the stack harder, sending the top box crashing into the one next to it. If he could clear a path, they might be able to get out before the smoke killed them.

Maddy coughed. Ripping fabric pulled his attention back to the women. Tara had pulled the tape off of Maddy's mouth and wrapped a strip of the bottom of her tee-shirt around Maddy's face, tying it in back. Maddy held the fabric to her nose and stood on shaky legs. Tara supported her aunt. She nodded to Gregore. "Can you get us out?"

"Trying," Gregore said. "If I can clear a path, we can..." he stopped. Peered closer at the golden orange flames. A shadow moved on the other side.

The fire parted for a dark, imposing figure. Not Jeffrey. Not Thomas either.

Nick Saints stepped into the ring of burning boxes with a sinister smile. The flames choked down to embers as he passed, as if shrinking away from him in fear. Seconds later, only the lit candles and smoke remained.

Gregore pulled the knife from his boot. Using preternatural speed, he flew forward, fist connecting with Nick's cheek, and slashing the blade with his other hand. Saints shot back with the impact, taking Gregore with him to the ground. Saints shook his head clear, gripped Gregore's elbows, and slammed a knee between his legs. Gregore choked, groaned, and gasped for breath. Saints knocked the knife away, then struggled to gain his feet, but Gregore locked onto his wrist and pulled him back, pitching the blond back onto his ass. Gregore rolled onto him, landing more blows against his head and chin. Blood spewed from Nick's nose and a cut above his right eye.

Saints growled. Struck punches into Gregore's exposed ribs. He used his speed to hit faster, landing twice as many blows to Saints as he took in return. Nick worked a knee up, pushing the space between them wider until he could kick Gregore away. He muttered under his breath as he shoved, and suddenly Gregore flew back, crashing into a stack of crates. They splintered and broke underneath him.

Pain speared Gregore's thigh. He cried out and reached for his leg. Hot stickiness met his fingertips, slick as he groped for the source. He touched wood, broken and sharp and protruding from his leg. Gregore drew in a shuddering breath, gripped the wooden shaft, and yanked it out. Black winked over his vision, and he was dimly aware of swearing long and loud.

He shook off the darkness and struggled to rise. Saints had turned away and blocked Gregore's view of Tara and Maddy, though Gregore could see both were still there. He staggered forward out of the crates, careful to avoid making a sound. Saints expected him to be down longer, underestimating the strength the curse granted him in human form. He'd take what advantage he could. His knife blade glinted in the candlelight, partially buried in the wood debris. Snagging it up, he crept closer.

"…culmination of this chase," Saints was saying.

Gregore lifted the knife and slipped forward, prepared to strike.

Two women stepped into the dim pool of light, one on each side of Maddy and Tara. One twirled a curved knife, spinning it on her open palm, yet not drawing blood. The other looked like the porn star version of a Catholic schoolgirl.

"It is unfortunate that this game had to come to an end so soon. I found I enjoyed it far more than I thought I would. Detective, you remember Deja?" Saints said, motioning to the porn star. "What a small world, don't you think? My other lovely here is Milla."

Gregore backed into the shadows. One knife against three wielding magic? Bad odds. Time to even them out. He slipped past the crates, praying Tara could take care of herself for a few more minutes, and sought out Jeffrey and Thomas.

He found Thomas first. He lay on the floor, curled in a fetal position, eyes closed. Curling white smoke slithered over his body. Gregore slid the knife in the sheath and laid a palm against his friend's forehead, careful not to touch the smoke. Thomas was sweating, shaking. Unable to help his friend, Gregore moved on, hoping Jeffrey was in better shape.

He was, but barely. Jeffrey and a brunette woman stood face to face. Jeffrey's eyes spit fire at her, though he appeared locked in place. He struggled, limbs held fast to his body. Much like an angry dog at the end of its tether with a threat less than a foot away. Scales covered his face, neck and arms, black talons clacking together as he struggled for freedom.

The woman held a hand inches from his chest, concentrating on holding him in place with her spell. Gregore expected to see the spell. Something shimmering in the air, at least. There was nothing, yet he could feel the magic as if it pointed at him.

Kicking into motion, he raced to the woman, wrapped his arms around her, and took her to the ground. Her concentration broke, releasing Jeffrey. The dark-haired giant grabbed her out of Gregore's arms, hauled her halfway to her feet, and landed a hard blow to her cheek. Wide red slices from Jeffrey's talons opened in her pale flesh and she crumpled to the floor, out cold.

"I'll deal with her. Go," Jeffrey said.

"Thomas is down by the door. Think you can handle a couple more without him? Two more witches are with Saints. They've surrounded Tara and Maddy. If you can take them down, I'll get Saints away. Give them a chance to run."

Jeffrey gave a wolfish grin. "Not to worry, mate. I can handle a couple of women."

Gregore looked pointedly at the girl on the ground. A dark bruise already formed on her face. He raised his eyebrow.

"And if they attack me, the others will receive the same care," Jeffrey said, disappearing into the shadows of the warehouse.

CHAPTER 38

Embers and tufts of smoke filtered through the warehouse. Gregore moved silently back to where Tara and Maddy faced off with Saints and the witches. The moment Jeffrey struck at the two witches, Gregore pulled his blade and launched his attack from the other side.

He slipped behind Saints, wrapped his arm around the man's throat, and yanked him back into the crate stacks, knife to his ribs.

"Get Maddy and Thomas and get out," he called to Tara over his shoulder.

Saints recovered quickly, slamming an elbow into his ribs. Gregore grunted and pushed his blade in, slicing his enemy open. Saints cried out, enraged, and sent a bolt of electricity into his thigh wound. Gregore sucked in a pained breath, his arm loosening around Nick's neck. Saints took immediate advantage and wrested his way out of Gregore's grip. He flipped to face him and stood on unsteady legs.

"Good move," Saints said. "Sneaky. Didn't think you had it in you. Especially getting your man to attack from behind." He flicked his gaze to the knife in Gregore's hand. "Did you actually think this strategy all the way through? That butter knife against me?"

Bastard had a point. Gregore wouldn't say so. He faced Saints and vowed to give the women as much time as possible to get out.

"Nothing to say? Disappointing." Madness gleamed in Nick's eyes. He closed his fist and punched the air right in front of Gregore's nose, snapping his hand back just as quick. Gregore flinched back and glared, as he realized Saints toyed with him.

Two could play at that game.

He slashed at Saints with his knife. His hand whirled and danced, keeping Nick off guard, not knowing where he'd strike. Saints fought back, blocking the blows with precision and surprising speed for an injured man. Gregore thrust, Nick parried, pushing away Gregore's wrist with one hand and landing a solid, brutal, magic-laced blow with his other. The blade clattered to the floor.

Gregore kicked into gear and shot forward with supernatural speed, wrapping his arms around Saints' waist and slamming him through the crates and back ten feet into the warehouse wall. Nick screamed in agony as he hit with the force of a train. Air rushed from his lungs, and he drew in short ragged breaths.

"Son of a bitch," Saints gritted.

Gregore punched and kicked every available patch of body he could reach on the madman. Saints blocked a couple. Most hit with well-honed speed and accuracy, bruising and bloodying his opponent.

Saints caught Gregore's fist in his. He squeezed, trying to break the bones with his feeble human strength.

Gregore laughed. "Is that all you have?"

Saints shook his head, blood from his nose dripping into his mouth. "I also had that."

Gregore cocked a brow. "What?"

Nick smiled and released Gregore's fist.

Further confused, Gregore paced back a step and felt more sticky warmth. He glanced down and saw his knife sticking out his other thigh. Somehow the wizard had drawn the blade to him while they struggled and managed to palm it without Gregore noticing. His distraction was all Saints needed.

Nick slapped his hands together and white powder filled the air. He blew it at Gregore and muttered an incantation. "Let's see your speed now."

Gregore tried to lunge, found himself moving at a snail's pace. Like fighting someone in a dream, his movements were maddeningly slow. His fist hit Nick's shoulder with hardly enough force to move him. Saints laughed it off.

"The strong gargoyle meets his match. If only you'd known that when you interfered with justice. Those men were mine to punish and you took them from me." Saints tossed a bolt of energy that struck Gregore square in the chest and knocked the air from his lungs.

"You took her from me. When Samantha was taken that night, I..." Nick refocused his gaze on Gregore. "It started all this into motion, didn't it? Hard to believe we're now at the end. That all those months of studying you, following you, have come to a climax."

Gregore struggled through the lethargy and pain wracking his limbs. He refused to back down or be cowed. He circled Saints, turning with him. Saints refused to stay put. They flowed right, then left. Each tried to outwit the other. Gregore prayed Tara was getting Maddy and Thomas to safety.

"This is where we finish the game," Gregore said. "You and I."

Saints smiled. "No. You, your detective and I. Let's not forget she's a player in this too. I will have my vengeance." He slashed out his hands, fingertips glowing black fire. He gripped Gregore's arms, pulled him close and shot lightning through his limbs.

Gregore jerked under the electrocution. His movements were slow, and the flowing blood from his legs made him weak. He despised that weakness. Shoving at Saints, he tried to force himself to a safer distance, but couldn't quite gain the strength to accomplish the move.

Shit! He should have been able to subdue the madman at the beginning instead of losing his grip on Saints. Jeffrey's growl sounded from Gregore's left, followed by the sound of flesh against flesh as his battle raged. Gregore couldn't see or hear Tara. Had he given her enough time? Had she gone as he'd asked?

Saints head-butted him, knocking Gregore to his knees. Gregore wrapped his fingers in Nick's shirt and pulled him down with him.

Nick looked him in the eyes. "Don't think she's sneaking out while you distract me. You and I both know her better than that. Even if she gets the others out, she'll be back. She can't turn down a chance to get her man, can she?"

Gregore swore. She couldn't and he knew it.

"I'll accept that as your answer." Saints untangled Gregore's fingers from his shirt. He pulled his fist back and smashed it into Gregore's face, knocking him back onto his ass. Nick reached down and ripped the knife from Gregore's thigh, twisting the blade as he pulled it free. Then kicked him over and over in the ribs. He switched to his injured thighs. Gregore couldn't hold back his cry of pain as a booted foot nailed him in the fresh cuts.

"Now for your girlfriend." Saints stalked out of Gregore's line of sight, bloody blade dripping.

Gregore rolled to his side, then his stomach. He forced his hands under himself and pushed up. Locking his elbows, he got his feet underneath him and shuddering to a stand, he staggered after Saints. He couldn't gather the speed he needed to run, so he moved as fast as he could to follow.

Saints stood facing Tara in the circle of candles. The flickering lights adding a demonic gleam to his face.

Gregore was out of time.

He turned back to Saints. Saw the blond raise his knife to strike Tara down. Those fingers sparked black death, and Gregore knew the pain they would bring. The electrocution, amplified through the blade, could kill her in minutes.

He'd never had the chance to save Zola. He could, no, he *would* save Tara. Gregore wouldn't allow another woman to die in his arms. Not when he could stop it. Saints thought he was down, underestimating Gregore in the worst way. He'd remarked that Tara was Gregore's girlfriend, but that was where he was wrong. Tara was the love of his life. That alone fueled him past the lethargy and pain in his limbs. Reaching for his speed, he found and used it.

He shoved himself between Tara and Saints.

Nick's eyes flashed surprise, then determination. He dropped the blade, wrapped his hands around Gregore's throat, and forced the magic through him. His body jerked like a live wire, absorbing all the energy Saints poured in. He smelled burning hair, skin, the noxious smell making him gag. He shuddered and twitched, the electricity eating him cell by cell.

Gregore thought he heard Tara yell. He felt her soft hands on his arm, but could do nothing but stare into Saint's eyes.

"This is too easy a death for you, Gargoyle. Sleep." He waved a hand over Gregore's eyes, and the lethargy in his blood quadrupled.

Gregore turned his head as much as he was able to find Tara. "Go. Run," he whispered. "I love you."

She shook her head. Stubborn woman. "No. I won't go without you."

"Go," he said. "Save your aunt." His eyelids were so heavy, he couldn't keep them open. He fluttered them in order to see her one last time. "Love you."

Darkness descended over his eyes and he saw no more. Gregore felt himself hit the concrete floor. It didn't matter. She had to go. Had to. His last thought was a prayer to God. That Tara's life be spared as Zola's was not. He loved her. Surely that love would account for something in the end.

Watching Gregore fall felt like watching her world collapse. Tara grabbed him and staggered to the floor under his unconscious weight. He didn't move. She tenderly laid his head upon the ground, brushed a hand over his brow. Saints moved. She saw him lurch awkwardly for the blade out of the corner of her eye and pulled her Sig Sauer.

She stood and squared off against Nick, weapon aimed at the widest part of his chest. At this distance, she wouldn't miss. Her aim was as steady as her resolve. If she couldn't arrest Saints, she'd make sure he couldn't hurt anyone else.

To her right, she heard the remnants of the fight between Jeffrey and the blonde witch. They seemed equally matched, but Tara knew Jeffrey would come out on top. Maddy hid near the exit, guarding Thomas. Only Saints remained. And by the look of him, Gregore had beaten the hell out of him before going down. Blood dripped from numerous cuts and his right cheek was swelling to twice its size. Seeing him like that made her smile.

"You're under arrest for arson and the murder of Hiroshi," she said.

The blond man laughed. "You can't seriously think I'll come willingly. And even if you forced me, would a jail hold me?" He winked and it drew her attention to one of his cuts as it closed before her eyes. "You know I'm stronger than that."

Tara nodded. He likely would escape confinement. She couldn't have that. "You would make me kill you?"

"I'd really like to see you try." He launched himself at her, slashing his blade in front of him.

She fired in rapid succession. The bullets bounced off an invisible shield, lodging in the crates and destroying a couple of candles. No go on the Sig Sauer, she realized, trying to shove it back in her holster. Saints raked his blade toward her middle. She slid to the side, blocked his blow, and landed one of her own. Nick laughed like a banshee.

He pissed her off. How dare he laugh when Thomas and Gregore were completely out and Jeffrey fought for his life. How dare he kill a man and burn her apartment. She'd done her duty of calling the paramedics for Samantha. It wasn't her fault the girl had died before she made the journey to the hospital. Gregore had punished those responsible, and this maniac decided to destroy him for it? Hell. No.

She fought for all she was worth, punching and kicking him. Still he laughed. His fingertips twitched and glowed deep ebony, like the fires of hell burned within. She knew what that meant. She'd seen poor Gregore's body electrocuted under the magic.

Tingles raced up her spine and spread through her limbs. Her innate magic, she knew. Dare she unleash it? What if she destroyed everyone? She couldn't lose Maddy. Or Jeffrey and Thomas, for that matter. She dare not think about Gregore right now. She'd crumble, break.

Pushing away from Saints, she let a bit of the magic trickle into her hands. What kind of spell could she cast? Most of what she'd done to this point was mixing potions for spells. Her tongue tingled. Like a word was there, waiting to be spoken.

Saints shot his hand out and snapped it back. A lightning bolt of energy hit her in the chest, knocking the breath from her. Tara gasped for air and locked her knees to keep from falling. He struck again, harder and faster. This time she was prepared. She staggered out of his way. The crate that had been behind her moments before crackled, flames catching on the wood.

Fire. Could she control it?

She held her hand out toward Nick. *"Ignis!"* Flames leapt from her fingertips and sparked on his clothes. He easily batted them out.

"So pathetic. I thought for sure that Gypsy heritage would gain you more power." Disgust dripped from his words. "I thought you were a worthy opponent. It must have diluted with your mixed blood." He shot more bolts at her, making her dive out of harm's way.

She tried to throw more fire at him. Her aim was off and a crate behind him exploded in a fiery conflagration. Damn. If she weren't careful, she'd burn the warehouse down. Just like in her visions. She didn't have time to think about that, though.

Saints attacked again. He kept her dodging his blows until she backed into a corner. His smile was pure menace. Waving a hand before her face, he leaned in close and said, "Sleep."

Her eyes suddenly felt weighted by anvils. They crashed closed. And she slept.

CHAPTER 39

Tara groaned, her eyes fluttering open. Her brain felt like it was stuffed with cotton and her eyes were grainy, like someone had rubbed sand in them. Each arm felt like lead. She drew in a breath and fought for each molecule of air through constricted lungs.

A hand caressed her cheek, slipping down to her chin and lifting it up.

Her gaze clashed with Saints.

Tingles shot through her limbs and face, and it became even harder to breathe. She gasped and fought to contain her spiking fear.

His blue eyes glittered under golden brows. "Good, you're awake. How are those bindings? Tight?"

Tara struggled and realized part of the weight in her limbs was the awkward position they were in. Her arms were bound behind her, feet secured by plastic wire ties to the legs of the chair. She glanced about for help and realized with a sinking heart that none would be coming.

Maddy, Thomas, and Jeffrey were all similarly bound in chairs seated haphazardly around her. In the bright grey light of dawn, she could just make out their eyes. Maddy's were wide with fear. Thomas's head lolled as he struggled to gain consciousness, and Jeffrey's eyes glittered with hate. Deja stood sentinel by him.

She looked at Saints. "Damn you."

He squatted down in front of her to keep eye contact. "I tire of your witty repartee. You need some new lines, Detective," he teased, and she wanted to head butt him until he bled.

She didn't.

"What, nothing to say?"

"Release them."

He shook his head. "I had kind of hoped for a little more originality. Although, at least you didn't say, 'You'll never get away with this!' Because I will. I have. The cops have left, in case you were wondering. Oddly enough, they couldn't remember why they'd come here in the first place. How do you suppose that happened?"

Tara pursed her lips, barely keeping her anger in check. Pissing this madman off was not ideal. "What do you want with us?"

"Ah, good. Now I can tell you my entire plan and watch you thwart it? No, this isn't a movie. I won't give away my secrets." He winked. "At least, not yet."

She had to get him talking. Maybe then he wouldn't hear her trying to work at the binding on her hands. "Do you plan to kill us?"

Nick cocked a brow. At first she thought he'd refuse to answer this question as well. He surprised her by replying, "I plan to kill the creature. Gregore the gargoyle. Sounds like a comic book character. I'm still deciding about you. You are far prettier than I thought initially."

Tara locked her jaw closed. She refused to respond.

"Maybe I'll keep you a little while. I wonder what sex magic would be like with you? Would all that Gypsy magic in your blood increase my power? It's so tempting to find out." He ran his hand down her neck slowly, dipping to just above her breast before sliding to her shoulder. "I bet you're a wildcat in bed. Especially after I kill your current lover. What do you think? Is angry sex better?"

"You'll never know," she ground out. Tara wanted to bite him. She seethed with rage. But if she didn't wait for an opportunity, he would kill them all.

"Oh, that's where you are wrong. I can make you come willingly to my bed and all the while, you'll be recharging my power." He chuckled and stood, pacing away from her.

Gregore.

She looked around wildly for him. He lay on the ground, face up by a stack of crates, utterly still. In human form, she should have been able to see his chest rise. Straining her eyes, she realized she couldn't. The sun hadn't touched gilded fingers to him, yet it was far too bright.

Her heart stuttered as she found the source of the light. Every window was broken. *Every* window. Dawn was moments away. Oh God, the dawn.

Oh God, oh God, oh God.

Today was his birthday and the anniversary of the curse. He'd known, for whatever reason, that today was his last day. That with the sunrise, he would turn to stone forever. She couldn't lose him. Not now. Not when he'd just said he…She swallowed over the knot in her throat. Not when he loved her.

Tara fought hard, squirming and yanking with both hands and legs, trying to force the bindings to stretch even a sliver so she could escape.

Harsh male laughter grated on her nerves. "You think I would make it that easy? No, this is my end game. Today I finally have justice."

"Justice for what? Your dead girlfriend?" Tara spat. Anger flowed like wildfire into her words, making them dark and ugly.

Red suffused Nick's face. He was across the short space and snarling at her in a blink. He grabbed a fistful of her sweater and yanked her close. "You will not speak of her. Ever."

Emboldened by rage and fear, Tara said, "Samantha Peters died last summer from a robbery gone wrong. Tell me, Saints, where were you then? Were you there? Did you let her die?" *Idiot! Don't antagonize him.*

Too late.

"You let her die," he roared. "You and that creature! You wouldn't let me go to her. You kept me on the sidewalk like the rest of the rubbernecking onlookers. Like I was nobody to her. I was *everything* to her. And that *thing* over there, he chased down the robbers before I could. He didn't kill them. He didn't take their lives as they took my Samantha's. He dropped them off at the police station. And you want to know what happened then? They were released. Not enough evidence to charge them for her murder. Where is the justice, Detective? Where?" Nick shouted. "It's right here. Right now."

"And where were you when she was attacked, Saints? Hiding behind her skirt?"

He backhanded her with all the strength in his body, knocking her head to the side.

"We didn't kill her," Tara mumbled, feeling a warm trickle on her chin.

"You all did. The robbers paid with their lives. The gargoyle will pay with his. And you? You will watch your lover die. Like I watched mine."

"Saints. Don't do this. You know we didn't mean to—"

Nick punched her, knocking her head to the other side. "Shut up. I'm done listening to you." He grabbed a roll of duct tape from a nearby crate, tore off a piece, and wrapped it over her lips. "Now you will watch."

He dragged her chair into a pool of light facing the east bank of windows. Facing Gregore.

"I've waited for this day for months. I found out about it from one of the priests who worked at that church. He didn't take too well to pain and spilled what he knew pretty easily." Saints kicked Gregore hard in the ribs. The flesh was already solidifying into stone.

Tara watched helplessly as the grey light turned to silver, then gold. The glimmer of first light washed over Gregore's feet, up his calves.

"Keep an eye on them," Saints said to Deja.

Tara stilled and continued working the plastic that bound her wrists behind her. She wished she had something sharp to cut the ties. No matter. She worked and worked at the ties until she became aware of an odd sensation. Tingles sharpened in her fingertips.

Magic. She had magic.

She didn't have good control, but she didn't have time to worry about it. If she set herself on fire, hopefully she could put the flame out before burning to a crisp or alerting Saints. Curling her wrists, she touched her fingertips to the end of one of the wire ties and whispered, "*Ignis.*" She smelled the noxious burn of plastic as a tiny flame sparked and felt the tension in the ties loosen.

"Now this is interesting," Saints said, looking at Thomas. He cocked his head. "He's literally fading. What is he?"

Tara glared daggers at him.

"A better man than you," Jeffrey said.

Nick scoffed. "Do you think I'd have had a woman like Samantha love me if I were a bad man? No. She was too pure."

Tara didn't want to hear about Samantha. She tugged harder on her restraints and felt them slacken further. She worked the melted plastic until it gave, until she could pull a hand free. Deja turned to look her way, eyes narrowed. Tara stilled and kept the hand behind her.

Nick cocked his head and studied Thomas a moment longer, watching him disappear from view. He faded until only a shadow remained and the restraints no longer bound him.

Thomas stood.

Tara's heart sank. Her ally was free but useless. He would simply pass through anything he touched, his corporeal form gone.

It was lighter now. Pink and gold spilled in from the open windows and colored Gregore in beautiful light. Knives of pain sliced through her, watching his warm skin turn grey. Her heart crushed inside her chest. She wanted to scream, to rage as the sunlight splashed and illuminated his wonderful body. They were too late. They were all too late.

As if sensing her thoughts, Saints returned to Gregore's side and squatted down. He poked Gregore a few times. "Fascinating, don't you think? I wonder if I should pose him. That way he can serve a more useful purpose than just a slab of rock."

Tara released the last binding around her wrists and shook them out, waiting. Jeffrey nodded to her, a single movement of his head. She took that to mean he was also free of his bindings. Thomas met her gaze and she could just make out the sadness in his eyes. The regret. She looked pointedly from Thomas to Deja. Taking her cue, he moved so that the witch turned to follow him with her narrowed gaze, effectively putting her back to Tara and Jeffrey.

Tara slid her hand forward and torched the ties on her ankles. The toasted plastic smelled awful and would alert Saints at any moment. She pulled the tape off her mouth, barely restraining her yelp of pain in the process.

"Get them out," she mouthed to Jeffrey. "He's mine."

Jeffrey frowned, but hedged his agreement. He extended a finger and a shiny black talon replaced his fingernail. He quickly cut through the bindings on his legs. "Three," he mouthed back. "Two...one."

Jeffrey slashed a hand full of talons out, catching Deja off guard. Scales swept over his skin, and his eyes turned an eerie red. He flew at her, and they tumbled in a blinding blur of arms, legs, and wings.

At the same moment, Tara launched herself at Saints, knocking him down. They rolled, punched, each wrestling for the upper hand. He was far stronger than she, but she had field training he didn't. Tara forced her way on top and settled all her weight onto his upper chest and arms.

Saints grabbed her legs, dug his fingers blazing with dark fire deep into her clothes. Holes burned under his touch until his fingertips touched bare skin. She struggled free, rolled to the side, and reached for her weapon. Her holster was empty. Shit. Saints must have taken the piece while she was out. He yanked her closer, crawled up her body and wrapped his hands around her throat, his fingers heating to painful levels. "Now you die."

Black winked over Tara's vision as electric bolts fried her insides. Tingles raced through her, and it took a moment to identify that these were different from the current of electricity. This was her magic, racing to save her. She was tired. So tired. But if she gave in now, Maddy would die.

Tears broke from her eyes, running down to her ears and mixing in her hair. Her wild gaze found Gregore. He lay so still. Completely unmoving. In that moment, she knew she'd failed. The curse had claimed him. Her heart ached with fierce loss. She'd failed. She hadn't been fast enough or smart enough to save the man she loved. Tara knew intrinsically that this was the same thing he'd felt for his entire life. God, how had he lived with the crushing burden of his failure? How would she?

Tara pushed the pain and fear down into her soul, then reached for her magic. She couldn't save Gregore now. She could save Maddy, Jeffrey, and Thomas. Her body was growing cold. If she waited any longer, she'd die. But she sure as hell would take Saints with her.

Over the last few days, tiny cracks had splintered the inner wall of her self-control, threatening to break through her fierce control on the magic she kept locked away, too afraid to let out. Now she prodded those cracks, pushing mental fingers into them until she could rip large chunks out of the wall. Suddenly, with an almost audible roar, the wall disintegrated. Magic sparked and flooded her. Warmed her until she felt like she glowed with it.

Saints narrowed his eyes, pressed harder to her throat.

Tara blinked. A tug of war raged in her body. Magic against magic. Saints was so strong. Little by little, his magic pushed hers back, overcoming hers. What she had wouldn't be enough. She needed more. Blindly she reached her hands out toward the witch battling Jeffrey. She could see Deja's aura now. She latched onto that with her magic, saw Deja's shock, and yanked. Hard. She dragged the power out of her body.

The woman crumpled to the floor. Jeffrey roused himself to his feet and shuffled over to Maddy to release her bindings.

Tara turned to Saints and seized his black aura. She pulled harder. Saints wrestled against her, grappling for control of his dark powers.

Not really even understanding how, Tara opened a channel between them, letting his power flow into her. She tapped in to the ochre ley lines of the earth. So many, right here. Crisscrossing the building in a fantastic star of power.

She grounded herself, pulled all the magic into a ball, and shoved it at Saints.

He opened his mouth to scream in pain. Tara shoved it down his throat and infused it in his molecules. Wrapped him in blinding power until she could no longer see his human form.

Holding him in place, she detonated the supernatural bomb she'd conjured in his body.

Nick Saints screamed and roared so loud she had to cover her ears. Tara broke the connection lest she get sucked into the whirlpool of magic tearing his body apart.

Eyes dead of life locked on her. "Die," he whispered and flicked his wrist.

Out of nowhere, Gregore's dagger sailed forward and slammed into her stomach all the way to the hilt. Tara doubled over in pain, unable to breathe as she watched the light fade from his eyes. Saints was dead.

Jeffrey knelt at her side. She could see Maddy's little tennis shoes and knew she was also there. "Out," she managed to gasp.

"We'll go. You too," he said.

She shook her head. "Not without him." She waved bloody fingers in Gregore's direction.

"Where's your fucking cell phone?" Jeffrey growled.

Tara patted her back pocket with the last of her energy.

Jeffrey snagged it up and called for paramedics. When he hung up, he grumbled, "We're not leaving until they arrive and help you."

Tara didn't listen. She scooted closer to Gregore and laid her head on his chest.

CHAPTER 40

Broken, bleeding, Tara pressed herself to Gregore and draped her leg over his. Held him close while trying not to move the blade protruding from her abdomen. Her shattered heart beat in halves. Why hadn't she been able to translate that stupid curse sooner? Why hadn't she thought to use the spell sooner that would bring the page back? Why wasn't she smart enough to figure out the riddle before they'd left to save Maddy? Why did she listen to him and wait until the last moment when it was far too late?

"Stupid. I'm so stupid," she cried.

Distantly, she heard someone—Jeffrey? Thomas?—deny her claims. She ignored them, knowing in her heart what was true.

Gregore's body was cold as marble. His chest still. He didn't breathe. Didn't move. His heart didn't beat beneath her ear. This was so different from the other times he'd been stone. She felt it in her bones.

"Wake up," she mumbled to him. She placed her hands on the pools of golden sunlight on his chest and tried to shake him. "You have to wake up. You have to be alive. I love you."

Nothing. Confirming what she wanted to deny. She'd lost him to the curse.

Tara laid her head back on his chest. She moved her hand, sliding it up his stomach, leaving a smear of red in its wake. Blood. Her blood. She looked at it, at the rapidly darkening line, and couldn't bring herself to care. So maybe she was dying. So what. She was so numb that she didn't care whether she did or not. She'd lost the one man in all the world she could love. Tears slid down her cheek and joined in the blood, mixing with it like little red pools. She swirled her finger in one. Drew a heart right over Gregore's heart.

Her cheek tingled and grew warm where her skin met his chest. She felt a slow movement.

She started. Was that...? Did he just...?

Shocked, afraid to move, Tara held her breath and waited. Sirens screamed in the background, getting closer. She tuned it out. An eternity passed.

Another slow rise of Gregore's chest. Followed by warming of the area under her fingertips. "Oh God," she choked out.

"He's gone," Jeffrey said and laid a hand on her shoulder.

"No. No...he isn't. He breathed. I felt it."

A sad exhale of breath. "No, he didn't."

"I'm not imagining it," she said. "He did."

A full minute later, Gregore breathed again.

"Shit. You're right!"

Gregore's body heated until it burned. Too afraid to move away, lest she break the cycle of whatever was happening, Tara waited and watched in awe. His wings crumbled away to sand. The grey of his skin darkened and tanned. Became flesh. The beak of his nose re-shaped into a normal human nose. Still he breathed.

Underneath her fingers, the heat blistered her skin. She kept her hand over his heart. "How is it possible?" she whispered, even as sunlight played over her hand. It was day and the curse—broken. "How?"

Suddenly she knew. The riddle of the counter-curse played in her head as if the old witch had spoken in her ear.

Only by my blood and tears
Freely given with no fears
Wrapped in a love you can see
Only then shall ye be free.

Blood. Tears. The heart on his chest. Tara was a direct descendent of the old Gypsy woman. Her blood flowed in Tara's veins. Her tears wet her eyes. Could it be so simple?

Gregore's eyes opened. He blinked, swallowed. "Tara?"

She cried harder. "I'm here." His skin cooled, back to the regular temperature of flesh. She slid her hand up his chest to cup his chin. Angling his head down, she pressed a gentle kiss to his lips. "I'll always be here with you."

Gregore lifted a hand into the golden ray of sun. "How?"

"She did it," Jeffrey said. "I don't fucking know how, but she did it."

"You? Thomas?" Gregore asked.

Jeffrey shook his head. "No changes here. Just you. Must be that she likes you more."

Tara choked on a laugh.

Gregore took her hand in his and immediately noticed the blood. "Are you hurt?"

"Just a scratch," she said.

Jeffrey snorted. "Sure."

A door banged open at the end of the warehouse and paramedics rushed in. They spread out to the different bodies.

"This one's dead," one called.

"She is too," another said.

A man crouched beside Tara and moved her arm away from Gregore, checking her stomach. "Got one," he said to the others. To Tara, "Ma'am, I'm going to need you to not move."

A couple of others joined him, setting their bags down and pulling out different medical instruments. Tara only had eyes for Gregore. He was alive.

"She's cold. Blood pressure is too low. We've got to get her to the hospital."

Tara looked up at them, then down at the handle of Gregore's knife sticking out of her stomach. She nodded. She had to live now. "Okay," she said as the medic began to work on her.

Jeffrey stood to the side. "I'll get the others home."

Gregore reached out to take Tara's hand. "I'm going with her."

>-+•>-•O-•<•+-<

Carson waited in the lobby the day Tara was released from the hospital. He offered to drive her back to Maddy's. Gregore had never left her side. She tucked her hand into Gregore's and then greeted her partner.

Carson held a pretty bouquet of pink blooms out to her. Tara took them and smelled the lovely scent. "Nice," she said.

"Sorry. I'm so sorry, partner. I should have believed in you. Should have helped you through this. You were right. Video was able to clean up the image of the guy from your apartment. It was Saints. The insurance company had no record of the documents we'd found. They were forged." He scratched his head. "I'm still not sure what happened back at the warehouse. We surrounded the building. Next thing I know, I'm home watching television."

Tara shook her head. He'd never believe her.

Carson waited for an answer. When one didn't come, he continued on. "Anyway, the captain was satisfied with your account of the events of the warehouse. The investigation into Saints and the death of those women will continue. Captain has reinstated you with the department's full approval. You can come back as soon as you're all healed up."

She nodded, unable to find words. She'd lied to the detectives about Saints and the women who'd held Maddy captive. She'd fed them a line of how Saints had killed the women for turning on him when he'd kidnapped Maddy, then mysteriously died as they struggled. So far, they believed her.

Carson shifted on his feet, then said, "I'll go get the car."

She waited for him to pull the car up, her thoughts in turmoil. Even when she was healed, she didn't think she could go back. She'd lied and she'd killed. She needed time to figure out where magic fit in her life. Needed to see where her relationship with Gregore was going now that the curse was broken. Not to mention the unfinished business with Jeffrey and Thomas.

As soon as they arrived back at Maddy's, Tara gave Carson a hug and sent him on his way. He went reluctantly and she promised to call.

Maddy was on her porch, rushing down the few steps as soon as she saw them. She threw her arms around Tara and Gregore, hugging both close. "Oh, I was so worried, dears."

Her cuts and bruises were healing, and she looked more like herself than the last time Tara had seen her. "Are you okay?" Tara asked.

"Don't you even worry about me. I'm fine. You come right inside and sit down." She ushered Tara and Gregore both into the warm comfort of the house. Maddy had tea waiting and put out some poppy seed cakes. She made Tara sit in the living room chair. Thomas and Jeffrey were both there. Thomas smiled, though he looked tired. At least Tara could see him, as dusk had just fallen.

"I'm sorry," Tara said to them both. "I promise to help you find the answers."

Jeffrey leaned forward and squeezed her hand. He nodded to her. "We'll find a way. Thank you for saving him. Even if he is a pain in the ass."

Gregore slugged him halfheartedly in the shoulder.

Thomas rose and came to stand before Tara. He bent and pressed a kiss to her temple. "You're a gift to us all, Tara. You're the gift of hope. Take care of him."

Tears stung her eyes. "I will."

Thomas straightened and pulled Maddy to her feet. "Maddy darling, I don't suppose you could cook up something? I'm famished."

Maddy giggled like a schoolgirl. "I'll see what I can do. Would you like to join us, Jeffrey?" she asked as she headed for the kitchen.

"I'm going to be as big as a house," Jeffrey grumbled. He winked at Tara and followed them out of the room.

Gregore lifted her out of the chair and carried her up to her bedroom. He set her on the floral bedspread, settled on the bed beside her, and pulled her into his arms.

"I love you," he whispered against her hair.

She smiled and relaxed against him. "I love you too."

"I want you to stay with me."

Tara snuggled into his welcome heat. "Always. But I don't have a place to live. And I'm not sure how the priests would feel about me living there if we aren't married."

"Then we should."

"Should what? Live there?"

Gregore chuckled. Lifted her hand and kissed her palm. "I want you to marry me."

She sat up gingerly and faced him. He was serious. They'd known each other such a short time, but the idea was appealing. More than that, they fit. Gregore was a man who saw her for exactly who she was and loved her. He understood her. It felt right. Had from the start. "Yes," she said.

He grinned and kissed her. He wrapped her in his embrace and held her close to his heart.

"But I still don't think we should live at the church."

"How about England?"

"England?"

A ghost of a smile traced his lips, chased by a touch of sadness. "I could never part with our old estate, yet could never go back. I'd like to take you there. I want you to see where I began this life. Unless you need to stay here? Go back to work? You don't need to work. I've got money. Whatever will make you happy."

"You make me happy," she said and kissed his lips.

As she pulled back, she looked around the room that was so like Grandma Rose's. At first, she'd not wanted to come back to Rose's house. The memories of Rose were too painful, especially in a room just like her bedroom. But now, Tara felt only peace. Rose would always be with her and it no longer hurt to be here. It was time to move on.

"I've always wanted to go to England," she said to Gregore. "I don't know about going back to the force. Maybe it doesn't make sense, but I'm not that person anymore. Through this journey with you, I've been broken down and reshaped into someone new."

"As have I. I never thought to see the sun again."

Tara laughed. "Maybe we should make a vacation stop at the beach on the way. There's nothing quite like the sunrise over the water."

"Wherever we go, so long as I'm with you." He tucked her back against him, and Tara was happy.

Epilogue

Two months later
Derbyshire, England

Bright, sparkling moonlight shone down on Gregore as he stood at the top of the steps of his English manor. Rolling lawns stretched out on either side of the drive. Trees dotted the grass and cast black shadows over the flowers peeking their heads up in the mild spring air.

He and Tara spent weeks cleaning the manor up, preparing for this day. Even though so much time had passed since he'd seen the home, he'd paid for caretakers, who'd done their job well. Not much was needed for repairs and all that the interior needed was a thorough cleaning. Marble floors shone, wood was polished, and every room aired out from neglect. It looked remarkably close to the day he'd left, though the laughter of his mother, sister, and brother no longer echoed within. He missed them, but it felt wonderful to fill the home with love once more. Tara's gorgeous smiled warmed even the darkest rooms.

Maddy had arrived last week and promptly settled into her new suite of rooms. She loved every inch of the house, just as Gregore and Tara did. After Tara had sent pictures, her argument to sell Maddy's house and come live with them gained merit. Maddy agreed and had come to stay.

"Grandma Rose would love this," Tara said, stepping into the circle of lamplight on the porch and wrapping her arms around his waist from behind. "I only wish she could be here for our wedding."

He wrapped her in his arms and held her close. "As do I." Still, she would make her grandmother proud. She practiced her magic daily in a workshop she'd set up for herself on the top floor and even dabbled in some tarot cards. Every day her magic grew stronger. This was life now, and one she clearly adored. Not once had she said she missed being a cop. She'd even mentioned using her powers for good. Like missing person's cases.

Gregore didn't care what she chose to do, so long as she was happy. As happy as she made him. He couldn't wait to make her his wife and said as much, just as an impossibly small car turned into the drive. "Looks like they are here," he rumbled in her ear.

"Finally," she mused. "I can't wait."

He kissed her head and went down to greet their guests. Jeffrey unfolded his legs and climbed out of the driver's side of the car.

Thomas followed from the passenger side. "Could you have found a smaller car, mate? One more bump and my knee would have gone through my throat."

"You made it, didn't you? Quit whining, you pansy."

"Next time, we travel separate. I had no idea I'd be flying Grumps 'R Us airline."

Jeffrey grinned at Gregore, completely ignoring Thomas's gripes. He slapped his friend on the shoulder and gave Tara a hug.

Darkness clung to the edges of his moods, but he'd lightened up a lot. And Thomas? Gregore hoped he never changed. Thomas bounded up the steps and muscled Jeffrey and Gregore out of the way to get his own hug from Tara.

"Sure you won't consider marrying me instead? I'd make a far better husband than that one."

She laughed and pulled him into the house. "Sorry. He's the only one for me." She turned and took Gregore's hand.

Gregore kissed her and replied, "She's magic."

"Perhaps you'll consider a tarot reading then? I have some questions."

Thomas looked so serious at that moment, Gregore knew she wouldn't deny him. "Of course. After."

Thomas clapped his hands together. "Then what are we waiting for? Let's get this wedding done."

Maddy came forward and hugged the new arrivals.

Gregore and Tara watched them ascend the sweeping stairs together.

"I never knew I could be this happy," she whispered.

"With you, my love. This is only the beginning." Gregore kissed her, slow and soft, and together they went up the stairs to join their family.

Turn the page for a special preview of

GAVRIL OF AQUINA

Coming soon from Aurrora St. James

The Kingdom of Aquina
Present

Gavril Khalon ducked under a yellow and red striped awning, leapt over a table piled with fruit, scattering oranges to the ground, and ran. The sweet scent of citrus filled the air, making his stomach growl but he couldn't stop. Heavy boots pounded the ground behind him, growing closer. He darted through a side alley and out into the next row of stalls, then back again to the original row, leading the guards on a winding chase. Onlookers parted as he ran. They stumbled out of the way, dropping their goods in his path. Gavril dodged the debris and ducked behind a stall. Pots of all sizes stacked high on the stall table, blocking the soldiers' view of his hiding spot.

He knelt in the dirt and held his breath, desperately trying to get his breathing under control. The proprietor of the stall didn't seem to be about, giving him a moment of relief. Sweat dripped down his brow, leaving a trail through the dirt caking his skin. He looked down at his filthy, ripped clothing, hating what he'd become. But not willing to die for it.

Four burly men in dark green tunics bearing the seal of Lorcan, ruler of Aquina, raced by. At their head was Captain Qadir. Qadir paused, looked left and right, then ran into the busiest part of the market. His men followed.

Gavril drew a shaky breath, stood, and ran in the opposite direction. A shout rose behind him and he cast a glance over his shoulder to see the Guard back on his trail. He ran as fast as he could, fear of getting caught pushing him hard. He wasn't the thief Qadir thought, but with the Captain of the guard, innocence didn't matter. If he was captured, Gavril would be taken to the dungeons. His secret would be discovered and then Lorcan would finish the job he'd started seven years prior. The people of Aquina would never have a chance.

He turned a corner and stumbled over a man carrying a load of fabric, falling to his knees. Pastel silks of all colors flew around him. He shrugged them off and gained his feet. The seconds lost were sure to close the distance with the soldiers. Gavril could practically feel Qadir breathing down his neck.

Shouts of "He's there!" and "This way!" rang out behind him.

Gavril turned another corner, ducked into the dark interior of a store, and collided with a woman. They went down in a tangle of limbs, rolling, and landing with her sprawled across his chest as his head cracked against the floor. Gavril gasped in a fragrant breath of peaches and cinnamon and blinked away the spinning room. His head began to throb.

Her breath came quick, blowing warm across his skin like a caress. She pushed herself up and helped him to his feet. Her hands were soft on his arm. For a moment, he was struck with the unexpected warmth of her skin on his. Gavril stared at the spot where she touched him. A shiver of delight ran through his body. It had been entirely too long since a woman had touched him.

Outside, the shouts of the guards grew louder, drawing his attention, and then passed right by the door he'd come through. The woman looked their direction, then back at him.

"Are they looking for you?" she asked.

Gavril nodded. Stars swam in his vision with the slight movement. He touched the back of his head, feeling a bump forming.

She stepped closer, brushing his hand aside. Her fingers gently stroked over the lump, then trailed down his chest to trace his bloodied ribs. "You're injured."

He didn't move. Just stared at the woman.

She was lovely, with midnight hair falling over her shoulder in waves and the plumpest pink lips he'd ever seen. Her skin was fair, unusual for their warm climate, and looked so soft he ached to touch it. A simple blue dress clung to her curves from shoulder to hips and then flared to her feet. She had amazing curves.

Something passed in her crystal clear green eyes as she looked him up and down. Those lips pressed into a brief line. He cringed at the image he must make. Dirty, beat up, and shaggy. Not the kind of man who would draw the eye of a woman like her unless it was filled with scorn.

She reached for him. "Come with me."

She took his arm and pulled him into the back room. She led him to a small closet. "Stay and do not speak until I come for you."

Gavril opened his mouth to respond when she pulled a curtain across the closet doorway and blocked him in darkness. He listened to her footfalls as she left the room. Why had she hidden him? Why not point him to the door? Or hold him for the guards? Perhaps that was what she meant all along. Maybe she would lead the guards to him. Could he trust her not to?

Suddenly weary, he sank to his knees. He didn't know this woman. But in that last moment, he thought he'd seen compassion in her eyes. He sent up a silent prayer he was not misguided and waited for fate.

About the Author

Aurrora St. James has loved ghosts, graveyards, curses, gypsies, magic, vampires, and haunted houses for as long as she can remember. Not to mention archaeology, pirates, lost treasure, lost lands, and pretty much anything paranormal.

As she got older, she started reading her mom's romance novels and developed a love for the happily ever after they promised, sexy heroes and the heroines who always got into too much trouble. Soon all of her daydreams centered around a boy, a girl, and an adventure. From there it was only natural to write those daydreams down and watch the stories unfold. Now she loves to incorporate all that magic and mayhem into a story where love can overcome anything.

She currently lives in the Pacific Northwest with her wonderful husband, co-dependent dog, and attached at the hip cat.

Aurrora loves to hear from her readers. To email her or find out about upcoming works, go to www.aurrorastjames.com.